About the Author

Larry Gibilaro was born into a family of Italian musicians settled in London, where he has lived for most of his life. He has five children from a long marriage which ended in 1998 with the death of his wife. He was previously Professor of Chemical Engineering at both University College London and the University of L'Aquila in central Italy; his book *Fluidization-Dynamics* describes a topic of his academic research there. His first novel *Serious Business* was published in 2006, *Holy Orders* is his second.

Holy Orders

Larry Gibilaro

Holy Orders

Olympia Publishers
London

www.olympiapublishers.com
OLYMPIA PAPERBACK EDITION

Copyright © L G Gibilaro 2023

The right of Larry Gibilaro to be identified as author of
this work has been asserted in accordance with sections 77 and 78
of the Copyright, Designs and Patents Act 1988.

All Rights Reserved

No reproduction, copy or transmission of this publication
may be made without written permission.
No paragraph of this publication may be reproduced,
copied or transmitted save with the written permission of the
publisher, or in accordance with the provisions
of the Copyright Act 1956 (as amended).

Any person who commits any unauthorised act in relation to
this publication may be liable to criminal
prosecution and civil claims for damage.

A CIP catalogue record for this title is
available from the British Library.

ISBN, 978-1-80074-453-0

First Published in 2023

**Olympia Publishers
Tallis House
2 Tallis Street
London
EC4Y 0AB**
Printed in Great Britain

Acknowledgements

I would like to thank Mike Windross and Joy Townsend for their careful reading of an early draft of this novel, also my son Jason Gibilaro for providing the black monk image shown on the cover.

Author's Note

Any resemblance of characters in this novel to real persons living or dead is purely coincidental, as is any resemblance of the fictitious educational establishments to real ones. Incorporated at times in the narrative, however, are real people, and real events in which the fictitious character Piers Denney has been assumed to play a part; and also real biblical research pertaining to the period in Palestinian history immediately following the crucifixion of Jesus in which Piers Denney is credited with contentious discoveries concerning James, the brother of Jesus, and Paul, the effective founder of the Christian religion. In reality, these findings follow the ground-breaking research of Robert Eisenman in which they emerge as credible outcomes in his exhaustive study ('James the Brother of Jesus'). Featuring importantly among Eisenman's sources are the Dead Sea Scrolls, biblical manuscripts relating in part to the period in question and studied by an international team; passages in the novel pertaining to these researches draw on the publications of Michael Baigent and Richard Leigh ('The Dead Sea Scrolls Deception') and Judith Anne Brown ('John Marco Allegro'). Events relating to the death of Pope John Paul I, the 'Vatican bankers' and associated criminality and killings are taken from David Yallop's comprehensive investigation into what he convincingly portrays to have been the Pope's murder ('In God's Name').

DEATH IN THE CATHEDRAL

It was in January 1979 that a brief item on an internal page of the *Standard* newspaper reported the discovery of the body of a middle-aged man in Westminster Cathedral. Cleaners arriving there for work early that morning had found him prostrated before the altar of one of the side chapels. They thought at first they were interrupting an eccentric worshipper's pious ritual, and it was only when they tried to rouse him that they realised he was dead. The following morning the dailies all touched on the story, again making little of it. But a day or two later, one of them carried a further piece fleshing out a little that bizarre discovery in the Cathedral. It wouldn't have meant much to most readers but in Stephen Hallam it gave rise to an emotional shock which left him breathless. For it named the corpse, Piers Denney, someone he had known well, and the sight of whose name was to awaken intense feelings of guilt — even then, some fifteen years after their having parted company under circumstances for which he would forever feel shame and regret. As the initial shock faded, images of that parting mingled with others. Of Piers, his first memory of him as Brother Carroll, the name he had adopted on joining the Roman Catholic teaching order that ran St John's College, the London boys' school Stephen had attended from the age of eight for ten fraught years of his life; of the kindness and understanding with which Piers had helped him come to terms with those religious uncertainties which had plagued his adolescence — uncertainties, it was to emerge, Piers had come to share, and which in their separate ways they had both eventually come to resolve; and years later of Natasha, the woman for whom Piers had abandoned his vocation and with whom for a brief poignant period Stephen had disastrously believed himself to be in love.

Standing there stunned, not knowing what to do next, sadness and regret enveloping him; and guilt, for in all that time never having attempted to heal the wounds he had caused. Piers was a forgiving soul; all it would have needed was the approach that, though thought of from time to time, was never to materialise. Now it seemed some action was required, some gesture of atonement. Not for Piers, he had to remind himself, too late for that now, just for himself; the perceived selfishness adding to his burden of guilt. Without thinking of what he was going to say, he phoned the Cathedral office, managing to blurt out he was an old friend of the deceased who wished to contact his family to express condolences, perhaps attend his funeral. They referred him to St Thomas's hospital where the body had been taken, and who in turn referred him to the police.

The phone was answered by an efficient sounding woman, who nevertheless appeared to have difficulty understanding what he was on about, making him think he had got through to a wrong number. But then, after a pause, a brusque male voice came on the line asking for his name and his reason for enquiring after the deceased. When told he was an old friend who had just read in a newspaper of the discovery of his body, the man appeared to take an interest, wanting to know when he had last been in contact with Mr Denney, and going quiet on hearing that this was some fifteen years ago. It was at this point that it first occurred to Stephen that there could be something suspicious about Piers's death. He hadn't really thought about it until then, tacitly assuming natural causes, a heart attack or something like that, the Cathedral setting perhaps pointing to a deathbed reconversion, a last-ditch attempt, on realising the end was near, to make final peace with the God he rejected years before. But as these notions surfaced their improbability became apparent, prompting him to toy with the possibility of other factors, perhaps of sinister nature, being responsible in some way for Piers's death. The police officer's tone, when finally he responded, had hardened, making clear he was intruding into an affair that was far from clear cut and the subject of an ongoing investigation. Without giving anything away, he asked Stephen if he would be willing to be interviewed with a view to providing background information on the man, implying as he did so that, should they decide this could be useful, he would have little choice in the matter. And yes, he would pass his name and contact details on to the family member or whoever would be responsible for the eventual funeral arrangements, though the way he agreed to this left little doubt that no response from that quarter would be forthcoming.

While wondering what to do next, the memory of a photograph came to mind. Did he still have it stashed away somewhere? Outside his bedroom door was a large chest, the bottom drawer of which had long been a repository for snapshots and letters, newspaper cuttings, articles culled from magazines and other such oddments that at times had appeared worth preserving. If the photo was anywhere it had to be there. The drawer hadn't been opened for years and he had only the vaguest idea now of what it contained. That evening he started rummaging through it, a slow process as items continually attracted his interest, stirring up long-buried reminders of times past. It was just as he was about to postpone the search to the following day that it turned up, in a tattered folder hidden among other papers. It was pretty well as he had remembered it: a formal group setting in the format of end-of-year class photographs, masters seated in the centre with the boys arranged symmetrically around them, and set against the wide steps that led up to the main entrance of the old school building. The group in this case was a small one, just ten twelve-year-old boys in blazers and short trousers; in the centre, the bishop — a slight, inconspicuous being — who had just officiated at their confirmation; and on either side of him, emphasising his visual insignificance, two giants — relatively speaking — wearing the black cassocks and stiff white bib collars of their calling. The one to the bishop's left was Brother Ignatius, the Deputy Headmaster, a man whose lumpen facial features had long passed through the sound barrier of ugliness to emerge 'interesting and full of character' — at least in the eyes of one parent he had overheard at a prize-giving, though probably not in those of any boy who would have crossed him; and there, to his right, was Brother Carroll, his boyish, strikingly handsome appearance in such contrast with that of Ignatius as to throw the whole composition off balance. And what was he doing there anyway? Stephen was one of the boys in the picture, seated on the far left, in line with the bishop and the brothers. He remembered wondering at the time why Carroll was there. He had played no part in the confirmation classes, nor in the ceremony itself, had just turned up for the photo, so it seemed, a popular intervention so far as the boys were concerned, his friendly smile and lighted-hearted comments easing the tension as the seating arrangements were being put in place, providing a welcome break from the stuffiness with which the business of the day was otherwise being conducted.

But after the picture had been taken, he had disappeared. Stephen was unaware of his presence in the school for a year or maybe more, after which he reappeared briefly to excited playground cries of 'Carroll is back,' only to vanish again in a matter of weeks. Rumour among the boys had it that he was engaged somewhere abroad in high-level activity for the church, though how true this was Stephen had no idea at the time; and it was a matter of five years or more after he had left St John's that he was to learn from Piers himself that this was indeed the case. A few weeks after Stephen had entered the fifth form, Piers reappeared again, for long enough this time to take over the history class, transforming what had amounted to a sterile, sleep-inducing recitation of dates, treaties and conflicts into the high point of the teaching programme, bringing alive the agendas, personalities, ambitions and fears of the participants in a way which held the entire class spellbound.

Memories came flooding back as he sat staring at that picture: of Piers, those pleasurable first glimpses of the man, of their relationship during his senior years at St John's, of the totally unexpected and unprecedented manner in which this was to develop thereafter, of the distressing circumstances that were to bring it irrevocably to an end. Provoked perhaps by the quiet complacency of the setting, other emotions arose unbidden: a sense of indefinable discomfort and, yes, the muted stirrings of anger. So innocent they appeared, so tamed and compliant. So dependent in their world view on that which had been instilled in them day after day, no alternatives on offer, no space for doubt. Confirmed now at twelve years of age, fully paid-up members of the one true faith, their lives pledged unquestioningly to its observance.

PART 1

St John's College
1948 – 1956

ONE

The bag containing bottles of wine for the party at Sarah's that evening made a disconcertingly loud clinking noise as he set it down on the stone floor next to where he had just knelt; a wave of irritation marred momentarily the pious expression of the unknown priest, viewed in profile through the screen in front of him. He had come well out of his way to attend the Sacred Heart of Jesus, so as to avoid having to confront Father O'Shea at the Blessed Virgin with his latest misdeed — one which had seemed a significant breakthrough at the time, though from an altogether different perspective from that in which it now appeared and, although not dwelling on the prospect, indeed keeping it securely stowed away in a quite separate compartment of his consciousness, one he looked to be in with a fair chance of repeating, perhaps even elaborating upon, in a few hours' time. But no thought of that now. Instead, concentrating his full attention on the matter in hand, he launched into the all too familiar preamble: 'Bless me Father for I have sinned, it is two months since my last confession, since then I accuse myself of...' The litany of disrespects, evasions, commissions and omissions that followed differing little, if at all, from that of two months before, representing, in fact, an established rote which had long served the purpose of getting the whole business out of the way with a minimum of soul searching and embarrassment. This time, however, there was this new one to add to the list, one which represented a radical departure from past form. Some thought had gone into how exactly to put it, the precise form of words to be tagged on at the end as though nothing out of the ordinary. This was a strategy that seemed to work well enough with Father O'Shea. But then he had never had to confess anything quite like this before.

'…and being immoral with a girl.'

For a moment he thought he was through, the silence that followed seeming the usual prelude to a brief homily, absolution, and a decade or two of the rosary. But then something seemed to awaken the somnolent figure behind the screen; bodily movements perturbing the settled folds of his cassock; his eyes opened — small bloodshot slits staring relentlessly ahead — then closed again as in measured tone he broke the lingering silence.

'And how many times has this immorality occurred?'

'Oh, only once Father. Just once.'

From somewhere close by, in the body of the church behind him, the creak of a pew and prolonged shuffling signalled the arrival of further penitents.

'And was it a completed act?'

Completed? Well, yes it was, in a way. But then… what exactly was he on about?

It had started pretty well by accident, or so it appeared at the time. Sarah had taken him to the roof of the block where she lived, encouraged by her mother who seemed to like him. The view, he had been told, was spectacular, major features of the London skyline distinctly visible on a clear day. The trouble that day was the fog which had enveloped the City all week. And anyway, it was getting dark by then, visibility extending no further than the far side of the High Street. He was in his skimpy school blazer and would have been feeling chilly if it wasn't for a consuming distraction. Sarah felt the cold terribly, she was always telling him. The grey woollen coat she had put on prior to the ascent sported a huge collar which effectively provided a further layer over the upper part of her body, making her look irresistibly cuddly. Although a couple of years younger than him, she was very well developed, mentally no less than physically. And she knew it. It could be quite intimidating at times.

'Your hands must be freezing,' she said, after he had taken in the view, such as it was, and commented noncommittally. 'Put them here, under my collar, it's warm there.' It was.

The sides of the priest's mouth had turned down, the prevailing silence becoming oppressive. There was no way out. He would just have to get on with it somehow. And anyway, whatever happens, it would be all over in a matter of minutes. The thought of sunlight on the busy street outside, people bustling along, going about their business with overflowing shopping bags, earnest dogs tugging on leads… A comforting vision which flickered on briefly to be set reluctantly aside.

'No, Father… no, no it wasn't… not really, no.'

Something in Sarah's manner had suggested the next move. Must have done. He would never have dared anything like that, not without explicit encouragement. A flicker of pleasure ignited at the memory: the dimly lit roof terrace of Westcliffe Mansions, his right hand little more than a hair's breadth from its position of a few moments earlier, but no longer between Sarah's coat and collar, under them both now, under the silky blouse beneath.

'Did this involve unchaste touching?'

Impressive, the speed with which the unknown priest had read his mind, homed in on his misdeed. And that word *unchaste*. That fitted the bill perfectly, clearing up at the same time a linguistic problem he had got used to living with. The opposite of *chaste*, that was it. The thing they sang about in that hymn to the Virgin Mary. *Thou art clement, thou art chaste, Mary thou art fair/Of all virgins, something something, none with thee compare.* It had never been clear to him before just what it meant, nor *clement,* come to that. But then they were all used to making responses in Latin which nobody understood a word of anyway — except for that little creep Hoskins. According to Philips, *chaste* referred to fact that the boys were always chasing after her — which caused a few guilty laughs but didn't throw any real light on the matter. These considerations sped with the speed of light through his brain. He thought for a moment of thanking the priest for his unconscious clarification, settling instead for,

'Yes, Father.'

Then he really laid into him. It was a mortal sin he had committed, no question about it, one that had set him on the slippery slope to eternal damnation, to the everlasting fires of hell. Was it worth it for a few moments of sordid, guilt-ridden pleasure? His only hope of salvation — a slim one, the tone implied — was to crave forgiveness and vow to curb forever his lustful ways. Then God in his infinite mercy would forgive him, allow him back into the community of the righteous. The options had been clearly laid before him. The choice was his and his alone. With seeming reluctance, the priest gave him absolution and a large number of decades of the rosary. And as he rose to leave, lifting the bag nestling guiltily beside him, the wine bottles gave vent to a discordant clamour — a veritable chiming of the bells of hell — and his thoughts turned again, despondently this time, to the party shortly to begin at Sarah's and his narrow escape from further participation in the devil's evil design.

His next problem was how to explain all this to Sarah. If she really loved him, and at the time he was quite sure she did, she would understand — a conjecture soon revealed well wide of the mark, her incredulous expression as she heard him out rapidly giving way to irritation. Following which she lost no time in directing her attention elsewhere. To Jumbo Gowers to start with, and then, when that proved heavy going, to Carlo Petroni, — widely regarded as proficient in such matters — who couldn't believe his luck. The party of high hopes a complete disaster; the loss, the rejection, a devastating blow from which it seemed he would never recover.

It was shortly after that fateful party that another embarrassing incident was to add to Stephen's growing unease. He had got into the habit of calling into the local library on his way home from school. As well as occasionally taking out and returning books, he would usually spend a few minutes, sometimes more, browsing through the magazines on display, including those of popular scientific content. At times this enabled him to make seemingly knowledgeable contributions to classroom discussions — a practice which generally went down well enough with the brothers but ran the risk of getting him lumped in with Hoskins as a know-all swot in the eyes of his classmates. Silence, he had come to realise, was the safer option. That day, however, when the temptation to air some recently acquired superficial knowledge had proved irresistible, it was not his classmates he would have reason to fear.

Brother Simon was conducting the religious instruction period with which morning classes always ended, his face a picture of serene contentment as he described the wonders of God's creation, the diversity of living creatures with which He had chosen to populate the planet. The chiming of the bell to signal the start of the eagerly awaited lunch break was minutes away when he paused in his delivery to cast an interrogative glance around the class, settling for a moment on Stephen, perhaps aware by his demeanour that there was something he wanted to say.

'Yes, Hallam?'

Clumsily, choosing his words with difficulty, Stephen started to suggest that certain creatures being talked about could have evolved from a common ancestor, seeing, as he did so, Simon's benign expression changed to one of indignant fury.

'Where did you get that idea from?' he demanded, his face turning scarlet. Then, as Stephen tried to explain that he had read something to that effect in the public library, screeching,

'Come up here.'

A platform some nine inches high ran across the front of the classroom under the blackboard, widening in its centre to accommodate the desk at which Brother Simon was seated. As Stephen came to it, he stood up, menacingly, fists clenched, inches in front of him at the commanding height provided by the platform.

'Just what is it you are trying to say?'

He searched in the frozen silence for words that would ease matters, eventually coming out with something containing the name Darwin — immediately realising his error as Simon's features set to explode.

'So... So you think you descended from a monkey, do you?'

This provoked a burst of laughter from the class, releasing the tension somewhat, Simon's features softening a little with the realisation he had made his point well, that it had been fully appreciated.

'Get away from me,' he bellowed. And at that moment, the lunch hour bell chimed loud, launching the slamming of desk lids and the scurry of feet on the stone floor, and blessed release from another morning of educational toil.

That evening Stephen called round to see Sam, a friend who lived in the next street and attended a local state grammar school. Sam had a scruffy nondescript dog — Fluff, half Yorkshire terrier so he claimed — that he would take for walks most evenings. Stephen would sometimes tag along, giving them the opportunity to chew over films shown at the local fleapit and exchange notes on school experiences. As they headed for the common, he told him of his clash with Simon over the evolution issue. Sam couldn't believe it. He was a year ahead of Stephen at school, studying science A-levels. His biology teacher treated evolution as an established fact, he told him, making the case for it overwhelmingly convincing, showing that most of the initial problems thrown up by sceptics had been resolved and that those remaining would undoubtedly soon go the same way. This, he assured him, was the near-universal view of the scientific community.

'What does your biology teacher have to say about it?' he then asked.

Stephen told him that biology wasn't taught at St John's.

'What! How is that possible? What sort of school is it? Sounds as though you're taught by a load of ignorant bigots.'

He wasn't having that. Standards at St John's were high, exam results comparing well with those of the best grammar schools in the country, better than the one Sam attended, a very respectable number of leavers going on to university. He put up a spirited defence for his school until interrupted by a dispute between Fluff and a larger dog on the cinder track that marked the boundary of the common they had been heading for. And when that had been sorted out, it seemed a good idea to change the subject, which had been getting a trifle heavy.

But he was later to reflect on what had been said. It was certainly strange, that absence of biology at St John's. Boys who needed it at A-level — in the main those applying for medical school places — had to attend a local technical college, special arrangements for this causing no end of timetabling problems. Probably nothing to do with the evolution issue, he told himself. But to what extent did Simon's views reflect those of the brothers in general? True, he was widely regarded as an eccentric oddball, so perhaps the rest of them, or at least some of them, felt differently. For reasons he could not explain, it seemed important to find out if this was so. There was only one person he could possibly ask about it, but even that might not be a good idea. Dissent, even a hint of it, could provoke a strong reaction at St John's, could lead to no end of trouble. With some reluctance, he turned his mind to other things.

TWO

The last lesson of the week for class 5A — Friday, three till four — was history, an arrangement that had the effect of finishing off the week's schooling for them on a high. This was particularly the case for Stephen and Stan Firbright, his closest friend there, both won over by Brother Carroll's inspired teaching. He had been covering the Industrial Revolution, the previous session ending with the introduction of the Corn Laws to protect the incomes of British farmers. What seemed to them special about Carroll's approach to this — indeed his treatment of the subject in general — was the way he would get inside the heads of the participants, showing how their opinions formed, why they behaved as they did, all convinced of their righteousness, sincerely believing they were acting in the general best interest; and that it was as a result of the narrow, seemingly impenetrable horizons within which they lived their lives that they were largely blind to the blatant self-interest so often apparent in their views and actions. This underlying theme, which he would turn to time and again, bringing it alive with colourful examples — plus, it was true, a fair amount of imaginative interpretation — did not signify for him a necessarily pessimistic prognosis for social development. For it was subsumed into the maxim which expressed what appeared to be the governing principle of his life: that religion — a belief in divine purpose, something above human knowledge and experience — had the potential to breach those limiting horizons. The repeal of the Corn Laws provided something of an illustration of this general principle. They were now to learn that this came about not as a result of the efforts of the Chartists — that vast, highly vocal working-class mass movement, which had been campaigning vigorously on the issue for years — but by those of the altogether more low-key Anti Corn Law League, which made the simple and, in the end, thoroughly effective case that the artificial maintenance of a high price for wheat was contravening the Lord's Prayer by denying the poor their daily bread.

At the sound of the Friday four o'clock bell, the classroom would empty at breakneck speed, not a second of the freedom stretching ahead to Monday morning to be lost. Stephen and Stan, however, would remain behind as the clatter subsided, awaiting the opportunity to get Carroll to themselves. The established pattern was that discussion would hinge on the just-completed history lesson, then turn to other matters. This was something Carroll actively encouraged, always taking pains to make his availability clear to all, ever ready to talk over matters of interest or concern with anyone at any time. They appeared the only ones to take regular advantage of this largesse. Looking back years later, Stephen would appreciate Carroll's influence as crucial to his educational development. And timely, too. Unlike Stan, a star pupil in all respects, his school performance at that stage could at best be described as mediocre. Now, for the first time, he was to feel the stimulus of academic curiosity and debate. Carroll had provided the impetus that would stir him from his lethargy and set him on his way.

On this occasion, Stan kicked off with a provocative query that went to the heart of Carroll's thesis, making Stephen wonder apprehensively how he would respond. It concerned the many examples that could be cited in which religion, far from exercising a benign influence, could be seen as the root cause of hostility and conflict, even furnishing a sense of moral justification to the perpetrators of some of the most heartless and bloodthirsty events of history.

'What about the persecution and murder of the Huguenots?' Stan went on, looking Carroll straight in the eye. 'After that, how on earth can you hold up religion as a panacea for enlightened behaviour?'

This was not, it seemed to Stephen, the most tactful example to come up with, given that those responsible in this case were the Catholics. But he need not have worried. Carroll just smiled, taking the point well.

'You are perfectly right, of course. Religion, like patriotism, can be a highly emotive issue and has undoubtedly been used by misguided people for evil purposes. But these are perversions of religious belief, abuses to be guarded against. Be careful though not to let that obscure the greater truth.'

He went on to expound that history was there to learn from, to see where things went wrong so as to be prepared next time, able to stop the same mistakes being made again.

'I know, I know this is a lesson that has not been well learned. But just think what things would be like in the absence of a religious dimension, with only self-interest as a guide to behaviour.'

The Catholic Church, he admitted, had been slow in the past to respond to zealous elements in its ranks. But times had changed. What was now in place was this vast and powerful organisation dedicated to human welfare, to the eradication of poverty and oppression, determined to learn from past mistakes, to right the wrongs and injustices in the world, and with the worldwide backing of over a billion devoted followers. He paused at this point before adding, in what seemed to Stephen, when he thought about it later, as something of a guilty afterthought, 'And with the stamp and authority of the true faith.'

Carroll was clearly anticipating in all this what he saw to be the inevitable outcome of the views of a growing minority within the Roman Catholic hierarchy, and perhaps a somewhat larger proportion of its grassroots, that the church should apply its formidable temporal power and resources to tackling the burning issues of the day, such as the appalling poverty in much of the undeveloped world. And that it should take a fresh look at its reactionary positions on such things as religious freedom, the intolerance of 'error has no rights,' and the explosively controversial question of birth control. The bitter struggle for the heart and mind of the church that these issues would spawn, and which the election a few years later of the liberal Pope John XXIII would bring fully into focus, had already drawn Carroll firmly into its embrace. An embrace from which, despite the raging torrents of doubt and temptation to which he would be subjected and would eventually succumb, he was never to break free.

But, of course, neither of them would have had any notion of this at the time. A silence followed in which Stephen could see Stan lost in thought, something bothering him for which he was searching for words to express. And something was bothering Stephen too. Something else: his tussle with Brother

Simon of a few days before, his disquiet at the violent reaction to what he had said, as though he were challenging the very foundations of religious belief. He had been back to the library a few times since then and had read more about evolution. Enough to convince him of Simon's utter ignorance and intolerance of what was clearly a well-reasoned hypothesis that was steadily gaining ground. Certainly not something that anyone with a smattering of intelligence could dismiss out of hand. So what did this say for Simon's other strongly held beliefs with which he was forever regaling them? Could they be equally irrational? And what about the other brothers? Sam's reference to a load of ignorant bigots had seemed gratuitously insulting at the time, and had angered him. But now those words kept coming back, naggingly, defying all attempts to dismiss them as simply the unconsidered spontaneous utterances they clearly were. It felt to Stephen as though the faith he had accepted unquestioningly all his life was being assailed from all sides. He was confused and disturbed. He wanted to talk to Carroll about it, was waiting for an appropriate moment to do so, worried that Stan's persistence with the topic in hand would leave no such opportunity.

Magically it seemed, as though reading his mind, Carroll broke the silence, coming right out with it himself. He couldn't believe it.

'Seems you have upset Brother Simon,' he said, giving him a look that somehow blended mild reproach with a glimmer of amusement. 'You should be more careful, you know. But perhaps you would like to tell me just what it was all about.'

'I wanted to talk to you. But... but how on earth did you

get to hear of it?'

What should have been obvious to him, would have been had he ever given it a moment's thought, was that the old school building — a high-security, no-go area so far as the boys were concerned — was effectively home to the close community of brothers. There, they dined together, shared a common room and other facilities, and there they would converse on matters appropriate to their calling — perhaps, on occasion, on other things as well. It turned out that Stephen's remarks in Simon's class had been reported, had given rise to discussion and some concern. Carroll's response, however, when he had heard what Stephen had to say, was to point out that a growing number of church members were coming to accept evolution as simply the expression of God's will, the fully intended consequence of his basic laws, set up at the moment of creation to govern the physical behaviour of the universe. And that there was no real problem with the biblical account of the creation; the Catholic Church, unlike many of its Protestant counterparts having long come to regard the stories of the Old Testament metaphorically — symbolic representations of God's special relationship with mankind, conveyed in terms readily comprehensible to the intended recipients, not in any way to be taken literally. The immediate effect on Stephen of this interpretation was one of relief, difficulties would surface later. For the moment only one further question remained, less fundamental to be sure, but disturbing nevertheless.

'Why then,' he asked hesitantly, 'did Brother Simon react with such violence to what I said? I was just repeating what I had read somewhere. It seemed interesting and completely related to what he had just been talking about. That was all. I wasn't attacking him or anything. It was just... I mean, just what scientists are finding out about things. What's wrong with talking about that?'

Carroll gave him a long look, clearly weighing his reply. He was in a uniquely difficult position of which they had no inkling at the time. The pressures of his other life — those long absences from school, of which so little was known to them — were tearing his soul. He was alone, tormented by doubt and ever-growing disillusionment. Perhaps Stephen and Stan, for all their juvenile naivety, were affording him a small measure of comfort, their uncertainties echoing, to some extent, his own. The fight for him, however, was still far from over.

'The problem we have to face,' he said eventually, 'is that Darwin's theory has been seized upon by atheists to attack the foundations of religious belief. Quite unjustifiably when you come to look at it dispassionately, but the fact remains. And Brother Simon is only human. People under attack, as he feels himself and his faith to be on this issue, should be forgiven for being less than open-minded about the weapons being used against them. It takes time to be objective under those circumstances. My view, for what it's worth, is that although there are still a lot of holes in the theory, a lot of essential evidence missing, many questions still to be resolved, enough is there to take very seriously indeed what is, after all, an elegant and ingenious hypothesis. Certainly, one with strong intellectual appeal. And why should we be surprised if God has chosen intellectually appealing mechanisms for his acts of creation? He never revealed the laws of physics to us directly, leaving it to people to unravel them for themselves — and marvel as they were doing so at their simplicity and beauty. Evolution may well come to be seen in that light, and likewise applauded as yet another example of God's wondrous ways.'

'So, you definitely believe in it then?'

'I think there is a lot to be said for it but we shall have to wait and see. More evidence is required, but that is going to be coming in now. Masses of it, from all over the place. When the scientific community is faced with a fundamental problem of this importance, no effort is spared in finding a generally accepted solution. But whatever that turns out to be has to be viewed as being in accord with God's plan. Nothing else. Faith has nothing whatsoever to fear from evolution or any other scientific theory. It operates on a quite separate plane.'

'And what about the other brothers?' This came from Stan, who had been silently watching and listening. 'How many of them do you think see it the way you do?'

Stephen couldn't see how Carroll could answer that, even if he knew. In fact, he started evasively with 'I can only speak for myself...', but then stopped abruptly. Something in his expression had changed as though he had come to a decision, was throwing reticence to the winds and the hell with it.

'None of them do,' he said at last.

He was looking somewhat dejected now that he had come out with it, an unaccustomed weariness threatening to envelop him. But then he collected himself, gave a coy half-smile and went on.

'But it's early days yet. One thing the Catholic Church has certainly learned by now is how to be flexible in dealing with intractable opposition to its doctrines. Its members will surely follow. Just give it time.'

Although spoken in a controlled tone, his demeanour giving nothing away, it appeared quite clear to Stephen that he applauded such flexibility, regarded it an essential virtue.

THREE

Stephen and Stan had started in the junior school at the same time, both at the age of eight. They moved up together into and through the senior school, but it was not until the fourth form that they were to become close friends. Stan was there, seated next to Ignatius in the confirmation photo, looking understandably uncomfortable with his hands on his knees and staring straight ahead; on his other side was Philips, his baby old-man's face set in a pinched smile that suggested he had just heard, or was about to tell, a dirty joke — he quite often looked that way; and next to him, at the end of the row, trying to look invisible, was Stephen.

Stan came from a well-off artistic family who lived in a large detached house in Muswell Hill. His father was an architect, partner in a thriving London practice, quite often abroad on business and a convivial presence when around — always seemingly pleased to see Stephen, making him feel at ease in their home. Stan's maternal grandfather had been a painter much in vogue in his youth, later less in the public eye but nevertheless a reasonably successful Royal Academician up to the time of his death. His daughter, Stan's mother, was also a painter who had likewise shown early promise, though had put it on hold to devote herself to bringing up her four children. At around the time that Stan, their youngest child, entered the fifth form she had started painting again in earnest, determined to make up for lost time. Stan chose to regard this development ambivalently, showing obvious interest, but at the same time going on about his needs being neglected and the house being a mess and smelling of turps — his mother's inevitable response being a good-natured laugh, in keeping with the family's reaction to all Stan's poses. For he was a consummate actor, ever experimenting with new roles and revamping old ones, managing in this way to draw some attention to himself in that bustling home environment.

Stephen always looked forward to his visits there, enjoyed the conversations that would develop over supper and sometimes carry on till late. He would occasionally stay overnight, sleeping in an unbelievably comfortable guest room with its own washbasin, into which he could indulge the unheard-of luxury of peeing at night without having to leave the room. A strong additional attraction of these visits, which he tried unsuccessfully to hide, was the possibility they provided for an encounter with Stan's beautiful sister Lavinia. She was three years older than them, and to Stephen all the more desirable for being totally unavailable, a goddess to be worshipped from afar and lusted over in private. On the rare occasions when she had nothing better to do than spend an evening at home, she would make a point of patronising Stan, treating him like a kid, at times also targeting Stephen with her teasing, adding to his infatuation. A positive aspect of all this was that it helped him get over his rejection by Sarah, something that had hurt badly and dominated his emotions for months. Lavinia had at least made him realise there were other delectable fish in the waters around him, even if the prospect of netting them at the time appeared remote. The other sister, Maria, the eldest child, was married and lived in France.

Stephen had never met her, but she was spoken of with reverence as a great beauty, particularly so by Stan when Lavinia was around — a thrust which only rarely struck a nerve. Between the two sisters came Albert, Stan's only brother, a witty, likeable rogue who did something clearly lucrative and probably dodgy in the city. Although he had his own apartment in town, he seemed to be always at Muswell Hill, driving over for supper in his sports car, often with a glamorous girlfriend — one of a string of these, each by all appearances oblivious of the existence of others.

Stephen and Stan saw a lot of each other during their fifth form year. It is difficult to understand just how such friendships come about. Their home backgrounds were very different, Stephen's dour and reserved, with nothing remotely resembling the sparkle and tolerance that so captivated him at the Firbright's — where nothing was taboo and even the most delicate-seeming topic could become the subject of uninhibited discussion and irreverent humour. Stephen remembers, on one of his first supper evenings there, reference being made to a Vatican pronouncement on birth control — something the Firbrights had strong feelings about. One after another they chipped in indignantly, the conversation then turning to ribald speculation on what would have led up to it, '…those celibate octogenarians in their ridiculous little red hats quoting Genesis and passing round French letters.' And the Firbrights, he had to remind himself, were conspicuously Catholic, ever active in the social affairs of the parish.

It was undoubtedly this liberal milieu that prompted Stan's forceful questioning of Carroll that so worried Stephen at the time. An example of this, one he would have strong cause to recall years later, arose during one of their Friday after-class sessions. It concerned once again the supposedly beneficial role of religious belief in settling major issues — something Carroll set great store by and which Stan was coming increasingly to question.

'Does it matter what religion we are talking about here?' he asked at one point, going on to say, 'I mean, do you see a belief in Islam or Hinduism as being helpful in this way?'

'Yes, I do,' Carroll had replied after the briefest of pauses. 'As I've said many times before, the absence of a religious dimension would leave naked self-interest effectively the only criterion in play. I know it may not seem like it at times, but the alternatives leave no room for hope.'

He looked a little disturbed, even indecisive, after having said that, as though struggling against a desire to say more. Stan in the meantime, keyed up, oblivious of danger, was warming to the debate.

'So, it's religious belief *regardless of its validity* that leaves room for hope. Is that what you're saying? That if there wasn't a God, we would have to invent one to preserve the brotherhood of man. I can't see Brother Simon going along with that. Nor any of the others.'

This time Stephen really thought he had done it, gone way too far, endangering the relationship that had developed between them. And indeed, Carroll's expression had turned very strange as if in confirmation of his misgivings. No trace of anger though. Puzzlement rather, together with something else, something undecipherable at the time that would require the benefit of distant hindsight for any hope of interpretation.

From time to time, when opportunities arose, Stan would try to question Carroll on his background and his long absences from the school. With regard to the latter, his reticence remained unshakeable, the inevitable response of a discreet smile making quite clear his unwillingness to be drawn. But some clues to his background were to emerge, which Stephen was later able to amplify from other sources.

He was born in Tunbridge Wells in 1915, his parents having married hastily at the outbreak of World War I. A few months after their marriage, his father had been posted to France, having volunteered for active service in the first flush of patriotic fervour to engulf the nation; soon to die alongside thousands of others in the Battle of the Somme, walking from his trench as instructed into a volley of German machine-gunfire. And so, Piers — Carroll — was never to see his father, and his young widowed mother was left in wartime Britain with an infant son and all expectations for happiness and a settled future dashed beyond hope. But help of a sort was close at hand. Her moderately prosperous family of Irish Catholic origin had been somewhat disapproving of her marriage to the son of an Anglican clergyman. They now rose to the occasion, supplementing the meagre financial settlement her husband had managed to set up and taking on full responsibility for Piers's education. In due course, he attended Downside, which he took to from the start, even coming to harbour a vocation for the Dominican priesthood. This he put aside, or at least on hold, when he won a scholarship to Oxford, developing there a passion for ancient history, which led him to the study of ancient languages, in particular Hebrew and Aramaic. On graduation, he accepted the offer of his tutor to remain at Oxford, researching into Palestinian history of the immediate pre-Christian period. But then world events conspired once again to shape the course of his life, World War II being declared when he was little more than a year into his postgraduate studies, bringing them precipitously to a halt.

To his mother's intense distress, Piers insisted on following in his father's footsteps, volunteering immediately for active service, doing so along with a cousin of the same age — son of his mother's elder brother — with whom he had shared a large part of his childhood. Both went on to serve in Africa with the 'Desert Rats', though in different units, and it was a matter of days following the fall of Tobruk before Piers was to learn his cousin had died there. He emerged from the war a changed man, beset by guilt at having encouraged his cousin's enlistment, and with the certainties which had previously conditioned his existence swept away with the comrades killed and maimed on the battlefields of North Africa. Returning to Oxford bemused, empty of emotion, he buried himself in his research. No longer the vibrant presence of his youth, a taciturn loner now, seemingly oblivious of all but his studies. Despite the travel and other difficulties of that immediate post-war period, he somehow managed to access key library collections in various parts of Europe and beyond, consulting manuscripts that had long laid forgotten and unread. And his thesis, when eventually it appeared, attracted serious attention from academic specialists in that field — not least among those of the Vatican, where some satisfaction, not to say relief, could be felt for the support certain aspects of his findings provided for endangered orthodox positions. He was invited to Rome, warmly received there, presented with the opportunity to confer with leading ecclesiastical scholars, and effectively enlisted as an authority to be called upon should the occasion arise. To him, this last provision appeared no more than a polite way of bringing discussions to a close, never imagining for a moment it would ever be taken up.

Piers had by this time largely come to terms with the horrors of his wartime experiences, recovered to some extent his previous sociability, and appeared well on track for a promising academic career — the possibilities of openings being hinted at by his Oxford advisors. But one thing he had decided upon in Africa was that, if he were to survive the war, his eventual role in life would be to teach. Not to the privileged few at places like Downside, but at the sort of schools his wartime comrades had attended — which they would talk about from time to time, for the most part disparagingly, but occasionally singling out a teacher who had got through to them, whom they felt had something worthwhile to convey. He had warmed to the notion of that role, convinced it was God's plan for him, and that nothing else, however tempting, should stand in its way. Shortly after his return to Oxford, unbeknown to anyone, he contacted a Roman Catholic teaching order seemingly dedicated to the values he had in mind. What he was reaching out for here amounted to compromise in several respects: members of the brotherhood were not ordained priests, though took solemn vows of poverty, chastity and obedience to the order nonetheless, and the schools they ran were not altogether typical of those his comrades had spoken of in the lulls between violent action. But it nevertheless all seemed to fit for him somehow, the senior brothers he spoke to appearing understanding of his vocation, appreciative of what he had to offer. So he laid the foundations for fast-tracking himself into their community at the completion of his academic studies. Which was how, as Brother Carroll, he came to St John's little more than a year after Stephen and Stan, apprehensive eight-year-olds, had entered the junior school.

FOUR

School education for the majority of St John's boys in the nineteen-fifties ended at sixteen, after the fifth form and O-level exams, following which they would enter the job market or family business or simply vanish without trace. Stephen and Stan were among the few to carry on into the sixth form — all part of a natural progression for Stan but for Stephen posing something of a problem. He had no idea at all what he wanted to do on leaving school, so the prospect of staying on, though not viewed with enthusiasm, at least had the advantage of putting off any fateful decision for another couple of years. Not completely, however, as a choice still had to be made between the arts and the sciences. For Stan, this involved no soul-searching, the arts having been his firm choice from the start. Stephen would have preferred a mixture, something involving no decision on his part, but this wasn't on offer and he eventually plumped for the sciences — helped along at the last minute by a mind-numbingly tedious Latin lesson from Brother Cornelius, who would be teaching the subject for the next two years in the Sixth Arts. And so Stan and he became separated in the classroom, their close friendship carrying on unabated nonetheless.

A few weeks into the sixth form, Stephen was railroaded into taking part in a dramatic performance, an outcome of which was to clarify for him the direction in which Stan's life was heading. He would soon forget the reason for the celebration — marked by the whole upper school attending a solemn service at Westminster Cathedral — but remembered well the joy and excitement at its announcement, involving as it did a day off school and a trip into central London. Stan and he made their way there together, arriving early and being shepherded to a pew somewhere near the front. There they sat for an age as the church filled. He could feel Stan getting fidgety beside him, the more so as the service progressed, and yet more during the oration that followed. The printed programme they had been handed on arrival indicated there were more of these to come, a bevy of dignitaries lined up to deliver them.

'I don't think I can stand much more of this,' whispered Stan. 'Let's get out of here.'

Stephen, getting seriously worried by this time, tried to caution against improvident action.

'Listen,' said Stan, interrupting him. 'I feel a fit coming on. You're going to have to carry me out.'

Before he could reply, Stan had fallen against him, saliva bubbling from his mouth, eyes pivoting upwards, only their whites showing beneath the lids. He stood, pulling Stan more or less upright, then somehow managing to manoeuvre him along the row, past legs hurriedly twisting out of the way, more urgently so as Stan started to retch. On reaching the aisle, he saw Stan's face the colour of chalk, felt his arm heavy around his neck, his full weight bearing down on him. While pausing there for a moment, Stan seemed to recover a little, his features settling into a picture of grim determination. Then, a first tentative step towards the daylight streaming in through the distant doorway. Slowly they made their way towards it, linked together, accompanied by a blur of fleeting images, expressions of concern, of curiosity, of gratitude even for the welcome distraction; of Ignatius's fixed gaze of undisguised hostility, Carroll's knowing look of mild amusement. On making it to the forecourt, Stan immediately broke away and bounded off, Stephen following hesitantly at first, then looking back as he ran, concerned that some sympathetic soul could have followed them out, could have witnessed the miraculous recovery. But no. Nothing untoward in sight. They were free. An intense feeling of liberation enveloped him, quite disproportionately so in view of the mere hour or two of freedom won, but a foretaste perhaps of that final departure from St John's, still too far into the future for conscious consideration, and an accompanying sense of relief that testified in large part to Stan's faultless performance which, against all the evidence for being just that, had begun to persuade him his symptoms were real.

Stan was popular and highly regarded among his classmates, not for any ability on the sports field — the usual criterion for acclaim at St John's — but because of his exceptional talent as a performer. His appearance, not an immediately obvious asset, helped here. At best it could be described as nondescript, his build and height average, his face rather puffy and featureless, someone who could pass through a room full of people attracting no attention whatsoever. Unless that is, he wished otherwise. Then the transformation would be immediate and remarkable, his features taking shape, the muscles hardening to the chosen form: the confident authority perhaps, expounding with unshakeable conviction, scanning the onlookers with a penetrating gaze that defied contradiction; or the seasoned cynic, pouring scorn on some expression of conventional opinion. The more bogus the stance, the greater the satisfaction he would draw from it. Later he would come to apply this talent in approaches to women, with a remarkable success rating that predated the celebrity status that would send it soaring. But the thing that really endeared him to everyone, set him indisputably in a class of his own, was his extraordinary skill as a mimic. He could assimilate and reproduce the accent and nuances of a spoken phrase, delighting his classmates with renderings of Ignatius or Simon or any other of the brothers pontificating on some well-worn theme, or engaging in improbable dialogue. *'Jesus! Look at that one over there, Brother Ignatius, the one in the short skirt and red jumper.' 'Holy mother of God Brother Simon, what a handful!'* The visual aspects of these performances were no less impressive, Stan's face contorting into recognisable features of whomever he was taking off, or, in the absence of such knowledge, into a seemingly appropriate appearance for someone who spoke in that way.

It was the school play, however, midway through their final year at St John's, that was to provide the occasion for Stan's talent as a performer to be appreciated by a wider audience, setting him firmly on the career path he was to follow for the rest of his life. A recurrent problem with the school play — an important annual event — was its almost inevitably requirement for females in the cast, a resource conspicuously unavailable at St John's. An approach to a girls' convent school close by could well have made good this deficiency; but, whether for reason of logistics or fear of exposing the boys — and, who knows, perhaps the brothers — to occasions of sin, was never explored, leaving as the only remaining solution that boys should play girls. In a more enlightened age this would have posed few problems, could even have been applauded for encouraging, among other good things, dramatic versatility. But Britain in the early fifties was far from enlightened in that respect, St John's being no exception: expression of the merest suggestion of femininity in that macho environment — possession of a smaller than standard male-size handkerchief, for example — being certain to elicit derision and contempt. Which presented a casting problem for Brother Leo, the overstretched director-cum-general-factotum of the production, whose repeated assurances that in Shakespeare's time female roles were invariably played by men were of precious little help. Resistance remained strong and deep-rooted, helped along by rumour and folklore regarding the pitfalls of any such involvement. A case in point, recent enough to be still very much on the minds of those concerned, featured a fourth former who, following glowing acclaim for his rendering of Hamlet's Ophelia, went on to display tendencies that, in roughly equal measure, entertained and scandalised the entire school, leading to his eventual expulsion. So one can well imagine Brother Leo's relief when, without the need for even a whisper of coercion or cajolement, Stan volunteered for the part of Lady Macbeth. What made this more interesting was that a classmate of his, Hamish Maclaren, star sportsman and paradigm of aggressive masculinity, — and, in Stan's view, as thick as burnt porridge — had been chosen for the title role. That he and Stan held each other in barely concealed contempt was widely known, fuelling wry speculation on how they would perform together on stage as man and wife. Hamish clearly felt he held the advantage here, his swaggering role and flash gear — battle armour and sword — in pleasing contrast to the soft gown or frock or whatever in which Stan would have to appear. So much so that he quite failed to appreciate the significance of what seemed to him no more than interminable nit-picking with which Stan would engage Brother Leo at rehearsals over every detail of the direction. The final rehearsal should perhaps have given him some inkling of the way things were going. But nothing would have prepared him for the first public showing, at which Stan abandoned his guilefully imposed self-restraint to let fly with a thunderous performance which held everyone enthralled. Whenever on stage, the action revolved relentlessly around him — her — the hapless Hamish relegated to a pathetic wimp, completely under the thumb of his contemptuous wife, his pained reaction to her taunts drawing relieved laughter from an otherwise spellbound audience — and a brief favourable mention by a theatre-critic alumnus of St John's in a local rag review otherwise devoted almost entirely to eulogising Stan's interpretation.

For Stan, perhaps the most significant outcome of the episode was in the reaction of his family, in particular his father, who, thrilled at what they had witnessed, dropped all objections to his auditioning for RADA rather than trying for Oxbridge as they had been pressuring him to do for some time.

FIVE

Carroll had effectively left St John's by the time Stephen and Stan entered the sixth form. He would still turn up from time to time on brief visits, though for no apparent reason, without any obvious school duties to perform. Enquiries about him to other brothers always drew a blank, indeed they were frowned upon as being none of their business. Rumour was rife, however, much of it stemming from Philips — a fount of insider information on all manner of things, many scandalous and salacious, often highly suspect, but enough turning out close enough to the mark to confirm his access to dependable, at times seemingly occult, sources. According to him, Carroll had been commandeered by the Vatican to help sort out a major problem the church was facing with the discovery of some ancient documents in the Holy Land. It was all very hush-hush because it appeared they contained accounts of the early days of Christianity that directly contradicted established belief. The Pope, according to Philips, was 'pretty pissed off about it because, thinking himself infallible, he took particular exception to being told he'd got something wrong.' Allowing for the usual embellishments, there was something plausible about this explanation for Carroll's absences. Certainly, ancient Holy Land documents were something they were aware he had made a study of at Oxford and, a few years before, there had been a great deal of excitement generated by the press at the discovery in Palestine of the 'Dead Sea Scrolls,' manuscripts which had promised to reveal much about events in that region at around the time of Jesus — only to fizzle out inexplicably and be largely forgotten. So, yes, there could be something in Philips's account, with which they looked forward to confronting Carroll, should the opportunity arise.

In the meantime, Stephen was to be made aware of another example of Philips's foreknowledge — not one that demonstrated particularly strong evidence of his powers this time, but of interest nonetheless, especially to him. This concerned a severe predicament being faced by fellow sixth former Carlo Petroni, news of which would shortly be entertaining the entire school. Carlo was a year above Stephen and about to sit his A-levels. It was he who, some eighteen months earlier, had accepted the favours of Sarah — something that still rankled with Stephen and still hurt badly. So, although he shouldn't really have blamed Carlo for responding as he did — the initiative would without question have been hers and the temptation considerable — any suggestion of misfortune befalling him would be sure to arouse Stephen's unsympathetic curiosity. Which was why, when Philips sidled up to him that morning, whispering from the corner of his mouth that 'your friend Petroni's plonker has really landed him in it this time,' he was understandably intrigued, eager to learn more. But all he could get out of Philips was a 'just wait and see,' and a knowing look. It didn't take long for the essential details to emerge.

The circumstances leading up to the Petroni debacle were crucial to its realisation. In considering these, it becomes necessary to correct the impression given earlier that St John's environment was completely women-free. Though a reasonable enough approximation for describing casting difficulties for the school play, this idea omits the existence of a substantial detached house in the school grounds, situated a safe distance from the other buildings, which housed a small community of Irish nuns. So that there should be no question of impropriety, members of this community were all ancient and, according to Philips, selected by means of a rigorous procedure — a sort of beauty contest in reverse — devised to prevent the remotest possibility of temptation perturbing the settled lives of even the most sexually repressed of the chaste brotherhood. So far so good. These nuns performed certain important tasks at St John's, including the preparation of all meals for the brothers and lunch in term times for the boys — the latter, it can be said, with appalling results, even measured against the abysmally low standards prevailing in early post-war Britain. More to the point, however, was that nobody was getting any younger with the passing years. Given their starting age of around seventy, the nuns were feeling this effect particularly strongly, finding it ever more difficult to cope. Meetings were held, the problem discussed, and a solution proposed by the nuns themselves and eventually accepted. Philips, when the saga had run its course, was, as usual, able to furnish details. It seemed that the nuns belonged to an order that had branches in poverty-stricken regions of Ireland, from where they were able to draw on the services of young women content to slave away without respite for no more than bed and board and assurance of the approval of the Almighty. The idea was simply to offer a few of them the opportunity of a working sojourn in London — perhaps put out as a reward for exemplary behaviour — so relieving the nuns of the more arduous of their duties. The girls apparently jumped at the prospect and it was agreed to go ahead on a trial basis. So relieved was the St John's administration at the negligible cost of the proposed solution that any doubts concerning its inherent dangers were brushed aside, and a first — and, as it turned out, last — batch of young women, one or two by no means unattractive, was duly installed in the convent precinct. It must have seemed to them that they had entered paradise, the modest facilities at their disposal sheer luxury compared with those left behind, their duties lighter and clearly appreciated, and regular entertainment provided from their rooms overlooking the playing fields by scantily clad young men engaging in exhilarating physical activity. The boys, for their part, spurred on by the attention of their well preened young admirers, responded with ever more ambitious performances, accompanied by frequent furtive glances at the windows framing their enthralled objects of desire. It was an accident waiting to happen, in the event not having long to wait: within a year of their arrival, one of the girls having to confess sobbingly to the sister-in-charge that she was pregnant. One can well imagine the horror with which this news was received in that chastity-obsessed enclave, and the further horror at the thought of it becoming public. This latter consideration may have played somewhat into the hands of Carlo Petroni, the soon-to-be identified perpetrator of the foul deed. Driven by forces he was unable or unwilling to control — perhaps, so Stephen liked to think, driven also to despair by the unsatisfactory outcome of his relationship with Sarah — he had breached the convent defences within a matter of weeks of the arrival of its nubile contingent; and unbeknown to anyone — other than Philips! — had entered into the ill-fated liaison. Summary expulsion was a not uncommon consequence at St John's for offences falling light-years short in perceived gravity of that of Carlo's. But in the confrontations that followed, involving Carlo, his father, the girl and the Brother Director, a deal was effectively struck: a discreet marriage would take place without delay and, in return for a pledge of complete silence, Carlo would be allowed to enter the school for the sole purpose of sitting his A-level exams, thereafter never to darken its doorstep again. And so the affair ended, the remaining girls returning to Ireland along with some of the more ancient nuns — the latter soon to be replaced by marginally less decrepit versions of the same. All evidence of the failed experiment expunged, the slate wiped clean.

Looking back years later, the Petroni affair and Stan's portrayal of Lady Macbeth would stand out among Stephen's few lasting memories of those final years at St John's. But dominating these, a result no doubt of later events unimaginable at the time, was that first tantalising glimpse of Natasha. The occasion was the annual junior school prize-giving ceremony of his first sixth form year. An assortment of spectators — boys' mothers mainly, interspersed with awkward-looking fathers and others — were assembling in the junior playground outside the door to the hall where the business was about to begin. It was a pretty nondescript gathering, totally ignored by the boys in the adjoining senior playground engaged in games and fights and whatever. Stephen and Stan were there, standing close to the boundary, chatting away, as was their habit in the break between lessons and barely aware of the dowdy group forming through the railings alongside them, until Natasha appeared on the scene. Stan was later to liken the effect to the cinematographic device of introducing a character in full Technicolor into an otherwise monochrome scene. Britain in the mid-fifties was showing few signs of the youthful awakening that was to transform its image some years later. But Natasha, it seemed, was in that vanguard, providing a foretaste of things to come, and splendidly incongruous in that dull disapproving setting. Stan was the first to notice her.

'Just look at that,' he said, under his breath; and, as Stephen turned to do so, she registered their interest and smiled at them gawping at her from no more than ten yards away. A lithe body clothed emphatically to draw attention to what lay beneath; chunky ankle boots accentuating the nakedness of long golden legs; a skirt scandalously short, a soft jersey highlighting firm, clearly unsupported breasts; her face little made up except round the eyes — dark with long mascaraed lashes; a swirl of blond hair escaping from under a rakishly angled cap. No sooner had they taken all this in than a loud clatter announced the opening of the hall door and she was lost in the surge that followed, swept away with the flow.

'Phew! Who on earth could that be?' said Stan, eyes ablaze. 'Somebody's sister, I suppose.'

Stephen nodded, lost for words. They had both reckoned her age to be twenty or so, on a par with Lavinia's.

'Did you see the expression on the face of the old bag next to her?'

Before Stephen could reply, the whistle had blown, signalling the end of the break and directing them in thoughtful silence to their separate classrooms.

It turned out that they were quite wrong about her age. She had been there as a mum, of her seven-year-old son in the junior school. Which placed her high in the twenties, perhaps even thirty — somewhere way over the hill from their adolescent perspective. This came as something of a shock to Stan.

'Bloody hell,' he said, on taking it in, 'she must be as old as Maria' — his eldest sister, indelibly ascribed to an altogether earlier generation. He seemed quite upset about it. As for Stephen, his feelings were confused. His social life, such as it was, revolved largely around a local youth club, attended with Stan, from where he had been dating a girl for some months, since shortly after his break with Sarah. It wasn't getting anywhere but lingering on from habit now, from want of any obvious alternative. Thoughts of Natasha — her assured body language with its promise of unimaginable delights, that amused receptive smile beamed in their direction — stirring up something inside, a tantalising concoction of guilt-ridden desire and forlorn aspiration. Is there something wrong with me, he wondered, to feel this way about someone's mum? Must be, he decided, and tried and failed miserably to banish her from his mind.

SIX

It was in his final year at St John's that another preoccupation would come to dominate Stephen's confused state. This concerned the religious faith into which he had been born and raised, his entire education devoted to its vigorous promotion, any doubt about it in his mind condemned as the lure of evil forces bent on his eternal damnation. Yet despite all this, seeds of doubt, planted over time without his knowing participation, were tentatively putting out shoots, though confined to a barely conscious level by fear of the enormity of what they implied, the terrifying emptiness to which they appeared to point. His only real awareness of their existence was through feelings of something-not-quite-right which were springing up now with increasing frequency, particularly during the daily religious instruction sessions. Doubts regarding fundamental aspects of the faith he had learned to suppress, putting them down to his ignorance of the rigorous theological arguments which, he had been led to believe, established them as unshakeable truths. But on peripheral matters, he was now feeling freer to question seeming inconsistencies and, though he would not have dared describe them in quite this way even to himself, plain absurdities. High on the list of these stood the matter of indulgences, a strongly promoted commodity at St John's, prudent investments guaranteed to mature promptly on arrival in the hereafter. The fact that Stephen was largely unaware of the massive sixteenth-century controversy on the issue that had led to the Protestant Reformation says much about the teaching of religious history at St John's. He had simply come to feel uncomfortable about the current practice of which he was directly aware, felt it trivialised the faith, and had voiced restrained misgivings about it in class. The response had been firm and unsympathetic: the power of the church to grant indulgences had been given her by Jesus Christ himself, the scriptures making this abundantly clear; and who did he think he was anyway, challenging the authority of the church, which had pronounced on the matter after prolonged scholarly examination? Rather to his surprise, Stephen remained undaunted by this rebuke and far from convinced by the perfunctory justification. So much so that he decided to examine the evidence for himself.

He found the justification to be based largely on a passage in St Matthew's gospel with which he was well familiar, the one where Jesus appoints Peter as the head of his church and bequeaths various powers to him, including the 'whatsoever thou shalt loose on earth, it shall be loosed also in heaven.' This was interpreted as giving Peter carte blanch to forgive sins, an act whose ratification in heaven would automatically follow, thereby enabling repentant sinners to achieve salvation. In fact, it was not only Peter to whom it was assumed this power had been granted; the other apostles, Peter's successors as head of the church, and anyone else he or they wished to appoint thereafter, were all presumed to possess it — spawning the ritual of confession, absolution and penance that occupies a prime place among Roman Catholic observances. This much Stephen had never thought to question. It was simply indulgences that had struck the discordant note.

These related to the doctrine that penitents whose sins had been forgiven did not then get off scot-free. Far from it. They still had to do time for their offences in purgatory — a penal institution which, by all accounts, rendered the most brutal of medieval torture chambers a holiday camp by comparison. But the catch-all nature of '*whatsoever* thou shalt loose on earth...' was taken to imply that, in addition to granting them the power to forgive sins, time to be spent in purgatory could also be 'loosed' by Peter and his successors in any way they chose. This they proceeded to do by bestowing indulgences — at times involving substantial cash payments — to remit part or all of the due sentences; partial remission typically being granted for engaging in some trite gesture of atonement, like wearing a particular holy medal; and total remission — a *plenary* indulgence, effectively a go-direct-to-paradise card — for simply turning up to receive a designated papal blessing. It crossed Stephen's mind that old-timers in paradise, who had had to suffer the torments of purgatory to get there, could well be excused for feeling resentment at the sight of newcomers, blatant serial sinners undoubtedly among them, swanning in with their plenary indulgence certificates straight from their deathbeds — a flicker of amusement at the thought interrupting his otherwise sober deliberations.

The more he read about the justification for indulgences, the stronger his feeling of something-not-quite-right was to become, gradually developing into severer, more focussed criticism: the sheer presumption of asserting God's participation in the banal practice coming to appear little short of blasphemy — akin, say, to the Temple money changers claiming God's ratification of their exchange rates. And alongside all this, a growing sense of incredulity at the tortuous logic with which the conclusion had been arrived at from the flimsiest of foundations: a few words, penned years after the event by a non-present clearly non-disinterested writer, on the basis of non-disinterested reports of what Jesus may have said and wild speculation on what he thereby intended. Stephen, at the time a firmly committed Roman Catholic, had confined his misgivings to the question of indulgences, not letting them spill over into other practices and doctrines of the church. But now, as a result of his probing, chinks were beginning to appear in the barrier bearing down on other more fundamental suppressed doubts, the muffled rumbling of dissent growing ever more persistent.

As the final sixth form year got underway, Stephen's thoughts turned reluctantly to what he should do next, not helped at all by lack of any feeling for what this should be, of any view of himself as other than the aimless, lost soul he had become. In this he felt quite alone, the enthusiasm of his classmates — all seemingly raring to set out along well-chosen paths to enticing careers — quite lost on him, their visions of status and success leaving him cold. He envied Stan, of course, could appreciate his excitement and share in it, though it served to rub in the fact that nothing remotely in that class of choice was available in his case.

But then one morning, after the deadline for Oxbridge applications had passed and those for other universities were drawing perilously near, his maths teacher asked him to remain behind as the lesson ended. He had no idea what he could possibly want with him, having had very few personal dealings with the man, a shy undemonstrative brother who in Stephen's view — not, by any means, a universal one — taught his subject with a clarity and precision that made for effortless understanding. As soon as the class had emptied, Brother Francis came straight to the point, asking if he had got round to applying for university admission; and, on being told that he hadn't, suggesting he might like to consider a degree in mathematics. Stephen was doubly surprised at this, never for a moment having thought that Francis had so much as noticed him in class, let alone singled him out in this way.

'In my opinion,' he went on, 'you have the potential for first-class achievement in mathematics, more so than anyone I have taught for quite some time.'

Stephen was dumbfounded. True, he had always done well in tests and homework exercises but never felt this to be of any significance, that it reflected only the commonplace nature of the assignments — a view compounded by Francis's distinctly low-key demeanour and lack of comment when work was handed back, in sharp contrast with the science teachers, forever vocal both in criticism and, less often, restrained praise.

Thanking Francis for his suggestion, he said he would think seriously about it and went away to do so, feeling his spirits rising. This could indeed be the answer it seemed, putting off for another three years, maybe more, dismal considerations of a career. Then, almost as a surprise, the realisation came to him how much he enjoyed wrestling with mathematical problems, finding a way through to a solution, developing new skills, learning new techniques. The idea that he could spend the next three years doing just that… it seemed almost too good to be true. Why on earth hadn't he thought of it before? Thinking about it now gave rise to a burgeoning desire to communicate his suddenly acquired enthusiasm to someone else.

The first person to become available for the purpose was Philips, who had approached him just as he was leaving the building, his expression revealing he had something salacious to report. But, before he could come out with it, Stephen got in first, announcing he had come to a sudden decision about a degree course. This was of interest to Philips, who, for reasons diametrically opposed to Stephen's, had also long agonised on what he should do next. In his case, the overriding concern being not to be left behind in the earnings and status stakes. But having made his choice on that basis, the worry remained: perhaps he had got it wrong, perhaps others had chosen more astutely. He regarded Stephen as something of a dark horse, whose dithering, confused manner was simply a cover for shrewd judgement. So he put his reason for approaching him on hold, remaining silent, his features betraying sudden anxiety, which Stephen noticed and was puzzled by; the more so when, after having come out with mathematics as his choice, he saw him relax, his expression reverting to that of a moment before.

'What on earth do you expect to get out of that?' he asked, going on without waiting for a reply, 'I've a bit of news that might interest you. We need to go somewhere more private. You're not going to believe this.'

Not for the first time, Stephen wondered about Philips, a strange bird by any reckoning. Very much a loner, inhabiting his private world from which he would only emerge briefly for well-defined purposes, such as the disclosure of intriguing, mysteriously-acquired inside information on the school and its inmates. Unusual also in appearance: a pinched and blotchy adult face — substantially unchanged from early junior school days — on a somewhat hunched, ungainly body. (He was destined to appear that way throughout his life, an unexceptional forty-five-year-old from early youth till well into old age). Perhaps it was Stephen's being also something of a loner that made him the most frequent recipient of Philips's bizarre revelations and impious asides — derogatory remarks typically aimed at one or other of the brothers or at something they had said in class. A striking example of this, one indelibly inscribed in Stephen's memory, concerned the question of Jesus' conception. This was a tricky topic for the brother taking the religious instruction course, not helped by the total absence of sex education for the boys either at school or, for the overwhelming majority, anywhere else — with the consequential proliferation of rumour and ribald speculation on the subject in general. St Joseph, it had been carefully explained, though a devoted father in all other respects, had played no part in this momentous deed: the fertilisation of the ovum in the womb of the Virgin that would develop into the divine embryo. This had been achieved by the direct intervention of the Holy Ghost, the mysterious third person of the Trinity, described as being a 'distinct person' and at the same time 'consubstantial' with both the Father and the Son — a relationship Stephen had some difficulty, both then and later, in getting to grips with. The precise manner in which this intervention had been brought about was not elaborated upon, the implicit assumption being simply of a miracle, an act of divine will. Philips, however, had in mind a more transparent mechanism.

'What did you make of that then?' he asked. 'The Holy Ghost playing mothers and fathers with the Virgin Mary?'

Then, chuckling away happily at the thought, 'Dirty old man!'

Stephen, a pious thirteen-year-old at the time, was left speechless with horror. Philips had clearly gone well beyond the bounds of mere blasphemy, 'sins against the Holy Ghost' being in a special category of their own, uniquely and, under all circumstances, unforgivable. And although some uncertainty existed as to what precisely constituted such a sin, there could be little doubt that Philips's lewd remarks fell well within its ambit. Philips was damned, no question about it, and Stephen had half expected the ground to open up there and then to swallow him into the fires of hell.

But that was all of four years ago and Philips was still very much around. When they had reached a suitably quiet spot, he stopped, and taking Stephen's arm, informed him with a twinkle of yet another illicit liaison that had come to his notice,

'Seems your great idol Brother Carroll has forgotten all about his vow of chastity.' He paused for a moment to see how Stephen was taking this. 'Seems he's been having it off with young Benjamin Fuller's mother. Wouldn't like to be in his shoes when Sir Edward…'

At which point Stephen angrily interrupted him, outraged at the scurrilous and absurd accusation.

'That's ridiculous! Whoever's telling you this is just having you on. Feeding your smutty little mind with whatever filth they know you'll swallow.'

But as he was coming out with this a connection clicked and he was lost for a moment, awash in a tide of competing emotions. For Benjamin Fuller's mother, he realised seconds after hearing her so referred to, was none other than Natasha — whose breathtaking appearance on the junior school playground some six months before was still lodged firmly in his imagination: a recurrent reminder of that dimly perceived world out there, persistently beckoning with exquisitely erotic promise. The notion that Carroll was in any way involved with her he dismissed out of hand, and not solely out of loyalty and of what he knew of the man; for he was well aware that, although Philips was undoubtedly privy to information, that at times proved largely correct, this was by no means always the case: the imminent elopement of Brother Lucius, the junior school head, with a plump bespectacled library assistant, confidently predicted by Philips more than two years earlier, had come to nothing and there were other, if less noteworthy, examples. But now, from beneath the raft of indignation, something else was stirring, loosed by Philips's absurd allegation and adding to his anger: a nagging awareness of the impenetrable barrier separating him from that other world, the world of Natasha and who knows what other exotic creations dimly visible through the fog, reclining languorously in rapt anticipation of the arrival... well, certainly not of himself, but, yes... Carroll he could well imagine being welcomed there. And this realisation hurt, compounding his unease, even though he was perfectly aware that only his imagination was in play, that any such scenario was unthinkable in reality.

Philips, in no way put out by the insults, was observing him calmly with an expression of smug confidence: just wait and see, it said, you'll find out soon enough. They walked on together a little way in silence, skirting the senior school building, heading for the gate to the street outside. On reaching an open doorway, however, Stephen turned abruptly into it, quickening his pace as though late for an urgent engagement, striding briskly down the dimly lit corridor with no idea where he was heading.

SEVEN

It was shortly after that encounter that a tragic incident would have the effect of stirring up Stephen's suppressed religious doubts, releasing them for cautious critical scrutiny. He first learned of it from his mother on returning home from school one grey, rain-drenched evening, it having fast become the hushed talk of the neighbourhood, casting a pall over the settled banalities of the suburban scene. A young woman, recently married, who lived in the next street to Stephen, two doors down from his friend Sam, had suddenly died. A massive haemorrhage, according to his mother, blood everywhere, nobody knowing what to do, the ambulance over an hour in getting there to carry her unconscious to the hospital, where she was confirmed dead on arrival. She had appeared anxious and unwell for some weeks, people were now saying; the adjustment to married life in her parents' home, the desperate saving for a deposit for one of their own, all taking their toll, so it had been assumed. But it would turn out there were more substantial reasons for her anxiety, reasons of which Stephen would soon learn, that would tear at his being, leaving him trembling with shame and impotent despair. For he had known Rosie Manning for pretty well all his life, from bright vivacious child some three years his senior, through steady progression without fuss or ostentation to a beautiful young woman. She had attended the local Roman Catholic church at which he would see her regularly at Sunday Mass and other religious and social occasions; and where, a matter of a few months earlier, she had married her childhood sweetheart. Shocked and distressed, Stephen set off to call on Sam, who had known her well, indeed had once entertained the possibility of progressing their relationship beyond adolescent friendship to something more intimate — sensibly chickening out before making any definite move and so avoiding the painful rejection that would inevitably have followed. For, apart from being too young, in a field far from short of eligible, well-heeled contenders, Sam was given to expressing uncompromisingly atheistic views and, worse than that, was of Protestant family origin. Whereas Rosie and her parents were devout, traditional-minded Catholics, quite impervious to the liberalising tendencies so apparent in the Firbright household.

Sam was in the first year of a degree course at Imperial College but still living at home, where he had converted a small spare room into a well-equipped study. He opened the door to Stephen looking pale and tense and not at all pleased to see him; hostile even, leaving him feeling he had intruded on private territory and not knowing how to respond to the mute awkwardness with which they faced each other over the threshold. The impasse was thankfully broken by Fluff rushing to the door in delight at Stephen's appearance, jumping up at him excitedly in anticipation of the walk his presence signified and providing him with the opportunity to break the silence.

'I came to see if you felt like a walk on the common.'

Sam didn't reply at once, remaining silent, his sour expression unchanged but, after a few moments, he nodded perfunctorily and went to fetch his coat. After walking a few paces, Stephen said softly,

'What's the matter, Sam?'

This time he elicited a forceful response.

'Don't you bloody know?'

'Of course, I do. It's why I came to see you. But why are you being like this with me?'

At which Sam exploded, anger and despair competing with one another, his face flushed and tearful.

'It's just as if they'd bloody murdered her, the bastards. The cold-blooded, ignorant, primitive, superstitious bastards. How can they have such power over people in this age? It's as though half the bloody population — you included — are still stuck in the Middle Ages. With beliefs and practices no better than those of some lost bloody African tribe with their witchdoctors and spells. Just the bloody same you are, and you can't see it. You still listen to that nonsense: yes, Father, no, Father, three bloody bags full, Father. It makes me sick. And now it has killed her. Bloody well killed her, just as if they'd hacked her to death there and then instead of simply making sure she would soon die anyway.'

Stephen didn't know what to say, never having seen Sam remotely like this before and with no idea what it was about and fearful to ask, not wanting to risk another outburst. But then Sam calmed a little, and as they walked, eyes focussed straight ahead, he explained with deadpan delivery just what had happened to Rosie, the full terrible story, which had Stephen speechless with shame and a confused simmering inside which was going to take time to unravel and interpret.

It appeared that some months after her marriage, Rosie experienced the first indications of the pregnancy she had been eagerly awaiting: a missed period together with some low abdominal pain which she took to be a normal symptom of that condition. But then one morning, she noticed a small discharge of blood from her vagina. Extremely worried, she hurried to her GP, who, after examining her, arranged for tests to be carried out at the local hospital — where it was eventually confirmed that she was in the very early stages of an ectopic pregnancy. The consultant involved was reassuring, explaining to her and Peter (her husband) that the Fallopian tube in which the fertilisation had taken place did not appear badly damaged, and if they acted quickly to remove the blocked section, there was every chance of her being able to conceive again soon after everything had healed. But, Rosie wanted to know, what about the baby? He explained that there was no question whatsoever of the embryo developing into a viable foetus.

'Just think of it as a false start,' he told her. 'Something we've been very fortunate to have identified early on, in good time to take effective action. If left, it can only lead to a rupture which at best would leave you very unlikely to be able to conceive again and at worst — and this is a real possibility — it could kill you. This is not a situation in which a difficult decision has to be made, there is only one valid option. Any doctor, any medical authority, will tell you the same.'

She was naturally very upset but with Peter's emphatic support agreed to be booked in for the operation the following week. On leaving the hospital, however, the significance of what had been decided came home to her in a different light: it was an abortion she had agreed to, something her faith as well as natural instinct deemed unspeakably abhorrent.

'But in cases like this,' Peter tried hard to assure her, 'it can't be considered that way, with no chance of the embryo surviving and the enormous risk to your own life if you simply wait until the inevitable happens. The doctors are perfectly clear about that. The church can't possibly raise any objection.'

And so it was decided to consult Father O'Shea, confident he would give his approval for the proposed intervention.

It was at this point that Sam abandoned the controlled objectivity he was forcing on himself, returning to the fury with which he had responded to Stephen minutes before.

'Can you imagine what that imbecile told them? That to remove the embryo before it was viable — that's before six bloody months gestation, way past the time when the tube would have burst anyway — is equivalent in God's eyes to holding a grown man underwater till he drowns. Can you believe it? The fact that the few-weeks-old bundle of cells was doomed in any case, that it couldn't possibly survive till viable, that the mother would be badly damaged, very possibly killed, none of that enters into it. Seems your idea of God is some sort of mindless bureaucrat with his book of rules which have to be followed blindly, regardless of circumstances, regardless of conscience, regardless of plain bloody common sense. And who wrote the rules in the first place? Those poor, deluded idiots believing themselves to be on a hotline to their creator, transcribing his imagined wishes into rigid laws to be imposed on all mankind. Could you imagine anything more plain crazy? And yet you still go along with it, with all that bloody nonsense. Your Father O'Shea said he would pray for her. Can you imagine it? Mumbling over his beads like a demented loony. While Rosie just waited there, refusing the help that would have saved her, letting it grow inside her, knowing it couldn't survive, waiting for the first sign of the rupture that was sure to come, that was certain to do her irreparably harm, and with only some tomfool plan to be rushed to hospital that predictably cocked up. And what now? I suppose you'll arrange to have Masses said for her and other meaningless rot. So you can all feel you've done the right thing, cared for her now she's dead, proud of yourselves for sticking to your absurd primitive principles. Well, it just makes me sick.'

Stephen was dumbstruck, overcome by the enormity of what he had heard and the intensity of Sam's feelings. Shocked too by the bitterness of the attack on his faith, on so much he had accepted without question as the spiritual foundation of his life. Sam had been in love with Rosie, that much should have been obvious to him before but was now clear beyond doubt. Religion had been the obstacle, as he had seen it, preventing their relationship from developing further. And now her religion, which he had long despised and now vehemently detested, had killed her. He was beside himself with grief and anger. Which was why Stephen couldn't contest his onslaught, his wild assertions. Even though he knew Father O'Shea to be a kindly man, undoubtedly greatly distressed by what had befallen Rosie, by her suffering and death. What had gone wrong? he asked himself. What breakdown in communication, for it had to be that, had led to the so easily preventable tragedy?

But no, there had been no misunderstanding. The church's position was crystal clear, as Stephen was to learn on bringing the matter up with Brother Anthony during the religious instruction class some days later. The ends can never justify the means, he was told, an act which involves the taking of human life — and in God's eyes an embryo is a complete human being from the moment of conception — can never be permitted regardless of what good is thereby intended. And so that there should be absolutely no doubt on the matter, the Tribunal of the Holy Office — the ultimate authority for the Roman Catholic church on questions of morality — expressly prohibits the removal of a foetus before it is sufficiently developed to survive, regardless of the motive being to save the life of the mother; and it goes on to state explicitly that ectopic gestations are not exempt from this ruling. So that was that. Poor Father O'Shea had had no choice in the matter: to not have proscribed as he did would have directly contravened the clear dictate of his church.

But as Stephen was taking this in, another moral issue came to mind, one which had perturbed him a few months before, events projecting it in high relief, unleashing torrents of anger and revulsion.

'But... but if that's the case,' he replied, 'that actions directly involving the taking of human life can never be justified... why then doesn't the church prohibit capital punishment?'

It was the previous summer, July 1955, that a young woman, Ruth Ellis, mother of a ten-year-old boy, had been hanged in Holloway prison for the murder of her lover. She had waited for him outside a pub where he had been drinking with a friend, calling to him desperately as he came out, and on being ignored, shooting him dead; then simply waiting passively for the police to come and arrest her. It was the culmination of a turbulent and violent relationship which, just three months before, had seen her miscarry as a result of his having punched her in the stomach. The case engendered intense public feeling both in Britain and abroad — where the lack in Britain of the concept of crime passionnel was noted with wry disapproval. Liberal minded people everywhere were up in arms, their reactions setting in train the opposition to capital punishment which would go on to ensure no further women would be executed in Britain, and lead to the effective abolition of the whole barbaric practice some nine years later. Stan's family were predictably distressed, the affair dominating their meal time exchanges for weeks; his mother and Lavinia getting heavily involved with the petition for clemency submitted in vain with 50,000 signatures to the Home Office; the church's lack of a firm stance on the matter receiving their unanimous bitter condemnation.

But Brother Anthony, it rapidly became apparent, saw things differently. After appearing briefly taken aback by Stephen's question, he responded at length with some show of aggression.

'That's quite beside the point. The infliction of capital punishment is not contrary to the teaching of the Catholic Church, the writings of theologians are quite clear on that point; the state has the right, indeed the duty, to defend itself and uphold its legitimate laws...' going on in that vein for some time, Stephen soon ceasing to take in what he was saying, wondering instead about those theologians, how they came to their definite conclusions, framed those immutable laws... about capital punishment, about ectopic gestations, about indulgences, come to that, about the whole catalogue of what was to be believed, of how precisely things appeared in the eyes of God, and of the Catholic Church as His sole infallible authority on earth. All, so it seemed, on the very flimsiest of foundations, which, in any other context, would be dismissed with derision. And then the self-serving aspects of so much of it, conclusions dovetailing conveniently with perceived temporal advantage: capital punishment being a clear case in point, because for the church to come down heavily on this flagrant, cold-blooded taking of human life — by threatening excommunication, say, to those involved in its practice — would be to challenge the authority of the state from whom it sought and obtained privileged treatment. A proposition clearly not in its interest to pursue. Whereas for a defenceless young woman carrying a doomed misplaced embryo, the sanctity of human life relentlessly invoked to prohibit action that would save her from certain serious injury, perhaps death.

Stephen's disturbingly subversive thoughts were interrupted by the realisation that Anthony had finished speaking and was fixing him with a cold gaze, clearly expecting a response to what he had been saying.

'But, but then...' he started, his mind racing blankly for a moment, then picking up on his immediate reaction to Anthony's opening words. 'But what you seem to be saying is that, in this case, the ends justify the means.'

Anthony remained silent, still staring at him, his features darkening.

'I mean,' Stephen went on, a determination not to give ground firming as he spoke, 'killing someone in order to defend something... isn't that what you said could never be justified?'

Stephen had long felt Anthony's hostility towards him without knowing the reason, simply accepting it as just another inexplicable manifestation of the natural order of things at St John's. To question anything there, he had learned, was almost never a good idea, the more tempting the desire to do so the greater the need for restraint. So most times he resisted the urge, acquiescing in silence, only very rarely taking issue and then invariably regretting having done so. But this time it had been different, two very real tragedies illuminating for him the inhumanity and self-serving partiality of the church's position. He would have liked to speak to Carroll about it, but he hadn't been around for some time and was unlikely to be so before Stephen had left St John's. Forever.

Something significant had changed for him, repercussions of which would inevitably follow — but what this was, and what they were to be, he had as yet no idea. The only immediate effect, a feeling of complete indifference to what Anthony, clearly wound up and angry, would now have to say. So that when it came — a recitation with embellishments of a catalogue of his failings — Stephen heard it out with equanimity, offering nothing in return. The following week, he would be sitting the first of his final examinations, the last one some ten days later. After that, come what may, St John's and all its works would be a phase of life irrevocably behind him. Appreciating this, perhaps fully for the first time, he settled back at his desk and switched off.

EIGHT

Exams over and done with. No unpleasant surprises, remarkable good fortune with precariously selective revision, all in all as satisfactory an outcome as Stephen could possibly have hoped for. But no feeling of elation, an emptiness rather, an unwillingness to do anything, see anyone. Those last frantic efforts seeing out an era, its successor featureless still, lacking all definition, void of promise.

A few days after sitting the final paper, Stephen returned to St John's. He had no purpose in mind other than mild curiosity at how it would appear now that his time there was over, the bonds finally severed. The place seemed deserted, apart from a sports field where groundsmen — an ancient retainer and his young assistant — were deploying machinery to no apparent purpose, and the junior playground where two small boys huddled in a corner regarded him guiltily as he passed near. Of course! Thursday afternoon, the whole school in the chapel for Benediction. It would be ending any moment now, the playgrounds swamped by the exuberant exodus. Time to be going.

For some obscure reason, that he could not afterwards recall, he decided to leave by the junior entrance — situated on the far school boundary and connecting with a side road leading to a drab housing estate. As he rounded the block of junior school classrooms, a door some yards in front of him opened to disgorge a young woman. It was Natasha, her sudden appearance causing his heart to miss a beat. It was the first time he had seen her following that unforgettable occasion months before. This second time, likewise dramatic and unexpected, differing notably from the first in that on this occasion there was no one else around, they were quite alone, figuratively speaking on top of one another. Satisfaction at this long dreamed of encounter completely overshadowed however by fear, fear of her finely-tuned sensibilities — with next to nothing to go on, he was quite sure she possessed these — somehow registering his carnal interest, provoking indignation at his impertinence.

He need not have worried; Natasha, giving every indication of not having noticed him at all, exclaimed angrily to the world at large, 'Where the hell have they all gone?'

Stephen, having come to an unsteady halt beside her, managed to pull himself together sufficiently to explain about Benediction, adding that it should soon be over.

'Thank heavens for that,' she said, looking him over carefully while continuing, 'I'd arranged to see Brother Lucius at four-fifteen. He'd better not be late. I have to be in Chelsea by half-five or there'll be hell to pay.' Then, changing down a couple of gears, she asked with a good-natured smile, 'What are you doing here anyway?'

She was wearing a fashionable short top, skin-tight blue jeans, brown leather knee-length boots, hair pulled back in a long ponytail. The jeans could well represent a practice, heard of from somewhere and mulled over approvingly with Stan, involving girls wearing them in the bath to shrink them accurately to the underlying curvature. Just the outfit, he thought, for a cosy session with Brother Lucius. While taking this in, he explained that he had just finished A-levels, effectively finished with St John's and, having nothing better to do, had wandered in to have a last look round.

'So, what are you going to do now?' she asked, managing to sound interested in what this might be.

'Depends on exam results. If all goes well, Westmoreland University. Mathematics. They've made me a conditional offer.'

He had discovered that people were in general baffled by this choice, explanations of sorts required. But instead, Natasha responded with seemingly genuine enthusiasm.

'But that's marvellous, you must be really excited.'

As she was saying this, a low rumble sounded from across the playground, growing within seconds to full-blown buffalo stampede, discordant cries rising above the pounding. Boys, brimful of pent-up energy appeared from all sides, transforming the placid landscape into a hive of frantic aimless activity. She turned away to peer through the glass panel of the door from which she had emerged.

'There's the little fellow,' she murmured. 'I'd better grab him before he takes off again.'

He thought at first she was referring to her son, then realised it was Brother Lucius — Poison Dwarf to the boys. Hesitating for a moment, her hand on the door handle, she turned back to him with a quizzical smile.

'You must be Stephen Hallam. Am I right?'

Dumbfounded, he nodded assent. How on earth could she possibly have known his name? Before he could even think to ask, she had responded with a warm knowing look and entered the building. He stood for some seconds, rooted there; then with a helpless shrug continued his interrupted progress to the junior gate, then through it into the world outside.

A phase of life indisputably behind him. That final exit from St John's marking definitive closure of a long chapter, the opening of a new one devoid of direction and constraint. Natasha's miraculous materialisation had imbued the transition with significance, both acute and indefinable, evoking an exhilarating sense of liberation, an unburdening of the spirit. But then as he walked the dismal streets, his thoughts turned to unfinished business, to troubled religious preoccupations to be aired dispassionately now in the first cool waft of freedom. So many doubts there had been, some fundamental to the faith, others less so, but sacrosanct nonetheless; all stowed away in the sealed compartment that was opening now, shedding its contents as he walked, aimlessly, no destination in mind, oblivious of all around him.

For a start, that 'limbo' business, *limbus infantium*, the eternal resting place for souls of infants dying unbaptised — subject of another of his something-not-quite-right feelings when expounded in class. To him, the idea of God — Supreme Being, creator of heaven and earth — deciding the eternal future of a dying infant on the basis of whether or not someone had got round to sprinkling water over it had struck him as absurd. The notion of some petty-minded clerk perhaps, with a barely understood book of regulations in hand. But God! It appeared gratuitously insulting, blasphemous even, to suggest such a thing. There being no way he could have voiced these misgivings at the time, he had looked into the doctrinal origins of limbo for himself, persevering only long enough to be appalled at what he found, at the wanton vindictiveness towards those innocents attributed to God by canonised

Fathers of the church. Far from providing the sought-after reassurance, his browsing only succeeded in raising questions bearing alarmingly on the very foundations of Christian belief — to be hurriedly vetoed and set aside. Until now.

The fate of unbaptised infants, he found, had been ruled upon unequivocally some four centuries after Christ by St Augustine: they went straight to hell. Although theologians would from time to time seek to qualify this inordinately harsh prescription, in obvious conflict with the notion of an infinitely just and merciful God, it was to remain the orthodox view for centuries, to be endorsed a thousand years later at the Council of Florence. Stephen was astounded at the fervour with which debate on the matter had been conducted, the confidence with which the various views had been expressed. These, to a large extent, dwelt on the intensity of the eternal torment the infants were to suffer; ranging, in the opinions of the diverse learned Fathers, from full endless exposure to the physical fires of hell, to mere frustration at being denied the supreme ecstasy that would have been theirs had anyone taken the trouble to baptise them. This latter lenient view was eventually to dominate, its most extreme expression even doing away with the pain of loss — the infants thereby experiencing eternal natural happiness, oblivious of having missed out on the infinitely more exquisite supernatural alternative.

But any reassurance Stephen may have felt at this reasonably happy, though by no means universally accepted, conclusion had by now become quite beside the point. For a start, there was that immense anguish to consider, inflicted on countless distraught parents through the ages who, for whatever reasons, had not managed to get their dying infants baptised; grief, in any case likely to be heart-rending, unbearably magnified by thoughts of eternal torment to which their offspring were being subjected, for which Sts Augustine and Anselm, Petavius, the African Fathers and the many other theologians responsible for promoting the brutal judgement, were clearly to be held to account. To which they would doubtlessly have responded that their conclusion, distressing as it may well appear to human reason, represented no more than the immutable consequence of divine purpose, revealed as a result of profound objective examination. For Stephen, the basis for such examination — in common with that for all theological discourse, certainly that for which he had become fleetingly aware — was something he had blocked off from further consideration, sensing vulnerability there, fearful of what probing might uncover. But not any longer. With mounting excitement, conditioned in part by awareness of dangerous ground ahead, peril to his immortal soul, he turned his mind to it, to what had to be the very crux of the matter: not just of limbo and indulgences and those other peripheral stupidities, but of the very heart of religious belief, the whole holy shooting match.

His thoughts were interrupted at this point by the sudden appearance before him of a substantial tree-spattered green space, identified after a moment's hesitation as an unfamiliar corner of the extensive common he was used to approaching from the far side with Sam and Fluff. It was practically deserted despite the fine day, a low sun projecting broken shadows over the sparkling dappled green. He set out across it, pausing at a bench beside a pool teeming with aquatic bird life; geese, ducks, moorhens and coots all engaged in watery displays of frantic aimless activity, reminiscent of St John's junior playground: spasmodic shows of sudden aggression, indignant protest, hasty undignified retreat. He sat down to watch, his mind emptying of its concerns, relaxing for the first time in this newfound freedom.

So far as he had been able to glean from his religious instruction classes, and what little he had read up for himself, theological discourse drew predominantly on two sources: the New Testament, in particular the four gospels reporting the words and actions of Jesus, and what was frequently and somewhat mysteriously referred to as *revelation*. With regard to the gospels, he had once received short shrift for suggesting in class that the events described perhaps only an approximation of what had actually taken place, that nobody could be certain of what precise words Jesus had used on any particular occasion, nor exactly what was intended. This incautious observation — which did him no good at all in the eyes of the brotherhood — had been provoked by the absolute reliance placed on the words reported in St John's gospel affirming baptism as a prerequisite for salvation: 'Unless man be born again of water and the Holy Ghost he cannot enter the kingdom of heaven.' Given that this was written years after the event — on the basis of no more than an evolving folklore, by an author clearly at one with the religious establishment in which the ritual of baptism had long played its part — was it wise to draw from it such immutable and far-reaching conclusions? That infants dying unbaptised be condemned to eternal damnation? And, more generally, that espousers of interpretations to any degree at variance with official views be deemed heretics — to be tortured and killed with impunity (as was the practice over long periods of church history) and likewise condemned to everlasting torment?

Considerations of this nature had disturbed Stephen with

growing frequency during his later years at St John's. Now they were to return with a vengeance, isolated fragments unifying into a terrifying whole, a new picture relentlessly taking shape. The books of the New Testament, it was now appearing abundantly clear, could in no way be regarded as historical documents, there was precious little reference within them to outside events that could support claims to authenticity; and independent confirmation of the stories was almost totally lacking, even with regard to the very existence of Jesus Christ. Rather, the gospels should be taken as no more than anecdotal accounts of various incidents, passed with inevitable embellishment between zealous supporters of the vigorously promoted religious movement, strung together and sifted for conformity to the developing view, *and then* — the shameless absurdity hitting him like a divine thunderbolt — taking their place as indisputable prime sources for theological study. So that St Augustine, for example, could quote those words in St John's gospel as irrefutable evidence for the eternal damnation of unbaptised infants — damnation in his view being the only alternative to salvation, for reasons Stephen by now felt little inclination to pursue further.

Up until that afternoon, seated there on that bench by the pond, Stephen's religious doubts had been those of a committed insider, concerned only with what he felt to be peripheral aspects of the faith, accepting fully what he understood to be its essential foundations. It could hardly have been otherwise. His whole life — at home, predominantly in the local community, exclusively at school — having been lived under the assumption of all truth and wisdom residing with the Roman Catholic church, a standpoint unthinkable, sinful even, to question, alternatives denied even so much as a look-in. But something unprecedented was happening now: a paradigm shift of which he was for the most part unaware, a mounting feeling of imminent deliverance, an escape route slowly materialising through the fog ahead.

His thoughts were interrupted at this point by a more than usually pronounced kafuffle as a fleeing mallard just failed to avoid the fast, descending beak of an enraged Canada goose — an intruder, one of a recently imported batch of these noted playground bullies. When the squawk of pain and the indignant protests of law-abiding witnesses had subsided, Stephen's thoughts returned somewhat refreshed to where they had been hovering moments before, then settling on to that other mainstay of theological discourse.

Revelation was a word that featured prominently in religious instruction classes at St John's, though in a manner implying its meaning self-evident, discouraging further enquiry. Stephen, duly discouraged but sensing something defensive there, had looked up what the church had to say about it to her lay followers. That was some months before, the reason for defensiveness rapidly becoming glaringly apparent, even embarrassing so, and 'revelation' hastily stashed away with other censored items too fragile to mess with. Recalling it now brought home the sea change that had taken place within him during the last few hours, so that, instead of embarrassment, a contemptuous dismissal of its self-evidently self-serving function. No wonder the brothers had appeared evasive when referring to it. Revelation, he learned, signified the transmission of some truth by supernatural means from God to man, either directly or via some pious intermediary. Oh yes! And how then to distinguish it from the myriad not-so-bright ideas, seemingly profound flawed intuitions and other spontaneous nonsense which, from time to time, invaded every person's thoughts? This was clearly where the church came in, specifically via the Pope's eight-lane-superhighway connection with his creator, enabling him to differentiate infallibly between the genuine article and its infinitely less significant simulacrum. The more he thought about it, the more mystifying it appeared that anyone could have got away with it. Why not simply present revelation as what the Pope states infallibly to be God's truth and be done with it? That was what the convoluted accounts in Vatican Council Decrees and Constitutions stripped of their foliage effectively boiled down to. And, because to Stephen, revelation now appeared the only remaining basis for theological enquiry, the absolute need for the absurd doctrine of papal infallibility became abundantly clear: without it the whole edifice was unsustainable, would simply come crashing down.

It was getting dark now. He set off for home across the common, its features growing unfamiliar in the fading light, the enormity of the upheaval taking place within him burning in his mind. No conscious decision had been involved. It was as though in that final exit from St John's every last vestige of what it stood for, its very purpose for existence, had been stripped away along with its physical presence. He felt light, unattached and unencumbered, neither elated nor yet fearful, and quite alone.

PART 2

London
1960 – 1963

NINE

Stephen returned to London in the early summer of 1960. Westmoreland, behind him by then, an evident success story that had spawned many friendships and a few, by and large, uncomplicated sexual adventures — the latter having succeeded in shifting that previously fraught area of largely theoretical speculation into a seemingly more rational, certainly more practical, perspective; and also, of course, the first in mathematics that secured the scholarship at Prince of Wales College London for research in number theory, in a field attracting close attention in the international mathematical community. All in all, a change in his fortunes unimaginable in the confused, confidence-lacking state in which he had left St John's little more than four years before.

    The nervous anticipation of exam results, followed by relief and joy at their arrival, had helped pass the time for Stephen in the interlude between St John's and Westmoreland, a period otherwise dominated by deliberations culminating in his final rejection of religious belief. A coming together and ripening of suppressed doubts accumulated over the last few years, and of withering appraisals of outlandish dogma bereft, as he now saw it, of reason and foundation. The more he thought about it, the more incredible it appeared that anyone in his or her right mind could take Christianity for anything other than a religious myth. The years of religious instruction diligently attended succeeding only in the end in exposing the absurdity. It was over and done with, all ties with Roman Catholicism, with religious belief in general, brought decisively to an end.

But the hold the church maintained on its members, on those raised in the faith, was to be brought home to him very soon after he had made that definitive decision. Up until that point he had continued with religious observances, in particular, attendance at Sunday Mass, regardless of doubts which had been growing steadily for months, perhaps years, reaching the stage at which the rituals had come to signify little more for him than unthinking habitual practice. But on the Sunday following the fateful decision, when, for the first time in his life he was set on committing the mortal sin of deliberate non-attendance at Mass, he was beset by feelings of severe unease and apprehension; and isolation, facing as he was the defection and its consequences quite alone. Could it be that he was deluding himself? he wondered. Or was it, as he had implicitly come to assume, that all around him were deluded? Either one or the other it seemed, which, put that way, didn't say much for his chances of avoiding eternal damnation, the inevitable consequence of such deliberate act of rebellion, as had been drummed into him for as long as he could remember. It was to be the final test of his resolve, the contest between what he saw as the inevitable outcome of rational thought and this enveloping fear; the dilemma persisting for the uncomfortable hours it took to ascribe the fear to those years of relentless indoctrination. Just that, nothing more. Only partially reassured but still holding firm; Sunday passing slowly, uneventfully, in mild discomfort; but waking the following morning to heartfelt relief, echoing that of final exit from St John's, the breath of liberation refreshing his being, blowing stronger as the day progressed. Occasional feelings of disquiet continued for a while, maybe a month or so, though progressively weakening, becoming ever easier to brush aside. And it was all but completely extinguished by the time of his arrival at Westmoreland, with only remnants of the accompanying anger remaining, flaring up spasmodically at the memory of his blinkered education. A little dazed perhaps, not quite able to believe he had finally broken free, but no longer any real question about it: the impenetrable barrier breached, the ties comprehensively severed.

So it was a much-changed Stephen that returned to London some four years later, to a social ambience also much changed and changing still, from a city of bleak stolidity, lingering in post-war austerity, to one displaying unmistakable signs of blossoming youthful creativity and pervasive sexual promise. Or so it seemed to him after the long absence, not entirely without justification. A taste for what this could imply was to be provided by an encounter engineered by Stan within a week or so of his return. They had maintained contact during his time at Westmoreland, Stephen having travelled down from time to time to see him in RADA productions, displaying his already considerable and fast-developing talent. The occasion this time started out as just a meeting for a drink in an Edgware Road pub, somewhere close to where Stan was rehearsing for a British Council sponsored theatre company tour of the Far East –something of a coup for him, the result of a well-established actor falling ill just as rehearsals were starting and Stan, having duly caught the attention of talent spotters at RADA, being brought in to substitute. Though this meant his having to forgo a walk-on part in a new television production — which could well have got him noticed and led on to something more substantial — he had no hesitation when the tour prospect was broached, regardless of the pitiful salary and little likelihood of anything to follow when it ended.

Stephen arrived at the pub first, bought himself a pint and settled down, resigned to a fair wait before Stan could get away. After some minutes, an abrupt change in the background hum of male chatter awakened him to his surroundings, its cause immediately evident: two young women of stunning appearance, models straight from the pages of some trendy fashion magazine, had entered the pub, bought drinks and taken possession of a vacant table. They seemed quite oblivious of the stir they had created in that quintessential male preserve, concentrating instead on giving each other undivided attention, talking and laughing contentedly together, in no way conveying the impression of awaiting a third party — Stephen's immediately assumed explanation for their presence. Stan arrived soon after in exultant mood, still, it appeared, immersed in the role he had been rehearsing. It was coming on for a year since they had last met, and once Stan had wound down, they were back to old times and catching up on each other's lives — Stephen's appearing numbingly tame in comparison, not that he minded particularly, or so he was able to persuade himself. A St John's reunion attended by Stan some months before provided snippets of interest, among them a sighting of Carlo Petroni dejectedly pushing a pram along Kilburn High Street, harassed wife beside him desperately trying to control the other three or maybe four (reports differing on this) unruly, snotty-nosed offspring. But heading the bill, the news that little Brother Lucius had left the order and married the plump bespectacled library assistant — as Philips had foretold God knows how many years ago; a child blessing their union soon after. Very soon after. Uncertainty about just when encouraging wry speculation.

'It could have been in the school library! Can you imagine it?' Stan clearly could and was eager to impart further. 'In the theology section. Her, sprawled over the desk, fat bum in the air. Him, behind her, standing on a thick sacred tome, lifting his cassock…'

Yes, thought Stephen, the evening was getting off to a promising start.

But then Stan noticed the two girls. He had set off to replenish their glasses, returning full of it.

'Have you seen those two over there? God, they're fantastic. Let's go over and say hallo. Come on.'

'Don't be stupid.'

In fact, Stephen, from where he was sitting, had had ample opportunity to view the young women, witnessing their contemptuous adroitness in seeing off unsolicited admirers. No way was he going to make a fool of himself like that.

'What's the matter with you? Nothing to lose. It must surely be worth a try.'

'No way.'

'Have it your own way then. I'll try on my own. I'll call you over if I get anywhere.'

'You must be crazy.'

Unbelievably though, after no more than a few seconds of awkward hesitation, Stan seemed to have won through; the girls giving every indication of warming to him, responding as though having been eagerly awaiting him all along. Seemingly engrossed in living up to the persona adopted for the purpose,

Stan appeared to have forgotten Stephen, who was watching him with incredulous admiration and just a touch of envy; how on earth does he manage it? Then Stan, all smiles, turned and waved him over and, rather sheepishly and in some trepidation, he wove his way across the by now crowded bar to join them. His reception astounded him. What on earth had Stan been telling them about him to elicit so enthusiastic a welcome? It was worrying, but there was no time to dwell on it.

'I'm Suzie,' said the one on the right, close-cropped auburn hair accentuating radiant femininity, eyes holding him in a steady gaze as she indicated he should sit beside her.

'And I'm Rebecca,' said the other one, leaning forward out of Stan's aura to welcome him into the fold, blond hair falling about her face. Stan, beside her, a picture of self-satisfied contentment. The smug bastard, thought Stephen, not without approbation.

'And I'm Stephen,' he managed to come out with, 'Stephen Hallam.'

'Yes, we know. The brilliant mathematician!'

'Oh, come off it.'

Embarrassment thankfully blurred by alcohol as, pint glass still in hand, he entered blindly into another world. Natasha's world? The thought of her flashing into mind as it was still wont to do on the least provocation, even after however many years since that one brief encounter; and, though the frequency had certainly diminished over the years, the intensity still there to tarnish incipient relationships, rendering them in some measure wanting, an affliction he had come to realise that was doing him no good at all. But could this be different?

'What are you thinking?'

Suzie's eyes hadn't left his face, her quizzical expression taking in his evident distraction.

'Didn't I warn you,' interjected Stan. 'He's performing massive mental calculations. Likely at any moment to rip off his clothes and run naked down Edgware Road yelling eureka.'

Rebecca laughed loudly at this. And Suzie's mouth curved into an affectionate smile, which appeared enchanting to Stephen, so much so that, on an impulse, he leaned over and planted a gentle kiss full on her lips. Her response was passive, neither participating nor pulling away, making him feel he should apologise for what had to have been a momentary booze-fuelled aberration. But before he could get round to it, her smile had widened.

'That was nice,' she said. And alongside the feeling of relief and heightening excitement, he was aware of Stan's delight at the way events were progressing: the big-time director basking in his ability to have his way, producing high-profile performances even from sub-standard material.

After that everything went swimmingly despite Stan's brashness, no trace of wariness on the part of the girls at the intrusion. Indeed, anyone observing them would assume their meeting to have been arranged, that they all knew each other well. Which should perhaps have bothered Stephen, given his well-founded misgivings at the outset. But so overwhelmed at the ease of it all, at the beautiful Suzie's apparent interest in him, that all else went by the board. The girls, they learned, were old school chums who kept in touch, meeting up as now to share reminiscences and update each other on career and love life developments. Which made for a pleasing symmetry, leading naturally into ice-breaking school-days reminiscences. After which the conversation turned to current concerns, Stan's theatrical activities, the impending tour, Stephen's research in mathematics — which he was able to dismiss without too much embarrassment.

Rebecca, they were to learn, held a prestigious position in the office of some industrial big-wig who had taken a strong fancy to her — nothing very surprising in that, thought Stephen. She kept them amused with tales of stringing him along to her advantage, keeping him at arm's length — responding furiously when Stan playfully questioned her success on this last claim.

'You should see him! Fat and bald and in his fifties. You don't seriously think I would go to bed with someone like that? Or do you?' She gave him a filthy look as she said this, driving him into a convincing routine of contrite apology. 'And anyway,' she went on when he had finished and she had calmed down, 'I find him quite easy to control, quite enjoy it really,' chuckling away as she said this.

Suzie had remained silent during these exchanges, Stephen likewise, aware all the while of her presence close beside him. The silence following Rebecca's disclosures lingered for some moments, to be broken eventually by Stephen picking up his glass and asking the others what they were having: pints of bitter for Suzie and Stan, Babycham with a cherry for Rebecca — this last eliciting a look of wry disapproval from Stan, which she saw, earning him another dirty look. At the crowded bar, Stephen turned with the intention of miming apology for the delay, only to see the three of them engaged in close, animated conversation, which had ended by the time he returned with the drinks. Then it was

Suzie's turn to say her piece.

Somewhat at a loss for what to do after graduating in art history, she had replied to an unusual ad in the personal column of a magazine with little hope of hearing back. Much to her surprise, however, she was called for an interview, sailed through a selection procedure and was taken on. It was an organisation with the supposedly altruistic purpose of promoting understanding and cultural exchange between Britain and the Arab world. But she was soon to learn that the particular target was the newly massively oil-rich Gulf states and that there was nothing in the least altruistic about it.

'The Arab rulers were looking to spend their limitless new-found wealth on Western goodies, and British businessmen were tripping over themselves to get their hands on the pickings. A few of them got together, co opted a number of high-profile public figures, including a cabinet minister, and set up the cultural exchange body. It was all part of the buttering up process, a prelude to potentially huge infrastructural and architectural contracts and the like that would earn millions and line the pockets of all concerned. The 'cultural' element was very much a sideshow, but that was where I was supposed to come in.'

'Oh yes,' said Stan with a smirk, at which Suzie went quiet.

'So what exactly do you do?' asked Stephen.

After another thoughtful pause, she told them.

'Well, on the face of it, it's quite straightforward. Important visitors arrive, a small group, usually two or three, sometimes just one. They're looked after incredibly well as you would imagine, put up in the most prestigious suites of the most luxurious hotels, lavishly entertained, introduced to government ministers, lions of industry, whatever of the great and the good can be rustled up. Then preliminary discussions with the business wallahs, setting the groundwork for further meetings, for vast contracts, golden handouts all round. My job is to fill in gaps in the programme, provide the 'cultural heritage' element, which in practice boils down to arranging private visits to stately homes, public and private art collections, sites of supposedly outstanding interest and natural beauty, and whatever else they may want to dip into. Helping them decide from what's on offer and making arrangements for anything else they may want to do — which is where problems can arise.'

'Are you going to tell us about them?' asked Stan, politely, in the pause the followed.

'Well,' replied Suzie, with a dry chuckle, 'there's this one I've got in tow at the moment...'

'Well, go on then.'

Which, after some moments, she did. Stan's face setting in eager expectation, Stephen totally enthralled, unable to take his eyes off her, Rebecca's smile letting on she had heard it all before and was happily resigned to hearing it again. It concerned the son of the ruler of a vastly rich sheikhdom. Young — early thirties, Suzie thought — suave, good looking with a wispy satanic beard and flowing milk-white robes and headgear. He had arrived alone, ostensibly to take soundings for a number of major initiatives in his father's kingdom, but more, so Suzie had surmised, 'to get away for a while, to experience a more open frame of existence.'

'Isn't that a rather euphemistic way of putting it,' said Stan, reverting to form. 'Don't you mean something more like delving into the fleshpots of decadent Western society?'

'Well maybe,' said Suzie with a light laugh. 'There's something undeniably sexy about him in a dark mysterious way. You could imagine him being quite cruel. Women are certainly attracted to him, you're aware of it all the time. You can practically feel his suppressed responses, the hormones coursing through his tissue fluids.'

'So, there you are,' said Stan, 'alone with this simmering sexpot, his personal escort no less, employed explicitly to satisfy his every whim. You're not going to tell us he hasn't made a pass at you?'

Suzie remained silent for an uncomfortable few moments; Stephen feeling he should intervene, should rebuke Stan for his hectoring behaviour, being on the point of doing so when Rebecca chimed in,

'Tell them about the envelope, Suzie.'

'I gave it back.' She came straight out with this. Then after a pause, 'There was no way I could have kept it. He became quite unpleasant, obviously unaccustomed to any sort of put down, which I suppose should have resolved any doubts I might have had about doing the right thing. But it still hurts, the way it turned out.'

Stan's face was glowing with excitement.

'So what was in it then? Are you going to tell us? A declaration of everlasting love, was it? The deeds to a five-star oasis and a herd of pedigree camels?'

'No,' said Suzie, ignoring his facetiousness, looking strained, struggling to maintain her composure, 'just five hundred pounds in cash.'

'Five hundred pounds!' Stan was beside himself. 'And you gave it back!'

Stephen was captivated. The sensation of unreality in this

encounter with the girls, which he had felt before, was quite obliterated; he was aware now only of a pressing need to come to Suzie's aid. Before Stan could say more, he told him to cut it out, to leave her alone and change the subject. Fearing a sarcastic put-down, he was surprised and relieved by Stan's unhesitating acquiescence. (Only much later, when all the fog had cleared, would Stan refer teasingly to 'Stephen doing his knight-in-shining-armour bit.') The conversation reverted to mundane matters, and Suzie's appreciation of his intervention, conveyed in an expressive fleeting look, gave rise to a rush of emotion that Stephen had difficulty keeping to himself. Something was happening here over which he had no control; all he needed to do was to sit back, relax, let events take their course. But his switched-off state was soon to be interrupted by anxiety brought about by Stan declaring that they should think about getting something to eat. With little more than two pounds on him, — all he had in the world till the following week when his grant cheque would be due — this appeared a problem. Stan was very probably no better off, and the girls gave every indication of having expensive tastes. He need not have worried though because Rebecca came up with an incredibly perfect solution. It turned out that she was 'cat sitting' for rich family friends who were away on holiday somewhere exotic. This gave her full use of their posh St John's Wood home, where she was at liberty to entertain friends and even had access to plentiful food and drink. All she had to do in return was look after Sebastian, their spoilt Siamese cat. Once again, it occurred to Stephen that it was all coming over too good to be true; but he put that thought aside however, accepting instead that he had simply entered a parallel universe of unlimited largess and promise.

The house, in a beautifully maintained white stuccoed Regency terrace, lived up fully to expectations. After rapidly taking in the resplendent ground floor living areas — from which Sebastian greeted them with a muted growl from his cushion on a sumptuous sofa — they settled on what looked like deconsecrated church pews around a pine table in the kitchen.

Rebecca produced a York ham, a selection of French cheeses and fresh bread rolls from the biggest fridge Stephen had ever seen, and, from somewhere else, bottles of Guinness and Worthington E; she offered to cook eggs and bacon, but this was declined as unnecessary. Stan set to work with a carving knife on the ham, for all the world as though he owned the place, and Suzie slid closer to Stephen, their thighs making contact beneath the table.

'This is the life,' said Stan, piling food on his plate and pouring himself a Guinness. 'All the joys of the pub without the riff-raff. And all this lovely food.'

A yowl announced the arrival of Sebastian, curiosity eventually winning out over aristocratic aloofness. With barely a glance at the others, he made straight for Stan, jumping onto his knee and settling there.

'Clearly, a discerning creature,' said Stan, stroking Sebastian's head. 'You see. He knows instinctively where the talent lies, don't you, my pet.'

'Yes,' said Stephen, feeling a put-down long overdue, 'your appeal to neutered males established beyond doubt. Must be quite an asset in your line of business.'

'Miaow,' said Rebecca through a smile, and after just a moment or two's hesitation, Stan gave vent to a burst of laughter.

A gradual pairing off developed after they had finished eating, Rebecca and Stan, who had been devouring each other with their eyes, slipping off upstairs, closely followed by Sebastian. Leaving Stephen somewhat apprehensively small-talking with Suzie, wondering whether he had misread her earlier allusions, had been mistaken in thinking his feelings for her reciprocated. Suzie, for her part, happily participated in the exchange, seemingly content to maintain it at an impersonal level. Their conversation ranged wide and shallow: over the music they liked, books they had read, touching on to the politics of the day. Then she asked him what he thought of the house they were in, of which it was clear she was well familiar, and then, after hearing of his amazement at its luxury and elegance, went on,

'The most impressive part to my mind is the main bathroom. I've never seen anything quite like it. Absolutely unique. Would you like to see it?'

He followed her up the stairs, along the thickly carpeted corridor, past closed doors behind one of which he supposed Stan and Rebecca to be disporting themselves, silently it seemed, no sound perturbing the enchanted stillness. She opened the door at the end, took his hand and led him into a slick, upmarket art gallery: white sculptured exhibits tastefully displayed against the marble-clad walls, among them the loo, a veritable throne, bearing little clue to its everyday function, and a gleaming white, free-standing bath poised on gilded lions' feet above the marble floor. Items of dark antique furniture — a long-case clock, an oak carver, a velvet upholstered chaise longue — interspersed the prevailing whiteness. Under more normal circumstances, Stephen could well have dismissed the whole thing as kitsch, an overblown effort to impress. But now, his hand still in Suzie's, it was simply a constituent element of the enchanted parallel universe he had entered, perhaps its very core. He turned to her, speechless.

'Well,' she said, 'what do you think?'

He made to kiss her.

'Hey, wait a moment.' She gently pushed him away with her free hand. 'Did you notice the shower?' He followed her gaze to a white archway in the wall over to their left, steps beneath it leading to a sunken mosaic-tiled enclosure. 'It's super, isn't it? Big enough for two, even more.'

She was looking at him expectantly and didn't resist this time when he kissed her, releasing his hand so that they could enfold each other, their lips coming together gently, repeatedly.

'Shall we try it then?' He could hardly believe he had said this.

'Um, if you like.'

Then into the dream, opening with her hands unbuttoning his shirt, him fumbling with the fastenings of her jeans, the long drawn out process conducted in silence, with frequent interruptions as mouths came together, hands fondled newly exposed flesh. Then in liberated nakedness down into the alcove, to soap each other's bodies under the steaming, gushing stream. But then, as he went to make a definite move — his feet between hers, her back pressed hard against the wall — he encountered some resistance, a stiffening of her body which halted him, causing him to draw back.

'I'm sorry. Is something the matter? Isn't it safe?'

'No, it's not that… Oh, Stephen…'

She hugged him close to her in the returning silence for the age before he could bring himself to speak again.

'What is it then? It doesn't matter if you don't want to go on. What's happened already is wonderful anyway.'

'But I do. It's just that I feel such a bitch. You're never going to forgive me.'

And then it all came out. He shut off the water as she began to explain. But almost before she had started, he knew pretty well what was coming; the misgivings he had felt at the outset, disingenuously pushed aside, crystallising now to what should have been perfectly obvious from the start: that it was all a set-up, and he had stepped right into it. God, how Stan must be beside himself with glee.

'There was no harm intended. Stan is really very fond of you. Often talks about you. You're probably his closest friend. It was just meant as a bit of fun. Something to set the evening off with a laugh. We should have come clean well before things got to this stage.'

The three of them had been fellow students at RADA, he now learned; Stan and Rebecca lovers who had been living together on and off for more than a year; Suzie and Rebecca close friends from school days — one of the few elements of the fabrication that happened to be true; both now out-of-work actresses.

'So that... that story of yours... the sheikh's son and all that...'

'All concocted. Did you really believe it? It seemed weak to me as I started playing it. But it got better. You see, we treated the whole thing like a drama class exercise in improvisation; first setting out in very general terms the underlying theme, establishing a few reference points, then letting things take their course. Something that usually ends in disaster. But it can be quite convincing when it comes off. I just got lost in it, persuaded myself it was for real, that I'd been picked up in a pub by a total stranger and was really turned on by the way it was developing. I should have told you long before, but it was going so well... seemed a pity to spoil it. Then in the end, I couldn't bear the idea of fooling you. Not that I wanted to pull out. Oh, Stephen, I've been such an idiot.'

Stephen was nonplussed, not knowing what to think. If she had strung him along before... but he believed her now, there seemed no reason not to. Yet the thought of Stan masterminding it all... that really got him, made him feel such a twit. But at the same time... What the hell! He took her into his arms, realising as he did so that something was missing, that the moment had passed, emotions near to bursting point minutes before now quite dispelled. Suzie, however, was in no mood to let matters rest.

'Turn the water back on,' she said, rubbing up against him. Then, 'Hey! What's happened down there?'

She kissed him and knelt down. He felt her hands pressing on his buttocks, her face against his groin; then her lips, gently at first, then more firmly... triggering his body's response, regaining the disrupted rapture of minutes before. He stooped, pulled back and lifted her forcibly to her feet, then entered her with an urgency that put pay to any possibility of further interruption. But no sooner had he done so than an uninvited image arose from somewhere in his subconscious: Natasha, there all the while, silently awaiting her cue. He was making love to Natasha, a realisation accompanied by a pang of guilt, soon to be overwhelmed in the fervour that followed; Suzie re-emerging through the haze, so that he was having them both, separately and together, lost in ecstatic vacillation as the intensity grew, gradually at first, then uncontrollably to the unsustainable limit.

Then it was Suzie, just Suzie in his arms... oblivious of all else but her presence... her body pressed against his as slowly, so slowly, he returned to earth.

She left him for a moment, returning with warm towels with which they dried each other and then dressed, all in an easy silence, signifying for Stephen that what had occurred between them was too perfect for words. But then, when he asked when he could see her again, she became evasive... not tomorrow, not the following week.

'Why on earth not, Suzie? What's the matter?'

'I've too much to do in the next few days, too many arrangements to make.' She was looking at the floor as she said this, then turned to face him. 'You see... I'm getting married next week. Next Saturday.' She gave a light laugh that contrasted with the sadness in her eyes. 'I should have told you, but once again, it seemed a pity to spoil things.'

'You can't be serious.' But he saw that she was. 'I just don't know what to think any more, what to believe. Stan knows about this?'

'They both do. Neither of them are very keen on Desmond, the guy I'm marrying. Maybe that was one of the reasons why Stan... No, that wasn't it at all. It was just thought of as a laugh, as I told you before. Something you would have realised soon enough, or we would have told you after a drink or two. Nobody thought for a moment that it would go on the way it has. That was just me. I was the one who decided not to let it go.'

'A last fling. Is that what it was? God, I know I should be grateful Suzie. Any man would be. But the thought of not seeing you again...'

'I didn't say that.'

'So, what are you saying?'

'Just to leave it for now. Get on with other things. There'll be opportunities for us to meet again. I'm sure of it. But not until things have settled. You'll have to be patient. And so will I.'

They came downstairs to find Stan and Rebecca sprawled on the sofa, both looking a little sheepish, Sebastian on Stan's lap.

'It's all right,' said Suzie. 'All revealed, show over.'

She was looking a little disconcerted though, leaving it to Stephen to give the best impression he could of having taken it in his stride.

'You bastard, Stan,' he said with a smile, 'I'll get you back for this.'

'Can't wait. You certainly owe me one. Judging by the sounds coming from the bathroom... Ouch!'

Rebecca, having kicked him satisfactorily, offered to make tea, but Suzie insisted she had to be going.

'Will you walk me to the tube, Stephen?'

'Of course.'

The leaving was friendly enough if rather abrupt, Stan coming out with something about inviting Stephen to a full rehearsal of his play, and Rebecca rising from the sofa to be kissed by them both and express the hope that they would all be seeing each other again soon — leaving out whether Desmond was to feature in this get-together.

They started down the road in silence, Suzie, after a few paces, taking hold of his hand, for all the world, he thought, as though they were long term lovers returning home from a night out. On reaching the station, he said he would leave her there, that he felt the need for a long walk. And with just a light squeeze of her hand on his, she entered the ticket hall, turning at the last moment to see him standing there, watching her, then blowing him a kiss before descending to the depths.

He headed down the Edgware Road towards Marble Arch, barely aware of the fine drizzle glazing the paving stones beneath his feet, unsure of the route back to Kennington and the seedy room he had rented as an emphatically temporary measure the previous week in his frantic search for somewhere to live; and feeling in no hurry whatsoever to get there, as he turned over and over in his mind the extraordinary happenings of the last few hours.

TEN

The following morning, his thoughts disengaging with difficulty from events of the previous day, Stephen set off for Prince of Wales College. It was to be his third visit to the Department of Mathematics, the second having been a week or so earlier, straight after his return to London, when a lone secretarial assistant, holding fort over the summer recess, had advised him to try again later. The first one had been some months before, when he attended for interview. On that occasion, he had been able to stay in what had been his home for as long as he could remember — which, in the meantime, had been sold and his parents ensconced in a retirement bungalow on the south coast, close to Eastbourne, where his father was hoping to engage in some consulting capacity with an offshoot of the company which had employed him for the better part of his working life. Though this upheaval had come as something of a shock to Stephen, signalling emphatically the end of an era, it was now a relief not to have to make excuses for not returning home and to be spared the guilt he would certainly have felt in having to insist on such a renunciation.

The departmental office this time was showing clear signs of having awakened from the summer hibernation: desks all occupied and seemingly busy, typewriters tapping away, purposeful intruders rummaging through pigeonholes, impeding the smooth functioning of the administrative machine with unanswerable queries, impossible demands. Stephen, among them, guiltily enquiring of the whereabouts of Professor Lambert, only to learn he hadn't been sighted and was unlikely to appear before the start of his course in October. If then. He stood his ground. Not in any way out of defiance, just bemused, lost for what to do next. Someone eventually took pity, consulted documents, made phone calls, then escorted him through a maze of dusty corridors and stairways to a room at the top of the building where Professor Lambert's postgraduate students were reputed to hang out. It was unoccupied. Left alone there, he began to wonder whether what he was letting himself in for was altogether a good idea. He put his bag on a desk — the only one of the four or five in the room uncluttered with books and paper — and took in his surroundings: walls lined with a shabby assortment of filing cabinets, stacked shelving and glass-fronted bookcases, a blackboard displaying the remnants of sloppily erased diagrams and equations, a high window, which appeared never to have been cleaned, from which dim light filtered in and which to see out of would entail climbing on a desk, a blue anorak hanging from a row of hooks on the back of the door through which he had entered. After a minute or two of just standing there, lost again for what to do, he took off his coat, hung it beside the anorak and wandered over to a bookcase. Hardly had he started a desultory examination of its contents, when loud running footsteps sounded from the corridor outside and a young man of dark Asiatic appearance burst into the room. Startled at first at the sight of Stephen, his expression changed rapidly from shocked surprise to hesitant greeting.

'You must be the fellow from Westmoreland?' And on

confirmation of this, 'Welcome to the madhouse. I'm Sharif, another of Emel's postgrads.'

'Emel?'

'Sorry. It's ML, for Malcolm Lambert.'

He was smiling as he said this and appeared about to add something before thinking better of it. Later in the day, when they had started to get to know each other, he was to explain the joke: that the letters also stood for Missing Link, which anyone coming across Lambert for the first time — as had Stephen at his interview — couldn't fail to appreciate. In fact, it had come as something of a shock to him. He knew of Lambert's immense reputation in his field of mathematics and had spoken to him on the phone. Gentle and precise, would be Stephen's description of his manner of speaking, rather fussy perhaps. Certainly, nothing to have prepared him for the face-to-face encounter. He had conveyed something of this to Stan in a pub on the evening after the interview, somewhat embroidered to be sure but nevertheless expressing well his initial reaction. 'You know those illustrations depicting the descent of man, a line of creatures striding across the page, at the tail end a small indeterminate quadruped, the others getting progressively bigger and more upright, ending with a perfect example of fully developed manhood — something like Brother Oswald arriving in the chapel. Well, the one before him, or perhaps the one before that, a hunched hairy body, heavy ape-like features, arms dangling down below his knees, hand gripping some sort of crude club — well, that's Professor Lambert to a T, he could have posed for it.'

Sharif in the meantime was eyeing Stephen thoughtfully, wondering what to make of him, how he would shape up as a colleague, as a companion perhaps.

'You've come at a quiet time, I'm afraid. Emel's at some workshop in Cambridge, taken Alan and Franco with him — two of the guys who share this room.'

Sharif's demeanour had changed, become somewhat distant, even a touch aggressive.

'It's on the great unifying conjectures — Badenski, Spalding, Taniyama-Shimura. You know, the search for formal links between seemingly unrelated branches of mathematics. Something he's been on about for ages. There's talk of setting up some high-powered international programme to coordinate the research. It's all pie in the sky though. Absolutely nothing's come out of it despite all the clever people working away at it for years. You'll be hearing all about it no doubt. Though if I were you, I'd stay well clear. That's if you want to finish your PhD before you're old enough to draw a pension.'

Having got that out of the way, his manner subsided to that of before.

'Oh, I nearly forget. Emel left some papers for me to give you, in case you turned up while he was away.'

He went over to his desk and produced a thickish file which he handed to Stephen with a wry smile.

'Something to thumb through when you've nothing better to do.'

Stephen was a little puzzled at Sharif's reaction to the Cambridge workshop. He knew something of the Taniyama-Shimura conjecture having attended a seminar on it given by a rising star from Princeton a few months before, at Westmoreland. It was a fascinating concept, all the more so as nobody it seemed could offer any explanation for the extraordinary analytical similarities between two so seemingly unrelated mathematical fields. But also puzzling was Sharif's suggestion that he, Stephen, might be expected to participate in some way in that programme. It was all so clearly way beyond his level of competence; something that if things went extraordinarily well for him, which he didn't for a moment believe they could, then perhaps… after his doctorate… What did occur to him was that Sharif could be feeling left out of whatever it was that Alan and Franco were getting involved in, that he was bitter about it. If that were so, it would soon become apparent.

He thought for a moment of referring back to Taniyama-Shimura, to see if Sharif could throw any further light on what little he knew, but decided against it. Perhaps later. There was something about the way he had closed on it, that inhibited further discussion and, anyway, it was a bit early in the relationship to get into technical stuff. Other things came to mind. As though reading his thoughts, Sharif brought up the question of lunch. It was about time for it. Had Stephen any plans?

'Not really. I just thought I'd try the refectory. What about you?'

'Well, the refectory's all right I suppose. But there are better ones. One advantage of this place is that there are plenty of cheap eating places around. Several University of London colleges are within spitting distance and we can use any of them. SOAS isn't too bad, if you like curry. It's just round the corner.'

'Sounds fine to me. What is it?'

'SOAS? The School of Oriental and African Studies. Then there's UCL, but that's no better than here, worse if anything. There are others, including ULU, the Students Union, which makes for a change now and then.'

SOAS it was. Over indifferent curry and rice, Stephen and Sharif put out mutual feelers, exchanging backgrounds and interests, ambitions and uncertainties — an exploration identifiable with hindsight as the beginning of the close friendship that was to develop between them. An immediate effect on Stephen was a diminished sense of isolation, a realisation that if Sharif was anything to go by, then the climate into which he had moved was very much one in which he could operate, could feel at home. Sharif's parents, he learned, had emigrated to Britain from Pakistan when he was four years old. Deeply religious Muslims, they had difficulty with his adoption of Western ways and gradual abandonment of the faith — things he played down with them, doing his best to imply no fundamental shift had taken place, a posture helped along by obvious devotion to his homeland, which he still regarded Pakistan to be, and to which he and his parents returned as often as they could afford, maintaining contact with countless relatives and friends.

'They're still set on an arranged marriage,' he said with a light laugh. 'Young virgins from the village lining up to be considered.'

'Well,' replied Stephen, 'when you're in your forties and getting fed up with what's on offer over here... could be something worth keeping in mind.' Sharif's dismissive laugh did not quite convince him that he hadn't been thinking along those lines himself.

It then turned out that he rented a room in Stockwell fairly close to Stephen's in Kennington, causing Sharif's eyes to light up expectantly.

'Do you drink?' he asked.

'Well, yes...' replied Stephen, hesitantly, quite surprised

at the directness, and as yet uncertain to what extent cultural inhibitions in this regard might still apply. To be on the safe side he was about to add 'in moderation,' only to be loudly interrupted,

'Well, thank goodness for that. Those other two are a dead loss, Alan is an out and out teetotaller and Franco seems afraid of even walking past a pub. Do you play darts?'

'Yes... but not very well. Why do you ask?'

Stephen realised he was holding back somewhat. He had learnt to play at Westmoreland, discovering he had what passed there for some natural talent for the game.

'You must come to the Pied Bull. It's only a few minutes' walk from Kennington station, about the same from my place. Not at all a bad pub, good for darts and to observe the natives in their habitat. What about tonight?'

Stephen had been planning to spend the evening alone, sorting out the mess in his room and brooding over Suzie. Now he jumped at the prospect of a sociable alternative, gratified yet again at the way his return to London was taking off. Perhaps Kennington would turn out less dreary than he had been assuming. And he was coming to appreciate that, behind the forthright manner, there was something strongly appealing about Sharif, a presence hinted at by look and gesture that held the promise of exotic adventure. As though to lend substance to this notion, a young woman of striking appearance, blond and feline, whom he had been admiringly taking in from across the room, approached their table. Hardly noticing Stephen, she addressed herself to Sharif.

'What happened last night?' she asked, receiving a dismissive shrug as though in resentment at the intrusion. 'I waited up all hours. Couldn't you have phoned or something?'

Without looking at her, he mumbled about having other things to do, business to transact that couldn't be interrupted. Surprisingly, she appeared satisfied with this explanation.

'When am I going to see you then?' she went on. 'It's been a long time.'

He shrugged. Then at last turned to her, though without change of expression.

'Could be tonight.' She seemed overjoyed at this. 'But not till very late. I really can't say when I'll be able to get away.'

'Doesn't matter, Sharif. I'll wait up for you.'

He nodded and turned away. And after an awkward few moments, she left them, threading her way back around the crowded tables and out into the street.

The silence that followed was eventually broken by Stephen, intrigued as well as shocked at Sharif's uncompromising display of power.

'You seem to be well in there,' he said, adding in the absence of a response, 'Bit hard on her, weren't you?'

Sharif chuckled, his features relaxing to their previous state.

'It's the only way with that sort.'

'Really?'

'Yes.' He laughed again. 'They get so used to men drooling over them that in the end the only thing that really gets through is a show of complete indifference. Particularly when they've spotted a likely candidate, felt some twinge of sexual attraction and fluttered their feathers. It doesn't always work, but when it does…'

It struck Stephen that the impression he had formed of Sharif minutes before could well come over as extremely attractive to women, helped along no doubt by his cool confident manner and dark-skinned physical appearance — indisputably handsome with a luxuriant black mane and somewhat heavy but nonetheless athletic body. And something else as well, an evident otherness that set him apart.

'Mystery-of-the-Orient,' said Sharif, as though reading Stephen's thoughts, at which they both burst out laughing.

Conversation then turned to the maths department. And Emel. Which was when Sharif let on to the origin of the nickname, to further shared laughter. It was becoming an altogether jolly occasion, as pleasant an introduction to his new position as Stephen could possibly have hoped for.

'When do you think he'll be back?' he then asked. 'I've no idea at all what I'm supposed to be doing here.'

'Don't expect any help from Emel with that,' replied Sharif, to Stephen's dismay. 'He's given you a sample of the relevant literature. It'll be up to you to decide what you want to do with it.'

'You mean... he's not going to specify my project?'

'No, he's not. No need to look so glum. It's the way he operates. It generally works out okay. And once you've found something and have started to take it somewhere... well you'll find then that he's only too ready to help. As I said, it's how he operates. Probably something he picked up in his cave.'

Though Stephen smiled at this, he was worried. It showed.

'Look, just take your time with those papers. Start with the one by Scheffer and somebody. It's relatively straightforward and doesn't draw much on specialised knowledge. We can talk about it some other time over a pint. But now I need to get some sleep. Didn't get much last night and doesn't look as if I'll get much tonight either.'

No, I don't suppose you will, thought Stephen with some

envy. 'Would you like to call off our darts appointment?'

'Good Lord, no. A few games of darts is just what I'll need to help me relax.' He took out a pen and sketched directions to the pub on the back of the till receipt. 'Seven o'clock, then?'

They parted in the street, Stephen returning to college in some confusion to open in trepidation the file of papers on his desk. Would he be able to make any sort of sense of them? And in the unlikely event that he could... well, that would only mark the beginning of God knows how many years hard toil, leading God knows where, and still the ubiquitous question of what on earth he was letting himself in for.

'Mystery-of-the-Orient five, Wisdom-of-the-West nil,' intoned Sharif, smiling self-satisfyingly as he wiped the board.

Smug bastard, thought Stephen, ruefully acknowledging once again his second-fiddle status in whatever activity he sought to pursue, but thanking Christ he had at least refrained from claiming proficiency in the game. Which was something of a near miss, as at Westmoreland he had played in the top league, such as it was, reliably able to give anyone a good run for their money. By that standard, he had performed well this evening but had been completely outclassed. The pub was starting to fill up by then, a few newcomers exchanging greetings with Sharif, one of them coming over and offering to chalk.

'No, I think we've had about enough for now. You go ahead.'

They moved to a corner table where Stephen, having spent the afternoon struggling to get to grips with the recommended paper, was hoping to question Sharif on one or two points. But they were interrupted by a seriously overweight bruiser —

mid-forties or thereabouts, pinched expression and lighted fag seemingly glued to his lower lip — who had come over and seated himself at their table. Completely disregarding Stephen, he addressed himself to Sharif.

'Did you hear about Rod? No? Fucking disaster.'

From what followed it turned out that Rod, captain and star player of the pub darts team, had been stopped by the police on his way home after their last away match, — 'in fucking Croydon' — escorted to the station, declared unfit to drive and would soon be appearing before a local magistrate — 'a fucking woman', retired headmistress and noted feminist bigot.

'Rod, unfit! Don't make me fucking laugh. Certainly, he'd had a few, but then he always has. It was minutes after that last game that he was stopped. Last three throws: hundred-and-fucking-forty, hundred-and-fucking-forty, — both as near to hundred-and-fucking-eighty as you could get – then treble seventeen, nineteen, double eleven to finish. And the fucking pigs say he was fucking unfit! Makes you fucking sick.' Then, after a thoughtful pause, 'It's not as though he wanted to compete in fucking Formula One. All he wanted was to drive his clapped-out Morris Minor to fucking Earlsfield. What's the matter with them?'

Stephen was cheered up no end by all this, his trivial academic concerns quite dispelled. Impressed also at the solicitous manner, with no hint of ridicule, with which Sharif was responding, and at his tact in later declining the invitation to take part in their next match, — clearly a major reason for the approach — citing with convincing regret the insuperable obstacles ruling this out of the question. While this was going on, Stephen was able to observe developing activity around the dartboard, where half a dozen or so local, middle-aged ex-hooligans were engaged in expletive-ridden chauvinistic repartee. Humorous enough on the whole, but with the occasional harsh, racist overtone and continuing indication that it wouldn't take much for the whole thing to turn nasty. And so to marvel at how black foreigner Sharif had been able to win their clear approval and indeed respect. By the time the intruder had left them, Stephen's glass was empty. He rose to replenish it, asking Sharif, whose glass was still half full, what he was having. Surprisingly, he replied that he was okay, that he needed to keep a clear head. A fuller explanation emerged when Stephen returned, which clarified some other things as well. Sharif, he was to learn, was a gambler. Not by any means a compulsive one, so he said, quite the contrary: he only played when he needed cash, it was the way he supplemented his meagre grant. A poker school which met in various West End apartments was frequented by certain Saudi fellow students 'with more money than sense. Lots more.' The stakes were high, 'much higher than I could be expected to afford. Last night was the first time for quite a while.'

'And did you win?' asked Stephen.

'Well, no,' he replied with a light smile. 'No, I lost a bit… or shall we say, I paid for information. Sometimes you have to do that. Tonight should be different.'

'I hope so.'

Stephen was worried. Though impressed by what little he had seen of Sharif, clearly identifying him as a competent operator, this sounded dangerous, particularly so in view of his air of utter self-confidence.

'What about the others?' he asked. 'Are they all rich students?'

'Good Lord, no. A very mixed bunch in every respect. Some quite shady customers, others seem okay... don't really know about most of them. It's not the sort of gathering where it's on to ask questions.' Which was where he clearly wanted to leave it. And so, Stephen turned to the matter of future plans, in particular Sharif's, as he was coming close to finishing his thesis, and learned that Emel had been trying to persuade him to stay on, to continue with his research for which funding could be made available.

'But it's peanuts. And in any case, I need a break. More than that, an exit. I'm finishing with mathematics research. It's been great in all sorts of ways but that's it. I need to get into something quite different. Among other criteria, something that will bring me in piles of cash.'

'Like what, for example?'

And then it came out that one of the Camels — his term, used affectionately, for the Saudis and other Arabs, to whom in like vein he was one of the Pakis — had come up with a business proposition which he was seriously considering. Initial soundings were apparently promising, but it was still at the embryonic stage, with much background probing to be carried out. Stephen was intrigued, but, seeing that beneath the assumed nonchalance Sharif was showing understandable signs of strain, thought it best not to question him further, nor to bring up the research paper. He put this off in his mind to however long it would be for Sharif to recover from his diverse assignations of the coming night. Instead, they just relaxed, observed the natives in their habitat, finished their beers and prepared to leave, Sharif exchanging warm salutations with those gathered round the dartboard as they made their way to the door.

ELEVEN

It was to be late in the following week before Stephen and Sharif were to meet again. The day before that, Stephen had arrived at college as usual at around nine to find his room occupied by two strangers, both seemingly absorbed in whatever they were up to among the jumble of books and paper littering their desks: Alan and Franco were back. Appearing initially put out at the intrusion, they went on to make some effort at welcoming him into the group, though he could feel their desire, particularly on the part of Alan — clearly identifiable as the dominant one — to get the interruption over as soon as possible. Stephen nevertheless asked about the Cambridge workshop, adding that Sharif had told him of it — though not of course what he had said — and that it sounded interesting.

'So you've met Sharif then?' Alan appeared surprised and somewhat disconcerted. 'We haven't seen him for weeks.'

'Only on my first day here. We had lunch together at SOAS.' Then, after a moment's hesitation that was just long enough for him to decide to omit mention of their pub session, 'He hasn't been in since.'

'I'm not surprised. He obviously thinks he's got better things to do than come into college.'

Stephen, much as he would have liked to allude to the knowledge of what these might be, remained silent. Alan's obvious antipathy to Sharif, which he knew to be reciprocated, made it prudent to feign unawareness of anything about him, in particular with regard to his extra-curricular activities. Compensating for that cravenness, however, by going on to press Alan on the matter of the workshop, which it was clear he was intentionally sidestepping.

'So, what happened at Cambridge then? Anything exciting? Any new unification conjectures coming out?'

'Yes, there were. Two quite new ones which nobody had heard of before.' This from Franco, suddenly quite animated. 'And it looks as if Emel could be coordinating the whole programme. It's as though...'

'Nothing's been decided.' Alan, angrily came out with this, cutting across Franco, who withdrew guiltily back into his shell. 'And Professor Lambert explicitly asked that nothing be said about the workshop until after the report of the proceedings has been prepared.'

Stephen was genuinely perplexed at this, as well as irritated by Alan's general pomposity and his put-down of Franco – looking sad and embarrassed beside him.

'Why was that, do you think?' he asked, feeling the need to respond. 'Did something controversial crop up? I thought it was supposed to be just an open academic get-together. All interested parties welcome to attend.' Adding, on sudden inspiration, 'That's what Julian Rush implied to me after his Westmoreland seminar back in February.'

This was a lie. No such conversation with Rush had taken place. Stephen had indeed attended that seminar and knew Rush to be a prime authority in the field, someone he could be pretty sure Alan would be in awe of. That was all, bogus name-dropping on a sudden whim. But it served the intended purpose of taking the wind out of Alan's sail for a moment, and the related unintended one of reanimating Franco, bringing him back into the picture.

'If only I had known about that seminar. I would have got to it somehow.'

'Westmoreland's rather a long way off. Practically in Scotland.'

'I would still have got there. I would so like to meet Julian Rush. I have read everything he has published. His work is beautiful. How was he to talk to?'

To Stephen's guilty relief, Alan interjected half-apologetically at this point, to remind Franco they had a deadline to meet.

'Yes, yes I know.'

And so the exchange ended and Stephen settled down to the 'relatively straightforward' paper Sharif had recommended, which was by now, in spite of initial misgivings, making some sort of sense, even providing glimmers of inspiration. That kept him busy till lunchtime, only distracted now and then by Alan's loud confident repetitions of Franco's quietly proposed suggestions for dealing with aspects of the urgent assignment.

'What are you two doing for lunch?' Stephen asked as he rose to leave, learning that they had brought in sandwiches to eat at their desks, Franco appearing unhappy at this arrangement.

'Then I'll see you both later. First, I'm going to see if Professor Lambert is in his room. They told me in the office they were expecting him back this afternoon.'

'Good luck,' said Alan, somewhat dismissively.

'Yes, he should be there by about two o'clock,' said

Franco. 'When he comes in, it's always at about that time. Do you know where his room is?' Then going on to explain how to find it: on the ground floor, whether fortuitously or by design, as far from that of his research students as it was possible to be within the building.

Following a stodgy refectory meal, which he vowed would be his last for the foreseeable future, Stephen made his way through the maze of ground floor corridors to Emel's room. He knocked and, on receiving no response, tried the door. It opened, revealing Emel facing him ferociously across his desk, in the manner he would later describe to Stan as that of a wild beast surprised over its freshly slaughtered prey.

'I'm sorry to disturb you, Professor Lambert,' Stephen just managed to come out with. And on receiving no response, 'I'm Stephen Hallam...' Still no response, — Emel's expression remaining unchanged, if anything darkening further — 'your new PhD student... from Westmoreland. I arrived here last week.'

To Stephen's dismay, Emel started to rise from his chair at this, intent, so it seemed, on violent reaction to the intrusion. But then to his heartfelt relief, a transformation occurred, Emel's countenance changing as he rose, passing from seemingly crazed aggression to concerned geniality.

'My dear fellow,' he said in a voice soft and comforting, 'however can you forgive me for not recognising you. Please, please take a seat.' He motioned to a small table in a corner of the room around which were arranged comfortable looking chairs. 'So pleased to see you. When did you say you arrived? Oh yes, you told me. Last week, wasn't it? I'm so sorry I wasn't here to greet you. A conference in Cambridge, you know. Got in the way of so many things. How did you manage to find your way around?'

Stephen shuffled over to the table and sat down, explaining as he did so that he had met Sharif and that he had been most helpful.

'Oh, Sharif,' replied Emel. 'Good, I'm so pleased.' He seated himself opposite Stephen, rubbing his hands together. 'A brilliant student, Sharif, one of the best I've had. I'm hoping he will be carrying on with his work here.'

Stephen muttered some further note of appreciation of Sharif, swallowing, of course, knowledge of his future intentions, then going on, 'Oh, and thank you for the papers. He passed them on to me. I'm working my way through them.'

Emel's expression turned blank for a moment, as though he had no idea what Stephen was talking about, then brightened up again.

'And what about accommodation?' he asked. 'Have you found somewhere to live?'

Stephen was grateful for Sharif's forewarning of this unwillingness to engage. It still felt strange though, still worrying.

'Yes, yes, I have. In Kennington.' Emel could not have looked more surprised if he had said Timbuktu. 'It's quite convenient really... on the Northern Line... not far from where Sharif lives.'

Emel responded favourably to this final phrase.

'Oh good, good. So pleased you two are getting along well. I'm so pleased.'

I never said we were getting along well, thought Stephen, petulantly, as he would later admit to himself. But it was painful having to think of what to say next. Especially as he was coming to appreciate the selection of papers Emel had assembled for him, realising it was by no means a simply thrown-together collection. Having by now got well into the first one, — following Sharif's prompt — he had been dipping into the others, some quite recent, others going back years. This casual browsing had helped resolve one of his problems with the Scheffer paper and had thrown up clues relating to others. He would very much have liked to discuss this. An awkward silence followed, broken eventually by Emel.

'I suppose you're still in touch with the department at Westmoreland. Give my regards to Barry Milman if you get the chance.'

'I'm afraid I don't know him,' said Stephen, feeling awkward and ill at ease. 'He's not in that department as far as I know.'

'Oh, really? Then maybe it's Newcastle. I get confused. It's been a long time.' Another silence. 'Well, I dare say you have plenty to do. Mustn't keep you. You know where I am now. Drop in any time you feel like it.' Again, that look, positively beaming with concern.

'Thank you.'

It was in low spirits that Stephen returned to his room to find Alan and Franco still slogging away. He settled back at his desk, not at all in the mood for work but getting down to it anyway, ruefully acknowledging the need to fill the vacuum. Soon losing himself in it however, with Alan's bombastic utterances and Franco's quietly offered words of apparent wisdom presenting little more distraction than the chirping of birds on a spring day in the park.

The following morning started out much as the previous one, Alan and Franco working away, hardly acknowledging his arrival. Then, just as he was getting down to work, attempting to derive for himself a quoted result in the Scheffer paper, the door flew open and Sharif burst in. Something very different about him was immediately apparent: a triumphant air, set off with new black leather jacket and jeans, expensive-looking shoes — these last a particularly welcome advance on the falling apart ones he had been wearing the week before, complaining bitterly he couldn't afford to replace them.

'So, it all turned out okay?' said Stephen, only to receive a look telling him to hold off for now, that all would be revealed in good time.

'Come into a fortune, have you?' said Alan, eyeing him disparagingly, Franco, in the meantime, smiling in clear approval.

'A lovely jacket that,' he said. 'Where did you get it? It must have cost a lot of money.'

'No, it was free. Belonged to a dead American. He obviously didn't have any further use for it so I helped myself.'

'Really,' said Franco, looking interested and about to say more, when Alan cut in.

'Don't take any notice. He's bullshitting as usual. Never believe a word he says.'

At which Sharif laughed and invited them all for coffee at the Green Spot, around the corner from college, saying he was feeling generous. Franco looked ready to accept but was put right by Alan reminding him they had a deadline to meet. And so Sharif led Stephen instead to the Grenville Arms, which was just opening, – for what he termed would be a celebratory beer, which went on to become several – bubbling over with stuff he wanted to talk about, the precipitous change in his fortunes he was only just beginning to take in.

Things had really moved for him, starting with the poker session Stephen had worried about, which, after a poor start and what could well have proved a disaster, had turned out dazzlingly successful.

'The cards just weren't running for me, seemed they were never going to. One guy, in particular, someone I hadn't seen before, though obviously well known to some of the others, was steadily coining it. Then I got dealt a promising hand, which went on to improve beyond my wildest hopes. At which point this guy decides to raise the stakes. Heavily. My first thought was that this is it, just what I'd been waiting for. I felt pretty sure he had pulled off a couple of successful bluffs before and was trying it on again. So I raised him, by a lot. And then, without a moment's hesitation, he raised again. Through the roof this time.'

Sharif paused at this point, laughing to himself, savouring the memory.

'So, you saw him?' asked Stephen, to bring him back.

'No,' replied Sharif with another laugh. 'No, I let him take it. Chickened out, in the view of those around the table. Quite understandably. The obvious interpretation. And just what I would have wanted them to think anyway — though that's very much in the way of a bonus. No — you're going to have difficulty believing this — but it suddenly came over to me crystal clear that he had the winning hand. A number of unmistakable indications, which I'd overlooked until that moment, all pointed to it. And it was confirmed by his immediate reaction when I dropped out: a fleeting wave of disappointment he just failed to hide before smugly raking in his winnings. After that everything went pretty smoothly. A gradual build-up followed by a string of really big ones. I ended up with more money in my pocket than I've ever had in my life.'

And that was just the beginning. It amazed Stephen, when he thought about it later, how far his friendship with Sharif had developed following that first meeting just a matter of days before. It felt as though they had known each other for years, nothing appearing in the least untoward in being the recipient of disclosures Sharif would have every reason for keeping to himself. Hardly giving time for the story of his poker triumph to sink in, Sharif went on.

'I got back late last night from Monte Carlo. Two days visiting casinos with the Camels. All pretty hectic but it looks as if things are taking off for me far faster than I could ever have thought possible.'

It wasn't to gamble that Sharif had gone to Monte Carlo, as Stephen could been forgiven for having assumed. True, he had played the tables, though in a desultory manner, 'Won a little, lost a little, nothing to speak of.' No, the reason for the visit had been to meet casino managers, one in particular, to learn something of how the business functioned and as a prelude to taking up what amounted to an upmarket apprenticeship. 'Seems I've been set up to spend time there, working as a general dogsbody, learning tricks of the trade. They want me to start next month.'

Gradually the full story came out. It appeared that the family of one of Sharif's Saudi friends owned a large share of the casino in question and had plans to expand its business interests in that lucrative field. After years of negotiation with the Malaysian government, approval had been given for the construction of a vast casino complex in a remote highland surrounded by mile-upon-mile of palm plantation;

construction of a highway, to reach it from centres of population, was about to begin.

'The scale of investment is mind-boggling. But then so are the expected returns. Seems that people in that part of the world are compulsive gamblers almost without exception, at all levels of society. No difficulty working out what it's going to make once it takes off. A dead cert winner however you look at it. Specially for the government. But also for those lucky enough to get in on it from the start.'

Staffing for the new casino — one of three, maybe four, planned for the complex — was a matter of concern for the Saudi investors, determined to maintain control of day-to-day operation and mistrustful of local involvement at anything other than clearly subordinate level. The fact that Sharif — quite inexperienced in a related, or indeed any, business venture — had been singled out for what appeared a major role in the enterprise should, perhaps, have surprised Stephen. That it didn't could be put down to the supreme competence he had witnessed in Sharif's handling of a succession of testing encounters during the brief period of their acquaintance: subjugation of an importunate female admirer, devastating proficiency at the dartboard and high-stake poker table, and alongside that, — something he was only coming to appreciate — outstanding achievement in an exacting field of mathematical research. So it came as no surprise that others who knew him would be likewise impressed and eager to enlist his services in a demanding undertaking.

'Well, it all sounds very exciting,' said Stephen when he had heard him through. 'But are you really sure you want to give up on academic research? Now that you've got so far? I've just been reading comments on that last paper of yours with Emel. God, what wouldn't I give to have things like that said about work of mine.'

'I don't feel I'm giving anything up,' said Sharif, looking serious for a moment. 'Nothing to stop me from carrying on with all that stuff if and when I feel like it. No, it's just taking on something else, something that should be fun and will bring me in some cash. That's important for me. And not just for me. You don't know what difference the sort of money I'll be able to send to Pakistan is going to make to the family there. We own quite a bit of land around the village, great potential if only it could be used more productively. It's a beautiful place, wild, unspoilt, great for riding and hunting. I can't get enough of it. One of the things I did with my winnings last week was to order a tractor for there. The difference that will make is enormous. And that's just the beginning. There's so much else that needs to be done.'

'I can see you're really hooked on the place. Do you think you'll settle there eventually? Back to your roots? With a young virgin bride? Maybe two?'

'Who knows,' replied Sharif with a light laugh. 'At the moment I can only see as far as getting right into this casino business, understanding just how it functions, the pitfalls and how to avoid them, all the tricks the punters get up to, and the management, come to that. I've got a pretty good instinct for what's involved but that's not nearly enough. Only a starting point, in fact. I need to get really into it, establish myself as an expert in the game.'

'And then what?'

Another laugh, fuller this time. 'Then I'll have to see what's on offer. Can't imagine there'll be any shortage of openings. You never know, I could even return to full-time academic research. Anything's possible.'

'In the meantime, what about your thesis? I assume you're going to go ahead and finish it.'

'Oh, yes. No way I'm going to leave that hanging over me. If I don't do that now I know I never will. A month may be a bit tight but a good bit's written already. And most of the rest is just a matter of editing my publications, pasting them in. Yes, I think I can just about get it done in a month.'

TWELVE

It turned out to be more than three months before Sharif's thesis finally got submitted. Stephen saw a lot of him over this period, mainly during the evenings after both had finished work for the day: once a week or so for darts at the Pied Bull, where Sharif would sometimes let him win a game or two, and on Fridays for more serious drinking, usually starting off somewhere near the college. A few weeks after Sharif had settled down to work in earnest, Stephen proposed an interruption which was gladly accepted, the occasion being the final rehearsal of Stan's play before its departure for the Far East.

The arrangement was for them to meet up with Stan in the same Edgware Road pub as on that previous, unforgettable occasion. They arrived some minutes before the appointed time, Stephen glancing over to where Suzie had been sitting as though expecting to see her still there. He had said little to Sharif of events of that night, just that he had met someone, a friend of Stan's girl, and had seemed to be getting on well with her until she had let on that she would be getting married the following week. Which was all true enough of course, if a decidedly limited account of what had occurred. He had tried to make light of it at the time, but Sharif suspected more than he was letting on to: that Stephen had been hurt and was accordingly holding back. Stan, arriving right on time, escorted them, after hurried introduction to Sharif, to a nearby defunct school, on loan to the theatre company for rehearsals and general administration.

'Good of you to fetch us,' said Sharif as they made their way through a maze of side streets, 'but we could have found it ourselves. You must have plenty on your mind just now.'

'Not at all. Getting away for a few minutes is just what I needed. And this way there'll be no problem getting you in. For some obscure reason, management are obsessive about keeping out uninvited guests — not that any have ever turned up so far as I know.'

Stan showed them into what would have been the school assembly hall, — line markings on the floor indicating additional use for indoor sports purposes — now serving as a stage and auditorium for rehearsals. A heterogeneous group of a dozen or so people were gathered against the far wall consulting scripts and conferring earnestly among themselves; some seated on folding chairs, some standing, one or two of them moving purposefully between the others. On spotting Stan, the buzz of business-like activity changed momentarily to a tone of relief, to which he responded with a wave while directing Stephen and Sharif to an array of chairs at which a smattering of spectators were waiting patiently for the show to begin.

'You'll be better off there, away from the mob,' said Stan. 'See you in the pub afterwards, as soon as I can get away.'

As he left them to join his colleagues, Stephen became aware of a further group seated alongside the 'mob', Rebecca's blond curls drawing in his gaze, then focusing beyond the bald man on her immediate right, on to Suzie, seated impassively, staring directly ahead. Rebecca waved, the gesture changing with a smile to signify meeting up later, to which Stephen responded with a nod, Sharif, all the while, taking it all in.

'Is that the girl you were talking about? That blond over there?'

'No. That's Stan's girl.' Then after a pause, 'Next but one to her. Trying hard not to look in this direction.'

'And the bald guy between them?'

'No idea. Could be the new husband.'

At which Sharif laughed, Stephen after a moment joining in. Thank Christ, he thought, I didn't let on what happened that night. Nor how I'm feeling about it now, about her.

For a while, nothing much happened, the consultations continuing with Stan now taking part. Then some movement, chairs being placed with much discussion in the centre part of the hall to represent the position of various props: a sofa, a sideboard, two of them a yard or so apart for a doorway. It all appeared so pathetically rudimentary that Stephen began to fear the performance would be an embarrassment, that he had dragged Sharif from his labours for no worthwhile purpose. A couple of false starts and indications that some of the cast would be reading from hand-held scripts did nothing to mitigate these concerns. But then, amazingly, as the action got underway, Stephen found himself growing progressively enthralled, hand-held scripts and the absence of props detracting nothing from the experience, if anything contributing to it by demonstrating their insignificance in the essence of what it was all about. The fact that the cast were clearly enjoying themselves contributed further to his own enjoyment. At one point, Stan was required to flop down on the sofa next to the female lead, who was fully occupying the folding chair serving that purpose — giving rise to a halt in the proceedings and some laughter while a further chair was hurriedly put in place next to her, on to which Stan gave a convincing show of flopping down — to further laughter from the cast before returning to the serious business in hand.

Sharif was the first to break the silence that followed the final curtain — marked by the director with an abrupt horizontal sweep of his right forearm.

'That was really something,' he said, clearly entranced. 'I can't remember ever enjoying a play so much.'

'Even without stage and scenery? You didn't mind that?'

'No. Or maybe a bit at first. But once it got going, it didn't seem to matter at all. The acting was so good. Particularly Stan. And the girl, come to that, and the rest of them. Really terrific.'

'The guy over there with the beard,' said Stephen. 'The one who's been taking notes all the time, that must be the author. He's talking to Stan now. Doesn't seem to be sharing in the general euphoria... Ah, that's better. Now he's grinning like a Cheshire cat. They're all looking pretty pleased with themselves. Not surprising really. They must feel they're on to a winner. Don't you think so?'

'Absolutely...'

Sharif was about to say more but was interrupted by Stephen gripping his arm and telling him they had company, Rebecca advancing on them, leading Suzie and, it had to be, Desmond across what, minutes before, had been the stage. My God, thought Stephen, how on earth am I going to cope with this. He needn't have worried, Suzie and Rebecca having it all in hand. Another drama class improvisation exercise, he concluded ruefully as Rebecca made the introductions.

'Hi, Stephen. This is Suzie, an old friend, and her husband

Desmond. Stan said not to hang around. He'll join us in the pub as soon as he can.' Then, as they made to leave together, 'Well, what did you think of it?'

Sharif was quick to answer this. He had introduced himself to Rebecca before Stephen had had a chance to, and now seemed to be making all the right noises, insofar as Stephen could take in anything other than Suzie's faultless performance, greeting him politely as through for the first time. An actress through and through, he decided, nothing there other than playing out the fiction of the moment. Wanting very much to believe otherwise though, that beneath the mask something was burning for him alone — absurd wishful thinking, dismissed no sooner than entertained.

In the pub, Stephen found himself concentrating his attention on Desmond – a defence strategy adopted spontaneously, which largely served its purpose. He worked in the city, Stephen learned, in the same outfit as Stan's elder brother Albert — through whom he had met Stan and Rebecca, and hence his wife-to-be Suzie, with whom he had just returned from honeymoon in the South of France.

'I know,' Stephen just managed to stop himself replying, the only near-miss in what he later felt to have been an otherwise pretty well-conducted performance — which, far from providing comfort, had the effect of making him feel worse than ever when he thought back to it. His firm resolve of banishing all thought of further contact with Suzie suffered, in the meantime, only two setbacks. The first, following Desmond's departure to the bar to buy drinks, when he had caught Suzie's eye, seeing something fleetingly there — a longing? an entreaty? — which brought back in a rush all that had occurred between them; later to be dismissed as overactive imagination feeding on buttoned-down desire. The second setback, more difficult than the first to discount, occurred after the pub encounter had broken up and he and Sharif were making their way back to South London. Sharif had clearly been much taken with Rebecca, which had provided some welcome distraction for Stephen as he wrestled with his allotted role. It was the first time he had witnessed Sharif in supplicant mode – quite a change from what he had seen of his previous dealings with women, charm resources and Mystery-of-the-Orient cards all in full play. It was to no avail, however, as he was laughingly bemoaning as they headed for the tube. Then he came out with it.

'You're really right in there with that Suzie, you know.'

'What are you talking about?'

'The way she looked at you when she thought no one would notice. I did, though. You had your back to her, talking to Stan. I thought for a moment she was going to rush up and throw herself into your arms.'

'You must have imagined it. Your mind befuddled by thoughts of the beautiful Rebecca.'

'Could be,' he replied, laughing again. 'Have it your own way.' Then, looking at his watch, 'If we get a move on, we could just about make last orders at the Pied Bull. What do you say?'

It was on a Friday evening in the Grenville some two months later, close to the time of Sharif's much-delayed departure for Monte Carlo, that Stephen was to meet someone who was later to play a significant role in his life. Sharif had pointed him out across the bar where he was seated in deep conversation with a young woman.

'That guy over there, the one chatting up that gorgeous creature, that's Karl Dembowski. He's a physicist, quite a whizz-kid. I'd introduce you, but he looks busy.'

In fact, Stephen had overheard reference to that name in the refectory, something to do with a recent publication that challenged established theory, a source of controversy that was giving rise to a lot of excitement.

'So that's what he looks like. God, he seems young. Do you know him?'

'Yes, 'replied Sharif with a laugh. 'We're the same age as it happens, started on our PhDs at about the same time. He finished his in less than two years and was immediately offered a lectureship, along with other inducements. Physics are expecting great things from him and are shit scared he'll clear off somewhere. Seems he keeps getting offers.'

Stephen was intrigued and was about to ask more when Dembowski and the girl got up to leave. Then, spotting Sharif, they came over.

'We're just off to the flicks. Some Swedish art film at the Everyman.'

Dembowski nodded to Stephen while saying this to Sharif, who had got up to greet him.

'Time for one more before you go?' he asked.

The girl was shaking her head, Dembowski consulting his watch.

'I think we can just about manage that. No?' he asked the girl, who, with some show of effort, nodded in resignation. 'It should help us get through it. Two and a half hours and no interval. Trouble with those films is if you go for a pee at the wrong time you can lose track of the whole plot. Remember that Polish one we saw the other week?' This to the girl who again nodded, her expression showing some concern. 'When I got back, they were all crawling through what appeared to be a sewer. No idea how they got there. Nor how they got out of it come to that because I fell asleep.'

'They didn't get out of it,' said the girl.

'Oh well, there you go. I didn't miss much then.'

Introductions followed, Sharif referring to Stephen as Emel's latest research student, at which Karl's face expressed interest.

'How do you find Emel?' he asked as Sharif set off for the bar. Then, without waiting for a reply, 'He's really something special you know, you're lucky to have got him. Could have got landed with... Oh, never mind. This is Liz by the way, from the Slade. About to take the art world by storm.'

'Don't be silly,' said Liz, smiling appreciatively.

It appeared to Stephen that the way he was behaving towards her was somehow reminiscent of Sharif's treatment of that girl in the SOAS refectory. Nothing harsh this time, in fact, all very cordial and jokey, so he was unclear quite why he was making that connection, unclear also why he was in no doubt that Karl's previous display of philistinism was bogus, put on solely for her benefit — and seemingly, surprisingly, going down all right with her.

'Ah, here he comes with the booze,' said Karl. 'Bless him.'

Sharif set them down and handed Liz, who had declined a drink, a packet of salted peanuts, which she happily accepted and opened.

'How did you know I wanted these?' she asked delightedly. 'I only thought to ask after you'd gone to the bar.'

'Sixth sense,' replied Sharif with a roguish smile.

'Mystery-of-the-Orient,' interjected Stephen, to laughter from Karl who appeared to be settling in well, drinking his beer and giving every impression of wanting to make a night of it; Liz, in the meantime, anxiously consulting her watch.

Sharif was right, thought Stephen, she is gorgeous. And then the nature of the connection made minutes before clicked: it was the unwavering confidence displayed by both in their hold over their women — beautiful women, who by the look of them would have little difficulty ensnaring any man who happened to catch their eye. As though reading Stephen's thoughts and determined to refute them, Karl acknowledged Liz's anxiety, looked at his watch, finished his beer and said they had better be going.

'You should come to Liz's opening at the Buckingham next Tuesday,' he said as they rose to leave, eyeing them both in turn. 'We'll be starting off in The Goose.' He explained briefly how to get to this Soho pub. 'Seven o'clock. Try to make it. Should be fun.'

'We will,' said Sharif, Stephen nodding in agreement, Liz trying to explain it wasn't her show at all, that she only had a couple of paintings in it, Karl brushing this aside with a laugh and guiding her out onto the street with a hand on her bottom.

'Why are you looking so worried?' Sharif asked after they had left.

'Sorry,' said Stephen, 'I was miles away.'

It was that confidence, or rather his own lack of it, that had given rise to that pang, the feeling he could never feel relaxed with a beautiful woman, at best would only be thinking it too good to last, doomed to imminent failure, thoughts of Suzie stabbing from the void.

'That Karl seems quite a lad,' he managed to come out

with. 'How did you get to know him?'

'That wasn't difficult. He's well known to everyone, gets into everything.'

Sharif went on to describe Karl's attendance at the fortnightly mathematics seminars.

'He used to come to them quite often. One of the very few people from outside the department that ever did. And always with plenty to say in the discussions, and not just in those for which you might expect a physicist to show interest. He seemed well up in everything, even the most obscure reaches of number theory. Really pissed some people off, the way he appeared to know more than they did about their own pet subjects. Not Emel, though. Emel really took to him. Got into heated arguments with him every time, which you could see them both thoroughly enjoying. Emel reckons the sky's the limit where he's heading. No doubt whatsoever that he's set to become a top player in whatever field he finally decides to dig himself into.'

'And that Liz. Is that a steady thing? They seemed quite together in some ways... but...'

'Good Lord no. Karl plays the field. No one's been able to pin him down yet, though quite a few have tried. Liz is just the latest. Been that way for some weeks now, but I still can't see it lasting. Sooner or later, they start making demands. Always do. Always the same.'

'Speaking from experience?'

'Oh God, yes.'

It occurred to Stephen that so far as he personally was concerned 'making demands' would be no cause for distress. Quite the contrary. If only Suzie had thought to make demands... Just another domain, a rather vital one this time, in which he felt himself deficient. Then, with a burst of resolve, he turned away from incursions of self-pity, changing the conversation to the inroads he was making in his research, the role Emel was now playing in this, and touching on Karl's admiration for Emel, expressed so soon after he had come to appreciate him in the same light. Sharif had been only too aware of this shift, something he had clearly predicted.

'I didn't tell you about my latest session with Emel,' said Stephen. 'Went even better than the one before, the one we talked about the other week. But he was holding back on that occasion. Very helpful up to a point, but not wanting to tell me what should have been the next move. Though it must have been obvious to him. I see that now. He wanted me to find it out for myself. In fact, looking back, I can see how he prepared the way, surreptitiously, all the while wanting me to feel I was getting there on my own. It's extraordinary. I can't imagine anyone else acting that way. It's only now that I can really appreciate what he was up to. It was that buzz I got on making that break. That's what really got me started, gave me the confidence to try anything that came to mind... It was as though he had planned it that way.'

'As I told you, it's the way he likes to operate. He did effectively the same for me when I was starting out. Doesn't always work. Not many people appreciate him. His appearance and general manner certainly don't help — or maybe they do, put people right off track, which suits him just fine.'

'But not Karl, you say? I would have loved to have seen that first encounter you were going to tell me about.'

'So would I. I only heard about it the following week, cursing myself for having missed out. Everyone was talking about it. Karl had apparently launched into a seemingly devastating criticism of something the invited speaker — quite a distinguished guy from Stanford — had been on about. Everyone was a bit taken aback, not knowing how to react. Then Emel waded in. And before you knew it, the two of them were going at it hammer and tongs. Constructively though. The Stanford guy then joined in, making something of a comeback. Then the three of them moved to the blackboard, covering it and themselves with chalk, everyone getting excited, coming eventually to some sort of amicable halfway house and arranging to meet the next day in Emel's room. And all in full view of the seminar audience, who had turned up mainly for the tea and biscuits and now found themselves witnessing this impassioned, high-level performance. The three of them are great buddies now, collaborating together, trying to take the whole thing further, exploring unexpected consequences...'

It was around this time that Stephen came to realise that, in a strictly limited sense, he had arrived, his work progressing in a manner unimaginable a couple of months before. And though saddened at the thought of Sharif's imminent departure, this now had everything to do with the close friendship that had developed between them, dependence on his advice having faded, their occasional technical discussions closer now to exchanges between equals, desperate appeals very much things of the past — especially since Emel had now abandoned his hands-off posture and was giving every indication of being ready to get involved, even coming close to expressing enthusiasm for the way the work was shaping up. In that respect, the future was looking brighter — more than could be said on the emotional front, with thoughts of Suzie, the hopelessness of it all, showing no sign of abating.

THIRTEEN

Come the evening of Liz's show, Stephen set off for Soho alone, Sharif having cried off at the last moment due to a summons relating to his impending appointment. Following Karl's directions, he made his way to a busy intersection of side streets lined with cafes, restaurants, sex shops and the like, also pubs, none, however, called The Goose. He wandered around for a while, convinced it had to be near, eventually asking a passer-by who gave him a strange, who's-this-idiot look before telling him he was standing outside it.

'But, but…' began Stephen, looking up at the sign, 'it says it's The White Swan,' thus seemingly confirming the stranger's first impression.

Hesitantly, and feeling a dimwit without knowing why, he stepped inside. It was crowded and noisy, a party seemingly in progress, on closer examination two parties, perhaps three. Everyone apparently celebrating something, making a great show of it. He stood for a while taking this in, still unsure if he had come to the right place. Then, across the horseshoe bar, over on the far side, he was relieved to see Liz, looking quite stunning, listening with what appeared rapt attention to an elderly man wearing an absurdly wide-brimmed hat and long multicoloured scarf wound around his neck, and going on about something with a good deal of dramatic emphasis. As Stephen watched, she eventually looked up and, on catching his eye, waved him over with a welcoming look that surprised him by its warmth and intensity, for all the world looking as though she had been waiting desperately for his arrival. He made his way to her around the bar, his senses firmly on hold, though awakened at a barely conscious level to possibilities not previously entertained. As soon as he arrived at her side, however, she scuttled off, with a feeble excuse, to join a cluster of exotically clad young people gathering by the door. Leaving him with a small pang of disappointment and the fellow with the hat — who, recovering swiftly from Liz's departure, introduced himself as Howard, a part-time tutor at the Slade, accepted the offer of a drink and, when this had been secured, continued with what appeared to be the monologue interrupted by Stephen's arrival. After trying hard for a while to make sense of what he was on about — falling standards in art education featuring prominently in whatever it was — he took advantage of a pause to comment favourably on the pub, letting on that this was his first visit — something Howard evidently found hard to take in.

'You mean... this is the first time you've been in The Goose?' he asked incredulously.

'Yes, and I must say I had difficulty finding it. Why does everyone call it The Goose when the sign outside says it's The White Swan?'

'But everybody knows it as The Goose. Have done for years.'

The silence that followed gave Howard time to work out that he hadn't really answered the question.

'You obviously don't know the story,' he said at last. 'Like a lot of people, I imagine. It's so long ago I'd almost forgotten myself.'

To Stephen's relief, his intervention had the effect of diverting Howard from his pet grouse onto a topic of conceivably more interest.

'It was years ago, before the war, well before. Early thirties it would have been, nineteen-thirty-one or thirty-two. I'd already been a regular here for a good few years by then. Since student days at the Royal Academy Schools. The publican at the time, old Bernie Oldgate, had decided the place could do with a facelift — he died last year, used to look in now and then after he'd retired, right up to the end as it turned out. Poor bugger. Anyway, the place had got pretty grotty, neglected for years. Then one day, out of the blue, Bernie announced that it wouldn't be opening for three days the following week, Tuesday, Wednesday, Thursday. Why? everyone wanted to know. For some, this could have posed real problems. Discovering it was to make way for decorators didn't help one bit. People were happy enough with things as they were, worried the place would lose its familiar scruffy appeal, perhaps that Bernie would use it as an excuse to put up his prices. He was a tight one, was Bernie. Never known to treat anyone all the time he was here. Got away with it though because, in other respects, he was all right. You just accepted he was a stingy bastard, probably born that way.'

Howard stopped at this point, Stephen wondering if he'd lost track of what he had started out on. He tried a gentle reminder.

'People called it The White Swan then, did they?'

'Of course, they did. That's the whole point of the story. Where had I got to?'

'The pub was going to be shut for three days for the decorators.'

'Oh yes. Well, it was before that, when Bernie first broached the idea of a clean-up and someone suggested a new pub sign wouldn't be out of place. The old one was falling apart. At first, Bernie wouldn't hear of it, it was going to cost money. But then he had a bright idea. This pub has always been a second home to artists, was even then. He put it about that, as a mark of affection for the place, perhaps one of them might like to produce a new sign. No mention of payment, of course, just the honour of having the piece permanently on display in this prestigious location. Well, as you can imagine, that went over like a lead balloon. It was professional artists he was talking to, for Christ's sake, some quite successful ones, not bloody signwriters. Quite a bit of indignation at the suggestion. But then Adam Courtney, a sly bugger and tight as they come — as tight as Bernie when it came to forking out for his round — somehow got hold of the idea that if he came up with the goodies, he'd be in for free drinks and peanuts for the rest of his life. Maybe Bernie had conveyed that impression. Anyway, that's what happened. Courtney produced his piece and Bernie had it mounted and hung without telling anyone, a pleasant surprise for his customers. Not how it went down, of course. Especially when it came out that Courtney had painted it. Well, you can guess the rest... someone suggesting Courtney's swan looked more like a goose... seized on delightedly by everyone. Then people started calling the place The Goose, jokingly at first, but it caught on... became the established name... nobody thinking to call it anything else... how it had come about lost in the mists of time.'

'It's a lovely story,' said Stephen. 'But what about Bernie and Courtney, how did they take it?'

'Well, Bernie was a bit put out at first. But when he saw

the business wasn't suffering – in fact, seemed to be doing rather better than before – he adjusted pretty quickly, eventually going on to give the impression he had masterminded the whole thing, which in a way I suppose he had.'

'And Courtney?'

'Oh, he just went off in a sulk. Never came back.'

While listening to Howard, Stephen had been taking in the general scene, people of all types continually arriving, adding to the diverse groups packing the place to bursting point. He was also aware of Karl Dembowski, at one moment with one group, then with another, thoroughly at home in all of them, clearly determined not to miss out on anything that was going on; catching Stephen's eye at one point, signalling he would be with him as soon as disengagement could be brought about.

Liz's companions then started to drift away, heading for the Buckingham, where a number of them were showing, Liz following in due course after first eliciting assurances from Karl that he would very soon be tearing himself away to join her. Stephen and Karl eventually set off from The Goose together, Karl in a garrulous mood, monopolising the first part of their journey without revealing what he had been holding back for most of the day. Then, it came out.

'I think I've pulled off the deal of the century,' he said as they reached Piccadilly Circus. 'Just got the final okay to accept an associate professorship in California, at Franklin Polytechnic, without having to give up my job here.' He gave a light laugh. 'So, it looks as if I'm in for a busy future. Only heard this morning. Haven't had time to fully take it in.'

This was indeed a remarkable achievement. Although precedents existed for such double appointments, they were very rare and only given to established luminaries with decades of achievement behind them. For someone as young as Karl, effectively just starting out on an academic career, it was quite unprecedented, certain to lead to raised eyebrows and all manner of jealous speculation. That it had come about testified to the extraordinary reputation he had built up in so short a time, the intense interest his published work had generated.

'Wait a minute,' said Karl, stopping abruptly and clasping Stephen's arm. 'This opening we're heading for. It's bound to be a pain in the arse, they always are. Let's have another drink and think of something better to do. I'm feeling the urge for a quiet celebration. And by the way, whatever it is it's going to be my treat... no, no, absolutely. I'm going to be really loaded, what with two salaries   one a whopping big one — and other incidentals, I'm not going to know what to do with it all.'

Stephen was having mixed feelings about this. He had been quite looking forward to the Buckingham, particularly now, having been taken by the number of attractive young women among the bevy surrounding Liz in The Goose. Also, he was broke, in the perennial situation of awaiting his next grant cheque and unhappy at the thought of not being able to pay his way — something that Karl had probably inferred. On the other hand, he had taken a real liking to Karl, as well as being in awe of him, and the opportunity for getting to know him better was certainly appealing.

'But what about Liz?' he asked. 'She'll be expecting you...'

'Oh, she'll survive. Plenty of admirers around to console her. Hey, that's a Fullers house over there. Quite a decent one if I remember rightly. Shall we give it a try?'

After a couple of pints, they were both feeling in need of something to eat and set off for a German restaurant in Charlotte Street renowned for its good cheap food and surly over-worked waiters: Nazi minor war-criminals, according to Karl, condemned to community service there as a result of a secret deal between the proprietors and the British government. On recognising Karl, however, the waiter serving them couldn't have been more accommodating, practically clicking his heels in greeting and making helpful suggestions for what was best on the menu that day. Stephen, by now experiencing few regrets at having missed out on the Buckingham, was thoroughly enjoying himself, the evening turning out more stimulating than he could ever have imagined. And Karl was in superlative form as raconteur and fund of information on the whole gamut of university affairs, both from within what could reasonably be regarded as his domain to way outside it, with hilarious accounts of cock-ups and near cock-ups in high places, scandals and near scandals simmering under the covers; and perceptive portrayals of ongoing research activity, at one extreme conducted in obscure nooks and crannies by dedicated researchers seeking enlightenment; at the other, group-based and generally banal, hyped-up to impress gullible funding providers; works of substance still being carried out by people such as Emel, for whom he once again expressed admiration. And so the conversation turned naturally to Stephen's researches, which he was generally reluctant to talk about in view of perceived difficulties – like, for a start, knowing where to begin. But this proving no problem with Karl, whose immediate grasp of essentials shouldn't have surprised him, given what he had been told of his interventions at mathematics seminars, but still did, and brought to mind Sharif's comments about people being pissed off at Karl's seemingly unbounded familiarity with their own specialised fields. Stephen, however, was far from feeling that way. He was delighted at being able to talk freely about his work and to take in Karl's constructive comments – one, in particular, setting his mind racing to a promising new approach he was eagerly anticipating following up the next day.

Karl then proposed a return to Soho, to a convenient dive providing for out-of-hours drinking, which he felt Stephen ought to know about. It was approached by way of an anonymous half-open doorway between seedy shops in a squalid side street; then along a dimly lit corridor and down shabby uncarpeted wooden stairs to a door bearing the incongruous legend, Paradise Club, Members Only.

Karl rapped on this sharply with his knuckles and, after a short delay, a small panel slid aside to reveal angry, bloodshot eyes, which visibly softened on seeing who was there. The door opened and Karl was greeted effusively by a dinner-jacketed bruiser, who escorted them through another door into the club. It turned out rather more inviting than prior indications had led Stephen to expect: a fair-sized room, softly lit with a bar in one corner around which were gathered a mixed bunch of some dozen or more members and their guests, standing or seated on high stools, chattering away among themselves; a number of alcoves fitted out with tables and chairs, some occupied, other miscellaneous seating scattered around; a piano tinkling softly from a larger alcove on the far side. On seeing Karl, the proprietor, Mavis — heavily formed and made-up, with dyed red hair — emerged from behind the bar from where she had been holding court to hug him to her substantial bosom; others likewise greeting him warmly, the pianist interrupting his performance to come over and shake his hand. All in all, a reception that appeared to Stephen appropriate for a war hero returning home, perhaps bearing the scars of his heroics. Stephen was then introduced and instantly accepted, 'Any friend of Karl's...' Then followed the hurried formalities — precautions in the event of a police raid — of signing the guest register and application-for-membership form, and the procuring of a dried-up sandwich — 'don't for Christ's sake think of eating it!' — to conform to the legal requirement of alcohol being served only with a meal. Time then for Stephen to take in more completely his fellow 'diners', conjecturing wildly on their identities, their roles in life: tarts relaxing between assignments, pimps, stage villains, dodgy customers in general furtively conducting their affairs, but mixed in with paragons of respectability — Rotarians, bank managers, family solicitors... the occasional wife or mistress in tow — taking time out from tedious workaday existence. What was particularly striking to Stephen, and comforting, the more so as the night progressed, was the easy camaraderie between them all: the well-heeled and down-at-heel, the respectable and disreputable, the successful and the just-keeping-heads-above-water; all ensconced in a cosy haven with social and cultural barriers suspended, the drink flowing freely, and the added joy of having thwarted repressive licensing laws.

'You seem to have got yourself well in with Mavis,' said Karl some indeterminate time later, when his social circumambulations had brought them momentarily together again. This was true. When Karl had been spirited away from Mavis's welcoming embrace, Stephen had remained, with no alternative but to submit to being pressed to give an account of himself. Which for some reason didn't come over nearly as badly as he might have thought, had he been given time to.

'Has she invited you to one of her parties?' Karl wanted to know. 'An experience not to be missed.'

'Not exactly. But she did mention something about parties at her house in Tooting. What's so special about them?'

'Maybe I should fix for you to get an invitation to one,' said Karl, laughing. 'Then you'll be able to find that out for yourself.'

Intrigued though Stephen was at the prospect, he decided on balance that it was probably best just to keep it that way.

The pattern of that evening's activities was to be repeated several times over the following months, in particular to mark Karl's returns from California, with Sharif joining them on rare occasions when his visits to London from Monte Carlo happened to coincide. Aside from all this, Stephen was finding his research ever more consuming, — racing ahead now with Emel very much on board, always on hand with suggestions — leaving little time for other activities beyond those necessary for survival. And although always looking forward to visits from Sharif and Karl and meetings with Stan, he was nonetheless grateful for their sparsity – welcome breaks from which he was always content to return refreshed to his explorations. God, what is happening to me, he would think, reflecting on the quite unforeseen shape his life was assuming, Westmoreland consigned to the distant past, St John's with its irresolvable preoccupations and concerns banished to beyond the boundaries of recall. Or so it appeared, quite mistakenly as he was set to discover, the past ever there, lurking in the shadows, patiently awaiting its moment.

FOURTEEN

It was getting on for a year after that first evening with Karl when a totally unexpected encounter would have the effect of disrupting irreversibly the ordered routine of Stephen's life. He was still living in Kennington, in the same house but occupying a much better room: larger, lighter, with a reasonably equipped cooking alcove and its own bathroom — the previous occupant for many years had suddenly accepted a job out of London, and Stephen seized the opportunity to transfer for a modest increase in rent. Travelling into college five, sometimes six, days a week when the worst of the morning's rush hour had run its course, remaining till seven or eight in the evening, sometimes later, with only a brief break for lunch. Although perfectly free to work whenever and wherever he pleased, this was the routine he had settled into and only rarely departed from. Exceptions /included occasional pub sessions with Stan, grown yet further in confidence following his successful Far Eastern tour and now settling into what had started out as a minor role that was becoming progressively more visible in a television soap drama – something to be lamented from his perception of himself as serious dramatic artist but nevertheless appreciated for the money and resultant attention, in particular from women; and reunions with Sharif, revelling in his new role of trainee casino manager, Monte Carlo and its allurements seemingly firmly in his grasp, developments in Malaysia drawing nearer to completion; and with Karl, buoyant as ever on his returns from California, his finger in countless pies, his scientific output and reputation growing by the day.

What the hell am I doing alongside all these fucking success stories, thought Stephen wryly, though without envy, contented enough with the way his own work was progressing, vistas of further satisfying developments ever opening before him.

And then there was Suzie. She had written to him exactly a year after that first intimate encounter, pointing this out and saying she often thought of him and wondered how his life was progressing, clearly opening the way for him to propose a meeting. Which, after agonising consideration, he declined to do, without however slamming the door; replying that he thought often of her, that his work was going well, that he had no girlfriend in tow, and padding it out with such things as Sharif's casino venture and leaving it at that. Still in the air. But he felt that their story was far from over, even months after hearing nothing from her following his reply. Or was that just wishful thinking? he wondered, uneasily, turning to his equations, losing himself in them, their therapeutic attributes easing his concerns.

But then, one freezing February evening, after a long day at college, everything was to change. A minor hurdle in his work, which had been plaguing him for the best part of a week, had just been overcome and he was feeling rather pleased with himself as he set off for home with a view to calling in at The Goose for a celebratory beer on the way. On a whim, however, he headed for another nearby pub which he had walked past many times without ever thinking of entering; wondering as he did so this time why this was so, why he had not heard mention of it before. The interior came over as welcoming as could be imagined: a substantial grate heaped with glowing coals, the massive, highly polished mahogany bar surmounted by beautiful glazed shutters at head level that could be swivelled for communication with the bartenders, large ornate mirrors in mahogany frames covering most of the walls, circular Britannia tables and other old rectangular ones, all with highly polished wooden surfaces, set out around the room. He bought a pint and took it over to a corner alcove, settling there to watch the regulars arriving, greeting one another, winding down. A place in which to relax at the end of a working day, in pleasing contrast for a change to the frenetic ambience of The Goose.

It was just as he was finishing his beer, preparing to leave, that he saw her, Natasha, approaching an empty table over on the far side and sitting down at it. It was a three-quarter-back view, so nothing definite, but necessitating confirmation one way or the other — taking him back to his time at Westmoreland where frequent similar sightings had, hardly surprisingly, all proved negative. But more likely here in London, he thought, smiling to himself at his absurdity. Then a man carrying drinks joined her at the table. There was something vaguely familiar about him, less to do with actual appearance — of which he had received only the haziest impression — rather than the way he moved. Who on earth does he remind me of? he wondered.

Their table was beside the door to the street. He would have to pass by it on his way out, which he set off to do, thinking to put pay to mildly aroused curiosity. But not getting beyond it: brought to a sudden halt there, thunderstruck, unable to adjust to the clear significance of what he was seeing.

'My God!'

Aware his exclamation had attracted local attention, he sought desperately to maintain self-control. The woman was indeed Natasha, quite unchanged from when he had last seen her some five years before; as desirable as ever, though with a fresh settled look about her, serene and contented. But the name that was on his lips, that he had just stopped himself bursting out with, was quite inappropriate now: black cassock and white bib-collar having given way to tweed jacket and corduroy trousers, check shirt open at the neck. Brother Carroll in mufti with the woman of his dreams.

For some seconds he stood there transfixed, embarrassed for the embarrassment he felt he must be causing them. But no. As recognition dawned, they both smiled at him, clearly unperturbed at the encounter, 'Brother Carroll' rising from his seat to come over and shake his hand, invite him to join them at their table, then setting off to buy him a beer, leaving him with Natasha.

'This is quite a coincidence you know,' she said after a short, awkward silence. 'We were just talking about you the other day, after watching Stanley Firbright on the telly. We're both great fans of his. Make a point of watching every episode we possibly can. Do you still get to see him now, now that he's becoming something of a celebrity?'

For a moment Stephen was lost, unable to adjust to what he had walked into, but then grateful for the lead she had provided, if for a moment uncomfortable at the notion of Stan being the focus of attention — but quickly dismissing such thought in easy exchange for its ice-breaking potential.

'Yes, we still manage to meet when we get the chance. Usually over a pint. I used to see him in rehearsal now and then when he was more involved with the theatre. That was always fun, often better in some ways than the actual performances.'

The 'now and then' was untrue of course. Only once had that occurred — thoughts of Suzie muscling in, along with an unaccountable feeling of guilt. But Natasha responded warmly, going on about how she also loved rehearsals, that she had often attended them with her ex-husband, who was associated with the theatre in some way that was unclear to Stephen — who thought for a moment to ask about it, but didn't, blown off course by that 'ex'. So, she was divorced from Sir Edward… a factor adding disturbing substance to her settled appearance with Brother Carroll. As though reading his thoughts, Natasha abruptly responded.

'You must be surprised at finding me with Piers like this.'

Piers? Of course. That was his name, Piers Denney.

'It's nothing new. We go back a long way. It was always going to happen.' Then lowering her voice to little above an intimate whisper, 'I'll tell you about it some other time.'

This, as Brother Carroll — Piers — approached, carrying a pint for Stephen and a half with which he topped up his own near-empty pint glass. Stephen, in the meantime, was trying desperately to come to terms with the bewildering shift in relationships, with Natasha treating him as an old friend, implying a familiarity by which she could confide intimate details of her life, and with Piers — he would have to get used to calling him that — for whom contradictory emotions were vying to take hold: a new affinity which Stephen could sense emerging from that of before, but tempered with criticism at his participation in the religious indoctrination to which he had been subjected at St John's, the shock of finding him with Natasha adding poignantly to his confusion.

'Well then,' said Piers, smiling serenely as he settled into his chair. 'Good to see you, it's been a long time.' And then, after a short and somewhat awkward silence, 'So, what are you doing with yourself these days?'

At which Stephen started to explain about Westmoreland University and Prince of Wales College, his PhD research in mathematics, becoming aware all the while of Natasha exhibiting more than could be put down to just polite interest, eventually interrupting to ask which branch of mathematics he was working in.

'Well, number theory,' he replied, somewhat surprised at her enquiry.

'Yes, but what in particular?'

Even more surprised, he started to tell her, realising it was coming over obscure, meaningless mumbo-jumbo, despite his efforts. And so he was relieved by her early interruption.

'Sorry, I'm no mathematician, but did I hear you right, that it's elliptic equations that you're working on?'

'Well, yes. A small class of elliptic equations that...'

'But this is truly amazing. I can't imagine why but I'd somehow got hold of the feeling you were going to say that. Does the name Alexandrovich mean anything to you? Yuri Alexandrovich?

'Yes, of course. He was a major player in that field, someone...'

'He's my brother. Well, half-brother, actually. A good deal older than me, same father though. We used to see quite a lot of each other. He's lived in America for ages now, but we still keep in touch, though it's probably two or three years since I last saw him. I used to think it so funny that he was an authority on something called elliptic equations. As a young girl, I used to tease him mercilessly about it — probably because I fancied him. And now you tell me you're working on them too, whatever they are. You'll have to explain it all to me sometime, what's so special about them. Yuri would only laugh when I asked him.'

It was indeed a coincidence. Stephen was well familiar with Alexandrovich's work, as would be anyone active in that field. It was back in the late forties when his seminal publications appeared. He was at Princeton at the time, could well still be there, though it was a good while since anything more of his had come to Stephen's notice. The overriding consideration for Stephen, however, was only obliquely related to mathematics: it was the tangible link that had magically materialised between himself and Natasha, something he could never have anticipated, and intriguingly flavoured by her admission of having fancied someone working on elliptic equations. Wow!

Speculation on this totally unexpected disclosure was cut short by Piers who had been smilingly taking in the exchange. Breaking a short silence, he asked Stephen what else he did with himself, what his other interests were. Questions that Stephen felt he would very much like to put back to him. And so they chatted away about this and that and nothing in particular until Stephen had finished his beer and offered to buy a round.

'I think we've had about enough for now,' said Natasha. 'And anyway, I left something cooking in the oven. What are you doing for supper, Stephen?'

'Well, I've some bits and pieces back home...'

'Why don't you join us? We're just across the road, on Percy Street. Plenty enough food for the three of us there.'

'Yes, do,' said Piers. 'It's been really good meeting up like this. Seems we've still quite a lot to talk about.'

Which was certainly true. In fact, virtually nothing had been said of matters clearly uppermost in both their minds. Not, it seemed to Stephen, because of unwillingness or embarrassment or anything like that. Rather as though the ground was simply being prepared, small talk paving the way for the sweeping reassessments that had to follow.

'It was as though a huge burden that had been weighing me down for the best part of my life had slipped from my shoulders. It felt strange at first, not having it there. Then wonderful. At last, I was free. All that nonsense I'd been conditioned to accept, forced to swallow. I could see it plainly then for what it was: base superstition and gullible acceptance of absurdity — all dressed up and presented as profound timeless wisdom. Things that in any other context would be laughingly dismissed as palpable gibberish. God! How on earth have they managed to get away with it? I felt as that child must have done; you know, listening to the great and the good going on about the exquisite clothes of the naked king. You can't imagine the relief I felt on arriving at Westmoreland, on finding people there, pretty well everyone I spoke to, untainted by all that nonsense, by those oppressive feelings of guilt. It was like emerging from the loony bin. Sanity at last. Surrounded by it, everywhere I looked.'

When later he thought back to that uncompromising outburst, Stephen was unable to recall precisely what had led up to it. It had taken place in the living room of the terraced house to which Piers and Natasha had taken him from the pub, the house in which they appeared to be living together. Natasha would have been in the kitchen preparing food, he left alone with Piers, who must have said something to set him off, provoking what would have come over as thinly disguised condemnation of his role in the St John's indoctrination agenda; jealousy at finding him cosied up with Natasha no doubt adding its pennyworth. But whatever the intention, Piers received it calmly, with no hint of displeasure.

'I understand your reaction. Believe me, I really do. But you have to realise that there are other ways of looking at these things, at the church. More positive ways, if you like, focusing on what is in place now, what it means to countless millions, this massively powerful structure firmly entrenched throughout the world, the comforts it indisputably confers, the further benefits for mankind it has the potential to deliver. In other words, to concentrate on the many positive aspects. And then on how it should be encouraged to develop, where it should go from here. In these respects where it comes from, what gave rise to it in the first place, is largely beside the point. Perceptions change dramatically over time, without people realising they are doing so. Myth or divine truth? Perhaps it doesn't matter too much one way or the other.'

Coming from Brother Carroll, that last statement should perhaps have rocked Stephen to his foundations. That it didn't testify to the shock he was still experiencing at seeing him with Natasha, seemingly intimately linked to her, and for the first time without cassock and bib collar. Circumstances under which nothing could shock him further. But still room for surprise at such an unprecedented volte-face: Brother Carroll seemingly unfazed by the notion of Christianity as a myth! Stephen was speechless, the ensuing silence finally broken by Natasha calling to announce supper, ending puzzled speculation on what on earth it was that Piers was driving at; and it would be quite some time before Stephen would be given some inkling of what lay behind that stance he was adopting, or indeed that anything pertaining to religious belief would again pass between them — Natasha's presence in some indeterminate manner ensuring this to be so.

That evening was nevertheless to see the beginning of the close friendships that were to develop in the months ahead. Thinking back later to the shift in his relationship with Piers — from devoted pupil and inspirational teacher to simple friendship — he would be amazed at the speed and ease with which this had occurred. And even more so with regard to Natasha, for whom the transformation from erotic icon to sisterly companion was likewise remarkable. Or so it appeared to Stephen, buoyed up by the discovery of such congenial soulmates residing a stone's throw from college. He was soon in the habit of calling at Percy Street after finishing work, typically two or three times a week, always feeling welcome there, at times just chatting for a while with one or both of them before heading home, now and then joining them for a drink in their local, or a meal at their home, or in a nearby restaurant; and to being introduced by them to aspects of the cultural life of the City that he might otherwise have missed out on.

It was some months into this by then established routine that Natasha invited Stephen home for lunch. Piers was away on unspecified business for the church, with which he was still involved in a manner that was difficult to fathom, and she had been having a hard time with problems of access to her son Benjamin, now in his teens and increasingly at odds with his father, with whom he had been living since the divorce. Stephen knew of this and thought Natasha wished to talk to him about it. But he was also aware of other things on her mind, including something to do with Piers's work that she had hinted at and was clearly worried about. But whatever that was would have to wait for another occasion. This time, it was mainly to do with clearing up misconceptions he could be harbouring about her and Piers: how they had got together, something she had surprised him by alluding to at that first meeting in the Fitzrovia pub. What she would have to say contributed a further thread to the potted biography of Brother Carroll that he and Stan had assembled from various sources while at St John's. And it showed up in a rather different light the story Philips had somehow got wind of and was selectively propagating. Natasha, clearly keen to put the record straight, lost little time in getting down to doing so.

'I've known Piers since I was fourteen, fell in love with him almost immediately. I was a big girl by then, could have passed for seventeen, eighteen. And very attractive. Boys were forever falling in love with me. It was a real pain. Then my father got this visiting appointment at one of the Oxford colleges and my mother and I went to stay with him for a few days. It was a pretty fraught time, full of talk of war about to break out. Which turned out to be true. It was the summer of 1939, a matter of weeks before it started. Anyway, I met Piers there at a reception following some boring lecture we'd been inveigled into attending. He had graduated the year before and was staying on to do research. We took to each other straight away. I'd never experienced anything like that before or imagined I could feel that way for anyone. It was quite overwhelming.'

They had finished eating and were sitting at right angles to each other at a corner of the kitchen table, Stephen feeling uncommonly relaxed, Natasha somewhat edgy.

'I don't want to keep you,' she said. 'You must be wanting to get back to your equations.'

'Not at all. I'm really appreciating this break. Makes a wonderful change from my usual routine. And anyway, I've always wondered just how you and Piers got together. The rumours going around didn't make any sort of sense to me.'

She smiled, resting her hand on his wrist, giving it a gentle squeeze.

'Well, it was a really long haul, us coming together. So many confusing factors, insurmountable difficulties. Some of them still unresolved.'

She removed her hand, turning away from him and leaning back in her chair.

'He took me to dinner. A pretty dismal restaurant, lousy food, but it was wonderful. I told him I was eighteen, had just split up with my boyfriend. All lies of course. There had never been anyone I regarded as a boyfriend, but I thought it sounded more adult that way. By the end of that evening, it felt as though my life had changed forever, everything seemed different, exciting. I was pretty sure he was feeling the same way. Then there was a bit of a setback after that bitch of my mother told him how old I was. I was furious. He was twenty-four and rather put out at first. "We'll have to wait," he would say. Which I suppose made sense but was not what I wanted at all. I wanted to stay with him in Oxford, not leave with my mother. But in the end, of course, I left. We kept in touch at first, both of us really determined to. But then the war started and everything changed.'

She stopped there, looking sad. Stephen eventually broke the silence.

'I know he volunteered for service as soon as that happened. With his cousin who went on to get killed.'

'Oh, you knew that?'

'Yes. Stan and I gathered together whatever we could find about him. He was pretty important to both of us. The only one of the brothers you could imagine existing outside the confines of the school, the only one you felt you could confide in. But sorry, I've interrupted you. Please go on. A lot must have happened between that first meeting and St John's.'

'Well, certainly for Piers. For me, it was mainly a question of waiting. Correspondence was difficult, close to impossible at times, though we somehow managed for a while. Then it gradually petered out. I thought he had been killed at one point, that it was being kept from me. By the time the war ended, I hadn't heard from him for nearly a year. But then I learned he was alive, had returned to Oxford. I was twenty by then, for Christ's sake. Six God-forsaken years. I went to find him.'

She went on to tell of the shock of that meeting, of Piers haggard and despondent, not recognising her at first, but then when he did... 'it seemed for an instant that everything was going to be all right, as though the old Piers was still there under the worn-out exterior. We hugged, and I felt him trembling. He told me he had aged beyond his years, that he had always been old for me and that now it was ridiculous for me to consider him in that way. I told him he was the only one, that I had waited six years and that for me nothing had changed.'

They became lovers then, but that only succeeded in fuelling his feelings of guilt: guilt for the death of his cousin and his comrades killed in Africa, guilt at being alive when so many around him had died.

'And now in addition he had this mortal sin to contend with. Yes, that's how he saw it. With me an agent of the devil, I suppose. We can laugh now but it was far from funny at the time. He was sick, desperately sick. And I knew I could get him through it if only he would let me. That momentary reaction when he recognised me. That showed me there was hope. And I was right. But it was going to take years, and he was going to have to confront it alone. At the time, it had come to appear hopeless. We parted badly. It seemed the absolute end for me, for him too.'

In desperation she took up with a dedicated admirer, married him and before she knew it had conceived his child. Piers, in the meantime, returned to his researches, gradually lost himself in them and, at the same time, laid the ground for what, in the midst of the carnage, he had come to believe to be God's plan for him: a life devoted to education and an untiring ritual of religious observances. Ironically, that period also saw the growth within him of religious doubt — to be repeatedly swept aside along with recurrent yearnings for Natasha. Some months after the separation, she wrote to him.

'I didn't expect to hear back. But the thought of him sick and alone was haunting me. Also, I still wanted him and was blaming myself for not having persisted, for giving up and bringing what we had together to an end. And my marriage wasn't working out at all. And I was pregnant. I suppose I was feeling pretty desperate, which made two of us.'

But he did reply, resulting in an exchange of letters that, though appearing a simple keeping in touch of old friends, came to signify much more: both expressing dissatisfaction with their lives, trapped by decisions made under pressures they no longer recognised.

'It kept me going, those letters; made me determined we would come together again. And we did. I saw to it that we did.'

She turned to him, searchingly, as though seeking

approval.

'And St John's?' he asked with a smile. 'Does that come into how you saw to it?'

She laughed, replacing her hand on his wrist, leaving it there.

'Yes, I suppose that's what you want to hear about. Well, there's nothing much to tell. Edward and I were living in Muswell Hill, just a short bus ride from St John's. That much was pure coincidence. But it seemed a signal to me, a call to action.'

They managed to meet on rare occasions. She saw to that too. Brief encounters arranged with considerable difficulty: a few minutes stroll in a park, tea in a cafe, nothing much more. But enough to set in train the possibility of their coming together again. Benjamin, her son, in the meantime approaching junior school entry age and Natasha insisting on St John's.

'Edward wanted him to board somewhere. Somewhere prestigious, which he could well afford. But I put my foot down, insisting on a Catholic day school, somewhere close by, St John's conveniently fitting the bill.' She gave a wry laugh, still staring straight ahead. 'I hadn't thought it out at all. It just seemed it had to happen that way, that it had been ordained somehow.'

Then came that look again, more intense this time, inducing in Stephen an overwhelming desire to go round and embrace her — quite platonically, he was able to assure himself. But he didn't do anything. Just stayed where he was, feeling the warmth of her presence.

FIFTEEN

Following that first lunch with Natasha, Stephen's visits to Percy Street were to become more frequent, both she and Piers forever encouraging him to call, to join them for a drink in their local, accompany them to films and plays. Occasionally, he would stay overnight, sleeping on a camp bed in their broom-cupboard sized spare room, Percy Street gradually becoming for him something of a second home. Lunch with Natasha was also to become a fairly regular occurrence, encouraged by Piers, concerned at leaving her alone, particularly when weighed down with worries about Benjamin. For Stephen, this provided gratifying interludes in his working week, her evident pleasure on seeing him always lifting his spirits, the inexplicable sense of well-being accompanying their commonplace exchanges persisting long after having left her. Piers's work activities remained a mystery, however. Natasha was seemingly aware of what he was doing and concerned about it but reluctant to bring it up. Stephen was content to bide his time, conscious of her desire to confide and expecting any day for it to find expression.

Following his initial outburst on that evening of their first meeting, Stephen was being circumspect with Piers, careful in conversation to avoid topics of possible contention. He was nevertheless curious about his dealings with the Roman Catholic church, also of where he now stood on the question of religious belief. It was all very intriguing, and Stephen was hopeful that Piers would eventually get round to opening up on these issues. Several months were to pass, however, without him showing any inclination of doing so.

But then one evening, as Stephen was sitting at his desk, feeling he had finished his day's work and trying to decide what to do next, the office phone rang. It was Piers, calling to see if he fancied meeting for a drink and perhaps a meal somewhere. Natasha had been unexpectedly called away — something to do with Benjamin — and he was feeling at a loose end. Perfect timing, thought Stephen, and they agreed to meet in the pub half an hour later.

Piers was already there when Stephen arrived, a near-empty pint glass in hand and clearly in a talkative mood. Something else about him too, an air of determination, impatience perhaps, as though a decision had been taken and he was anxious to get on with it. After getting through the business of exchanging greetings, buying beer and settling at a table, Piers came straight out with it.

'I really owe you an apology, Stephen. I've been holding back on you all this while.' Stephen couldn't imagine what this could be about, where it was leading. 'The way you described your loss of faith... hanging on to it for years in the face of growing doubts... fearful of taking the plunge... finally doing so. Then that all-consuming sense of relief. Well, I went through much the same. I should have admitted it from the start. Though I have to say it was probably more difficult in my case... those firm commitments I'd made... burying myself in deep. But on the other hand, I did have some help. Rather specialised help as it happens. And then of course Natasha. If it hadn't been for Natasha...'

Stephen was intrigued. What on earth could that 'specialised help' have been? He was about to ask, then instead offered to buy a round. And having done so,

'Well, are you going to tell me about that specialised help?'

Piers gave a light laugh.

'I suppose so. But it's a long story. I haven't told anyone before, not even Natasha. Let's go and get something to eat first, then come back with me to Percy Street. I'll tell you the whole sorry story over a glass of wine. It may take a while.'

What had finally persuaded Piers to talk about the Scrolls, Stephen could only surmise. His account of his rejection of religious belief, the fact of it seemingly mirroring Piers's own experiences, perhaps having something to do with it; and also, Stephen liked to think, his confidence that sensitive matters would go no further, that whatever he would reveal would remain secure. Also, of course, his sense of isolation must have been extreme, the desire to confide increasingly more difficult to resist.

'It came quite out of the blue,' Piers began, pouring a small quantity of wine into his glass, the larger remainder of the bottle into Stephen's, 'that urgent summons to Rome. I didn't know how to respond. There was the question of my teaching duties at St John's, my obligations there in general. My immediate thought was to decline, though the way it had been put didn't seem to leave much room for that. But then it turned out the whole thing had been fixed up behind my back. Oswald was quite chuffed about it, the fact of one of his brothers being sought after by the Vatican — God alone knows how they put it to him. It seemed to have quite made his day.'

'I can well imagine it,' said Stephen in the pause that followed. 'They always loved recounting special qualities or achievements of one of their own, boasting about them even, though not at all in a brash way; with affection for the most part, a sort of family pride they could share in.'

'I know.' Piers looked sad for a moment, reflective. 'I often miss that sense of community, even though I didn't experience it for long. But anyway, that's all well in the past now. Things move on, certainly did for me.' Again, that fleeting look of sadness.

'At the time, it seemed ordained I should go to Palestine, the coincidence too much to credit. After all, it was only a matter of months after I'd completed my thesis that the Scrolls were discovered, a few months later that word got around. It was all so obviously right down my street. Few in the world could have been better prepared for making sense of them. I had been steeped in the history of that period for over three years, had seen pretty well all the available sources, such as they were, had studied most of them in depth. Then suddenly these new ones turned up, with the promise of much more to come. At the time, I didn't imagine for a moment how earth-shattering they would turn out to be, how the whole history was going to have to be rewritten. No, I just thought they might add some snippet or two to the general picture, something I would have to include as an addendum in my thesis. Instead, when I finally got to grips with that new material, got to study it in detail, my initial thought was to throw the whole thing out of the window, start again from scratch. Then it gradually dawned that various uncertainties that had bothered me along the way, things that hadn't quite fitted in, which I had somehow managed to sweep under the carpet, were now beginning to make perfect sense. It was a strange feeling: exhilaration at the beautifully coherent picture that was emerging, mixed in with embarrassment at having missed out on it for so long. And, alongside all that, fear: fear at the implications, how they would be received. But I'm jumping ahead of myself, we'll come to all that in due course. What I want to do now is simply describe the overall picture in plain language, showing just what the discoveries are about, the truth they reveal about the earliest days of Christianity.'

It became clear to Stephen at this point what his role was: he was there as a sounding board; Piers had gathered his thoughts in isolation and was trying to fit them into a comprehensible narrative that he wanted to try out on someone — someone with no axe to grind, who could be trusted to keep it to himself. Stephen was more than happy to go along with that.

'Even without any real idea of just how radical the implications were,' Piers went on, 'the church was worried. It has always sought to control information, to issue clear instructions on just what was to be believed and don't you worry yourselves about why. And now it had good reason for thinking a loose cannon could well be about to fire off disconcerting revelations about the very beginnings of Christianity, things that would perhaps conflict with long-established tradition and belief. Which was where I was supposed to come in. Though exactly how was never clear — neither to me nor, I suspect, to them. But I felt flattered nonetheless. And what was being proposed was certainly intriguing. Getting me right back into the academic studies I thought I'd seen the back of for good.

'Ironically, what they were worried about — still are for

that matter — is as nothing compared to what the Scrolls actually reveal on close examination. It's a time bomb awaiting its moment. There's no way the truth can be obscured forever. Eventually, other scholars are going to get access to that material, it can only be a matter of time before someone else draws the obvious conclusions.'

'So, you're keeping quiet about what you found. Is that what you're saying?'

'Well, yes. Certainly, for the time being. There are other considerations you see, well beyond the purely academic ones which have been driving things for me till now. This just happens to come at a time when the whole future of the church is at stake, when it must decide where it goes from here. Does it cling to its imperious, superstition-riddled role or start transforming itself into a rational force for good in the world? It's at a crossroads, no question about it; decisions will be made quite soon that will set its course one way or the other. The last thing I want to do is provoke a reactionary backlash, something that could foul up any hope for real reform. You're looking puzzled.'

Stephen was. He had no idea what Piers was going on about, nor for that matter where he stood, neither at a personal level — a new start in life? with Natasha? — nor regarding the big picture he was alluding to, those mysterious impending changes within the church and his role in them, which he gave every indication of preparing to follow through, and which for a fervent, self-confessed, recently converted unbeliever was certainly puzzling. Stephen turned to him in silence, his bemused expression an adequate response.

'I'm sorry,' said Piers, laughing understandingly. 'I'm pretty confused myself, as you can well imagine. Forget about that last bit. I was just thinking aloud about a rather unlikely scenario that's been put to me, where I could fit into it somehow. Better if we stick to something more concrete. Let me just tell you about the Scrolls.'

'You will have heard the story,' he began, after taking a thoughtful sip from his glass. 'The Bedouin shepherd boy searching for a lost goat on the shores of the Dead Sea, finding the Scrolls in a cave. Well, the entrance to that cave is visible high on an almost sheer cliff face, quite inaccessible to even the most agile of goats. But never mind. It's easy to imagine it attracting the curiosity of any half-adventurous youth with time on his hands. What makes it rather incredible is that it has taken some two thousand years for someone to check it out. The lad who eventually did found these earthenware jars inside. No great effort taken to secure or hide them in any way; just left standing there, looking rather spooky. The lad got scared and scuttled off, returning later with some mates. Some of the jars were quite heavy and sealed. On opening them, the boys were disappointed to find nothing of obvious value, just these tight parchment rolls. There were apparently broken pots and scattered fragments of parchment lying around as well. Anyway, they took some of the complete Scrolls back to their camp, where they unrolled one, finding it to be several metres long and covered in strange writing. Somebody thought they could be of interest to a cobbler in nearby Bethlehem who ran a lucrative, illegal side-line selling unreported archaeological finds to private collectors. Well, when he saw them, he didn't know what to think at first but, sensing their antiquity, he bought them for a few dollars, then sold them for a good few more, to someone who hung on to them for a while and eventually went on to make a small fortune out of them. But well before things had got to that stage, word had got around. The Bedouin and others had come to realise there could be big money to be made and the search began in earnest, in other caves in that general area and all over the place, leading to many other finds and spawning a thriving business in Scroll fragments — real and faked — which shows little sign of petering out. God alone knows how much immensely valuable stuff has been spirited away into private hands, effectively lost to the academic community.

'So, you may well ask, what's all the fuss about? Well, for a start, a good number of the initial finds consist of books of the Old Testament, in the original Hebrew and Aramaic, some thousand or so years older than the previously oldest available versions. You can imagine the excitement, their enormous importance to scholars everywhere. So much so that it was to leave the other findings somewhat in the shade at first — the so-called sectarian material, which related directly to the community to which the Scrolls belonged: its day-to-day activities, laws, rituals, rules for worship, theological works and the like. Together with the biblical texts, clearly a library of immense value to its owners. So, we can be sure it must have been under pretty fraught circumstances that the decision was made to stash the whole lot away in remote caves, seemingly in a great hurry, presumably with a view to retrieving it all once whatever had led to the panic had run its course — something that clearly never happened. So, there it all remained, slowly mouldering away.

'But the really electrifying discovery turns out to be those sectarian Scrolls. Why they have been so played down is a question worth pondering. After all, we're talking here about a Palestinian Jewish community functioning, by any reckoning, at around the time of Jesus. And with a lot to say for itself. Precious little source material exists for that period, certainly nothing coming near in importance and authenticity to this stuff. And yet we see every effort being made to downplay its significance. Why? Another question of crucial importance concerns the precise dating of those documents — you'll understand why later — and just what the community producing them was about. What bonded its members together? How, if at all, did it relate to the earliest stirrings of Christianity? Or, if it predated Jesus — the view promulgated vigorously by the international team working on the Scrolls — what, if anything, do its written records tell of the circumstances leading up to Jesus' appearance on the scene? It was fear of dissension on this last point that led to my being asked to participate. All a red herring as it turns out. The truth of the matter being far more fundamental to the faith than anyone could possibly have imagined, going right to the heart of the very foundations of Christianity, absolutely mind-boggling in its implications.'

Stephen could feel his excitement mounting as he listened. For some time, he had been aware that Piers had discovered something of great importance there, something he had decided to keep to himself. Stephen had great faith in Piers's judgement, and now it seemed he was going to be let in on the secret. He felt immensely privileged and, unaccountably, somewhat nervous.

'How about opening that other bottle,' said Piers. 'I could do with another glass. What about you? And by the way, I didn't say anything before because it was implied anyway. But you do realise that what I'm going to tell you now must go no further. It will all come out eventually but just how that's managed needs to be thought through very carefully. As it stands it could do great damage in all sorts of ways —

including to my plans for where I go from here. You have to accept that.'

'Of course. I realised that from the start. You don't have to worry, Piers. I won't breathe a word to a soul.'

Stephen went over to the sideboard where a bottle of wine stood still in its wrapper, opened it and poured into the two by now empty glasses. Then he sat down again, waiting for Piers to continue.

'I didn't know much about what was being done with that stuff before the summons to Rome, just bits and pieces picked up here and there. Well, a meeting had been arranged in some church property. Not in the Vatican this time, somewhere nearby. A couple of people I knew were there — friends of mine by then as it happens. The few others I didn't know at all. I was introduced to this chain-smoking French Dominican in his white robes, Roland de Vaux, of the Palestinian Ecole Biblique, leader of the international team cobbled together to work on the Scrolls. He greeted me effusively enough, though I sensed a guardedness which he tried hard to conceal. He spoke enthusiastically of the team gathered under his wing and the progress they were making in the 'Scrollery' — a large room in the Palestine Archaeological Museum where the Scroll fragments were laid out on trestle tables. Working on them was an extremely tedious business as many were tiny, the result of them having been torn up, apparently at the time of their concealment; it was like putting together massive jigsaw puzzles with the pieces of various pictures all jumbled together and God knows how many missing or not belonging there at all. Although de Vaux spoke of his team as experts, it soon became apparent that this was by no means the case. Experts had indeed been consulted, but largely to solicit names, actual recommendations being made for all sorts of reasons — some, predictably, with a view to getting troublesome juniors out of their superiors' hair. Only one of them turned out to have any sort of academic track record — the problem child, as it happens. I'll come to him in a moment. The rest were effectively nothing worth speaking of. Funding for the work was patchy to say the least; my first impression being of a disorganised amateurish shambles over which de Vaux exercised tight control. He was quite skilful in this, encouraging vigorous debate but never, in the end, conceding ground. The other thing he had managed to achieve was to ensure that the supposedly interdenominational composition of the team was in fact dominated overwhelmingly by Roman Catholics — largely priests and theology graduates with priestly aspirations. In fact, he boasted this much to me at that first meeting in Rome, no doubt feeling it to be something to which I would approve.

'All outsider access to the Scrolls was rigidly blocked, even to scholars clearly eminent in the field. An effect of this was to imbue a sense of proprietary importance to the team, its members confident that, as they alone had access to the source material, anyone else's opinion that deviated in any way from the consensus could be imperiously dismissed. And with de Vaux firmly in control, there was always consensus. Or was, until a member of the team took it upon himself to upset the apple cart — the action anticipated by de Vaux, which led to those urgent consultations in the Vatican.

'The problem was all down to a young researcher from Oxford, John Allegro. We must have overlapped there for a while, though when we met in Palestine, I couldn't remember having come across him before. I have to say that I rather took to him when we did get to meet, regardless of the far from glowing picture painted by de Vaux. Much more outgoing and independent-minded than the others. And by then a professed agnostic, standing out as the only one of the team without strong Christian affiliation. Also, for that matter, the only one with a credible academic record and publications to his name. An interesting background too, which I was to learn about during those early encounters.'

Piers went on to talk about this, about John Allegro in general, the man who had set the alarm bells ringing in the Vatican. It seemed that, at the age of seventeen, one year into World War II, he had volunteered for the Royal Navy, serving from the following year on an escort vessel in convoys on the perilous North Atlantic run, later transferred to the eastern Mediterranean. It was there, moored off Alexandria, that treatment in hospital for a minor ailment triggered a chain of events which was to set the future course of his life.

On being discharged from hospital, he found his ship had sailed without him, and it was while awaiting its return that he learned it had been sunk by German warplanes with the loss of all on board. The days following that traumatic discovery were harrowing indeed, but he managed to find solace in a Protestant church stumbled upon in the course of lonely, depressed wandering through the alleyways of Alexandria; his welcome reception there recalling comforting memories of just a few years before in the Methodist chapel back home. Heartened by this experience, he went on to set up a Methodist group on his next ship, on which he served for the remainder of the war as a sub-lieutenant — having successfully applied for a commission while stranded in Alexandria. On demobilisation he followed up what had, by then, become a consuming vocation, enrolling for training at the Methodist college in Manchester. The course incorporated the early languages of the bible, which he studied at Manchester

University, rapidly becoming absorbed in these, in particular with the tantalising flexibility of the Hebrew script, which could only be interpreted in the light of the context in which spoken words or concepts had been transcribed. This opened so many possibilities for ambiguity that he found his previous confidence in the veracity of the scriptures gradually slipping away; the more he got to grips with the intricacies of the language the greater his misgivings were to become. He was well aware that the received view of Christianity, with its deeply moral prescriptions, enlivened with fanciful tales from the life of Jesus and of the saints and martyrs, counted far more for believers than questions of reliability of its historical origins. But for him, these very questions were of fundamental importance. How could he continue espousing a religion the foundations of which he was finding ever more critically flawed?

He withdrew from the Methodist training college, transferring to the degree course in theology at Manchester University — a move leading on to a succession of scholarly achievements: a first in Oriental Studies, an MA, academic publications, prizes and scholarships; then going on to register for a PhD on the dialects and colloquialisms in biblical Hebrew, soon to transfer this study to Oxford University under the supervision of the country's foremost scholar in Semitic languages. Then came the opportunity for him to join the international team in Jerusalem, working on what was undoubtedly one of the most significant and exciting archaeological discoveries of the century — an irresistible prospect for which his academic studies could not have been better suited.

Having got this far in preparing the scene, Piers paused. He was looking somewhat distant and just a trace uncomfortable, as though having woken up in unfamiliar surroundings. Or so it appeared to Stephen, who felt it best to say nothing, to wait for the moment of awkwardness to pass.

'I know I've gone on about him a bit,' said Piers at last, 'but he was the first to identify the striking similarity of the community at Qumran — from where the Scrolls originated — to that of early Christianity; and though it turned out he was largely wrong in the way he went on to interpret this, enough was on the right track to point the way ahead. But that all came later. It still seems strange thinking back to that first encounter in Rome. Even now, when I can appreciate what was going on there. De Vaux was clearly worried, though nothing had happened yet to give him real cause for alarm. But he was foreseeing trouble with Allegro, as were others present at that meeting. Not all of them, though. You know, the Vatican gives every impression of speaking with one voice, clear and authoritative, no possible room for doubt. But inside, it's not like that at all. You'd be surprised at the extent of liberal expression to be found there under the reactionary covers, the range of dissent from the expressed orthodoxy. But all held in check, of course. No hint of it in the impression that gets out. On the need for that, there is indeed complete agreement. Recognition that the extraordinary power the Vatican wields in the world depends on it and none of them, whatever their views, would wish to see that in any way diminished.'

Much later, Stephen would have reason to recall this digression. With a smile and a shrug, Piers signalled its passing, returning to the matter in hand, to the realisation of Fr de Vaux's worst fears.

SIXTEEN

It seemed that John Allegro fitted in well with his new colleagues to begin with, participating in the studies with enthusiasm and accepting the consensus on the Scrolls' authorship and dating: that they were the work of a community of Essenes, a fundamentalist Jewish sect inhabiting the isolated settlement of Qumran, close to the northernmost shores of the Dead Sea; and that the Scrolls themselves long pre-dated the birth of Jesus. On these issues, agreement within the team was to remain firm. The consensus also extended to the nature of the Qumran community, placing it far removed from the mainstream of violent political and religious turmoil that had characterised the region for generations and would continue to do so until well after the fall of Jerusalem in 68 AD: the Jews, constantly at loggerheads with their Roman rulers, their priest-kings relentlessly imposing their authority, at times with unspeakable cruelty, rival factions forever plotting and warring among themselves. The Qumran community however, — uncompromising maintainers of the Law of Moses, which they saw repeatedly and comprehensively flouted by the Temple establishment — supposedly remaining insulated from all this; regarded as a deeply religious order of celibate pacifists (with no women), eschewing all pleasures, holding all possessions in common, engaging in daily rituals of purification, prayer and labour, and patiently awaiting the coming of the Messiah.

'As we'll see later, a mass of compelling evidence conflicts with this passive portrayal of the Qumran community — all overlooked by the international team, including for the most part by Allegro himself. But in his case, something else had come to dominate his attention, a bombshell in a Scroll he was examining. He could hardly contain his excitement, especially after finding its highly controversial significance echoed time and again in the Qumran documents. What he was seeing there appeared to him to be nothing less than a pre-enactment of the life and times of Jesus Christ some hundred years earlier — though he was chary at first of expressing it in quite those terms, inhibited no doubt by the company he was keeping. But it was all there, the first Christians talking in the language of the Essenes, the Scrolls mirroring repeatedly the language of the gospels. I could give you no end of examples, the Scrolls are riddled with them: both their leaders regarded as being in direct communion with God, their sufferings seen as atonement for the sins of the world; both communities in anticipation of the imminent final battle between the forces of good and evil; the Qumran sect portraying themselves as the elect of God, '...the precious cornerstone whose foundations shall not be shaken' — almost word for word anticipating St Peter's address to the early Christians: '… a cornerstone chosen and precious… God's own people.' And there's much more. To cap it all though, the leader of the sect, the Teacher of Righteousness — referred to repeatedly by his followers as 'begotten by God' — is persecuted and eventually put to death by order of the "Wicked Priest", very probably, so it seemed to Allegro, by crucifixion. There was no getting away from it, he concluded: Christianity, far from springing from a singular divine intervention, was simply following established Jewish tradition. This was something that de Vaux and the Catholic church in general were quite unwilling to even contemplate.'

'But you agree with him, don't you? Allegro, I mean.' Stephen came out with this in response to the pause that followed, to the strange look Piers was giving him, clearly inviting comment. 'From what little you've said,' he went on, 'it sounds obvious enough.'

Piers smiled. 'Well, that's how it seemed to me when I first confronted the evidence. Certainly, the objections raised by de Vaux and the others didn't make sense at all. They were clutching at straws, plainly rattled, not knowing what to do next, then turning to me in desperation. But I have to say that my sympathies, by that time, were firmly with Allegro. He was the only one approaching the studies objectively, with an open mind, prepared to change direction when additional factors came to light. And though rather brash at times and quick to jump to provocative conclusions, this was more to do with trying to get stimulating discussion going than anything else. But when I came to consider the whole business in detail, I couldn't escape the nagging feeling that something was wrong. It just didn't add up somehow. I had made copious notes on the background to all that at Oxford, which I read through again. Then back to the Scrolls. Then back and forth all over the place until eventually something clicked. And from that point, it all started to come together. They were way off track, all of them. The truth of the matter was startlingly obvious once the initial break had been made. And fundamental to the origins of Christianity, and far more serious for the church than anything de Vaux could have dreamed up in his blackest nightmares. What the hell, I thought, was I going to do about it.'

Right on cue, it seemed, a door slammed in the hallway and a moment later Natasha entered the room.

'Has something happened?' she asked, anxiously taking in their solemn expressions; then, on being assured that all was well, going over to Stephen, kissing him affectionately on the cheek, pressing a hand lingeringly on the small of his back. Then she did much the same to Piers, though less thoroughly, or so it appeared to Stephen. He had been aware in the last few days of a coolness in their relationship and had wondered what if anything lay behind it. Then she saw the wine bottle and her eyes lit up.

'Just what I need,' she said, fetching a glass from the cabinet. 'What about you two? Though, you know we have an early start in the morning.' This was to Piers. 'Not a good idea to make a session of it tonight. It's already past two o'clock.' She was still holding the bottle though, invitingly.

Piers nodded, mumbling agreement, holding out his glass, as did Stephen, looking disappointed. Piers turned to him.

'Don't worry. I'll finish off next time. Which I'm afraid will have to be tomorrow evening. Is that okay with you? I'm tied up the next day and leaving for Rome the day after.

'Yes,' said Natasha, 'back to the bloody Vatican. I'm beginning to think you must have a woman there. Some randy dolly nun who just can't wait to break her vow of chastity. I can't think what else you could be getting up to.'

Piers laughed. 'You should see them,' he said. Then, turning to Stephen, 'More like that lot at St John's. I should be so lucky.'

All very jokey and good-humoured, thought Stephen, but the tension between them palpable, the coolness he had noticed earlier now explained.

'Tomorrow should be fine,' he said, 'if you're sure it's okay with you. How long do you expect to be away?'

'Bloody ages,' interjected Natasha, clearly angered and upset.

'I can't say. It could be quite a while. I've really no idea.'

He too was looking upset, and sad. But Stephen knew him well enough to recognise the determination. Whatever it was he had got himself into there, he was going to see it through, regardless of anything. Little wonder Natasha was acting up.

'So, next Thursday's off then?' he asked. They had bought tickets weeks before for *Plays for England* at the Royal Court — two contentious pieces by John Osborne they had been looking forward to.

'Not for me, it isn't.' Natasha was trying hard to keep her anger under control. 'You're going to have to put up with just me, Stephen. I wouldn't miss that for the world.'

'I'm really sorry.' Piers had drained his glass and moved over to her, putting an arm around her waist. She responded, resting her head on his chest, her anger evaporating, leaving only sadness. 'But there's nothing I can do about it,' he went on. 'Maybe you can find someone to use my ticket.'

What on earth is he up to with the Vatican? Stephen was asking himself. Is it to do with what he had just been talking about? Or, more probably, what he is going to be talking about tomorrow? — a waft of irritation at Natasha's untimely interruption momentarily intruding. But why all the mystery? For a start, about how long he was going to be away. It almost seemed he was saying it could be forever. There must be something else going on there. Something of which perhaps even Piers himself is not fully aware. In the meantime, where did this leave him with Natasha? She was obviously upset about it and who could blame her? His mind then returned to Piers's story, recounted with the usual flair and precision — still the inspirational history teacher of his school days — and breaking off tantalisingly in the time-honoured manner of popular crime fiction just as the crunch could be sensed stumbling into view.

The following evening Piers and Stephen had the house to themselves again, Natasha off visiting friends with Benjamin, not due back till the following afternoon.

'Allegro thought he had identified the Wicked Priest of the Scrolls as the Jewish priest-king Jannaeus of the Hasmonean dynasty: a bloodthirsty tyrant who ruled for some thirty years from about 100 BC and was renowned for acts of extreme cruelty.' Piers had picked up directly from where he had broken off the night before. 'On one occasion, following an unsuccessful rebellion against him, Jannaeus had had some 800 Pharisees crucified — a popular method of his for dealing with adversaries. As it appeared to Allegro that it was Jannaeus who had had the Teacher of Righteousness put to death, he went on to speculate that crucifixion could well have been the method adopted — a reasonable enough hypothesis, which nevertheless elicited extreme indignation from de Vaux and the Roman Catholics in the team who felt it detracted from the perceived uniqueness of Jesus' suffering and death. This was quite at one with their refusal to acknowledge any common ground between the Qumran community and early Christianity, even where the most obvious similarities were staring them in the face.'

He paused at this point, seemingly lost in recollection.

'You know,' he then went on, 'it's really well-nigh impossible for a believer to take an objective view of these things. I should know. There was so much I ignored before, shut my eyes to, the automatic censor switching on at the merest hint of heresy. Reactions of which one is for the most part unaware.'

This was something Stephen could well appreciate, those final years of his at St John's, the doubts that would surface repeatedly amid all that certainty, their guilt-ridden suppression. He was on the point of interjecting something of this, when Piers took off again.

'As we have seen, what Allegro felt he had discovered was a long-established tradition displaying the essential characteristics of what was to blossom some hundred years later with the coming of Jesus. Let me just give you some examples of the practices of the Qumran community which appeared to him to mirror those of the first Christians. For a start, both were ruled by a council of twelve members, three of them being accorded special authority — in the case of the church, the twelve Apostles led by James, John and Peter. Both attribute prime importance to the ritual of baptism, the rules of the Qumran community stipulating that new members be cleansed of their sins with purifying water — rings a familiar bell? Both insist on all wealth being held in common, that new adherents donate all their possessions, selling what they are unable to bring with them and handing over the proceeds — harsh punishments prescribed by both communities for the holding back of anything whatsoever. And, of course, both drawing inspiration from a charismatic leader — the Teacher of Righteousness in the case of the Qumran community — put to death by their enemies. I could go on, there's plenty more, but I think you will have got the general picture: the Qumran community appearing to provide a near-perfect blueprint for the early Christian church of Jerusalem.

'You can imagine Allegro's excitement at his discovery. And the source was indisputably virgin — unlike the Gospels, which were produced long after the events they describe, with clearly partisan additions, deletions and general editing. He would regale members of the international team with his findings, naively expecting they would share his enthusiasm, the evidence he was holding before them seemingly in overwhelming support for the case he was making. And he didn't see in it anything subversive: that Jesus had emerged from a background steeped in the values and rituals that would influence his teaching and much subsequent Christian doctrine appearing far more plausible in his view than the hitherto accepted notion of these having materialised out of thin air. Overlooking in his excitement the fact of this latter view — with "out of thin air" amended to something like "by a unique act of divine will" — being incontrovertibly that of the Roman church, for whom any suggestion of human participation in the process would constitute heresy of the highest order.'

Piers paused here, his expression again inviting comment.

'You seem to be putting Allegro's case so strongly that I just can't imagine what it is you find wrong with it. Am I missing something?'

Piers laughed. 'Well, yes, you are, but in your case, you have every excuse. I can't say the same for the others though. You see, the problem is essentially that of de Vaux and his acolytes adopting every possible means to distance the Scrolls from the origins of Christianity. Whether consciously or unconsciously it's difficult to say — that automatic censor again. That's why they were so put out by Allegro storming in as he did, disrupting the consensus. But even he was taken in on what was perhaps the most crucial issue of all: the question of dating.'

Stephen listened in silence while Piers outlined how this had been carried out. Carbon dating, the only strictly scientific method, setting a span of some two-hundred years or more — from before about 100 BC to a little after 100 AD. De Vaux and his team, relying mainly on their interpretation of archaeological and palaeographic data, settling for the early end of the range, back as far as perhaps 150 BC.

'As safely removed from the Christian era as could possibly be swallowed.'

Piers was also scathing about the palaeographic methods to which de Vaux paid particular heed.

'These involve dating the manuscripts on the basis of how writing styles change with time; but as handwriting varies widely, both among individuals and according to the purpose for which a document is being prepared, its application over the time scale of interest, in this case, is effectively useless. As for the archaeological evidence, also much trumpeted by de Vaux, far from supporting his position on dating and other matters of key importance, it more often than not points in the very opposite direction. No, the only way dating can be achieved with any confidence is through the internal evidence: what is in the Scrolls themselves; interpretation requiring a thorough knowledge of the history and culture of the region against which the recorded events can be lined up and compared.'

Piers then spoke for a while about the nature of the Qumran sect as revealed by the internal evidence of the Scrolls. For a start, this demolished the monastic-style, celibate, male community hypothesis by providing a record of precise laws governing marriage and permitted sexual practices — with the supporting archaeological evidence of women's and children's graves. And then going on to dispose of the notion of a community of passive contemplatives, the "War Scroll" providing both a manual of military tactics and a propagandist tract exhorting armed resistance to enemy invaders — again with the archaeological support of the remains of a substantial forge for the clear purpose of weapons production.

'Make no mistake about it, there was nothing pacifist nor accommodating in its make-up. Qumran may well have started out that way, but by the time to which the Scrolls refer, it had developed into a passionate warlike sect, uncompromisingly opposed to what it saw as corruption and apostasy in the rulers, its members ready to fight and die for their beliefs – closer in nature to the combative Zealots than the supposedly peaceful Essenes. Incidentally, these labels — Zealots, Essenes, and a whole string of others associated with that society — shouldn't be regarded as relating to well-defined entities; they simply represent idealised aspects of the seething religio-political brew that was Palestine. It's important to appreciate this point if you want to make any sense of what was going on there.'

He then went on to show how the adversaries of the Qumran community had to be Romans and, in particular, of *Imperial Rome*, citing references in the texts clearly pointing to this conclusion — including reports of victorious soldiers "sacrificing to their standards".

'This was what first clinched my doubts regarding the assumed dating. The practice was only introduced after the creation of the Roman empire, of which the emperor, portrayed on the standards, was regarded as a god. It would make no sense whatsoever during the pre-Christian conflicts when Rome was still a republic. This, along with many other factors, places the Scrolls firmly in the early Christian period, during the time of the revolt in Judea (AD 66–74), its brutal suppression by the Romans, leading to the sack of Jerusalem and the destruction of the Temple. Once this had become clear all the inconsistencies, things I had felt to be wrong but couldn't quite put my finger on why, fell into place. Yes, the production of the Scrolls had to be contemporaneous with that of the earliest books of the New Testament, dwelling like them on momentous events of recent history.'

'My God!' Stephen, who had been listening spellbound, couldn't believe where this appeared to be leading. 'Sorry for that. But just what are you saying? The Teacher of Righteousness...'

'Go on. So, who do you think he could be? Go on, have a guess.'

'Not... not Jesus Christ?'

Piers laughed, clearly pleased with himself for having led Stephen into this. 'Well, not quite, but not bad for a beginner. Just a little early in your dating. No, the events described in the Scrolls relate to the period after Jesus' crucifixion, to the community of his followers led by his successor, his brother James.'

'Jesus' brother?' Stephen was getting more confused than ever. 'But I thought...'

'I know what you thought. But it's perfectly clear from the historical evidence, even from the New Testament, the Letters of Paul: "James the brother of Jesus", referred to often enough.'

'Yes, but we were told that "brother" there implied only close relation or something of the sort, that there was ambiguity there, overlooked in the translation.'

'The usual prevarication, ambiguity claimed where the obvious is difficult to stomach, absolute cast-iron certainty for anything that seems to conform to entrenched belief. No, the surprise is that occasional mention of awkward relationships managed to survive at all in the New Testament. Mostly they get brushed aside. So that Mary, for instance, acquires a sister called Mary, enabling Jesus' siblings — there were several of them in addition to James — to be taken for cousins, so avoiding conflict with the doctrine that was to be concocted years later of her perpetual virginity. The texts are full of such evasions. You need to be continuously on the lookout, always ready to take them into account.'

He then proceeded to outline the detailed comparisons leading to the inevitable conclusion that events described in Acts and other early Christian documents tied in precisely with those referred to in the Scrolls.

'James, the "Teacher of Righteousness",' he went on, 'was eventually killed by order of the "Wicked Priest" — by stoning incidentally, not crucifixion as Allegro had suggested. This villain was clearly a member of the Temple establishment — abhorred for its acceptance of Herodian rule, what was seen as the profanation of the Temple, the quisling subservience to the occupying forces of Rome. The Qumran sect was unmistakably a Jewish nationalistic movement, xenophobic and overtly aggressive, its members unshakably "Zealots for the Law", James their revered leader. James was also the universally acknowledged first leader of the "Christian" church in Jerusalem, the undisputed successor of his brother Jesus. Everything points to the conclusion that the Qumran sect and the early Christian church were effectively one and the same.'

SEVENTEEN

These disclosures were almost too much for Stephen to take in. He was aware that Piers had simplified things for him, revealing only bare essentials, but he still needed time to digest what he had been told. One thing did occur to him almost immediately though: nothing Piers had said about Qumran appeared specifically related to Jesus. Did this reflect the general picture? If so, it seemed strange. He put this to him.

'Yes, I know. With the hindsight of the phenomenal growth of Christianity throughout the world and the investiture of Jesus as the human embodiment of God, it appears incredible now that following his death the succession would simply shift to his brother. But for his followers, the community to which he belonged, it was a perfectly natural outcome, just what they would have expected. For them, Jesus was no God but simply a leader in the bitter struggle against what they saw as the abasement of their religion, the imposition by Rome of corrupt Herodian rule. Nothing of this changed with his death. If anything, one would expect their anger and frustration to increase. As indeed they did; the struggle continuing under the leadership of James until his death some thirty years later, by which time the influence of Jesus was very much in the background. Jesus was certainly a charismatic preacher with an avid following. But there was nothing particularly unusual about that. There were other charismatic preachers both before and after him, which is hardly surprising given the long-running universal resentment to the impositions of Rome. John the Baptist was one — the only one acknowledged as such in the New Testament, where he is portrayed simply as a precursor, his role limited to preparing people for the coming of Jesus. But that wouldn't be in any way how he saw himself, nor how he appeared to his followers. The historian Josephus, by far the most comprehensive source for that period of Jewish history — himself living and participating in events leading up to and following the sack of Jerusalem — lumps them all together: troublemakers, for the most part, stirring up the populace in revolt against Rome, Jesus no exception, in no way singled out for special mention.'

'Is Jesus referred to at all in the Scrolls?' Stephen asked, his mind spinning.

'Well, nobody is referred to by name. Personal references are invariably in terms of attributes: Teacher of Righteousness, Wicked Priest, The Liar — I'll be coming to that one in just a moment — and so on. There are effective allusions to Jesus though, to a leader "hanged from a tree" — a term for crucifixion — but nothing more specific. This is to be expected though because things had moved on by then. We're talking here of some thirty years after the death of Jesus, a period beset by extreme political turmoil and mounting religious tension, warlike confrontation with Rome and its quisling supporters growing inexorably towards the inevitable explosion. What is abundantly clear is that by then the central position in this embryonic "Christianity" was held by Jesus' brother James, a man of unparalleled piety and righteousness as testified repeatedly in the historical documents of the time, including those of the early church. Referred to variously as James the brother of Jesus, James the Just, James the Righteous — in the Scrolls, the Teacher of Righteousness — he was the undisputed leader of the early "Christian" church, first bishop of Jerusalem, "bishop above all bishops".

'But what about Peter?' Stephen, trying hard to keep track, throwing this up from his confusion. 'I thought he was the one appointed to lead the church after Jesus; "...keys of the kingdom of heaven" and all that. Now you're saying it wasn't him at all. We hardly heard anything of James at St John's. How on earth could that be?'

'Not at all surprising. Peter's, was a late posthumous appointment to head of the church, to first Pope; part of the programme to write James as far as possible out of the picture — for reasons I've touched on and will become clear in just a moment. But what's perfectly obvious, even from Paul's letters and the Acts of the Apostles in general, is that James was the first leader of the early "Christian" church to whom all then deferred, and that he continued in that role up to the time of his death. In fact, from a historical perspective, James emerges far more clearly than Jesus himself — for whom precious little is to be found outside the accounts in the Gospels. But James and what he stood for were to become acutely embarrassing to the Pauline faction from which the new religion, the Christianity we know today, derives. There's a crucial and perhaps rather obvious point I must emphasise here. Nowhere is there any suggestion whatsoever of the Qumran sect being open to outsiders, to flouters of the Law, to the uncircumcised. Everything it and James stood for would be totally opposed to even the suggestion of such adulteration. Nor, of course, is there anything there remotely related to the concept of Jesus' divinity. That was to emerge much later and from what would have been a completely alien source. So far as Qumran was concerned, it would be difficult to imagine a more blatantly blasphemous heresy. And yet this was the first "Christian church" of Jerusalem, consisting of the very people who knew Jesus personally, his immediate followers, his disciples, his heirs: the "Christian church" for them being nothing other than a fundamentalist Jewish faction campaigning relentlessly for a return to the strict observance of Mosaic Law. You see where this is leading? Its implications? That, if they thought in those terms, it's difficult to conclude other than that Jesus did so as well. You'll understand now what I meant about the truth of the matter being far more serious for the church than anything de Vaux could possibly have imagined.'

'But this is absolutely fascinating Piers.' Stephen was feeling quite stunned at the enormity of what he had been hearing. 'Have you spoken to anyone else about it? Not to de Vaux, I would imagine.'

'Good Lord, no. But yes, there are other people involved in what to do about this, where it should go from here. But look,' he broke off, looking a trifle uncomfortable, clearly not wishing to be drawn further on this issue. 'I'm hungry. I believe Natasha's left us something in the kitchen. Let's eat, then we can get back to it. There's something else there I want to tell you about.'

They finished the food laid out for them by Natasha: cold meat, salad, cheese and fruit. Stephen had been worried that Piers would have other things to do, preparations for his impending journey, his mysterious open-ended commitment in Rome, that he was taking up too much of his time. But there was no sign of this as they ate, reminiscing happily enough, no sense at all of Piers wishing to hurry things along. Then, refreshed, they went back for the final lap.

'Something had bothered me in passing, long before all this. But then the New Testament is full of such things when you come to consider it critically. You're puzzled by something, ponder it a while, then give up and move on. This one concerns Paul, the driving force behind the evangelising of Christianity beyond its Jewish origins, its presentation and promotion to anyone who would listen: to flouters of the Covenant, to the uncircumcised, to citizens of the occupying-enemy empire — the last people in the world with whom members of the Qumran sect would wish to do business. An odd thing I had noticed about Paul in his letters is the number of times he proclaims himself not to be a liar, the context giving no clue to why he feels the need to keep going on about this: "I am no liar" and "God knows I am no liar" and so on. A pertinent example of this, for reasons that will become clear, occurs in his first letter to the Galatians. Immediately after having said that *he had been with James, the Lord's brother*, he goes on to assure them that in what he is writing "I lie not." Why on earth, you may well ask, would he feel they needed such assurance?'

Piers paused here, giving Stephen a sidelong glance, perhaps inviting a response, to which Stephen could only shake his head in mute anticipation of what was to follow.

'As I said, it was something I had puzzled over long before. But then, when I got to see the work-in-progress on the Scrolls, there it was staring me in the face. There were two great villains that the Scrolls show the Teacher of Righteousness having to contend with. One we've seen already, the Wicked Priest, who harasses him relentlessly, eventually having him put to death, soon after to be murdered himself in reprisal and his body mutilated by the Teacher's enraged followers — a further example, if one were needed, of their Zealot rather than Essene leanings. The Wicked Priest can be readily identified as the high priest Ananus of the despised Temple establishment. The other high-profile villain is referred to simply as The Liar, someone who had clearly been closely associated with the sect and had subsequently defected:, a traitor with whom the Teacher had been involved in long and bitter controversy. I have to say that when I first saw those references to The Liar in the Scrolls, it immediately called to mind those New Testament protestations of Paul's, but that was before the question of the dating had been resolved, so I had to dismiss it as one of those flashes of insight we all have at times that turn out to be off-target. But by the time I had the dating finally sorted out, the Scrolls firmly attributed to the early Christian period and their provenance fully appreciated, then the notion of the link with Paul came hurtling back, and this time it fitted perfectly into the revised picture.'

Piers went on to describe how this was so, setting Paul's interactions with the early church as described in Acts against those of The Liar as recounted in the Scrolls, each from its own point of view covering the same ground.

'That there should be extreme antagonism between James and Paul is hardly surprising given what we now know: that the original "Christian" church led by James, to which all the immediate followers of Jesus belonged, consisted of a fundamentalist Jewish sect, its members believing themselves the chosen people, alone destined for salvation, uncompromising "Zealots for the Law" and bitter enemies of all who transgressed it. And then there is Paul — an outsider, a convert who joined the early church never having known Jesus personally — disparaging the Law, declaring that it "will not justify anyone in the sight of God"; rather that salvation is to be attained solely through faith in Jesus Christ, and that anyone at all willing to accept this is welcome aboard.

'Both in Acts and in the Scrolls we learn of James's repeated attempts to impose his authority on Paul, on The Liar, summoning him to Jerusalem to be berated for preaching to "everyone everywhere", for his failure to demand adherence to the Law, at one point obliging him to undergo a period of purification, after which he apparently agrees to mend his ways, only to return to them almost immediately, precipitating an attempt on his life by the enraged "Zealots for the Law" and his branding as The Liar, the name by which he is always referred to in the Qumran documents — which are nothing other than original records of the early "Christian" church in Jerusalem. Little wonder then at the bitter antagonism, exacerbated by Paul's evident success in attracting adherents. So much so that the Pauline faction would go on to swamp all opposition, the heresy to become mainstream dogma; the new religion founded by Paul promoting Jesus as God, concocting the doctrines of his virgin birth and resurrection, commissioning from within its ranks authorised accounts of his life and teaching which would go on to attain the status of gospel truth, and growing relentlessly in power and influence throughout the empire and beyond.

'Which brings us more or less to where we are today. But now you see the problem these discoveries have thrown up. There's simply no getting away from it. It's there in black and white, untainted by subsequent editing and special pleading to promote a cause. In cutting itself off from its Jewish roots, Christianity succeeded in cutting itself off from the community and cause for which Jesus laboured and died, from his lifetime followers and everything they stood for, from the very person that was Jesus Christ. A posthumous betrayal unparalleled in human history.'

The silence that followed was broken by Piers noisily pushing back his chair and striding out of the room, to return moments later bearing two glasses of wine, clearly in no hurry to bring the session to a close. Then fixing Stephen with that familiar interrogative look he had been half-expecting: the accomplished teacher as ever, drawing out responses from the class, getting them involved. Stephen, smiling to himself at the recollection, thought hard of what he could say.

'I seem to remember reading of a claim that Jesus was just another Jewish prophet along with the others; it was probably in a book that came out while I was at St John's, I must have seen a review somewhere.'

'Oh, there have been plenty of highly plausible theories along those lines, often involving well-reasoned argument based on the available evidence. The church soon discovering the most effective way of dealing with them being to turn a deaf ear. The difference this time is that we have the direct evidence of this irrefutable primary source: the manuals of the first "Christian" church in Jerusalem. And though discord with its embryonic Hellenic offshoot is apparent enough in the New Testament — clashes between James and Paul — this is so watered down as to appear no more than disagreements over points of detail and procedure. Instead, what we now see clearly in play, is a bitter struggle between two fundamentally opposed religious ideologies: on the one hand an exclusive, fiercely uncompromising Judaism, espoused by James and the other brothers and direct associates of Jesus — and by inevitable implication by Jesus himself — and on the other, a breakaway heretical faction, open to all comers that would go on to evolve into a completely new religion, bitterly hostile to its Jewish antecedents. So much so that it would spawn the virulent anti-Semitism that has persisted to this day. The supreme irony is that the focus of this new religion, the person at its centre regarded as God-Almighty-made-flesh, was not only a Jew, but a Jew passionately committed to the fundamentalist Jewish cause.'

Another thoughtful silence, broken again by Stephen.

'But don't the actions and teachings of Jesus themselves support at least some of the views of the breakaway faction. I'm thinking of the Sermon on the Mount, the tolerance and humanity of those concepts. Something one associates with Christianity. No?'

'Not a good example for the point you're trying to make because those very sentiments are mirrored time and again in the Qumran documents: the poor and the meek portrayed as receiving the particular favour of God, and so on. That was one of the things that inspired Allegro to read foretastes of Christianity in the Scrolls. It seems to relate to the passive Essene aspects of the community, which as we have seen coexisted with those of belligerent zealotry. But you're right nevertheless. There are indeed passages in the Gospels that stand out as being quite at odds with what Qumran stood for, along with others that emphatically support its values — even at times where these appear quite contrary to the tenets of the breakaway movement. An example of the latter is Jesus' adamant defence of the Law, his declaration that he had come to fulfil it in its entirety, that not one bit of it could be changed in any way — effectively the subsequent war cry of "Zealots for the Law" and fully in accord with James's unwavering stance in his disputes with Paul. Another episode that bears all the hallmarks of Qumran is the attack by Jesus and his followers on the money changers in the Temple, overturning their tables and setting them fleeing for their lives — an overtly violent action in marked contrast to Jesus' gentle, peace-loving image in the Gospels, but completely in keeping with the Qumran sect's furious indignation at the profane practices of the Temple establishment.

'When it comes to the other side of the coin — those passages appearing in conflict with the Qumran ethos — you have to bear in mind once again the provenance of the Gospels, their role as promotional material for the victorious faction by then largely severed from its Jewish roots and evangelising relentlessly throughout the Roman empire. Under such circumstances, anything construable as hostile to Rome in the written records was clearly to be avoided, and acquiescence with impositions of Roman rule not at all a bad thing to lay claim to. Such considerations must surely have led to the insertion of the "Render unto Caesar the things that are Caesar's" passage, which — regardless of its being portrayed as a smart response by Jesus to a question framed to condemn him however he answered — is quite inconceivable, given the climate of the time: the virulent opposition to Roman rule, contempt for its pagan religious practices, and unremitting hostility to the imposed taxation. Jesus' credibility among his followers would, without doubt, have been lost, his very life endangered by so treasonous a pronouncement — which in any case ran counter to everything he and his followers stood for. Its insertion in the Gospels, however, would have well served the purpose of reassuring Rome it could come to terms with this new religion blossoming on its doorstep — a welcome change from the fanatical hostility endured for generations from its predecessor.'

EIGHTEEN

Although it was more than five years since Stephen had renounced his faith — the couple of months or so of unease that followed quite a thing of the past — Piers's account had shocked him deeply. Why? he was asking himself. Because even before Piers had finished, he found himself accepting the basic plausibility of the revised picture of Jesus' popularity among his followers being a result of his charismatic espousal of the Jewish cause in the face of corrupt leadership and alien occupation: to a return to Judaic righteousness and obedience to the Law, and for his being part of a vigorous fundamentalist movement — for a while its leader — devoted to those ends. Why then the discomfort? A good part of it, he decided, resulted from the imagined reaction of believers, in particular the brothers at St John's, how they would respond — realising almost immediately that they wouldn't at all, that the only authority for them on this issue, as on any other, would be the church, which if it felt the need to react would simply draw on its formidable resources to rubbish anything that conflicted with the authorised view.

But still the discomfort, its focus wavering for a while before settling on Piers — so apparently at ease with the results of his researches. It had taken long enough for Stephen to come to terms with Piers's defection from the brotherhood, with his liaison with Natasha. But quite adjusted to all that now, his relationship with them both quite transformed from whatever it had been before into close friendship. Nothing more and nothing less, or so he had come to persuade himself; his adolescent infatuation with Natasha consigned to history, occasional reminders, like last night's lingering pressure of her hand, always competently brushed aside; her relationship with Piers fully accepted and welcomed – so much so that the turn this was now taking, with Piers's imminent departure for Rome, a cause for deep concern: concern for them both and also, for reasons unclear, for himself. And along with all this, his recollection as though it were yesterday of Brother Carroll's persuasive insistence on the absolute need for a belief in God, the bleak prospect he held out for mankind in the absence of such conviction. Yet here he was, decrying the inception of the religion to which he had devoted his life, showing it up as what amounted to an opportunistic confidence trick that had spectacularly come off, and to all appearances quite unabashed at so prodigious a U-turn.

But what in the face of all this was quite inexplicable was Piers's continuing involvement with the church. That he was no longer a believer Stephen was in no doubt whatsoever. So, what was he up to with the Vatican? And who were these people there he was confiding in, people he had found sympathetic to his findings? It crossed Stephen's mind that perhaps they were simply stringing him along, playing for time while planning how to neutralise the damage his discoveries could cause — immediately dismissing the notion, confident that Piers was not one to be misled in such matters, would have no difficulty in recognising insincerity. He would very much like to hear something of this from Piers himself, however; fearful of asking though, only too aware of his reluctance to be drawn. But perhaps now as good a time as ever to try, the momentum for disclosure stronger than ever likely to occur again.

These issues raced through his mind; Piers's expression fixed, inviting a response; the silence in danger of becoming an embarrassment. Until... abandoning caution on a whim...

'The thing I can't get hold of at all, Piers, is just where you stand in all this. I mean, I thought you'd finally ditched religious belief. But have you? Sorry. You've already told me the answer to that. But then what on earth are you up to now? With the Vatican? With Natasha, come to that? It seems so natural, you and her together, the fresh start you both longed for. So just what are you playing at?'

He's probably regretting having confided in me, was Stephen's immediate thought on coming out with this, Piers's expression remaining unchanged, immobile; but then slowly softening, a tinge of sadness momentarily discernible as he gathered his response.

'It's nothing new you're witnessing. Natasha has known all along of my vocation, my unshakeable commitment to the church. In that respect, nothing has changed. I tried, obviously successfully, to separate that from what I've been talking about: the foundations of Christianity, the revised account of its historical beginnings — for which stark objectivity is the only respectable option, of course. But, as I've said to you before, what we must face up to is the fact of the church's present existence, its massive presence throughout the world, drawing together people of all nations, of all cultures. And the fact of its immense influence and stability, both greater than that of most, perhaps all, nation states. It's all there, staring us in the face. It's not going to go away. It's quite immune to anything that may emerge from research into its origins or indeed anything else; a witness to mankind's overwhelming desire for an ideal that transcends personal and national interests; an alternative to purely selfish concerns; a focus on something above all that: a perception of universal goodness that imbues human existence with comfort and hope.'

'Yes, but all based on myth and superstition.' Stephen, as he came out with this, was experiencing a faint aftershock of the anger he had felt years before on cutting loose from religious belief, anger at the years of relentless indoctrination — brainwashing, no less — to which he had been subjected, which had clouded his childhood and adolescence. 'You seemed to have accepted that,' he went on, 'so what are you saying now? That the church should ditch the mumbo-jumbo, transform itself into some sort of humanistic, do-gooder organisation that will continue to attract a mass following, enable it to cling to power? Doesn't sound very realistic to me. In fact, a dead-cert loser, given that its whole appeal lies in its very irrationality, in its exploitation of the desperate wishful thinking of its followers, their unwillingness to come to terms with the spectre of their own mortality, with the loss of loved ones, with their insignificance in the cosmic order. And the whole thing so elaborately put together, so wrapped up in pious posturing and pseudo-scholarly gibberish as to obscure the fundamental absurdity at its source.'

Although Stephen had articulated something of these sentiments to Piers before, after that first meeting with him and Natasha in the Fitzrovia pub, he had since kept them very much to himself and was relieved to see that Piers was not in the least put out by the outburst.

'Well, that's not exactly how I would put it,' he replied

with a smile. 'But it isn't helpful to focus solely on the past, on the negative. What is now in place, this massive structure that permeates the world, has an immense potential for good, for transcending the cold self-interest otherwise conditioning our existence. In that respect, its origins are largely beside the point, serve only to emphasise the extent to which perceptions have changed: a one-time belief in the supernatural gradually giving way to something else, to awe perhaps at the multitudinous wonders of nature. The church must come to accommodate such shifts of perception, accept the notion of a spirituality that stops short of belief in the supernatural. And at the same time, to be seen to identify irrefutably with the poor and vulnerable, with the oppressed; to be working constantly on their behalf, wary of cosy accommodation with the rich and powerful. Its arrogant assertiveness and ostentatious displays of wealth need to be phased out; the mumbo-jumbo, as you put it, the ritual, trimmed and accepted as no more than respectful acknowledgement of tradition. It's going to have to open its doors to all, to those with other beliefs, of other faiths, to unbelievers, to all seeking solace or tranquillity or escape from the senseless greed of the well-to-do, to anyone concerned at injustice. It's a gradual transformation that is needed, not something that can happen overnight. But then many practicing Catholics have already come to feel much this way about their religion — on the whole without being aware of any conceptual shift having taken place. To them and countless others, both within and outside the church, the term Christian has come to be regarded as synonymous with goodness, decency, consideration for others. This is something positive to build on, a basis for rational development away from superstition, petty proscription, absurd obsession with chastity and the rest of it. It's going to take time and immense effort on the part of those working for change. It goes without saying how important it is that these efforts should not be in vain.'

Stephen, with growing unease, was feeling his long-held confidence in Piers's judgement slipping away. Not that his sincerity was in doubt, far from it; nor the appeal of the ends to which he was committed. But did he really believe that the countless priests and bishops, monks and nuns and lay workers, dedicating their lives to the service of the church, would be doing so in the absence of that towering supernatural stimulus? Without belief in that all-seeing, all-knowing, obsessively judgemental creator of the universe, who appeared two thousand years ago in human form in a conflict-ridden outpost of the Roman empire? It passed through Stephen's mind that he would have found it quite impossible to accept that persons demonstrably sane and intelligent could be subject to such a delusion, were it not for his having suffered it himself — and for the struggle he had undergone in breaking free. But that was beside the point, which was now how to respond to Piers, so obviously committed to his pipe dream?

'I wish you luck,' was all he could come up with after a longish pause.

'You don't sound very convinced.'

'Well, I'm just trying to imagine the reaction of the brothers at St John's, if you want to know: Ignatius, Anthony, Simon, the rest of them. Can you imagine any of that lot going along with your vision of... what do you want to call it? Spiritual atheism? Sounds fine to me, but then I'm not one of those you're going to have to sell it to.'

Piers remained silent for a while before replying.

'Nobody will need to sell anything to anyone, other than tolerance of diverse views. I know that seems a formidable task given the church's past record, but by no means impossible now that the spirit for change is firmly in the ascendant. And let's be absolutely clear that no one's calling on anyone to abandon anything, certainly not deeply held belief. It's simply, as I said before, just a matter of opening doors, acknowledging that nothing is certain except that what is in place is of immense value — potentially priceless, embodying the concept of a universal goodness capable of embracing the full gamut of belief: from faith in Jesus Christ to humanism, from accepting the Gospels as authentic historical records to regarding them as fables expressing a universal moral message.'

Stephen, far from convinced, was on the point of adding some further note of perplexity; sensing an opportunity however, he steered instead to a related matter.

'You know Piers, there's something that has puzzled me, that I've wanted to ask you about but have kept putting it off. When you were teaching at St John's... had you already given up the faith? I only ask because there were certain things you said then, or rather it was more the way you said them, that seemed strange at the time, but perhaps make some sort of sense now.'

Piers didn't answer; he was looking at him strangely, perhaps waiting for him to go on.

'When did it happen? Was it when you discovered the provenance of the Scrolls? What they had to say about the origins of Christianity?'

Still no answer.

'I'm sorry, it's none of my business.'

'No, it's all right, it's a perfectly valid question. It's just that I'm not sure how to answer it. It's not a thing that happens on the spur of the moment — at least it didn't for me. Did for St Paul of course, in the other direction, but then he had to fall off his horse.' His smile reassured Stephen that all was well. 'But perhaps even in that case, deep down somewhere, the ground had been prepared, suppressed notions had accumulated, were awaiting an opportunity to burst out. In my case, it all took a long time. I don't think I can identify precisely when the definitive switch occurred. Though no, it would have been after St John's. Probably quite soon after. I remember well some of the things you and Firbright — particularly Firbright — would come out with. They tied in pretty well with my growing doubts. But I was still clinging to belief at the time, despite everything. If it hadn't been for Natasha... but then you know that story.'

'Yes, I do. That's why I can't understand what you're doing now. Risking all that. I'm sorry, that's certainly none of my business.'

'No, it's mine. And believe me, the decision was by no means easy. But then, the alternative was to throw away everything I have built my life around — much of which I still passionately believe in. What I have to do now is work to see those parts strengthened, the whole made acceptable — both to the growing band of disillusioned insiders and to those outside who, in its present guise, wouldn't touch it with a bargepole. Natasha understands all this. She knows me well enough... my feelings for her... my feelings for what I have to do. We've gone through it all before... years ago. She knows perfectly well that it simply isn't on for me to give up, to throw in the towel; she understands the consequences that would be certain to follow — not only for me but for what we have together.'

He went on in this vein for some time, trying hard — too hard, it seemed to Stephen — to justify the course on which he was embarked. It was getting late, time to call it a day.

'You must have a lot to do. I've been taking up too much of your time.'

'Not at all. You're one of the very few people I feel I can talk to about all this. It helps, even though you probably can't see that. But I can assure you that it does.'

'You've eased my conscience. So, you're off on Wednesday then. Any idea when we're going to see you again?'

'I'm afraid that's out of my hands. But I won't be leaving till Thursday now. Other things have materialised. I've a lot of running around to do over the next couple of days.'

'Can't you put it off another day? Then you could keep our Thursday theatre date. Or is that too much to ask?'

'Well, it wouldn't be for me,' Piers answered with a dry laugh. 'But I'm afraid that's also out of my hands.'

Well, in whose hands is it then? For although there could be no doubt of Piers's vow of chastity having been spectacularly cast aside, that of obedience still appeared very much in evidence. But obedience to whom? For a moment Stephen thought to ask, but something in Piers's laugh told him it would be futile.

And so to the leave-taking, a somewhat awkward exchange of words followed by a warm shaking of hands and then, on an unprecedented mutual whim, a full-bloodied Latin-style embrace — a gesture, though satisfying the emotions both were feeling at the time, destined to lodge painfully in Stephen's memory, augmenting the burning guilt he was to feel for his role in events set shortly to unfold.

NINETEEN

Stephen set off early for college the following morning, getting to his desk before anyone else had arrived. A number of things were bothering him, preventing him from getting down to work, leaving him just sitting there staring into space. He had upset Emel the other day, declining an offer he had apparently expended some effort in setting up. What had been proposed had so much going for it that he couldn't understand now his reason for turning it down. It was for him to spend the fast-approaching final year of his PhD studies in California, at Franklin Polytechnic — an arrangement he felt sure Karl Dembowski would have had a hand in. He was to prepare his thesis there, returning to London for the viva; then, all being well, back to Franklin on a postdoctoral appointment with unlimited possibilities thereafter. What on earth is the matter with me? he was thinking. Also on his mind was the fraught situation at Percy Street in which he was finding himself embroiled, Piers's imminent departure for Rome sending perplexing waves he was unable or unwilling to interpret. Somewhere on the horizon was the hazy notion that perhaps these separate matters were interlinked. He was interrupted at last by the arrival of Alan and Franco, forcing him into simulation of concentrated study — eventually to transform into a half-hearted version of the real thing, which helped pass an hour or so until he could no longer carry on with it and left.

    On Thursday morning, while preparing to leave for college, he was startled by a loud knock on his door; there was a call for him on the communal payphone in the hallway. It was Natasha wanting to confirm arrangements for that evening, Piers poised to set off with his one-way train ticket to Rome. It seemed to Stephen that she was making a determined effort to confront the pain of his departure, her voice bright, cheerful even, her manner efficient, well in control.

'The show's going to end quite late. It's probably better for us to eat beforehand. I thought I'd prepare something simple here. What do you think?' Then going on without waiting to hear what this might be. 'If you could get here by about six, it'll give us plenty of time. There'll be no need to rush. Is that okay with you?'

It was, he assured her.

He had been thinking a lot about that evening, originally planned by Piers and Natasha, to which he had at first felt included as something of an afterthought. He was looking forward to it though, and genuinely sorry that Piers was not to be with them. But that, of course, was but a trifling consequence of the situation Natasha was having to face, for which he was feeling the compelling need to provide comfort and support — a prospect coming over as inexplicably pleasurable, which should perhaps have set alarm bells ringing. That it didn't testify once again to his conviction that the infatuation had been brought firmly under control, subsumed within the unaffected friendship dating back to that extraordinary encounter in the Fitzrovia pub some eighteen months earlier; all inklings of former cravings brushed aside, along with any suggestion of Natasha's signs of fondness for him — increasingly evident of late — signifying anything other than just acknowledgement of that friendship. But perturbed now, as he put down the phone, by a confused cocktail of emotions of which the dominant flavours were exhilaration and apprehension.

He changed his mind about going into college, not wanting to see anyone now, persuading himself that papers brought back the previous evening required his uninterrupted attention — but giving up on that after twenty minutes or so of not making head or tail of them. A long walk, he decided, could clear his mind, restore his concentration and, more importantly, help pass the time to evening. With no direction in mind as he set out, he found himself on automatic pilot for college, turning abruptly on realising this, heading now for Regent's Park. There he came to a pond where old men, revelling in the joys of second childhood, were deploying beautifully constructed remote-controlled model sailing boats — a serious business from their expressions, but less so than the imminent races to which he overheard them referring, for which the present performances were but a limbering up. Glad for the diversion, he stayed for a while among the smattering of spectators: lonely drifters filling the day as he was, harassed mums with hyperactive pre-school-age children, a group of animated foreign girls — Italian or Spanish by the look of them — that, on other occasions, could well have absorbed his attention. He checked his watch, only half-eleven, how slowly time was passing. It was getting dark however, a realisation engendering a moment of panic: that time had overtaken him, that his watch had stopped, that he had missed the six o'clock appointment. Then, rationality returning, he saw it was just the clouds, grown extensive and dark by now, blocking out the sun. It was coming on to rain. A few drops — perhaps imagined — sending him hurrying home, where he made toast and opened a can of beans. Then, with some reluctance, back to those papers, making some sort of sense of them this time, selecting a likely couple for more detailed attention. Time speeding up as he worked; it was nearly five when he broke off to prepare for setting out.

She called out when he rang that the door was on the latch, to come on in and shut it behind him. He found her in the kitchen, looking more desirable than ever in a faded T-shirt and raggy jeans; sad, red eyes adding the note of vulnerability that made the urge to hug her to him all but impossible to resist; her smile acknowledging his concern, at the same time gently discouraging further moves, sticking instead to practical matters.

'Everything's ready. Just waiting for the water to boil for the pasta. Why don't you pour some wine? There's an opened bottle of Frascati in the fridge, glasses in the cupboard behind you.'

While doing this, he started to bring up Piers's departure, realising almost at once his mistake, her face darkening as he spoke.

'I'm sorry, Stephen, but I'd rather not talk about that now. I know you're trying to help, but let's just concentrate on other things. Maybe later…'

But then she looked as though about to cry, and this time didn't resist when he came up to her, pressing her head to his shoulder as he held her, not daring to move. After several long seconds, she pulled away, squeezing his wrist as she did so, wiping her eyes.

As they ate, Stephen tried hard to concentrate on other things; he talked about college, the way things were going for him there, getting on to the offer he had been made to spend a year, maybe more, in the United States.

'But that's wonderful,' she interjected, 'when do you plan

to leave?'

'I turned it down. I didn't feel ready for it somehow.'

'Why on earth not? It sounds like a perfect opportunity. What's the matter with you?'

'I just feel I don't want to leave London, that's all.'

She was looking at him strangely as he said that, the 'especially now' he had just stopped himself adding perhaps registering anyway, or so he was later to imagine. Time was getting on. Natasha got up to go and get changed, telling him to leave everything on the table where it was, that she would deal with it the following morning. He had nevertheless just about finished rinsing and stacking the things by the sink when she called to him from the living room.

She was standing across the room from where he entered, by the open door to the bedroom, looking somewhat dishevelled in a long blue gown, her left arm raised and bent, the hand seemingly grasping at something behind her neck.

'You're going to have to help me with this zip,' she explained, smiling at his puzzled expression. 'I should have thought before buying the thing that I was going to need help in putting it on.'

He realised then what she was doing, that it was only her hand holding the figure-hugging creation in place. She turned as he approached, revealing a slender back, bare from her neck down to where the gown opened across the tops of her buttocks, the offending zip fastener nestling there in the cleft. Stupefied, he felt his body responding, his mind turning numb. With no thought for what he was doing, he came up to her, taking her arms lightly from behind and planting a gentle kiss on her neck. Her reaction was immediate and unequivocal: a sharp intake of breath as she pressed back hard against him, feeling his erection through their clothes, his hands tightening their grip on her arms. She let the dress fall, first to her waist, then, after a brief struggle, to her feet where she kicked it away. Completely naked now, her hands groping behind her, grasping his penis, grappling with the buttons of his flies. He tried to turn her to face him, but she resisted with a harsh '*no, this way,*' and pulled him with her to behind a nearby low sofa and bent over its back. He stood for some moments in unbelieving rapture, gazing down on her body, his hands moving to her hips, holding her there, letting his penis — firmer and more extended than he had ever known it — lightly brush her buttocks, her thighs; savouring the moment, willing it never to end. Until she called to him, her voice hoarse and urgent, 'Come inside me, Stephen. Put your finger in my bum and come inside me.'

Mesmerised, he obeyed, her hand guiding him into her, her body rising to receive him.

Afterwards, they embraced and kissed and did the loving things fantasised by Stephen in the desperate longings of his adolescence; bafflingly aware of having exceeded even the most wanton of those imaginings, surmounted an impregnable barrier, entered unwittingly into an altogether other state of existence. Or so it seemed. He couldn't quite believe it. Images of those distant, first glimpses of Natasha, the unattainable goddess of his dreams, flitting through his mind as he held her naked in his arms. Elation and triumph deflected to a holding zone all thoughts of Piers that could be vying to get through. Brought back to earth then by Natasha, partially disengaging herself to unbutton his shirt, which along with his socks, had managed to evade the frantic disrobing of the previous era.

When these had joined the tangled heap on the floor, he felt sufficiently clear-headed to come out with the banal observation that they were on course for missing their appointment at the Royal Court.

'Fuck the Royal Court,' was Natasha's whispered reply in his ear, the lobe of which she was holding between her teeth and then bit.

'Ouch!' said Stephen, rubbing the wound. Then, feeling it was about time he simulated some sort of control of the situation, he took her arm and guided her through the open doorway to the bedroom.

It was on the verge of sleep, an hour or so later, that Stephen was driven wide awake by the unmistakable sound of the front door being opened and then gently closed. From beside him came a poignant gasp and a whispered 'my God,' as footsteps sounded in the hallway and light from the living room beamed from under the bedroom door. He started to rise, aware of his vulnerable nakedness, of Natasha's restraining hand gripping his arm, of their scattered clothes way out of reach, but in full view of Piers — it had to be Piers — silently taking in the betrayal. The lingering silence was broken after an age by Piers's voice, unaccountably calm and restrained, 'Well, you certainly didn't waste much time.' Then his retreating footsteps and the opening and closing again of the front door.

All feelings of triumph and elation swept away in a consuming wave of guilt and self-loathing. What had possessed him to behave in that way, to destroy what had become perhaps the closest friendship of his life? And following so soon from those intimate disclosures, that free bestowal of trust. Natasha's hand was still gripping his arm, her eyes tightly closed, features frozen in a tragic mask. As he pulled free, she rolled over onto her stomach, smothering sobs in the pillow, perhaps soliciting some gesture of support he felt unable or unwilling to provide. Instead, just leaving her there, gathering up his clothes and making for the bathroom, his head in a confused whirl of shame and remorse. Some clarity returning as he showered, frantically seeking impossible answers, paltry justifications. How had it happened so suddenly, so out of the blue? Nothing had been planned — at least not by him. His attention then turned to Natasha. She had been completely naked under that dress... hardly preparation for a chaste evening at the theatre. And then her unhesitating response to his touch. Yes, he had touched her, but could hardly have done otherwise given the set-up. And her ambiguous behaviour on his arrival, refusing what would have amounted to their usual affectionate greeting as though somehow inappropriate in the light of her grief at Piers's departure; then, moments later, using that grief as reason for burying herself in his arms, igniting the slow-fuse. He was coming to see himself the victim of a carefully thought-out strategy of seduction into which he had unwittingly been drawn — a convenient view, seen through almost immediately as pathetic evasion of clear culpability; in no way had he resisted the approach, indeed had seized the opportunity. And although never before having made any sort of direct pass at Natasha, muted intimations would have made her aware of his desire for her, as well he knew. They were in this together, his shame only compounded by craven attempts to shift the blame.

She was in the living room when he returned there, in a crumpled dressing gown that was somehow matching her face, the creases around her eyes, her hair lank and unkempt; looking her age, quite different from how he had ever seen or imagined her. The initial revulsion reverting after a moment to guilt-ridden tenderness.

'What are we going to do?' he asked, pathetically.

She had been watching him through half-closed eyes, taking in his reaction.

'You'd better go, Stephen.'

It was what he wanted, easier now at her request. He took a step towards her, feeling the need to soften the separation, but she shook her head impatiently.

'Just go.'

It was raining heavily when he stepped outside, something which, after a moment's hesitation, he welcomed, as though the water could flush away his guilt. For a while it seemed it could, his mind emerging from a crippling numbness to grasp at a practical course of action, a means of escape: that offer he had turned down, to Emel's barely concealed irritation, perhaps it was not too late to change his mind. California was a long way from London — hardly the major feature of what had been proposed but, for the moment, the one presenting the most powerful attraction.

Rain falling in buckets now as, in sodden clothes, he waded on through deserted streets; shoes filling with water, water streaming over his hair and down his neck. Lost in the enormity of it all, of the explosive climax to another phase of life drawing irrevocably to a close.

INTERMISSION

Franklin Polytechnic
1963 – 1964

TWENTY

Things moved fast after Stephen had told Emel of his change of mind. Fortunately, nothing had been done to revoke the agreement for his secondment at Franklin, the offer still open and, with little difficulty, brought forward a couple of months to satisfy his desire to get away from London as soon as possible. If Emel was surprised at these changes, he showed no sign of it, simply confirming the arrangements and wishing him well. And turn out well it did, in many respects, not least in terms of his mathematical development in a department brimming with inspired expertise, into which he had found himself welcomed and soon absorbed; and also emotionally, for a start by helping put behind him the squalid event that had pushed him into being there.

Karl had been on hand to greet him on his arrival at Franklin. Before dashing off on one or other of his countless assignments, he had taken the time to introduce him to congenial colleagues. One of these, with whom Stephen hit it off from the start, was Percy Mattingly, an associate professor from the English department. He turned out to be an ardent anglophile, delighted at meeting someone from London — which he knew quite well and was forever talking of returning to. At their first meeting, he suggested Stephen join him for a beer that evening in a hotel bar close to the campus. This went well and was soon to become a regular occurrence, Percy's wife Patsy sometimes joining them for a while. She was quite a bit younger than Percy, very attractive and clearly devoted to him. It emerged that she had been a student on a graduate course he ran — still did — on creative writing. This seemed a strange concept to Stephen at the time, how on earth, he wondered, could you teach that? How it functioned would in time be explained to him by students on the course — clearly a popular one and quite different from anything Stephen could imagine being in place back home. This was to be his first acquaintance with what he took to be cultural differences in the British and North American universities. Others were to follow. He found himself gradually forming the view that, with few exceptions, they managed things rather better there, something he felt the British could well take note of.

When later he would think back to his time at Franklin, it would more often than not be to episodes directly or indirectly associated with Percy Mattingly. Much of Percy's and Patsy's social life appeared to revolve around the creative writing course, and quite soon after his arrival Stephen was invited to a gathering at their home attended by fifteen or so of his students — perhaps the whole contingent. They were a mixed bunch, over half of them female, mostly about his age, two or three rather older. One of the older guys — cool looking and rugged, seemingly in his mid-to-late thirties — gave the impression of having got around a fair bit and of knowing how to take care of himself. He was clearly something of a star, deferred to by most of the others and targeted relentlessly by the most striking girl there — the one Stephen was having difficulty taking his eyes off. Lawton was her name, though whether a first name or surname he couldn't say. Even if a first name, it would have been impossible to tell without knowing in advance whether of a man or a woman, but this was a problem he was finding himself coming up against quite often in the United States. His name — the cool one — was Branson, to which the above remarks could also apply. It was a relaxed and friendly setting, snacks and crates of beer on hand to which guests helped themselves and wandered about eating and drinking out of bottles. Stephen, feeling inhibited at first, was quickly put at ease, soon mixing freely, becoming the object of some interest. Groups formed and intermingled, eventually settling into a large, approximate circle with some, including Stephen, on chairs, others sitting or squatting on the floor. Someone had rolled a huge joint which was passed round, and Stephen relaxed happily in the laid-back togetherness. After a while, he became aware of a girl sitting opposite him and fixing him with a direct gaze. He smiled at her and she looked away. Then, without his having realised how it happened, she was sitting on the floor in front of him, between his legs, eyes closed, an arm over his thigh. Percy, he noticed, was watching this development, smiling to himself. For some minutes he did nothing, just sat there, then he placed a hand very softly on the girl's head. She didn't respond in any way, so he left it there. It all seemed natural somehow, even when someone nearby spoke to him, asking about courses at Prince of Wales College, to which he responded as informatively as he could, for all the world as though nothing else was going on. Which, in a sense it wasn't. Then he became aware of some movement around him, whispered consultations, the circle starting to break up, people leaving the room, though not in a way that suggested they were leaving the party. Someone offered him something which he politely declined. It was to be Stephen's first experience of the drug scene, which he had heard about, knew existed in specialised circles in Britain, but here appeared the norm, the equivalent perhaps of a glass of brandy to round off a dinner party. The girl hadn't moved. His hand was still on her head. He started to caress it, gently, behind her ears, the back of her neck, feeling all the while he should be doing something more, saying something, but not wishing to disrupt the languorous state into which he had settled. He was feeling mildly aroused by then, though not in any way as though wanting to do anything about it. Just aware of the fact — as she must have been. But still no reaction. He stopped caressing her head, a little later removed his hand. They stayed like that for he had no idea how long, until the girl pulled away and stood up. Half turning, she muttered something indistinct, which he took to mean she was leaving.

'I expect I'll see you around,' he said, or something to that effect.

'Guess so,' she replied and left.

The next day, over a beer in the hotel bar, Percy remarked that he appeared to have been hitting it off well at the party with Kate Guthrie.

'Is that her name? Is that what it looked like? Well, to me it seemed pretty weird. She just came over and sat there. Didn't say a word. I've no idea what it was all about.'

'She's a deep one, Kate,' Percy replied with a laugh, 'as well as being a bit strange. But very talented as it happens. One of the best on the course, probably *the* best. Doesn't say much but her work is quite exceptional. I think she's going to go far.'

'Really!'

Stephen couldn't work out how he felt about this,

eventually deciding to put the episode behind him, to forget it. It appeared unlikely — without any effort on his part, which he didn't feel inclined to make — that their paths would cross again. But eventually they did, providing a further bizarre recollection of his time at Franklin to take back with him to London.

It was a few weeks later that Stephen sighted Kate Guthrie on the Franklin campus. He had just emerged from the block containing the science faculty office, heading back to the maths department, as she was approaching in the opposite direction with a sizeable group of what looked to be fellow students. Pretending not to have noticed her, he was negotiating his way through the group when he heard his name called.

'Hi Stephen, how you doing?'

He turned, badly simulating surprise, to find her smiling at him, giving the impression of being pleased to see him. It was the first time he had seen her smile. Quite an improvement, he thought.

'I wanted to see you,' she said, 'but didn't know how to get in touch.'

The group had moved on by then, leaving them alone on the sidewalk.

'Some of the guys you met at Percy's are meeting up Friday evening at Lawton's place. I thought you might like to come along.'

He would probably have liked to whatever, the fact of it being at Lawton's place something extra, an irresistible inducement.

'Look, I can't stay,' she said. 'I've a class starting in five minutes.'

She gave hurried directions for meeting her outside Karlswells — a popular eating place just off campus — and hurried off. He continued on his way, aroused at the prospect of meeting Lawton again, though recognising the impossibility of any progress in that direction; at the same time aware of distinct possibilities with Kate, her welcoming demeanour reawakening something dimly felt before, overriding subsequent misgivings.

He arrived on time at Karlswells, she half an hour or so later. It had felt awkward standing there clutching a six-pack, a lone figure subjected to curious glances from people hurrying by. Not the perfect start to whatever he had been thinking the evening could throw up, and not helped by Kate's sombre arrival: no smiles this time, no apologies for being late, back to the mute bloodless encounter at Percy's some weeks before. Things improved somewhat on arrival at Lawton's place where the party, or whatever it was supposed to be, was underway; Lawton greeting him as though overjoyed, unable to believe her good fortune that they should be meeting again — though all the while keeping a watchful eye on Branson, lording it over a bevy of admirers across the room. Stephen's appreciation of this reception blunted though by a recent experience that had left a deep impression.

It had been a week or so earlier, on a visit to a supermarket to stock up on things for his room. The checkout girl was very pretty — something he had been pleasantly aware of while queuing to pay. She had looked up when it got to his turn, her face on seeing him bursting into a display of pure delight, '*Well, hi there. How you doing?*' He hadn't recognised her, he thought, guiltily. Must have been one of the girls at Percy's party, or maybe someone he'd rubbed shoulders with at a seminar or some other Franklin event; perhaps she looked different in this setting, working to pay her way through college. She turned away from gazing at him adoringly to check in his items, take his cash; then, another radiant smile and out it came, *'Thank you for shopping at Optibuy.'*

The trouble with that sort of thing, it seemed to Stephen, though for sure an improvement on the surly service habitually handed out back home, was that it put in doubt the genuineness of all effusive greeting, like that of Lawton's just now, which was something he very much wanted to believe in – and so decided that he would, and the hell with it.

'Have you met Madison?' Lawton asked him.

'No.' He hadn't. And so, turning to a big guy standing broodingly beside her, he said, 'Hi, I'm Stephen.'

'Grayson, Matt Grayson,' he replied as they shook hands. Then, somewhat suspiciously, 'You a friend of Lawton's?'

'Well, eh...'

The guy clearly wasn't Madison. This was getting confusing. At which point Lawton broke in to introduce a girl who had materialised beside her. This it turned out was indeed Madison, who lost no time telling him that she'd heard all about him, had been dying to meet him, and just loved his accent — all of which he made a point of accepting at face value. Why not? The memory of that first meeting long ago with Suzie intruded momentarily: that feeling of having no control over pleasurable events perhaps set to unfold. Madison was really something. Almost on a par with Lawton. Scantily clad over a curvy bronzed body, most of it showing: bare feet, a skimpy, loose T-shirt that stopped well above minute shorts, nothing else, nothing else at all. While taking this in, he learned that she shared the flat with Lawton, who was her closest friend, but not a lot more because Kate, assuming proprietary rights, was suddenly there at his side to shepherd him away.

'There's someone I want you to meet,' she said.

She was being quite friendly now. Not exactly smiling but maintaining a faintly amused expression as she set about questioned him on what he was doing at Franklin, how he felt about life here, how different was it from England. Then came the introduction to Branson, who had been involved with a small group close by and had come over to join them. Surprisingly, Stephen found himself taking to him straight away, not at all what he had expected. His background was unusual. It turned out that he had graduated in chemical engineering a good few years back, then worked for a large chemical company producing a range of environmental poisons for as long as he could stand it, — 'about a year I guess' — before dropping out and travelling: some years in South America, then for a while in South East Asia, living rough most of the time, the occasional odd job providing the few bucks necessary for survival. He had written some pieces related to his travels, some submitted for publication, a couple appearing in magazines. Percy had seen something of this and encouraged him to enrol on his course, going on to fix for him to do so at little or no cost — a covert arrangement which Stephen could just see Percy enjoying setting up. Branson then went on to question Stephen on his research, surprising him by a show of knowledge of mathematical subjects far removed from those of obvious interest to an applied scientist. They chatted away happily together, observed all the while by Kate, at Stephen's side, saying nothing but giving the appearance of taking it all in.

It was getting late and quite dark outside, people drifting away. Then someone suggested a move to the pool, to Lawton's loud cry of approval. Kate asked Stephen if he wanted to swim, to which he replied, stupidly, that he didn't have his swim trunks, at which she laughed, telling him he didn't need them. The pool was a facility of the condominium in which Lawton and Madison rented their apartment. It was open-air, surrounded by a grassy bank and a wall, from which lamps provided subdued illumination. On reaching it, they found Lawton in the final stages of stripping off, then cavorting naked at the pool's edge, exhorting others to follow.

'Aren't you going to take your clothes off?' asked Kate, as she squatted on the grass.

Others were following Lawton's example, including Madison, for whom the procedure was pretty well over before she had started.

'Yes, I suppose so. What about you?'

'No, I'm not. I'll just sit here and watch.'

'Then I won't either.'

'Yes, you will.' She was looking up at him standing beside her, her expression deadly serious. 'I can't, but I want you to.' That feeling again, of being taken over, relinquishing control.

He left his clothes in a heap and went over to the pool. Branson was in the water swimming strongly, others splashing about. He jumped in and swam sedately for a while, then stood in the shallow watching Branson talking to Madison at the pool edge, Lawton pulling herself noisily out of the water. Feeling more relaxed now, initial awkwardness all but passed, he swam again, underwater this time. As he surfaced, he heard someone proposing 'horse wrestling', Lawton excitedly agreeing. She approached Branson, but he had already teamed up with Madison.

'Stephen is over there,' he told her. 'Go and grab him.'

Horse wrestling, Stephen was to learn, involved a girl sitting on a man's shoulders in the water and 'wrestling' with another horse-and-rider couple until one or the other falls over. Lawton came splashing up to him, her naked body wet and golden, her face gleaming.

'I want to ride you, Stephen. Can I?'

He had to be dreaming, no way could this be for real. She took hold of his hand and led him into deeper water where he helped her clamber onto his shoulders. Then stood in bewilderment, his torso squeezed between her calves, her pubes pressing softly on the back of his neck.

'Right, let's get them,' she said.

At which, Stephen realised that for her the intimacy of their bodily contact was quite incidental: it was the contest that was driving her, the challenge ahead. Which was a pity because it was quite clear to him that they didn't stand a chance. And indeed, they fell at the first encounter, to Madison's exuberant cry of joy. He helped Lawton mount again — perhaps the most rewarding feature of the performance — then back to the fray, Branson being careful this time to go easy, not to take advantage of his superior strength. So much so that when Stephen felt himself falling again, with Lawton hanging onto Madison, he was pretty sure that Branson let Madison go, so that the three of them — Stephen, Lawton and Madison — fell together in a sublime entanglement of flesh and the round was declared a draw. They fared slightly better after that, not winning any rounds but staying upright for a bit longer each time, eventually agreeing to call it a day. When he got back to Kate, he found she had procured a towel for him, for which he thanked her.

'You weren't much good, were you? she said, derisively.

'Oh, I don't know. I thought it went rather well. It's not just about winning, you know. The game's the thing.' Which he felt to be rather good at the time, but got no reaction.

Miserable cow, he thought. But what exactly is she playing at? Then something Percy had alluded to came back to him, something that could perhaps explain what she was up to: that she was gathering material for an epoch-making first novel. That had to be it. A sure bestseller, in which he was set to appear in a small but highly visible role: an English twit, easily recognisable as himself to anyone who knew him. For a while, that thought would keep turning up to bother him.

A pool, similar in appearance to that of the horse wrestling antics of some months before, was to be the setting for another of Stephen's recurring memories of Franklin, his role this time being simply that of an observer. And although nothing of any consequence was to take place there, he would in time come to realise that the tranquil scene he witnessed provided a prophetic foretaste of previously unthinkable developments in the evolving mores of Western society.

Percy had access to the pool, which was close to his home. He had offered to take Stephen there on a number of occasions, and one sweltering afternoon they set off for it together — Patsy due to join them as soon as she could get away from whatever it was that was occupying her at the time. If not exactly crowded, there were nevertheless many more people there than Stephen would have expected for a weekday afternoon. They changed in cubicles — Stephen having his swim trunks with him this time — and made their way to a vacant patch of grass. It seemed to Stephen that there was an air of something odd about the place, though he was unable, at first, to figure out what this was. Then it came to him: there were no women present — in itself nothing remarkable, except that the men were for the most part distributed around the grass in pairs, their demeanour, as they conversed and preened themselves and each other with lotions, coming over strange to him and a little disturbing. He conveyed something of this to Percy, who brushed it aside with a chuckle, — 'Yes, it's becoming a popular haunt of the gay community' — then carried on with whatever it was he had been talking about before. Stephen, for his part, was feeling far from comfortable: an intruder in an alien society, the extent of which, even its very existence, he had been hardly aware of up to that moment. The openness of it particularly surprising, especially coming from Britain where all male homosexual behaviour was still strictly illegal and, if reported, more likely than not to result in criminal prosecution. And that word *gay*! At the time, just emerging as a term for homosexual, still a poor contender with its established usage for carefree, joyful. After sunbathing for a while, Stephen left Percy to go for a swim, on the way glancing discreetly at the assembled bodies stretched out in the sun. They all looked remarkably fit and well-groomed, most of them of about his age, with the occasional somewhat older man and younger partner — to all appearances like himself and Percy, he realised with mounting embarrassment. He swam, remaining in the pool longer than he had intended, reluctant to leave it, until he spied Patsy wending her way between the bronze bodies to Percy's side. Relieved, he joined them; her presence helping him adjust to his surroundings, come to terms with a previously hidden sexual phenomenon set to emerge from the shadows and demand acceptance from the world at large.

But it was the arrival of a letter, getting on for a year into his first appointment at Franklin Polytechnic, close to the time for his return to London to defend his doctoral thesis, that for Stephen was to be the far and away most memorable event of that period of his life. It was from Suzie, her second letter to him, some two years after the first. She and Desmond had separated, it now transpired, divorce terms amicably agreed, the marriage accepted by both as a mistake almost from the start. Or so she maintained, giving Stephen little cause or desire to doubt her word. And removing in a trice the block which, from the day they had first come together, had been holding them apart.

PART 3

London
1978 – 1979

TWENTY-ONE

Newspaper reports of the discovery of the body of Piers Denney in Westminster Cathedral were to send Stephen's mind racing back some sixteen years: to his research studentship days in the mathematics department of Prince of Wales College, where he was now a lecturer, and to the guilt-ridden termination of his relationship with Piers and Natasha. So much had changed for him since that time, but the memory of that betrayal forever hovered, liable at any moment to descend and dispirit him. He wanted to speak about it to Suzie — away on tour somewhere in the north of England and not due to call him until late that evening. Not knowing what to do next, how to fill in the time, he made a series of phone calls, eventually being directed to the police — whose reaction to his enquiry led him to surmise that Piers could well have been murdered.

Suzie phoned a little after eleven-thirty in high spirits, soon to be deflated. He had given her an edited account of the Natasha debacle years before, after his return to London from Franklin. She had been sympathetic, not at all critical, in a way thankful for him having experienced something of a failed relationship to set alongside hers with Desmond. Now she was appalled and upset by his news, knowing how it must be affecting him. And though by that time he had got over the initial shock, it was a relief to talk it over with Suzie, to let her steer him into putting it into some sort of rational perspective.

'It was ages ago, that business of you and Natasha. This has absolutely nothing to do with it. Obviously, you're upset, but there's nothing you can do, nothing you need feel you should get involved in.' Sentiments which before long were to be overtaken by events.

'Have you spoken to Stan yet?' she had asked at one point, a tinge of coldness in her tone: relations with Stan being strained since his desertion of Rebecca, with whom she was still close.

'No, I haven't. I suppose I should get in touch with him. It's months since I last saw him. He's not going to believe this.'

That he felt better after having spoken to Suzie was something he had expected, relied upon. And thinking about her after hanging up had him feeling better still. It was now over ten years that they had been together, their fifth wedding anniversary just a few days away, the limbo that followed that unforgettable first encounter in an Edgware Road pub consigned to the distant past. Though thoughts of Suzie had continually invaded his mind during that period, he had put this down to wishful thinking, something he could dwell upon without expecting anything to come of it; he still had difficulty at times believing that something eventually had.

A week or so after learning of Piers's death, Stephen's phone rang late in the evening. Though a little earlier than expected, he thought it must be Suzie having somehow managed to call from the theatre straight after the final curtain. But the woman's voice that replied to his greeting wasn't Suzie's — though instantly recognisable nonetheless, regardless of the anxiety blurring her speech and the passage of some fifteen years since he had last heard it.

'It's Natasha, Stephen. I was given your phone number. I'm sorry, but I just have to speak to you. I'm desperate and there's no one else I can turn to.'

Stephen was lost, unable to think, rocked by a spasm of guilt at the memory of that last encounter with Natasha — echoing that of the previous week on learning of Piers's death. And alongside that, a recollection of long-buried adolescent fantasies brought on by the sound of her voice, and curiosity at her desperation to talk to him about what had to be Piers. He replied after some moments of uneasy silence.

'God, Natasha, I don't know what to say. I can't believe I'm speaking to you. It was terrible hearing about Piers... terrible... I can only imagine how it was for you. It brought it all back... what happened that time. It's never left me, the way things finished up. And now this. I'm so sorry, Natasha.'

'I know, Stephen. We both felt that way too. But this is something else. Look, I can't talk on the phone. Can you come here?'

'Yes, of course. Where are you?'

She gave directions to a house in Camden Town, telling him not to speak to anyone, anyone at all. He agreed to call the following morning.

So, she was still in London. On his final return from Franklin, he had checked out her old Percy Street address, cautiously, fearful at the thought of her seeing him — only to find the windows boarded up and an estate agent's sold notice on the wall. It was the only time he had made any attempt to trace her whereabouts, a mixture of relief and disappointment — predominantly relief — following the discovery that she had moved irrevocably out of his life.

Suzie phoned later that evening as expected. He found it difficult keeping up with their usual exchanges without mentioning Natasha's call, persuading himself that this had just to do with her demand for secrecy, that he would confide all after the meeting the following morning, but feeling guilty nonetheless for reasons surely related to that initial reaction on hearing Natasha's voice.

The house to which she had directed him turned out to be in a row of small terraced cottages a few minutes from Camden Town tube station. The doorbell bore the name Natasha Denney, which surprised him. So they had got married, it seemed; until yesterday, he hadn't even known whether they had got together again after that disastrous evening.

He rang. There followed a long delay, leading him to wonder whether she had had second thoughts about seeing him. But just as he was about to ring again, the door opened.

It took a moment or two for him to recognise the dishevelled middle-aged woman standing before him, her lined features further distorted by anxiety, or perhaps fear. She appeared not to recognise him at first, relaxing somewhat when she had, a veiled trace of the Natasha he had known just about showing through as she greeted him.

'Oh, Stephen, it's good to see you. I'm sorry, but with what happened last night… I'd almost forgotten you were coming. It's chaos here, but come in.'

He followed her into the hallway, where a desk lay on its side, its contents — papers, folders, books, other miscellaneous objects — scattered over the floor. Through the open doorway to a living room, he could see chairs and a sofa overturned.

'It all happened last night after we had spoken. I went out

and this is what I found when I got back. I called the police. They came and told me to leave everything as it is, till the forensic people have finished with it. They should be round later today. Oh God, I've no idea what to do, where this is going to end.'

She was looking disturbed again, prompting Stephen to come up with something, anything to break the silence.

'Did they get anything of value, do you know?' he asked, feeling it a stupid question.

'They weren't looking for valuables. It's Piers's journals they were after. He told me to keep them somewhere safe. They were here until a couple of weeks ago. Then I thought it best to move them, thank God. They're well out of the way now.'

He needed time to take this in, what it implied. In the meantime, he spoke to fill space, improvising with no idea of what was involved.

'Strange they didn't take anything though. Could have made it seem like an ordinary robbery.'

He was aware as he was saying this of being drawn in; intrigued, and at the same time fearful of where it could be leading.

'They're not interested in covering up what they're doing,' she said. 'Quite the contrary.'

It seemed a dream. That he was floundering in an alien world. Then he saw she was on the verge of losing control, trembling, face screwing up, eyes filling with tears. He went dutifully to her, pulling her towards him, pressing her head to his shoulder, holding her there. The memory of the last time he had done this came back, what it had led to then, the emotional turmoil that had scarred his life. And though there was no question this time of any such thing reoccurring, he felt guilty nonetheless; guilty too for not having told Suzie of Natasha's call the previous evening, making it seem he was up to something there, revisiting the scene she would probably have correctly surmised to have been the culmination of the overriding erotic fantasy of his adolescence. Ridiculous as this now was, he saw only too clearly how it could appear. His mind then turned to Piers, thoughts of whom had continued to haunt him since learning of his death: to what had become of his relationship with Natasha, of his dealings with the Vatican and researches into the origins of Christianity; most of all, of course, the manner and circumstances of his death. Natasha was clearly in a position to provide answers, as well as indications for those matters for which she lacked complete knowledge. He felt himself wanting these, a growing desire to understand just what it was that Piers had been devoting his life to.

When he felt her tremors subsiding, he pushed her gently from him and led her to the dining area, which had withstood the worst of the upheaval. They sat there at the table, regarding one another in silence that was eventually broken by Natasha.

'I felt bad calling you, bad about everything. But I needed to talk to someone, someone who knew Piers, who could make some sense of what he was about. There didn't seem to be anyone I could turn to. Then I got passed your phone number. It seemed a miracle. I couldn't believe it.'

She went on to tell him that she and Piers had often spoken of him, had wanted to get in touch, but with him being out of the country… and then with one thing and another… they had never got around to it; and that she had told Piers that what happened between them had been unplanned, spontaneous and on her initiative: a sudden consequence of her desperation at his departure for Rome. He had been understanding, she said, and wanted to draw a line under the whole sorry episode.

'When was that?' he asked, uncertain of how much of it to believe, Piers's departure that night having a finality about it, certainly so far as he was concerned.

'When he arrived in Rome. He phoned after what had been a miserable journey — as you can imagine. But we already had a long history of impossible situations to come to terms with. We'd been there before. Believe me. Nothing was going to do us any lasting damage. We were both quite sure of that.'

It came home to Stephen how little he knew them; the picture he had put together over those few months, when he would call at Percy Street, just a snapshot it seemed, an untypical fragment of their life together into which he had intruded. How on earth, he wondered, had it progressed after his guilt-ridden departure?

'It all seemed to be going so well for him there, all they had been working away at for years coming together at last. I'd never seen him so buoyed up. Then, out of the blue and right under his nose, the whole thing blew apart.'

It was what he had been waiting for; without the need for any prompting, she was talking about Piers's involvement with the Vatican. He felt his excitement rising, together with the need to keep it in check.

'I'm sorry, but I'm not with you. What was it that happened to ruin things for them?'

'They killed him, that's what happened.'

This didn't make sense to him. It was before Piers's death that they were talking about. Wasn't it? He'd lost track somehow. She was looking at him with incredulity, then anger at his bemused expression.

'The Pope. The bloody Pope. You must have read about it, it was only a couple of months ago, the papers were full of it. Just a month after they'd moved heaven and earth to get him elected, the bastards murdered him.'

Of course, he had read about the newly-elected Pope's sudden death. It hadn't meant much to him at the time, except perhaps by way of uncharitable amusement at the thought of the convoluted ritual for the election having to be repeated — those geriatric cardinals from around the world, barely recovered and settled back into their cosy routines, having to head back to Rome to go through the whole tedious performance yet again. But no connection with Piers had crossed his mind at the time, which he wondered at now. And yes, there had been talk of something suspicious about the Pope's death — which, along with most others, he had simply dismissed as the predictable reaction of conspiracy theorists.

Natasha was staring at him wide-eyed, looking quite demented again. Though it appeared unwise, he felt compelled to push on.

'And Piers?' he asked, quietly, worried how she would respond.

With relief, he saw her pulling herself together, her features relaxing.

'They killed him too,' she said. 'The police are pathetic. They've quite made up their minds it was suicide.'

'Is that what they told you?'

'It's obvious from the questions they ask, their attitude in general. It's the easy option so far as they're concerned. They're so condescending when I try to tell them that Piers was the last person in the world who would consider suicide.'

'There must have been an autopsy?'

'Yes, there was. Some injury to his face and head, as though he'd been in a fight. Nothing serious though, certainly not the cause of death. But then they found he'd been poisoned. Massively. Enough to kill him several times over.'

'Did they say with what?'

Stephen didn't know quite why he asked this. He couldn't have expected the answer, if she had one, to have meant much to him. When it came however — phenobarbitone, a well tried suicide drug as even he was aware — he found himself coming to appreciate what she dismissively regarded as the view of the police. And later, after he had had time to digest the rest of what she went on to tell him, to conclude that, on the face of it, suicide appeared by far the more likely possibility. True, along with Natasha, he found it difficult to accept that the Piers he had once known would resort to suicide — and draw attention to it with the bizarre cathedral setting. But her conviction that both he and the Pope had been murdered by order, or at least with the connivance, of the church hierarchy appeared to him beyond the bounds of belief. For whatever evil design he might be prepared to attribute to that lot, collectively or as individuals, he drew a line at the murder of the Pope. And regarding the suicide option... well a lot can change in fifteen years. But still...

As he was mulling this over, considering what to say next, conscious of Natasha eyeing him in exasperation, her composure of a few moments before quite obliterated, they were interrupted by a loud hammering on the door. It was the police: a uniformed officer and two men in plain clothes come to check out the break-in. They looked suspiciously at

Stephen, who introduced himself embarrassingly as a friend who had called to see if there was anything he could do to help.

'I'd better be going,' he said, feeling awkward and unwelcome and in the way. And so, with a nod to the officer, and a promise to Natasha to phone later, he made his way back to the tube.

He had much to think about on the journey home. In the first place, Natasha. Though he had expected changes, nothing had prepared him for the extent of her ageing and general deterioration, which he had at first tried to put down to grief at Piers's death. But then it seemed to him that, underneath it all, she wasn't mourning for Piers at all; that her obvious distress and erratic changes of mood were the result of something else — though he couldn't for the life of him imagine what this could be, nor even make out what it was that made him feel this to be so. Perhaps, he now wondered, it could be to do with her assertion that Piers had been murdered — something he hadn't responded to, his implied scepticism perhaps fuelling her anger. But now, reviewing his earlier impression, suicide was starting to appear no less improbable. It was a mystery all right, the cathedral setting posing confusion to whatever line of speculation he could turn his mind to. When the police arrived, she had tried to cover her anger, though clearly holding on to it; making him feel she regretted having solicited his support in the first place, that she couldn't wait for him to leave. Which, in a way, was all right by him. Though in other ways not all right at all.

He tried to phone Natasha that afternoon, getting no reply, which was something of a relief, other matters looming large. Like Suzie, their wedding anniversary the following week, which they still hadn't got round to working out how to celebrate. Then, on an impulse, he phoned Stan, not really expecting to get through to him. It had been some time since they had last been in touch, and it came to him as he dialled that Stan would be almost certainly unaware of Piers's death. To his surprise, the phone was answered promptly, though by someone with a strong, what sounded to be, East European accent.

'Abracadabra Enterprises. How can we help you?'

He was about to apologise for having misdialled, when something clicked.

'You'll have to do better than that, Stan. I could tell it's you a mile off.'

'Stephen, you bastard! Good to hear you. It's been a while.'

'I know, I'm sorry. I should have called before. Some things I need to tell you about. I thought perhaps we could arrange to meet up sometime.'

'As a matter of fact, I'm going to be in London next week. Tuesday to Thursday. Quite a lot on… though I could probably stretch it to Friday… Yes, how about the Thursday then? I could stay in London that night and go back the next morning. We could meet in some pub early on, perhaps around six or so. Then go and eat somewhere later. Give us time to talk.'

'Sounds fine to me. Good.'

'But what are these things you want to tell me? You've got me intrigued. Though, as it happens, I've got some news too. Something that will amuse you. But go on. You first.'

So, Stephen told him about Piers — or Brother Carroll, or just Carroll, as they would always refer to him. Stan had read the strange tale of the discovery of a body in Westminster

Cathedral and was now thoroughly taken aback to learn that it was Carroll, making Stephen feel guilty for not having made the effort to get through to him before.

'God, that's terrible. And weird. Have you any idea how it happened?'

'Not really. But we can talk about it when we meet. I may know more by then.'

'You know, when I read of it, even without knowing who it was, it reminded me of that time at school. When I had to do that sickness act to get us out of that mind-numbing performance there. Remember that?'

'How could I ever forget it?'

'I had to act something similar in an episode of Broadlands. Did you see it?'

'No. I must have missed that one.'

'Pity, because I played it as near as damn it to how we did it then. Had it in my mind all the time. Really took me back. People kept going on afterwards how convincing it was.'

'Well, it didn't seem to convince Ignatius, from what I remember. Nor Carroll come to that.'

'Oh, come off it,' Stan replied with a laugh.

After which they talked briefly of other things, including Suzie's success in continuing to land good stage parts, which Stan admitted to feeling envious of — ridiculously so in view of his lavish earnings and celebrity status in television soap, but reflecting his growing regret at being unavailable for — and to some extent excluded from — more aesthetically satisfying roles. Then something happened at Stan's end which meant that he had to hang up — so having to put off imparting his amusing news until their pub date the following week.

Hardly had Stephen replaced the receiver, when the phone

rang again. It was Suzie, complaining bitterly that she had been trying to get through to him for the last half hour, and going quiet for a moment when told he had been on the line to Stan. She couldn't talk as she was due on stage in ten minutes, except to tell him she had managed to get a couple of days off the following week, so they could celebrate their anniversary in London. This was good news to Stephen, who felt the occasion warranted something better than his traipsing up to Wigan, or wherever it was, for what would probably turn out to be a God-awful meal somewhere after the show. Now they could visit their favourite haunts, spend two whole days alone together doing what they liked best. After hanging up, he realised with a pang of unease that he still hadn't got round to telling her of his dealings with Natasha, her call last night, their meeting that morning. Perhaps, he thought, the whole thing would just fizzle out, that he would hear no more about it. But no, that wasn't how it was going to be, nor how he wanted it. That business with Piers, which he had run away from all those years ago, was never going to stop pursuing him. Natasha didn't enter into it, not any more. And he had stopped running now. All he had to do was sit back and wait for events to catch up with him.

In the meantime, Stephen had other things to turn his mind to. Among them, some analysis he had carried out some years before and published in a mathematics journal. It was an esoteric piece, seemingly of little interest to anyone outside his specialised field. But much to his surprise, he had just learned that it had been picked up on as having relevance in the search for a solution to a problem in number theory that had been baffling mathematicians for centuries. It was Karl who, quite by chance, had discovered this during private discussions he had witnessed following a mathematics seminar at Princeton. How and why, he had got in on this was anyone's guess — though, knowing Karl, of no great surprise. He had written straight away, telling Stephen that the fact of his having produced what appeared to be a breakthrough in the resolution of Fermat's last theorem — the most famous and unsolved mathematical puzzle of all time, *without his being aware of having done so,* had been a source of amusement to those taking part in the discussions — "some of whom are sure to be busily at it now, working out how to take the credit for it for themselves." He had then gone on to jot down notes on the gist of the *strictly secret* exchanges that had taken place, and to say that he would shortly be back in London with perhaps more on the matter which they could discuss then.

Stephen found this news upsetting at first, bringing to mind Emel, who, had he still been around, would have certainly been conversant with his work and most probably able to advise on such wider implications. But Emel had died shortly after his return from Franklin to Prince of Wales College and the lectureship he had been instrumental in setting up for him there — a tragedy that had shaken him badly, casting a cloud over that homecoming.

He was also unhappy at the thought of having to divert attention from the fruitful line he was pursuing at the time and direct it to an area he had vowed to avoid from the outset of his entry into mathematical research — the image of Sharif warning him off involvement in 'Emel's pet unifying conjectures' on his first day at college some eighteen years ago bringing a wry smile to his lips. Now it was looking to him as though this latest development was pushing him in that direction. But he realised, as Karl clearly had, that such a move — which he was able to persuade himself would be temporary — could have the effect of removing the block his career had run into. His problem was that, following Emel's death, number theory research in the mathematics department had gone into near-terminal decline, giving ground to areas perceived as being of more practical value to science and society in general. This hadn't bothered him over much. For though the absence of Emel was undoubtedly a blow, he was already sufficiently independent to be able to follow his own inclinations, present his work at international conferences and generally interact worldwide with specialists in his field. His progress, measured in terms of quality publications and general reputation within his area of research, was without doubt good. The trouble was its lack of visibility outside that small and largely insular academic community. This was the reason, he felt, for his having been stuck at lecturer grade while others with less to show by way of academic achievement had been promoted. It now appeared that there was something he could do about this.

Reluctantly, he gathered up the pile of loose sheets on which he had been happily working, appended brief notes on points to bear in mind when he came back to it — with a prayer that this wouldn't be long — and consigned it to a filing cabinet. He then read through his paper which had been the cause of amusement, quite enjoying doing so, but still clueless when he had finished as to what the fuss was about. He turned back to Karl's letter, his hastily scribbled notes at the end of it. On further reading, something fell into place. That elliptic equation he had been dealing with — a small variation of one in a class first considered some thirty years ago by Yuri

Alexandrovich — Natasha's half-brother! He could just about see how it could possibly be recast to relate to Fermat's last theorem. He would have to check it out, but from how it now looked to him, and from what Karl had told him of that meeting, he was as near as damn it sure that this was so. Not that it necessarily cleared the way to the long sought-after proof everyone was frantically seeking. But if it indeed turned out that the problem could be transformed into one on elliptic equations... that was certainly something. In fact, quite enough, so far as he was concerned. He transferred a wodge of plain paper from a drawer to the surface of his desk and sat staring at it, working out where to begin.

TWENTY-TWO

Suzie was due back again in London on Tuesday evening of the following week, Stephen to meet her at Euston station. He spent the best part of that afternoon going through the motions of tidying up the house, then taking pleasure in the preparation of a meal to celebrate her return home. On arrival at the station, he found her train had been delayed and had to hang around for nearly two hours until it arrived.

'God, it's good to be back,' were her first words as they embraced. 'You know, Stephen, I've had enough of living like this, away from you and everything. Time to pack it in.'

He thought at first that this had just to do with her tedious journey – the train, after a delayed start and then proceeding at snail's pace, having stopped repeatedly along the way for no apparent reason. But he was later to realise that there was more to it than that: that it was the decision he had long been waiting for her to come round to. He had never brought the subject up, however, knowing how much her acting career meant to her. And, along with the problems it caused, there was also something positive to be said for the way her work had impacted on their life together, giving it an edge which he wasn't at all sure he wouldn't miss were it to end. They needed to talk this over carefully, along with other things. But not just yet. Tonight, they would eat, drink a little, make lazy love and fall asleep in each other's arms. Thinking of this in the taxi ride home, with Suzie dozing, her head on his shoulder, it came to him once again how incredible it was, this thing they had together. Who could have believed it would have come out of that frivolously engineered one-nighter all those years ago?

She woke up shortly before they arrived home looking sleepily content. He had been wondering when and how to tell her of his meeting with Natasha, worried again at his delay in doing this. But it was Suzie who brought it up, her first words on waking in the taxi.

'You didn't mention it when we spoke on the phone… but have you found out anything more about Piers… about how he died?'

Oh well, he thought, that resolves that one.

'Yes, I have. Quite a lot. I was going to leave it till the morning. It's a long story.' She was fully awake now. The taxi was pulling up outside their house. 'Let's just get in and I'll tell you about it.'

He paid the fare and trundled the suitcase to their front door, Suzie holding on to his free arm.

'At long last,' she said as they stepped in from the cold. Then, taking in the table, the opened bottle of wine, 'Oh, Stephen, that looks marvellous. Pour me a glass then I'll go and tidy myself up. You can't believe how good it feels to be home.'

They embraced and kissed, hanging on to each other until she pulled away to head for the bathroom and he went to attend to things in the kitchen. It was not until they were seated at the table, food in front of them, glasses refilled, that he felt able to take the plunge.

'Natasha phoned. I couldn't believe it. Seems she and Piers had got married. The police had passed her the contact details I left with them. She was sounding pretty desperate. And frightened. Wouldn't say much on the phone, said she couldn't. But wanted to see me, said there was no one else she could turn to.'

'When was this?' Suzie asked.

'Wednesday evening. It was just after I'd spoken to you.'

This was untrue, of course. It was before he had spoken to her. But his actions sounded less evasive that way.

'And you saw her?'

'Yes, the following morning. At the address she gave me in Camden Town. It was all pretty weird. I didn't recognise her at first when she opened the door. My God, how she's changed.'

He started to describe what had taken place, first with Natasha's unstable behaviour and the raid on her house.

'Was anything stolen?' Suzie interjected at this point.

'No. She thought they were only looking for Piers's journals, which weren't there. She'd moved them to somewhere safe some time before.'

'And you believed all this?'

'Well, yes. It didn't occur to me not to. What are you getting at?'

'Only that tipping up chairs and desks and all that doesn't sound to me like searching for journals. Sounds more like some demented loony letting off steam.'

The idea of Natasha causing that upheaval herself had simply never occurred to him.

'Well, she called the police. In fact, they turned up while I was there. That's when I left. But look, let me tell you the rest of it. You could be right, but wait until you've heard the whole story. Or rather what little I know of it. It's all quite incredible.'

This wasn't going at all how Stephen had imagined. His concern at her suspecting his motives was quite dispelled now, replaced by the realisation that he wasn't alone in this any more, that someone else was involved who could help in working out what was going on.

'I'm sorry,' she said. 'I'll try not to butt in again.'

'No, please do. I'm kicking myself for not having considered that possibility. It's just that I've been so bottled up with all this since first reading about Piers's death. Then Natasha's call out of the blue and what she had to tell me the following day. Perhaps I should have tried to contact you that evening, but that's always difficult. And anyway, you were coming home, and it's easier like this than on the phone.'

When he started up again, with Piers's vision of a reformed Roman Catholic church gradually discarding the dogma, the implausibility struck him again, as it had when Piers first confided in him all those years ago at Percy Street; and harder this time, with Suzie there in front of him, trying her best to maintain a neutral expression. But when he got on to Natasha's belief that Piers — and the newly elected Pope! — had been murdered by order of Vatican insiders she could contain herself no longer.

'For God's sake, Stephen! She's just a deluded nutcase. How on earth can you even begin to take her seriously?'

He was feeling pretty dim now for not having thought to dismiss the allegation from the start. But still confused. The alternative, that of Piers committing suicide, still a problem for him.

'But… but what about Piers? His death in the cathedral? That's something you can't just put down to Natasha's ravings. I know the whole thing looks pretty crazy…'

'The cause of death must have been established by now. Do you know what it was?' she asked.

'Yes. He was poisoned. A massive dose of phenobarbitone. The police are convinced it was suicide.'

'Well, obviously,' she snapped. 'What on earth else could it be?'

The following evening, after a day in which all mention of the Piers affair had been carefully avoided, Stephen and Suzie set off for The Goose. He had booked a table for later at a nearby French restaurant as a fitting conclusion to their day together — not quite their wedding anniversary, Suzie having to be back at work for that, but close enough. Most of that morning they had spent in bed, among other things talking over plans for when Suzie's tour was due to finish in a few weeks' time. She told him she was adamant that this should mark the end of her long absences from home, and that she had turned down an offer for a good part in another touring company production. Though pleased to hear this, he found it somewhat surprising, until she came out with what had clearly been much on her mind.

'It seems hard to believe, but I'll be forty next year. Which means if we don't do something about it pretty soon, there'll be no hope for us ever having a child.'

She was looking at him as she said this, watching for his reaction, which was to hug her and tell her it was what he had been thinking too, but had been holding back, waiting to hear it from her. It was ages since they had last talked about this. Right at the start of their relationship, following his return to Britain from Franklin and her separation from Desmond, she had told him that it appeared extremely unlikely that she could conceive. It was something that had added to her problems with Desmond, who had been very keen to start a family and who, after several months during which she had failed to get pregnant, had insisted on seeking medical advice. After numerous consultations and tests, she learned that the problem was with her, and that treatment was available that stood a fair chance of resolving it. But by then their marriage was on the rocks. Her acting career, on the other hand, was progressing well, and little had changed there by the time she and Stephen had got together and eventually married. At the back of both their minds all along had been the thought that sooner or later something would have to be done about this. Now it seemed the time had come. She would arrange to see a specialist when she next returned home. Stephen was feeling quite dazed at the thought of the new phase of life into which they could be entering: a muddled feeling of love and anxiety as he took her into his arms.

They arrived at The Goose a little before seven. It was already quite crowded but they managed to grab a couple of stools at a corner shelf just as the previous occupants were leaving. Stephen left her there to go to buy drinks, recognising as he was doing so a familiar face across the other side of the bar: Karl. What on earth was *he* doing here? He wasn't due back from the United States till the following week. There was a young woman with him, blond and expensively dressed, for whom it was clear — Stephen having seen it all before — Karl was pulling out all the stops. Their eyes met, initiating a series of hand-signal exchanges, which resulted in Stephen and Suzie leaving their comfortable perch to squeeze in around the table that Karl had in the meantime rearranged to accommodate them.

'This is Kaylee,' said Karl, as he got her to move closer to him on the bench to make room for Stephen on her other side. A chair had arrived from somewhere for Suzie. 'We're both a bit jet-lagged. Arrived this morning from Los Angeles. It's Kaylee's first time in Europe.' Then, 'Stephen, Suzie,' introducing them to her. 'Old friends. I guess we'll be seeing more of them in the next few days.' Then, to Stephen, 'What are you two up to this evening?'

At which Suzie leaned over to explain that they were celebrating their fifth wedding anniversary and had just dropped in for a quick drink before going to eat. And without giving offence — she got on well with Karl, most of the time — managing to convey that on this occasion they wanted to be alone.

'Pity,' said Karl. 'I'm taking Kaylee to Penelope's. You could have joined us.'

'Another time,' said Stephen. 'Suzie's going back up north tomorrow for another couple of weeks. I'll be on my own till she gets back.'

'And game for anything,' interjected Suzie with a laugh.

Kaylee had remained silent during all this. It looked to Stephen as though it was more than jet-lag that was affecting her. Could it be that The Goose was falling short of expectations? In which case Penelope's was hardly likely to improve matters. He wondered for a moment if Karl knew what he was up to — immediately dismissing the thought of him being in any way deficient in such matters; the contents of an untouched glass in front of Kaylee perhaps an element in his strategy for smoothing the process.

Stephen was later to discover that everything had indeed turned out in accord with Karl's plans: Kaylee installed in his pad, looking as though she belonged there. He also got to hear how they had first met. It was at a party in Los Angeles, just three days before that meeting in The Goose. She had arrived there with her boyfriend, with whom she had fallen out, determined to end the affair. Finding Karl a sympathetic listener, she had poured out her troubles, further bemoaning the fact — on learning he was English — of having reached the advanced age of twenty-five without having got round to visiting Europe; at which he had suggested an immediate remedy and the next day proceeded to rush through the necessary arrangements. Never one to hang about was Karl. And as though that wasn't evidence enough, just as Stephen and Suzie were preparing to leave, he brought up the matter Stephen had been waiting to talk to him about as soon as he could get him alone.

'I know this is neither time nor place, but have you got anywhere with that Last Theorem stuff since I wrote?'

'Yes, I have,' said Stephen. 'Nothing earth-shattering but it opens up a number of possibilities...'

'Can you get something on paper in the next day or so?' Karl cut in. 'I only ask because I'm chairing a conference session in Texas in a couple of months. San Antonio. Nice venue. I could fit you in to give a presentation. Some of the people taking part could well have interesting things to say about what you're up to there. Could be useful.'

'Yes, I could... but... but I haven't any travel money to draw on...'

'Oh, don't worry about that. It's very well-funded. All expenses will be taken care of. And with the deals currently on offer from the airlines, it'll cost little or nothing to bring Suzie along as well, if she's free that is.'

The next few days saw Stephen busily preparing his presentation for Karl's session, with the prospect of an all-expenses-paid jaunt with Suzie to the United States as an added bonus, and slotting in perfectly with her decision to give up on acting engagements, at least for a while. In addition, Karl had promised to arrange for him to give seminars at Franklin, for which he would be paid fees and expenses, and which would enable him to show Suzie something of his old haunts and meet old friends, some of whom he hadn't seen for years. One way and another, things seemed to be shaping up well for them.

The arrangement with Stan for the following Thursday was to meet in that Edgeware Road pub, scene of Stephen's first encounter with Suzie, the memory of which had him feeling unaccountably ill at ease. He got there about ten minutes early to find Stan already seated at a table, reading an evening paper.

They were now in their early forties; Stan, Stephen noting with a touch of envy, looking remarkably young and well turned out. He jumped up in greeting as Stephen approached, causing a flurry of attention in the pub, of which Stephen was aware without appreciating the cause; until, on seeing the covert glances and head turnings that Stan's going to buy drinks gave rise to, the penny dropped. He had been recognised. And, try as many of them might, people of all sorts were finding themselves unable to resist the temptation of staring at the apparition — familiar to all from twice-weekly appearances on a popular television soap — now walking the floor of their local pub. Stephen was finding this a little discomforting, until Stan, giving a credible impression of being unaware of anything out of the ordinary, had returned with their pints and immediately brought up the matter that had been occupying him since Stephen's phone call.

'So, any developments on the Carroll business? You know, after what you told me last time, I couldn't get it out of my mind. It's quite unbelievable. I keep thinking back to those sessions we used to have with him. How important they appeared to us, standing out in the midst of all that nonsense we had to put up with there.'

'I know.'

Stephen was in a quandary. He had never said anything to Stan about having met up with Piers after leaving St John's; nor, of course, anything about Natasha. This seemed strange now. But at the time things had been moving fast for both of them, Stan's career taking off exponentially, Stephen digging himself deep into his research. So that, by the time of Stephen's fateful encounter with Natasha and his precipitous escape to Franklin, they had been out of touch for a matter of several months. And it was hardly surprising, he was now telling himself, that following his final return to London — to Suzie — the Piers/Natasha debacle should remain buried; which was why he had never mentioned anything of it to Stan, nor to anyone else come to that. This was something he was now going to have to put right. The question being just how much to come out with.

'There's a lot I haven't told you,' he started off, uncertain of where the disclosures were going to end. 'I'm not talking about Piers's death now — sorry about the change of name but I've got so used to thinking of him as Piers that Carroll sounds almost a different person. No, it was well before that, donkey's years before. In fact, it was quite soon after that affair you cooked up for me with Rebecca and Suzie in this pub —

which, don't get me wrong, I'm not complaining about.'

'No,' replied Stan with a laugh, 'I'm still waiting for the reciprocal move you promised at the time.'

'Well, from what I gather, you're in little need of help in such things. What I do feel bad about though, is not letting on about my meeting up with Piers. It seems terrible now, seeing how we were both so involved with him. But I'd got myself into a real mess with him and the last thing I wanted was to be reminded of it. And now, with what's happened... seems I could be getting involved again.'

Stan was looking understandably intrigued. He said nothing for a while as though lost in thought. Then,

'Well, Hallam, I think you've got some explaining to do.'

It was Piers's voice. So perfectly tuned that Stephen experienced a momentary shudder as though Piers had indeed called to him from beyond the grave.

'My God, Stan,' he said with a forced laugh. 'How on earth do you do it? It could have been him.' Then, after another pause, 'Okay, I'll try to do that explaining. I come out of it really badly.'

And so Stephen launched into his account of meeting Piers and Natasha in a pub near college, Stan straight away interrupting him.

'I can't believe it. So, Philips was right about them all along.' He was shaking his head, smiling in disbelief. 'This leads into something else, something I wanted to tell you about. But carry on for Christ's sake. That can wait.'

'I joined them for a beer,' said Stephen, 'both of them treating me like an old friend. Quite amazing really. It all happened so suddenly, so naturally, no awkwardness at all. I went back with them to where they were living together — a house very close to college, just off Tottenham Court Road.'

He described his friendship with Piers and Natasha, how it had taken off after that first encounter. Then on to what he had learned of their first meeting and falling in love in the run-up to the declaration of war with Germany — which showed their much later coming together in a rather different light to the opportunistic seduction scenario insinuated by Philips. Then, on to Piers's participation in the Dead Sea Scrolls studies at the behest of the Vatican, something of what he found there, touching on to its implications. 'Just the sort of thing he was supposedly there to stop coming out!'

They were seated in a relatively secluded corner of the busy pub. Stephen had been speaking softly, not wanting to be overheard; Stan listening attentively, leaning forward to hear him over the small table they were sitting at.

'It must have worried him terribly,' he said as Stephen paused to take a drink. 'I don't quite know what it is but… but at times, when he was speaking to us, he appeared to have something else on his mind… something that was making him think twice about what he was going to say next.'

'Well, yes. That's exactly how it was. He was going through the final stages of abandoning his faith. Something he'd been agonising over for months, maybe years. He told me all this after hearing my account of escaping from the brainwashing he had had a hand in. I hadn't been very tactful in the way I came out with it, but he seemed to take it okay. Didn't say much at the time. But later confessed to me how he had gone through much the same himself.'

They were interrupted at this point by two young women, whom Stephen had noticed staring at them from a nearby table. For a moment, the thought passed through his head that Stan was up to his old tricks again. But no, it was just that they wanted his autograph, which he signed for them in the name of the character he was playing on television, to their evident delight. When this had finished, Stephen went on to what he had learned of Piers's recent dealings with the Vatican, — going over what he had described to Suzie the previous week – the whole thing sounding even more implausible to him than before. Then on, with some misgiving, to Natasha's claim that Piers had been murdered on the orders of members of the Curia. He had decided to say nothing of her further contention that they had just previously conspired in the murder of the Pope, feeling the less said about it the better. But, much to his surprise, Stan came right back at him on that.

'It's funny, but I was talking just the other day to a friend of mine who's a journalist. Quite an impressive guy. For a while, he was the Rome correspondent for one of the posh dailies — the Telegraph I think it was. He told me that a reliable contact of his out there firmly believes that the new Pope had been murdered.'

This disclosure had the effect of stopping Stephen in his tracks.

'It appears,' Stan went on, 'that straight after he had been elected, he wanted to bring about sweeping changes that were going to thoroughly upset, and unseat, powerful figures in the Vatican hierarchy. I know it sounds crazy, but according to this guy a number of people there are taking that possibility quite seriously.'

This was precisely what Natasha had been on about, that 'sweeping changes', and indeed the election of a Pope they believed could be instrumental in achieving these, were what Piers and his mates had been working away at for years. He was feeling a surge of excitement, and the need to keep it in check. Time was needed, he was telling himself, to take in the implications of this totally unexpected support for Natasha's wild assertions. And so he decided to steer the discussion on to the topic he would have preferred to avoid, but which he felt Stan should know about.

'Let me get some more beer,' he said, 'then I'll tell you what completely screwed things up between me and Piers... well, between me and both of them.'

When he got back from the bar, as he was putting the glasses and peanuts on the table, he came straight out with it.

'Piers had left for Rome for an indefinite period. The way it sounded it could have been forever. But he didn't get far. Something, God knows what, caused him to miss his train. So he came back and found me and Natasha in bed together.'

'Well,' said Stan, after the briefest of pauses and with a large grin, 'congratulations.'

'Yes, I expected that, and I suppose I asked for it. But it was no cause for celebration I can assure you. It was a fucking nightmare. Still is, when I think back to it. You might find this hard to believe, but it was the only time anything even remotely close to that had occurred between Natasha and me. Nothing had been planned. She was desperately unhappy about Piers leaving like that. And I was there... and it just happened. I never saw Piers again. Never. And now he's dead. Nor Natasha, till the other week... and God, what a mess she's in.'

'I don't know what to say,' said Stan.

'Better just leave it. Change the subject. Tell me about that other thing you were keeping for me.'

What Stan had to tell concerned Philips: that he was in

jail, put away for a long time for fraud.

'Something to do with a dodgy investment fund he had set up and soaked for millions. It was in all the papers, but you probably wouldn't have taken in the connection because his name was always reported as Luzac Philips. In fact, his full name *is* Robert Luzac Philips — R L Philips at school. Remember? Understandably, he kept quiet there about the Luzac. It stems from his mother, who was part French. He probably came to think it sounded more impressive than Robert Philips or just plain Philips — which is all he ever was at St John's, of course; Robert, or even Bob, never getting so much as a look in. Anyway, I saw his photo in a local rag and there's no doubt about it. He looked exactly as he did then — not a compliment in his case.'

Stan went on to describe how Philips had hit the big time.

'...luxury pad in Mayfair, private jet, villa in the Bahamas, the lot. And all paid for by the poor sods foolish enough to entrust him with their life savings on the promise of everlasting, super-fat dividends. Serves them right in a way.'

'It was just what he'd planned for himself from school days,' said Stephen, reminiscing. 'Isn't it nice to see hard work and honest ambition earning their just reward? Something St John's can be proud of. Remember Ignatius's advice as we were leaving? "Aim for the top," he told us. "Always aim for the top."'

It was a few days after that session with Stan that Stephen was woken with a start early one morning by what turned out to be a phone call from Natasha. She was in Bristol, she told him, staying with her son Benjamin.

'I'm sorry to trouble you, Stephen,' she said, 'but could

you do something for me? I wouldn't ask but there's no one else I can call on for this.'

She was sounding as though speaking was an effort. There were background sounds, a distant muffled conversation, perhaps the radio.

'Of course I will,' he replied sleepily, feeling as he was doing so that it would have been wiser to first hear what she was asking of him.

'It's Piers's journals,' she said. 'They're in a suitcase in a left-luggage depository in Victoria. Not in the station itself but quite close by. They need to be taken to someone who will know what to do with them.'

Stephen was fully awake now. He jumped out of bed to fetch a notepad on which to write the details required for the collection. Natasha would in the meantime contact the depository, telling them to expect him that afternoon. He also noted down the name and South London address of the Roman Catholic parish priest to whom he was to deliver the suitcase. It was all done quite quickly, Natasha seemingly in a hurry, discouraging his attempt to question her further. After hanging up, he realised he hadn't asked for her phone number. There was no way of contacting her if something went wrong.

He set off for college in a state of burgeoning excitement. This was something for which he had all but given up hope: an opportunity to get close to, perhaps even learn something about, whatever it was that Piers had been so involved with in the days leading up to his death.

TWENTY-THREE

As Stephen was leaving Victoria tube station, on his way to picking up Piers's journals, it came to him that he was within a stone's throw of Westminster cathedral, that he would be virtually walking past it on his way to the left-luggage depository. It was all of twenty years since he had last been there, the droll memory of that occasion — refreshed only a few days ago by Stan's reminiscences — shrouding its melancholic association with Piers's death. On an impulse, he made a small change of direction and within a matter of minutes he was there, standing in the nave, staring up the central aisle. It was as he remembered it, little or nothing changed in twenty years.

Then, from somewhere, came the desire to find out just where it was that Piers's body had been found. He made a tour of the side chapels, all, he noted, dedicated to saints associated in one way or another with Christianity in Britain. Nothing very surprising about that. Then he spied a man wearing a dark suit and dog collar, a curate perhaps, who was moving purposefully about as though he belonged there. Stephen approached him.

'I wonder if you could help me, Father?' he said. The man gave him an unfriendly look, but Stephen carried on. 'It's about the man who was found dead here... in the cathedral... two weeks or so ago.'

'Well?' said the man, looking even more unfriendly.

It was probably an embarrassment for them, thought Stephen. Something they didn't want to be reminded of.

'He was an old friend that I hadn't seen for years... Piers Denney. The newspapers said he was found in one of the side chapels. I would just like to know which one it was.'

The man said nothing for a while, just stood regarding him with a puzzled expression. Then,

'Why do you want to know that?'

It was a good question. Why on earth do I? thought Stephen. But he did. As for why... that would need to be thought over later. But how to respond? The answer came on a wave of profane inspiration.

'It's just that I want to pray for him,' — he was feeling quite pleased with himself for coming up with this, tarnished with just a modicum of guilt — 'at the place where he died.'

It worked. It was in the chapel of St Gregory and St Augustine, he was told, the first one on the right as you enter the cathedral.

A printed notice on a column at the side of the chapel explained that St Augustine had been sent to Britain in the year 597 by Pope Gregory 1 — with whom he now shares the chapel — to convert the pagans to Christianity, an undertaking in which he had proved conspicuously successful. But wait a minute! The name rang a bell. Wasn't he the one...? No, he wasn't. The notice went on to point out that this St Augustine was St Augustine of Canterbury, not to be confused, as was often the case, with St Augustine of Hippo (Hippo being a source of some amusement to the boys of St John's) who lived some two hundred years earlier. It was this latter St Augustine whom Stephen remembered for his steadfast insistence that babies dying unbaptised would be consigned to the eternal fires of hell.

The church of St Anthony of Padua, where Stephen was to deliver Piers's suitcase, stood at the end of a long, uphill road of semi-detached dwellings that branched off from Norbury High Street, close to the bus stop where Stephen alighted that evening. The light was beginning to fade, a fine drizzle threatening to develop into something more substantial. He trudged his way to the church, getting progressively wetter and more fed up. Why on earth couldn't Father Legrand — the intended recipient of the suitcase — have collected it himself? he wondered irritably. Metal gates under a brick archway opened onto a path running between the church and the presbytery to what appeared a sizeable garden. He went through and rang the presbytery bell. The door was opened by a casually dressed man of about Stephen's age, clean-shaven, longish dark hair lightly streaked with grey, jeans and a roll-necked sweater. Obviously expecting Stephen, he greeted him warmly.

'Alain Legrand,' he said, taking hold of the suitcase with one hand and shaking hands with the other. 'Please call me Alain. You must be Stephen. Come in, my dear chap. Goodness, you're soaking. Let me put your jacket by the fire, and you go and sit by it too.'

He led the way to a dimly lighted room containing various pieces of mismatched dark wooden furniture. A coal fire was burning brightly on the far side, with wing chairs on either side of it. Alain placed a dining chair between them and hung Stephen's wet jacket over its back. On the tiled fireplace stood a clock, a few gloomy photos of saints and what could have been previous incumbents, and a statue of the Virgin Mary; centrally above it the statutory crucifix.

'Sorry about all the religious paraphernalia,' said Alain on seeing Stephen taking this in, 'but Mrs. Chadderton — my housekeeper — refuses point blank to have it diminished it in any way. She's at her sister's now but will be back in the morning to make my breakfast and get me up in time for Mass.'

Stephen was quite taken aback at Father Legrand's friendly flippancy. He was feeling better now.

'I'm going to have to leave you soon to hear confessions. Shouldn't be too long on a wet night like this. Then we can talk about Piers and have a bite to eat. Can I get you a cup of tea before I go?'

'I'm okay for now, thanks.'

'You must be intrigued about these journals and everything. And so am I. And by the way, you're welcome to stay the night if you care to. It will give us more time to talk. There's a spare room here, always ready for the unexpected guest.'

This was all going quite differently from what Stephen could possibly have imagined. Almost too well it seemed. Just where did this genial priest fit into the general picture? He was a good-looking guy, quite athletic in the way he moved and held himself. And not a trace of French accent, which Stephen had been expecting.

'In the meantime,' Alain went on, 'let's just have a surreptitious look at what's inside that suitcase.'

He produced a key from somewhere and opened it, revealing a stack of large envelopes, some quite bulky, and other assorted folders and notepads. The envelopes were unsealed, some having a year date written large on the front. Alain flipped through them.

'No 1978,' he remarked. 'Hardly surprising, but that's the one some people could be particularly keen to get hold of.' He took out a slim folder, checked its contents, then closed the suitcase and locked it. 'Better to leave this until someone from the community has had a chance to vet it,' he said. 'In the meantime, here's something you may like to read while I'm away. We can talk about it when I get back. It puts a somewhat different slant on a well-known tale.' He handed Stephen the folder. 'And now I need to change into my working togs.'

He left the room, returning a few minutes later transformed, in cassock and dog collar, looking completely the part.

'See you in a bit,' he said as he left the room.

Stephen waited until he heard the front door closing behind him, then opened the folder and started to read.

THE DEATHS OF JESUS AND HIS BROTHER JAMES

From the time of his baptism by John in the waters of the Jordan, Jesus believed the Kingdom of God to be at hand — an everlasting, deeply religious Jewish state, governed in accord with Mosaic Law; and that he had been chosen by God as instrument for this momentous event, which would deliver the Jewish people from the pagan clutches of Rome and overturn the corrupt religious leadership under which they were compelled to worship. Jesus gave every indication of believing this divine intervention should be solicited by peaceful means, by repentance of the masses, their abandonment of sinful ways and their unwavering adherence to the Law. Then God would unleash His power, vanquish their enemies and restore the sacred birth right of His chosen people. And so Jesus set out across the land, his words and tales of his deeds rousing the multitudes who flocked to him in their thousands, his influence and prestige growing by the day, his very presence a portent of impending freedom. For though his exhortations were not fully understood — he spoke often in parables, unclear to even the closest of his disciples — they resonated with the yearnings and emotions of his ever-growing body of followers.

In his mission, he was by no means alone. As the leader of a fundamentalist community, united in the belief of its unique standing in the eyes of God, Jesus commanded a substantial force, one that hung on his every word, patiently awaiting his call to action. For beneath the passive exterior — his utterances, for the most part, extolling meekness and poverty, exhorting absolute obedience to the Law — lay a violent undercurrent, with those among his community ever ready to take offence at the slightest perception of idolatry or blasphemy, prepared at all times to take up arms, to fight and kill and die in God's cause. But they were kept in check by Jesus, awaiting a clear signal from God that the time for action had arrived, and concerned that accusations of incitement to insurrection could in the meantime reach the Roman authorities, who would react mercilessly to the merest suggestion of revolt, while remaining indifferent to peaceful religious manifestations of whatever magnitude. This latter forbearance was by no means shared by those Jewish religious authorities who owed their power and status to an accommodation with Rome, and were feeling increasingly intimidated by the growing popularity of Jesus with the Jewish *people, and by the ever-critical and uncompromising fundamentalist movement which he led.*

The extraordinary popularity of Jesus was feeding growing expectations in his followers. They believed him to be of the house of David, directly descended from the second king of Israel — slayer of Goliath and deliverer of the Jewish people from the superior might of the Philistines. Could not then the descendant of David likewise deliver the Jewish people from the superior might of Rome? For along with talk of his miracles, — of the driving out of demons from the possessed, of curing the sick and deformed, even of raising the dead — his words, though little understood, were redolent with concealed power. But with the months slipping by and the Kingdom of God no nearer to realisation, the patience of the more militant among his followers was beginning to wane. Jesus, however, was not to be rushed, was ever awaiting a sign.

Then, at the approach of the spring festival of Passover, with pilgrims in their thousands flocking to Jerusalem to worship at the Temple, a sign of sorts did indeed appear. Not at all what Jesus had been anticipating, but one unleashing fury and righteous indignation among the Jews, a portent of inevitable violent protest. The Roman governor, in an act either of crass insensitivity or overt provocation — more probably the former, but in effect mattering little which — had ordered standards bearing the image of the emperor to be erected in the immediate vicinity of the Temple: an idolatrous, highly visible imposition on holy ground, guaranteed to infuriate worshippers of the Living God. And so Jesus, perhaps with some misgivings, led his followers towards Jerusalem, their numbers swelling as they approached the Holy City, his confidence in God's support in whatever awaited them there blossoming with the frenzied acclaim from the triumphant procession which now accompanied him, voices in their thousands hailing him King of the Jews. They gathered beneath the massive walls of the Temple complex, then through its portal into the vast forecourt, by this time teeming with pilgrims. Although no plans had been prepared, many of his followers carried arms — swords and daggers concealed beneath flowing robes. Their moment, it seemed to them, had come; their God, smarting under this latest flagrant Roman insult, certain now to intervene, to guide them to ultimate victory.

It was a thoroughly hopeless and doomed expectation, but, for a while, in their euphoria, they believed they would prevail. They routed the profane traders — the money changers and sellers of sacrificial beasts — who had turned the precincts of the house of God into a common marketplace. The multitude, soon to occupy the entire Temple precinct, fervent in their support of Jesus; the Temple authorities fearful to intervene. And so it remained, until the arrival of a Roman cohort, summoned by the harassed Temple authorities, which moved in with the Temple police to regain control. It was a bloodthirsty, one-sided intervention, resulting in deaths and countless injuries.

In the ensuing confusion, Jesus and leading members of his community made their escape, fleeing the Temple and taking refuge in a dwelling well removed from the Holy City. But its location was soon to be made known to the authorities — the result of a betrayal, it seemed, perhaps under torture, by a captured disciple. Jesus was arrested, the outcome of his trial before the Roman governor a foregone conclusion. He was crucified, along with other participants in the insurrection, the legend King of the Jews *on his cross, a stark warning to potential insurgents, his death agony intensified by the realisation that his God had forsaken him.*

Jesus' mission had ended in abject failure, the Kingdom of God a shattered dream. The existing, emasculated, Roman-controlled Jewish state, centred on Jerusalem and the Temple, was also doomed: Jesus' insurrection and death setting in train the slow campaign of resistance to Roman rule which would eventually result in its annihilation.

It appeared to Stephen that this was a good place to pause and reflect. There was a lot more to come. He placed the folder on the chair bearing his, by now, almost dry jacket and closed his eyes. Yes, the text did indeed present a new slant on the story; one that, on the face of it, resolved many problems glaringly apparent in the established versions. It was a long time since he had read the New Testament Gospels, but he remembered feeling uncomfortable at St John's at their many inconsistencies and sheer implausibilities. This was certainly the case with regard to Jesus' trial, with its portrayal of Pontius Pilate, against his better judgement, giving in to the Jewish mob to condemn him for some ill-defined offence. It didn't ring true at all. For one thing, it was quite at odds with what was well known about the man, his arrogant, authoritarian disregard for the views of his Jewish subjects. Nor did it accord with the evident popularity of Jesus with the Jewish people. He had thought at the time to say something to this effect but had wisely refrained. That Jesus had been crucified for leading some sort of insurrection against the Roman-imposed establishment — for which crucifixion would be the inevitable punishment — appeared far more plausible. As did the notion of Jesus as leader of a fundamentalist movement, intent on liberating the Jewish state from the occupying forces of pagan Rome.

He picked up the file and continued reading from where he had left off.

The death of Jesus had dealt a mortal blow to his followers, unable at first to accept it. Rumours developed and persisted of sightings of Jesus, that he had not died at all, that he had risen from the dead. Then followed the painful process of adjustment and accommodation, leading to the appointment of a new leader: James, a brother of Jesus, a choice welcomed unreservedly by the community. For though very different from his brother, lacking his charisma with the public at large, James was venerated by all who knew him for his legendary piousness and unshakable adherence to the Law.

And so the teachings of Jesus continued to reach the multitudes, promulgated now by James and the community of which he had become undisputed leader. He would preach to the people from the steps of the Temple, attracting them in their thousands as his brother had done. Also disputing from there with the high priests of the Temple establishment, who, though resentful of his popularity, as had been the case with Jesus before him, would from time to time solicit his help in calming the restless masses, acknowledging thereby his moral authority and the esteem in which he was held by the Jewish people. James would dispatch members of the community to wherever Jews were to be found, exhorting them to prepare themselves by pious works and strict adherence to the Law for the elusive, long-delayed, but eventually inevitable realisation of the Kingdom of God.

But then James's preaching would turn at times to criticism, both direct and by implication, of the conspicuous vices emanating from the house of Herod — the kings imposed by Rome on the Jewish people. For the Herods were foreigners, overt fornicators and idolaters, their imposition as rulers, particularly as religious rulers, deemed a grotesque travesty by their subjects — with the exception, of course, of those of the religious and administrative establishment who benefitted in no small measure from accommodation with the imposed order. Such criticism by James could hardly escape the attention of his enemies. And before long, bands of Herodian henchmen would take to disrupting his discourses, resulting at times in violent disorder, bloodshed, even death. A particularly vehement leader of one such band, enraged at James's outspoken criticism of the Herodian dynasty, was a kinsman of Agrippa II — the then king of Galilee — and a powerful and privileged Roman citizen by virtue of that relationship. His name was Saul, a fervent opponent of James's fundamentalist Jewish message. Saul would lose no opportunity for harassing James and his followers, on one occasion attacking him as he preached at the Temple, causing him to be thrown down the steps to where he lay unconscious, his legs broken, seemingly dead to those who witnessed the assault. But James survived, and, when fully recovered, he returned with undiminished *vigour to his sacred mission.*

There was no shortage among the community of James of those well prepared to repay with violence the violence to which they were being subjected. The fact that the seemingly inevitable major conflict failed to materialise was due to an extraordinary and quite unforeseeable event that was to change the course of history. Saul was quite suddenly and without warning struck down by a cerebral seizure that left him both blind and emptied of the raging antagonisms which had previously dominated his existence. And the vacuum this left was filled with an all-embracing religious certainty, totally at variance with anything he had ever felt or imagined before. Out of his confused state had arisen a lucid vision of Jesus — the crucified revolutionary leader whose followers he had relentlessly persecuted — as the supreme supernatural being, with whom he now believed himself to be in direct spiritual contact, and in whose service he would henceforth dedicate his life.

To go some way towards understanding what could be behind this momentous transformation in Saul, it becomes necessary to appreciate the prevailing religious environment under which he was raised: the ready acceptance in the Hellenic world of 'mystery religions' involving god-like figures, being both man and supernaturally endowed — at times the result of impregnation of a human virgin by a god. The city of Tarsus, where Saul was born and grew into manhood, was at the time a major centre of one such belief, Mithras, then the predominant religion of the Roman empire. Saul's upbringing could not have avoided prolonged and intimate contact with the beliefs and manifestations of this flourishing creed — involving the birth of a man-god and the rituals of baptism and of meals in which the consumption of bread and wine symbolised the ingestion of a divine force.

The new religion which Saul was eventually to found would turn out to be heavily influenced by these early exposures to Mithras. But his immediate concern, following recovery from his seizure and the restoration of his sight, was to make peace with James and the community of the family of Jesus — which included two sisters and three brothers in addition to James — and his disciples, who had all been intimately involved with Jesus up until the time of his death and were now dedicating their lives to the promotion of his teaching. Given the violent hostility to which Saul had previously subjected them, this was to prove no easy undertaking. But he somehow managed to persuade enough of them of the genuineness of his conversion to their cause and was, before long, to become an active member of their community: changing his name to Paul, submitting to the leadership of James, and preaching the gospel of Jesus to the multitudes with noteworthy success in recruiting to the cause.

Fault lines in the relationship of Paul and James were soon to emerge. These came about as a result of Paul's success in attracting adherents to what was fast becoming the cult of Christ Jesus. Such was the appeal of Paul's preaching that he was recruiting Gentiles as well as Jews, all attracted by the promise of redemption and everlasting life in return for nothing more than a profession of faith in Christ Jesus.

News of this and other, what would have been disturbing,

developments were soon to reach James, who at first reacted by sending emissaries to make clear to Paul that the mission of Jesus was directed solely at Jews, fully compliant with all aspects of Mosaic Law. Gentiles who wished to join the movement would first have to convert to Judaism, the men having to undergo circumcision. He then summoned Paul to Jerusalem to receive direct instructions on just how he should proceed with his evangelising activities. Paul was submissive at first, underwent a ritual of penance and rededication and agreed to comply fully with all of James's directives.

Such accommodation was not to last. With growing confidence, fuelled by the number of Gentiles joining his ranks, and his conviction that the spiritual relationship he had established in his mind with the Christ Jesus he had never known as a living man was in every way superior to that of James and the other of Jesus' relatives and disciples. And so Paul returned to being a bitter enemy of James and the community which he led, losing no opportunity to disparage both them and all aspects of Mosaic Law — in direct conflict with the teachings of Jesus. And he was soon to become known within the community as The Liar for his broken pledges to James to uphold their rules and observances. And he went on to found a new mystery religion — with, as man-god, the resurrected crucified Christ Jesus — which would sweep the earth.

James, in the meantime, was dispatching disciples to broadcast the gospel of Jesus to wherever Jews were to be found, exhorting them to prepare themselves by pious works and full adherence to the Law for the coming of the Kingdom of God, and preaching at the Temple to the multitudes flocking to his presence — to the irritation of the Herodian-imposed high priests, who could only wait in hope of hearing him express a treasonous sentiment which could be used to bring about his downfall. But they waited in vain, James's exhortations being confined to matters of little concern to the Roman authorities. And so James continued for some thirty years with the mission inherited from his brother, up until the time when a bitter enemy — the high priest Ananus — seized an opportunity to silence him forever. This occurred by virtue of a change of Roman governor — the person who under normal circumstances would have to approve far-reaching actions of a high priest. In the interval between the departure of the existing incumbent and the arrival of his successor, Ananus arranged for James to be arrested on a trumped-up charge of blasphemy. The subsequent trial and the implementation of the sentence for the inevitable guilty verdict —. death by stoning — were carried out in great haste, not giving his followers time to gather their resources and prepare a defence. It was a bitter blow which left the community stunned, unable at first to take in the enormity of what had transpired. But not for long. Shoots from the seeds for momentous repercussions, planted long ago with the crucifixion of Jesus, were now to burst forth with the murder of James, and nothing on earth could arrest their development.

When the insurrection finally erupted, all hell was let loose. The Herodian-appointed high priests were relentlessly targeted, they and their families forced to flee or suffer certain slaughter, their palaces set ablaze, the Roman cohorts stationed for their protection quite unable to cope with the intensity of the onslaught. Ananus — architect of James's judicial murder — was himself brutally murdered, his naked mutilated body thrown from the walls of Jerusalem to be ravaged by wild beasts. The palace of the Herodian princess Bernice — a prime target of James's denouncement of fornication and incest — was burned down, along with others of the Herodian kings and their courtiers, in the frenzied orgy of destruction and revenge.

Any satisfaction the participants in the uprising and the Jewish people in general may have felt at this taste of liberation from the Roman yoke was predictably short-lived — lasting no longer than the time required for Rome to marshal the substantial force required to end once and for all the violent insubordination of her Jewish subjects. The campaign was first led by Vespasian, until his return to Rome to further his ambition for the imperial throne, thereafter by his son Titus. Encouraged, no doubt, by his mistress Bernice, Titus oversaw the complete destruction of the Temple and the sack of Jerusalem: countless slaughter of the population, women and children herded into slavery, and all expectations of a Kingdom of God buried forever under the ruins.

Stephen was feeling quite overwhelmed by the time he had reached the end of this extraordinary document. The second part, dealing with the pivotal role of James, following the death of Jesus, was particularly illuminating — adding substance to what he vaguely remembered of the situation described in the letters of Paul, but almost totally excluded in later documents of the New Testament. It also corresponded to what Piers had told him all those years ago about his Dead Sea

Scrolls findings. The identification of Saul/Paul with the Herodian dynasty being particularly interesting, providing a justification for his bitter, and previously unexplained, antagonism to Jewish Christianity — ever vocal in its criticism of the conspicuous vices of the Herodian rulers and their families — as well as for the, also previously unexplained, fact of his Roman citizenship. All in all, it was a devastating rewrite of what Alain had referred to as the well-known tale.

The fire was looking in need of attention. He got up and poked it and added more coal from the bucket standing alongside. Then he started reading from the folder again, from the beginning, with more care this time, hoping to get through it once more before Alain returned from his ministrations.

TWENTY-FOUR

Alain came back to find Stephen deep in thought, not having heard him come in, looking surprised at seeing him standing by his side.

'I'm sorry if I woke you up,' he said.

'I wasn't asleep,' replied Stephen with a chuckle. 'Just musing on the implications of this document you handed me.'

'Good. So, what do you make of it?'

Stephen thought for a moment, then:

'More to the point, I think, is what you make of it. I'm afraid I gave up on all that stuff years ago. What I can't get though is where it fits in with whatever Piers was supposedly trying to achieve for the church. Am I missing something?'

It was Alain's turn to laugh. Quite good-naturedly, Stephen was relieved to hear.

'Well, maybe,' he said, 'but first I need a beer. What about you? There's light ale, Guinness… or would you prefer something stronger?'

'Guinness sounds fine.'

'Good. It's what I'm having.'

He left the room, returning minutes later with a tray loaded with bottles and glasses and a large packet of crisps.

'Mrs Chadderton has left a pan of soup on the stove,' he said, as he placed the tray on a side table, pushing it with his foot to where they could both reach it. 'There's also cheese and other bits and pieces for when we feel like eating. In the meantime, let me try to answer your question.'

'Don't get me wrong,' said Stephen. 'I found the document quite fascinating, really enjoyed reading it. It seems more plausible than the established versions, from what I remember of them. And it seems to tie in with what Piers told me about his Dead Sea Scrolls findings. But, as I said, I can't see its place in any sort of reform programme. Seems more like a brutal exposure of the very foundations of Christianity. Isn't that a problem for you? It isn't for me, but then I'm a complete outsider. It's just that I can't imagine how it could possibly go down with you lot.'

A silence followed, making Stephen feel that perhaps he should have been more tactful. But Alain was simply considering his response.

'It caused a lot of trouble,' he said eventually. 'Even upset people Piers thought had been thoroughly won over. As for the others... Trouble is that, although many of them claim to be gung-ho for reform, their views span a wide spectrum of perceived outcomes. Which is hardly surprising. Not many go along with Piers's long-term vision of an effectively secular organisation, concerned exclusively with human welfare and open to all shades of belief, including none.' He broke off to open a bottle and pour into two glasses, handing one to Stephen. 'But despite all that,' he went on, 'there's been a fair measure of consensus in a number of fraught areas. For a start, with the question of the observances: Mass, confession, baptism, the rest of it — customs and rituals that effectively define the church for its adherents. Strangely enough, no real problems were encountered with these. Almost everyone agreeing it was simply up to individuals how to take them, with the expectation of the few rituals standing the test of time eventually coming over as no more than ceremonial acknowledgement of where it all started. Rather in the way that in Britain, ceremonies relating to the monarchy continue to play a popular and arguably important role in public life, regardless of nobody any longer believing in kings being appointed by God. A similar view was taken with the books of the New Testament — which was what got us on to this. Again, it was generally felt that it had to be up to individuals. They could be taken as gospel-truth or fanciful myth or perhaps something in-between. Again, no real problem. But then Piers and one or two others — those who had been involved with him in research into that period of history — felt that a voice should be given to their findings. And not just for publication in academic journals. And in a style readily accessible to the general reader. Hence what you've just been reading, which was intended as an illustration of the openness Piers had in mind, a trial if you like, something to pass round the group to solicit comments, stimulate discussion. As I said, it caused no end of trouble.'

'Hardly surprisingly,' said Stephen. 'But just how credible is it anyway? I know I said it looked plausible, which it does, but what evidence is there to back it up?'

'That's part of the difficulty.' Alain signalled a pause, while he drank from his glass. 'Nothing in that document is by any means certain. Which provides plenty of leeway for dismissing it by anyone who feels the need to. You can say the same, of course, and with a lot more justification, about the established versions. But when you look at the way in which Piers and those working with him went about it, the sheer scope of their studies, their detailed assessment of all available sources — including those previously dismissed for whatever reasons or otherwise overlooked — it's hard to dispute the gist of their conclusions. Particularly where they show just where and how the established versions have been doctored to support the developing dogma. But look, before we get on to that, I haven't had a chance yet to tell you how I met Piers and got involved in all this. Perhaps you'd like to hear that?'

'It's certainly something I was wondering about.'

Alain topped up their glasses, helped himself to a handful of crisps and handed the packet to Stephen.

'I was following in Piers's footsteps,' he said, when he had finished munching. 'Studying for my doctorate at Oxford under the same advisor. Piers would drop in to see him now and then. That way we got introduced... took to each other... hit it off from the start.'

This came as a surprise to Stephen.

'So, you met Piers before you were ordained?' he asked.

'Oh yes. It would have been just a year or so after graduating. Thoughts of the priesthood were vaguely in my mind, but nothing definite. That all came later. In fact, after I'd finished my doctorate. I started on a postdoc fellowship, then abandoned it after a few months for the seminary.'

'Despite having hit it off with Piers?'

'What do you mean? No, you've got it wrong.' Alain gave a light laugh. 'It was largely due to Piers that I took the plunge.'

This was once again to bring home to Stephen just how little he really knew of Piers, of his faith, or lack of it, his relationship with the church, with Natasha even, everything. He said nothing for a while. Then:

'It seems strange, that's all, given the doubts he would

have been living with at the time. But then I suppose one shouldn't be surprised at anything with Piers.'

'No,' said Alain. 'But what he had to say quite shocked me at first. It took quite a while for me to come to terms with it. You see, I felt emotionally drawn to the priesthood — strongly so, no question there. Alongside that, though, was this recurring doubt about the whole basis of religious belief, making it seem absurd for me to continue with my vocation. But then I got to speak to Piers. I'd known him for some time by then. In addition to the academic stuff, we would chat happily about this and that when we got to meet, nothing of any real consequence. I knew he was involved in some way with the Vatican, but he always steered clear of any reference to that. It was only when, on a whim, I told him of my dilemma that it all came out. He persuaded me that the doubts I held in no way excluded me from my vocation. On the contrary. That the church was in dire need of people in its ranks able to think the unthinkable, adjust to massive changes in the perception of its role. Without these shifts it was doomed; its members destined to wake up eventually to the absurdity of it all — things previously accepted blindly, without question. It was happening all the time. The immense benefits the church was in a position to confer on mankind were in danger of being lost forever.'

What Alain went on to say, Stephen had heard before — all of seventeen years ago. He had been sceptical then of Piers's vision of the church's progressive secularisation, the dogma gradually giving way to a rational agenda. But if Alain was anything to go by, Piers's vision would appear to be taking root. Perhaps to the extent — it fleetingly came to him — that the threat he posed to powerful interests could have been felt sufficient to warrant the extreme measure he had previously dismissed as unthinkable. Rapidly dismissing this notion, he returned instead to where they had started, to the "different slant on a well-known tale" — the revised account of what had to be the very foundation of the Christian religion.

'I know it sounds strange,' said Alain, 'but much of what is in that document follows from little more than a careful reading of the New Testament: the letters of Paul, the Gospels themselves.'

'Jesus as leader of an insurrection against Roman rule! Where on earth is the evidence for that?'

'In the Gospels,' replied Alain. 'But you need to know how to look for things there... to understand the circumstances under which they were written... where the authors' got their information from... what message they were setting out to convey... what they were desperately trying to conceal.'

Stephen settled back in his chair. Memories of schooldays perplexities with the Gospels — for the most part brushed aside — coming back as he sat there, intrigued at the direction the conversation was taking.

'Very few people,' Alain went on, 'very few Christians, realise just how little is known about Jesus the man. There is virtually nothing written about him outside the Gospels, and precious little in them about his background, his family, what he did before that brief period from the time of his baptism by John till his crucifixion. The Gospels are all we have. And these were written by far-from-disinterested authors long after the events they describe. The first one, Mark, some forty years after the crucifixion. The others ten, twenty or more years later. Think what this means.'

He paused to drink, carefully replacing his glass on the

table while fixing Stephen with an interrogative gaze.

'I suppose...' began Stephen, uncertain how he was expected to respond, but recalling his own doubts at St John's about just what Jesus was supposed to have said concerning baptism as a prerequisite for salvation. 'I suppose it means we can't be sure of anything reported in the Gospels.'

'Well, yes, there's that,' said Alain. 'Think what the authors of Mark had to go on. Nothing written down, nothing concrete at all. Recollections in abundance though. Fragments heard or misheard at first, second or third hand; excitedly discussed and passed on with inevitable embellishment. A mishmash of truth and half-truth and imaginative speculation, which rumbled on for some forty years. But despite all that, despite great uncertainty in all the details, much of the underlying picture would have been clear. It would have shown, for instance, that during Jesus' lifetime, there could have been no question of him being regarded other than as a pious Jew, born of natural parents and with several brothers and sisters — who, along with everyone else who knew him, would have been amazed at his metamorphosis from humble carpenter to charismatic preacher with an immense following. It would also have resolved any possible doubt as to Jesus' message being directed other than at the Jewish people. It was only later, after the crucifixion, that Paul was to come along and contentiously claim otherwise. To maintain so at the time though, in addition to ignoring completely the evident politico-religious climate, would have been quite contrary to reported statements of Jesus himself, which have somehow managed to survive in the Gospel records. A notable example of this is his response to a Gentile woman who asks him to cure her daughter: "I was sent only for the lost sheep of the house of Israel", he tells her. And when she persists: "It is not right to take the bread of the children and cast it to dogs." Although, after that overtly racist put-down, he eventually relents and cures the girl, it couldn't be clearer that it was to Jews alone that he saw his mission directed.'

Alain paused at this point, taking in Stephen's questioning expression. 'I think I know what you want to ask,' he said with a smile. 'It's about my accepting what is written here, after warning you against trusting the details. Is that it?'

'Well, yes,' said Stephen with a laugh. 'That's just what I was thinking.'

'Good,' said Alain. 'But a general rule to follow with the Gospels is to be deeply suspicious of anything that conforms to the line the authors are trying to promote — on the basis, of course, that those bits could well have been inserted for that purpose. But when you come across something that runs counter to their agenda — like the example we've just been considering — it's much more likely to be genuine. This is something always to be borne in mind.

'Following the crucifixion,' he went on, 'Jesus' brother James was to take over as leader of what, for lack of a better term, can be called "Jewish Christianity". This was the fundamentalist movement *within the Jewish religion,*' – Alain emphasised these words – 'consisting of the disciples and other followers of Jesus who believed him to be the Messiah: the man chosen by God to restore His kingdom to the Jewish people. The conversion to their cause of Paul, following the fall from his horse, occurred sometime later, well after the crucifixion. It's a well-known story. So is Paul's subsequent split with Jewish Christianity. This has been put down to understandable contention at his admittance of non-Jews to that fundamentalist Jewish faction and his renouncement of the Law — the Law of Moses. But perhaps an even more compelling reason for the break-up concerns the central plank of Paul's enduring vision: the further metamorphosis of Jesus to God. This was something that James, the Jewish Christianity community, all who had known and supported Jesus during his lifetime, and indeed all pious Jews, could regard only as blasphemy of the highest order. The break up was inevitable and irreversible and exceedingly bitter.

'The problem now facing the authors of Mark — and subsequently those of the other Gospels — was that the picture which would have emerged from their sifting and sorting of the recollections of witnesses to Jesus' sermons and deeds would be in direct contrast to the message they wished to convey.' Alain paused for a moment, taking in Stephen's puzzled expression. 'Because the new religion had fully taken off by then, its adherents overwhelmingly non-Jews who worshipped Christ Jesus as their God. The last thing on earth they needed to hear was of him as a pious Jew, a mere man, and with a message addressed solely to the Jewish people.'

Stephen was aware that a feeling he was experiencing had a familiar ring to it. Then it came back to him. It was with Piers, all those years ago, the feeling that what he was telling him about the Dead Sea Scrolls had been well prepared, that he had been waiting to try it out on someone, someone uninvolved with the issues at stake. It was like that now.

'I'm not boring you, I hope,' said Alain, giving Stephen an enquiring look.

'Good Lord, no. I'm finding it absolutely fascinating.'

This was true. Stephen was hooked. Other things he needed to ask... about Piers... about what Alain knew or suspected concerning his death... they would have to wait.

'But what about Jewish Christianity?' he asked, as Alain was getting up to put coal on the fire. 'Jesus' direct associates, his disciples? Didn't they have any say in what went into the Gospels?'

'None whatsoever. By the time Mark first appeared, around the year 70, Jewish Christianity was dead. Literally so: its remaining members killed or dispersed in the massive Roman offensive which had just taken place against the Jewish state, culminating in the sack of Jerusalem and the destruction of the Temple. It was solely from Paul's new religion, the initial stirrings of the Christianity we know today, that Mark and the other Gospels were written.'

Alain had returned to his chair and was pouring the remains of a bottle into the two glasses.

'So how,' said Stephen, 'did the authors of Mark go about resolving their problem?'

'Creatively,' Alain replied with a smile as he settled back, glass in hand.

'They would have started off with the jumble of material passed down by word of mouth from recollections of supposedly direct witnesses some forty years earlier. Selecting carefully from this, resolving inevitable ambiguities and contradictions, working it up into some sort of coherent narrative with plausible-sounding dialogue. But regardless of how selective they would have been, the underlying problem would still be there. A thorough editing would be needed, with judicious deletions and insertions, to bring it as near as possible into line with the evolving dogma.'

'To cook the books, in other words,' said Stephen.

'Well, yes. You could put it that way. They would have

been under immense pressure to come up with something acceptable to the Church Fathers.' Alain went quiet having said this.

'Are you going to tell me how they went about it?' said Stephen.

'Yes, of course. But I was just wondering whether you would like a break. A bite to eat?'

'If it's all right with you, I wouldn't mind hearing a bit more first. I'm finding it quite fascinating. What you've said so far confirms feelings I had years ago, without appreciating where they came from.'

'Good,' said Alain. 'It's all fairly obvious when you come to look at it objectively — something believers find well-nigh impossible to do.

'The editing process,' he went on, 'would have been carried out for various purposes. One would have been to blur the image, which would have come down overwhelmingly, of Jesus as what we would now regard as a liberal Jewish preacher; another, to suggest, quite unrealistically, that his message was directed, at the very least equally, to non-Jews. When, for example, you read of such inconceivable things as Jesus and his followers disregarding the fast-days; or the passage in Matthew which quotes Jesus as saying that it will be the Gentiles who will lie down with Abraham in the kingdom of heaven, and the Jews who will be expelled to the outer darkness, you can be quite sure that these are bogus insertions. It's simply a matter of following the general rule. The Gospels are riddled with such passages, clearly totally at odds with what would have come down from the recollections of the Jewish witnesses.'

'That reminds me of something,' said Stephen. 'About

Jesus being criticised by the Pharisees for dining with "publicans and sinners". I remember it because "publicans" was a source of amusement to us sixth-formers at St John's. I suppose they would have been Gentiles?'

'Very probably,' said Alain with a laugh. 'And if Jews, certainly not practicing ones. You've hit on another example of where to apply the general rule. In fact, there can be no question whatsoever of Jesus, a pious Jew, engaging in table fellowship with such people. Paul, maybe. As you're probably aware by now, "publicans" is an inept translation of the term for the hated tax collectors, not your landlord of the Dog and Duck. The primary tax collectors for the Romans were the Herodians, and the very least that can be said of Paul's relationship with that lot is that it was a cosy one. But we'll come on to him later.'

'Good,' said Stephen. 'It's another thing that intrigued me in that account: what it said about Paul.'

'I'm not surprised,' said Alain, 'but one thing at a time. There were other reasons for the editing, including the often ham-fistedly contrived one of trying to relate Jesus' words and actions to Old Testament prophecies. But perhaps the most important one — which brings us back to your question of evidence for the insurrection — was to fudge, or at best eliminate, anything that could be construed as hostile to Rome. Nowhere is this more evident than in the treatment of events leading up to the crucifixion. Christianity, even by the time the first Gospel had appeared, would have severed its Jewish roots and was taking off across the Roman empire — including, importantly, in the city of Rome itself, where Mark was most probably written. The Romans, though tolerant of widely varied religious beliefs, would surely have to draw the line at a creed which worshipped as God someone they had executed as leader of an insurrection against their rule. This posed a seemingly insurmountable problem to the authors of the Gospels. That Jesus had been crucified by the Roman authorities was unfortunately indisputable. The best that could be done would be to try to shift the blame as far as possible away from the Romans. And where better than on to the Jews, bitter opponents of the new religion, and who throughout the ages had never ceased to cause the Roman occupiers of their land no end of trouble? The fact that the Jews had been overwhelmingly behind Jesus, had come to regard him as their saviour, ordained by God to deliver them from the Roman yoke, would have to be simply ignored.'

Alain paused here to drink. Stephen, saying nothing, was lost in anticipation for where this was all leading.

'Consider for a moment the beginning and end of those final few days of Jesus' life,' Alain went on as he set down his glass. 'Starting on a high with his triumphant arrival in Jerusalem, the vast ecstatic crowd, many carrying arms, surging into the Temple, keyed up to fever pitch, hailing him King of the Jews: "Hosanna to the Son of David", they cried, "Blessed the coming Kingdom of our father David". It was the moment the Jewish people had long been awaiting: their Messiah primed and ready with God's blessing to drive the Roman invaders from their land. And ending a few days later with his crucifixion by the Romans, the words King of the Jews, pinned above his head for all to see, leaving no possible doubt to the reason for his execution.

'These events are indisputable. There was nothing the authors of the Gospels could do about them. If they were to have any hope of shifting the blame for the crucifixion to the

Jews, they would have to concentrate on that intervening period between Jesus' triumphant arrival at Jerusalem and his death. Bear in mind that, along with virtually everything else that was to appear in the Gospels, no other record of what had transpired existed or could conceivably be produced to conflict with what the authors would have to say. In this respect, they were safe to write whatever best suited their purpose.'

Alain paused again, this time giving Stephen an appealing look. 'If you don't mind, we could carry on with this after a break. Right now, I'm feeling quite hungry. What if we go and see what Mrs. Chadderton has left for us?'

With some reluctance, Stephen nodded in agreement.

While Alain was arranging things in the kitchen, Stephen was able to ponder the extraordinary turn this meeting had taken. It seemed unbelievable that a Roman Catholic parish-priest — a good one, Stephen felt, certainly regarding his evident humanity and approachability — could hold such subversive views, which clearly must have stemmed from Piers. He was looking forward to hearing more. Then perhaps they could get round to talking about Piers himself.

The "bits and pieces" left for them turned out to be a very agreeable meal: onion soup followed by a pork terrine with French bread and a mixed salad, then a selection of cheeses and fruit.

'Like me,' said Alain as they were eating, 'Mrs. Chadderton is half-French. Though, in her case, on her mother's side. That's from where she learned to cook. I'll invite you back some time when she's preparing something special.' He certainly appears to have got himself well-sorted, thought Stephen, not without a touch of envy. 'I didn't offer you wine this time as it seems we've still a good bit of ground to cover. Maybe a glass when we decide to call it a day. You will stay the night, won't you? You're very welcome to.'

So, it was agreed. They stacked the plates by the sink and left the kitchen, returning to the fire, which Alain poked and added more coal to. Then, settling back in his chair:

'The dominant impression that emerges from Gospel accounts of Jesus' triumphant entry into the Temple is one of unbelievable anti-climax. You have this immense throng, worked up to fever pitch, streaming into the Temple courtyard, vociferously acknowledging Jesus as their leader, son of David, and rejoicing in the imminent realisation of his kingdom — which would of course signify defeat and expulsion of their Roman masters. And then? Well, according to Mark — the first Gospel and source material for the other three — nothing at all. Jesus just looks around, sees that it's getting late, and heads off to Bethany with the twelve. No mention of what his tens-of-thousands of keyed-up followers were to make of this abandonment, how they would have reacted: an anti-climax that is utterly inconceivable. Nowhere are the traces of the censor's scissors more evident.

'So, what did really happen? Well, despite that pathetic attempt at evasion, it's abundantly clear that the Temple was indeed invaded and taken over by Jesus and his followers. And that they held it for several days, with Jesus preaching to the spellbound masses, to the evident distress of the authorities who found themselves powerless to intervene. This much is clear from Luke, which reports the Herodian-appointed chief priests wishing to destroy Jesus, but being unable to do so because of the multitudes there hanging on to his words. That it had come to this was no mean achievement. The Temple, far from simply a place of worship, consisted of a massive fortress covering some twenty acres of land. It was staffed by many thousand personnel and protected by a Roman cohort of several hundred men. The Temple police, a substantial force at all times, would have been further strengthened to deal with the huge influx of pilgrims flocking there for the Passover festivities. And yet, with all this at their disposal, the authorities were unable to resist the invasion and several-days occupation of their territory — an intrusion which would certainly have involved acts of violence.

'Care has been taken in the Gospels to portray Jesus as a man of peace and gentleness, opposed to all forms of aggression. But disjointed fragments, that somehow managed to survive, point to a rather different picture. Matthew, for example: "Don't think I came to bring peace on earth, I didn't come to bring peace but a sword." And Luke: "Anyone who doesn't have a sword should sell his cloak and buy one". Where such phrases uttered by Jesus appear in the Gospels is probably quite arbitrary. They would have been remembered for the impression they made at the time and passed on to reappear wherever the authors felt to be appropriate. But the message is clear enough: when the time was ripe, Jesus, the Messiah, promised deliverer of the Jewish nation, would be ready to lead his people to armed victory over their oppressors. We can assume that many of those invading the Temple were armed, and this is even borne out in the Gospels by the account of Peter drawing his sword and severing the ear of a servant of a high priest — the part of a violent encounter that probably evaded censorship by providing an opportunity for demonstrating once again Jesus' miraculous healing powers. And then, of course, there is the famous incident, reported in all four Gospels, of the routing by Jesus and his enraged supporters of the legitimate traders in the Temple courtyard — money changers and sellers of sacrificial beasts. Again, an overtly violent incident, and a further indication that for a while — indeed, for several days — Jesus and his followers had taken control of the Temple fortress.'

Alain then went on to talk about the many absurdities and contradictions in Gospel reports of the trials of Jesus following his arrest: accounts in Mark and Matthew of a Jewish trial — in the middle of the night! — before the Sanhedrin, at which he is condemned to death for blasphemy; the decision of the Sanhedrin the following morning to take him to Pilate — who, they must have known, wouldn't have been the slightest bit interested in this religious offence; the account in Luke of the charge being changed to include "preventing the people from paying tax to Caesar and claiming to be King-Messiah," which Pilate hears and to which he declares Jesus to be innocent; then the Jewish mob, whose ecstatic devotion to Jesus had been preventing the authorities from intervening in his occupation of the Temple, screaming for him to be crucified — with no explanation whatsoever for this incredible volte-face; Pilate unbelievably acquiescing to their demand, and "washing his hands" of the blood of an innocent man — an essentially Jewish gesture, inconceivably that of a Roman governor.

'Nowhere is the blatant disregard for the truth, or even remote plausibility, more evident. The whole treatment of that intervening period, from Jesus' invasion of the Temple till his death, being little more than a far-fetched invention to cover the embarrassing fact of a forlorn insurrection — perhaps engineered or perhaps merely stumbled into by Jesus — and its eventual suppression by the forces of order; the crucifixion of Jesus, along with others caught up with him in that final reckoning, the inevitable Roman penalty for rebellion against their rule.'

TWENTY-FIVE

Stephen awoke the following morning little more than three hours after having gone to bed. It took him a few moments to determine where he was, for memories of the previous evening, which had stretched well into the night, to come seeping back. Alain, he could imagine as being in a worse state, probably not having slept at all, by now immersed in the ritual of seven o'clock Mass. They were due to meet downstairs for breakfast at eight-fifteen.

It had been a mammoth session to which Stephen had contributed very little, just the occasional interjection, reminiscences of long-discarded religious perplexities. By the early hours, Alain had got on to Piers's intriguing uncovering of Paul's familial connection to the Herodian puppet rulers — which the author of Luke, at least, must have been aware of, yet chose not to reveal. This relationship clarified certain events concerning Paul, reported in Acts, providing explanations where none was available before. For example, his early persecution of the Jewish Christianity community, — when he was known as Saul — violently breaking up their meetings and arresting adherents, men and women, and throwing them into jail — though with what authority and for what reason never divulged. But then in the Scrolls appears the bitter condemnation by the Teacher of Righteousness — James, Jewish Christianity's leader — of sexual practices clearly identifiable as relating to the Herodian rulers, in particular that of uncle-niece marriages — a practice habitually adopted by the Herodian dynasty to consolidate the succession: to keep it in the family. As a powerful member of that family, Saul's infuriation with Jewish Christianity, the authority for his punitive actions, and indeed his possession of Roman citizenship, all become clear.

Another example concerns the extraordinary sequence of events, reported in Acts, set in train following an attempt on Paul's life by zealots of the Jewish Christianity community, sworn to kill him for preaching against the Law. He is rescued, following a tip-off, by a Roman cohort and, for his safety, dispatched with an escort to Caesarea, the Roman capital of Judaea. Acts describe the escort: two centurions, two hundred soldiers, seventy horsemen and two hundred spearmen! At Caesarea, he appears before the Roman governor, Felix, who treats him with great courtesy. He resides there for some considerable time, — in Herod's palace! — consorting with the king, Agrippa II, and his sister, the princess Bernice. Even the Roman governor, it turns out, had been adopted into the Herodian clan: Felix being married to Drucilla, another of Agrippa II's three sisters. All this high-level effort and concern for someone, so Acts would have us believe, that, from the Roman perspective, would appear no more than an extreme religious propagandist, a potential source of trouble; his treatment as a person of consequence, the consideration afforded him at the highest levels of society, making no sense at all. Until that is, we learn of Piers's researches into Saul's antecedents: of the close line of descent from Herod the Great he shares with Agrippa II.

When Stephen arrived downstairs, he found Alain already seated at the table, looking jaded. He was introduced to Mrs. Chadderton, who had come into the room bearing a pot of coffee and a jug of milk. She was quite different in appearance from what Stephen had expected, much younger — mid-thirties, it seemed — and undoubtedly attractive; not at all the dour, religious widow he had been led to believe. She watched with an amused smile as Alain poured coffee into his cup with a shaking hand, then asked what they would like for breakfast. A little later, over scrambled eggs on toast, Stephen broke the easy silence into which they had settled.

'It was really good of you to take so much time for me,' he said, '…and all this hospitality… I don't know how to thank you…'

'Not at all,' replied Alain. 'My pleasure. Seriously though, I only saw a draft of that document of Piers's about a month ago. It tied in with what I knew of his research — and with his desire for openness in presenting and interpreting controversial findings. And it was useful for me to spell out something of the justification to you… helped me sort it in my mind.' Stephen smiled to himself at having already come to that conclusion. 'And it helped that it was you, someone who had known Piers, knew something of what he was on about. And an outsider. An interested unbeliever.' He laughed having said that. 'The ideal audience.'

'Well, thank you for that,' said Stephen, genuinely grateful for having revisited, without hang-ups this time, those religious perplexities of his school days – but at the same time concerned that what he had set out wanting to hear from Alain had been side-tracked. Now was the time to put that right.

'I really can't get over the way this meeting of ours has

turned out,' he said, as he helped himself to coffee. 'It feels really strange being brought right back to things I thought I'd seen the back of years ago… to see them treated objectively. I really appreciate that… really do. But what we haven't talked about yet is what happened to Piers.'

Alain was spreading butter on his toast as Stephen said this; he continued doing so in the short silence that followed. Mrs. Chadderton, returning with a tray, paused in the doorway looking concerned.

'Natasha is convinced he was murdered,' Stephen went on. 'The police apparently regard it as suicide. I've been waiting for an opportunity to ask what you think it was.'

'Yes,' said Alain, quietly, as though to himself. 'I knew we would have to get on to this.' He reached for the marmalade, started spreading it on his toast. 'The problem though, which you may have difficulty believing, is that I'm probably as much in the dark about it as you are.' He looked up at Stephen. 'Both suppositions appear extremely unlikely. But then I suppose it has to be one or the other. It's something that's been bothering me, keeping me awake at night… the idea of Piers committing suicide.' It seemed to Stephen that he was about to say more, then changed his mind. 'But then,' he went on, 'to have him killed… I know he had upset some pretty powerful people there… but nothing, surely, that could lead to that.'

The silence this time was longer, broken eventually by Stephen.

'Natasha said he had been injured, as though he'd been in some sort of fight…'

'I know. Could it have led to him being poisoned? Is that what you're saying? When he was unable to defend himself? But then the autopsy would have shown that up. Wouldn't it?'

This was clearly something else that Alain had been brooding on.

'I don't know,' said Stephen. 'Depends, I suppose, on how hard they were looking.' This just slipped out, to be immediately dismissed. 'No, you're right. It would have to have been obvious to whoever was carrying it out... there must be a record of their findings...'

Mrs. Chadderton had come over to clear some of the mess from the table, the tender look she was giving Alain noticed by Stephen, shunted aside for future consideration.

'It's only that...' said Alain, still lost in thought, then deciding to come out with something, then changing his mind, leaving it hanging there. It was the second time within minutes he had done something like this.

'Only what?' said Stephen, feeling some encouragement to be in order this time.

'It's probably nothing,' said Alain, pulling himself together. 'It's just that I can't get anything out of Piers's colleague in the Vatican, the one I thought I was on easy terms with. Almost impossible to get through to him. And when I managed to, by subterfuge, it was as though he was someone else, someone who didn't know me and refused to respond at all. He's the one who's supposed to call here for Piers's journals. I've no idea now when he proposes to do this.'

For some reason, this called to mind for Stephen Natasha's and Stan's journalist friend's suspicions regarding the death of Pope John Paul I – something Alain must certainly have views on.

'Could he have been frightened, do you think?' he asked. 'Afraid of being overheard speaking to you about Piers?' Stephen was feeling mildly aroused now, as though something of significance could be slipping into place. 'They must still be in shock there at that sudden death of the last Pope... and now this.'

Alain was looking a shade uncomfortable. 'I don't want to jump to conclusions,' he said after a short pause. 'But yes, it could be that, or something related... the undercurrents of that death... all very mysterious. We'll have to wait till he gets here, when I can speak to him face-to-face. I know him quite well. I can't imagine he'll be like that with me then.'

At least this is something, thought Stephen. Some thread, however tenuous, to latch on to. He felt concerned then that he would be excluded from that encounter and was wondering how best to ensure he would be kept abreast of whatever was to come out of it, when Alain interrupted his thoughts with an unexpected proposal.

'I'll get you to meet him when he eventually arrives. You'll like him. He was very close to Piers.'

Satisfaction at this offer was clouded by the thought that whoever it was would be unlikely to agree to such a meeting: to a complete outsider muscling in on sensitive matters of acute concern to the secretive faction to which he belonged. Stephen tried to convey these misgivings to Alain.

'That's no problem at all,' he replied. 'He'll be only too happy to meet you. He knows all about you from Piers.'

This came over as scarcely credible: that Piers, with good cause to regret ever having befriended him, would so much as mention his name.

'I can't believe that, Alain,' he said. 'There could be no earthly reason for Piers to want to talk about me. We parted not exactly on the best of terms. And I've had no contact with him since, none whatsoever since he first set off for Rome.'

Stephen immediately regretted coming out with this, with perhaps drawing attention to matters he had every reason to wish would remain buried. He was therefore more than a little put out by Alain's response.

'You're referring to what happened between you and Natasha?'

How on earth, thought Stephen, stunned, did he know about that? He said nothing, lost for how to respond.

'I'm sorry,' said Alain with a light laugh. 'Sorry to spring that on to you like that. But Piers did talk about you. He saw you as a prime example of that vast mass of people out there he particularly wanted to reach. And... no wait a minute,' — this was in response to Stephen's attempt to interrupt — 'that business with you and Natasha, it didn't come as a surprise to him. It had occurred before. More than once, as it happens. Believe me. It was something he had come to terms with, a facet of her personality — her deep-seated needs if you like — that he knew he would have to face up to in their relationship. And, believe me, there were many things she had to face up to with him.'

Stephen was having difficulty taking this in. But then it evoked those last words he had heard from Piers, words etched painfully in his memory: 'You certainly didn't waste much time.' He had assumed this to have been addressed to himself... or perhaps to both of them. But, from what Alain was telling him... could it have been Natasha he was speaking to? That he expected no less from her, that it was just her haste he was remarking upon? Pushing such patently self-serving fantasy aside, his thoughts returned to the perennial notion of how little he understood Piers. It then occurred to him that this meeting with Alain had been planned, that he had been purposefully inveigled into more than just the matter of delivering a suitcase. He put this to Alain, who was clearly prepared for it, ready with his response.

'Yes, you're right. I've been waiting for an appropriate moment to tell you. You've just provided it. Piers did want us to meet. He first brought it up some years ago. Then other things intervened, we never got round to doing anything about it. He brought it up again quite recently, not long before he died. I could obviously have picked up those documents myself. But Natasha, who knew about this, saw the opportunity. I'm pleased she did, though I'm not sure exactly what she had in mind. As you've seen for yourself, she's been in quite a confused state since Piers's death. And, anyway...'

'But why?' Stephen interrupted. 'What earthly reason could Piers have for wanting us to meet? If you're trying to tell me he was relaxed about finding me in bed with Natasha...'

'No, I'm not saying that, not at the time he wasn't. But later, when he had had time to reflect, when the bitterness with Natasha had run its course and he learned from her how she had led you on. She would have been quite open about that. As I told you before, it wasn't the first time something like that had happened. Their relationship was strong enough to withstand it.'

'But you haven't answered my question.'

'No, I haven't. Well, it was to do with re-establishing contact with you — something he very much wanted to do. After all the time that had elapsed, he thought a third-party approach might be the best way of achieving this. That's when he first spoke to me about it. You have to realise that you were the only outsider he had ever discussed his vision with, his commitment to achieving it. Those conversations with you had come to mean a lot to him — the only ones he ever had with anyone outside the church.'

'As far as I can remember, I was pretty sceptical about the whole business, I made no attempt to hide it.'

'Yes, you were sceptical of his chances of getting anywhere with it. But he knew you very well, both from your school days and later as a close friend. He was in no doubt that you would welcome what he was setting out to achieve if only you could see it as having any likelihood of success. It was when he got to feel that things were moving for him, colleagues in outposts of the church, even in the Vatican itself, joining him in what was becoming a sizable movement, that his mind turned to contacting you again. Quite apart from anything else, he would have wanted this for past friendship's sake, and so would Natasha.'

And so would I, thought Stephen in the silence that followed, a wave of sadness reminding him again of never having made the approach to Piers which could have ended their estrangement. And now there was this contributing to his dejection, the affair with Natasha being made known and talked about behind his back, rekindling the shame. He thought to say something of this to Alain, deciding against it, concerned now to bring their exchange to an end. And so it was agreed that they would be in touch again soon. If not before, certainly when the emissary from the Vatican had confirmed the date of his proposed visit.

For the next few days, Stephen's thoughts kept turning to Piers, — his biblical researches, what he was setting out to achieve... what he was up against... his death — interfering with other concerns, in particular his mathematical research, which had all but ground to a halt. Although scepticism for

Piers's vision — or, as Alain would have it, the likelihood of it ever selling to the faithful — remained undiminished, he couldn't but be aware of glaring instances of the secularisation of Christian affairs, transformations having come about independently of conscious influence or pressure, spiritual significance simply having faded to become no more than an optional add-on. A prominent example was the festival of Christmas, now celebrated unreservedly by everyone, believers and atheists alike, its Christian significance happily subsumed, along with Santa Claus, turkey and Christmas pudding, into an orgy of unspiritual indulgence and conspicuous consumption — an undoubted boost to the capitalist economy. Easter too, with its chocolate eggs and Easter bunnies, testifying to a universal appeal little to do with its solemn foundation. Probably not quite what Piers had in mind, he decided, but clear examples nonetheless of secular phenomena that had shunted off their religious origins and were clearly flourishing and here to stay. Something of this also had to be said for Europe's immense Christian heritage: its cathedrals, symbols of sublime human achievement; the churches of its towns and villages, cherished for their architectural beauty; its paintings, sculptures, music, even its literature, valued for aesthetic attributes quite independent of religious belief.

This is all very well, thought Stephen — remembering past anger, feeling it returning — but rather beside the point when it comes to the church voluntarily relinquishing power. Power that stemmed from its claim for authority deriving directly from a supposed Creator of the Universe and, perhaps even more bizarrely, supported by some billion or more adherents professing to believe it. Power that was formerly maintained with unbridled ruthlessness, with countless burnings at the stake and forced drownings and all manner of unspeakable torture meted out to those who dared question, or were thought to have questioned, even the minutest detail of the dogma: actions that must rank the church among the world's foremost perpetrators of crimes against humanity. Though such excesses had now passed, power maintained nevertheless by methods that include brainwashing of the young and vulnerable, instilling in them terror that their common "sins" — dwelling on impure thoughts, for example, non-attendance at Sunday Mass — were exposing them to everlasting torment in the fires of hell. Though this absurdity appears laughable now, it was no laughing matter, some thirty years ago, to a group of terrified eleven-year-olds gathered for a "retreat" in St John's chapel.

Stephen well remembers the occasion. The affair was conducted by a young Irish priest, smoothly proficient in the art of mass persuasion. Thinking back to his performance, Stephen, in spite of himself, has to appreciate the skill with which he pursued his aim. Brother Ignatius, having introduced him, had retreated to one side, leaving him centre stage, erect and motionless, waiting for silence. And when it came, when you could hear a pin drop, continuing to wait, the air heavy with foreboding. Then he started up, low-key, quietly friendly, nothing remotely threatening; the boys relaxed, giving him their full attention. He talked of this and that, making little jokes — on the dogma even, on phrases in the gospels. The one coming back to Stephen being his take on *not by bread alone that man shall live*.

'Course it isn't,' he proclaimed, soft Irish brogue upping in volume. 'What about the bacon and sausages, the toast and marmalade he has for breakfast?' Peals of relieved laughter. The boys thoroughly won over, loving it; no less so in view of the imagined disapproval of Ignatius, scowling in the wings. Then, with seeming reluctance, he moved on to the serious stuff, managing to sound almost apologetic about having to do so. But duty-bound, he insists, for their own sakes, so they can be forever on their guard, ready at all times to resist the devil's subtle attempts to bring about their downfall. And so to the warning of the peril they face every moment of their lives, the peril of an eternity of horrendous suffering in the unquenchable fires of hell. The laughter stilled and forgotten, the fraught silence returning. The boys, a completely captive audience now, waiting transfixed.

'Try to imagine what this means,' he said. 'Many of you may have experienced the pain of a burn, an accidental touch of hot metal, a splash of scalding fat from a pan. Quite painful it can be. Treated with a soothing ointment perhaps, maybe a bandage. Well, there'll be no ointment or bandages in hell. And the burning will be ten... a hundred times more painful. And covering every inch of your body. And the bodies of the countless thousands around you, all writhing there in agony. And you'll know that your suffering will never end. Never. Not after a day... not after a week... a year... a thousand years. Never. It will last for all eternity. Just think for a moment what this means.' He had then now, spellbound, terrified, waiting in trepidation for what was still to come. 'Think of a sphere of steel the size of the Earth suspended in space,' he went on, breaking the nerve-racking silence. 'Imagine that every year a dove flies up to it, brushing it with a feather of its wing. Each year, just one light brush with a feather. How many billions of billions of billions of billions of years do you think it would take for that brush with a feather to wear out that sphere of steel the size of the Earth? No, you can't imagine it. But let me tell you that when that time comes... when that sphere of steel the size of the Earth has been completely worn away... eternity will not even have started.'

Years later, Stephen was to read of strikingly similar accounts of the church's efforts to terrorise the young — most notably, and with knobs on, by James Joyce. But by that time he had come to regard the whole edifice of religious dogma as little more than superstitious nonsense, with its visions of hell the sick fantasies of deranged minds — conveniently exploited nonetheless to consolidate the church's power. At the time of the St John's retreat, however, Stephen, along with his classmates, would have been quite incapable of questioning the existence of hell. To even think of doing so, they had been led to believe, would be to imperil themselves still further. They trooped out of chapel pale and dumbstruck; even Philips uncharacteristically subdued, contemplating perhaps his particular predisposition to eternal damnation — Stephen calling up this image with a sudden rush of amusement. No laughing matter at the time, though. Then his mind turned disparagingly to Piers's vision. How on earth, he wondered, in the face of all this swallowed insanity, could Piers and Alain and others in the movement have believed for a moment that their aims could ever be fulfilled? Why hadn't they simply cut their losses? Just got out of it and into something else? Anything else: Piers back to his academic studies and an unencumbered life with Natasha. What was the matter with them?

He returned to college in perplexed despondency to his neglected researches, which would help him pass the time while awaiting the call from Alain.

TWENTY-SIX

Although the deadline for submissions to the Texas conference had long passed, Stephen set to work immediately on the short paper with which Karl had assured him he would be able to wangle him into it. At least this was something to turn his mind off the Piers saga for a while. Within a couple of days, he was close to completing what promised to come over as an innovative approach to the Last Theorem problem. Although harbouring reservations regarding the delivery of that promise, it could nevertheless achieve the desired effect of displaying his work to a wider audience than the specialised circle he habitually addressed. As he was tidying up the final draft, his office phone rang. It was Stan, calling to say he would be in London the day after next, meeting up with a journalist friend — the one with informed speculation from Rome on the death of Albino Luciani just thirty-three days after his election to the papacy. He had been intrigued with what Stan had told him of the Vatican connection with that other bizarre death in Westminster cathedral and wanted to meet Stephen to talk about it. Could he join them for a drink that evening, perhaps a bite to eat? Could he indeed! Thankful for having all but concluded the paper for Karl, he wrapped it up and sent it off; then settled back to fevered anticipation of what this unexpected encounter would reveal.

The meeting was to be in a little-frequented pub, recalled by Stan from his RADA days, in an alleyway off a Fitzrovia side street. Stephen arrived first, bought a beer and settled himself at a secluded table. It appeared a well-chosen venue for their purpose, empty but for the barman and two regulars slumped at the counter. He hadn't long to wait before Stan arrived with his friend, who turned out to be somewhat older than Stephen had expected — mid-to-late fifties, perhaps a bit more — and smartly dressed in a brown suit, checked shirt and a tie suggesting prestigious association: public school perhaps, or regiment or London club. He greeted Stephen warmly, with no trace of pretentiousness, introducing himself as Ennis Leary and saying how much he had been looking forward to this meeting. Following further convivial remarks and the buying of beer, they were set to go, seated around a small circular table, deciding how and where to begin. It was eventually agreed — largely at Ennis's insistence — that Stephen should start off by outlining what he knew about Piers: as Brother Carroll at St John's, his biblical researches and their implications, what was known of his Vatican connection, views regarding his mysterious death, anything else. Ennis had been fascinated by what little Stan had already told him and was eager to hear more. After that, they could get on to Ennis's "informed speculation" on the death of Pope John Paul I.

Stephen's outline of the Piers saga went on for quite some time, due in part to Ennis's interruptions with queries and requests for amplification. Stephen didn't mind this. In fact, he was grateful for the opportunity to string together the various strands into some sort of coherent picture before a clearly perceptive listener. Stan, apart from chipping in early on with school-days reminiscences, had remained uncharacteristically silent, content just to listen attentively to what the other two had to say. Ennis was clearly enthralled, becoming particularly animated towards the end when Stephen alluded to Piers and his Vatican associates scheming for Albino Luciani in the papal election.

'Where on earth did you get that from?' he asked, clearly excited.

Stephen had to think for a moment before recalling Natasha's frenzied outburst about them "moving heaven and earth to get him elected."

'This is amazing,' said Ennis. 'I'll be getting on in a moment to the mysterious circumstances surrounding his death. But there is also something of a mystery concerning his election, something that's been completely overshadowed by his dropping dead a month later.' He stopped to drink, raising his hand at the same time to prevent interruption. 'Outside the Conclave, nobody gave a moment's thought to Luciani as a candidate. He wasn't cited in any Vatican-watcher press articles, which were full of speculation on all those thought to be in with any sort of a chance. Nor did his name appear in bookies lists of potential winners — in which Britain's Cardinal Hume appeared as a rank outsider at 30–1 but Luciani wasn't even thought to be worth a mention. And yet, once the election process got underway, he featured strongly right from the start and ended up romping home an easy winner. An amazing outcome in view of the strongly fancied candidates he would have had to contend with. More to the point, it suggests a formidable undercover operation in play. But what nobody appears to have any idea of is where this could have come from. Which makes what you've just said about Piers's group campaigning for him so interesting.'

Stephen was getting used to the feeling that something or other he had just picked up on could have bearing on Piers's death, Ennis's disclosure another case in point.

'I didn't think to question Natasha about it,' he said, acknowledging to himself what would have been the futility of such an attempt. 'She must have had good reason for coming out with it. Perhaps someone should speak to her.' By someone, Stephen had in mind someone other than himself.

'Yes,' said Ennis, 'that's obviously worth following up. But look, I don't know about you two but I'm beginning to feel quite hungry. What do you say to another beer and then off for something to eat? In the meantime, I could start filling you in with my part of the story — supposing the various things we're talking about here to be parts of a single story. Or is that too much to ask? Just a coincidence could it be? Two very mysterious Vatican deaths a few weeks apart? Two unrelated incidents? Anyway, whatever it is, it's an extraordinary tale I've been getting from Rome. Stan's heard some of it already.'

'Yes, I have,' said Stan, 'and I can't wait to hear the rest. Whichever way this turns out, we seem to have the makings of a superior mystery play here. Or spooky film perhaps' — his expression indicating exploration of this notion. 'Just so long as I get to play the lead.'

'I'm sure that can be arranged,' said Ennis with a grin as he made for the bar.

He returned, clutching his round, obviously wound up with what he was about to disclose.

'The Vatican City State is an extraordinary entity,' he said, as he set the glasses down on the table. 'An island of about half a square kilometre in the middle of Rome, with some thousand inhabitants. Size and population of a small village.

Yet it qualifies as an independent state — like the USA and China! It's got all the trappings of an independent state: ambassadors and diplomats and passports and border controls, a police and security corps, the lot. And the Pope is an absolute monarch. There are loads of functionaries, of course, with fancy titles and impressive-sounding responsibilities, but they're all appointed directly by the Pope, and he's quite free to get rid of any of them on a whim. None of your independent judiciary, separation of legislative and executive functions, all that. The Pope controls everything. From the moment of his election, he becomes the absolute ruler and remains so for the rest of his life. It's a quite unique and bizarre set-up. But, in spite of all that, the analogy of a village can still hold good. The citizens live, in many respects, in a village-type community; there's little that goes on in one part of the Vatican that doesn't rapidly permeate the rest of it. This was something I used to make good use of when I was working in Rome. Stefano, my main Vatican contact, had it well sewn up: internal sources who reported anything of possible interest pretty well as soon as it happened. Lovely guy, Stefano. A former priest who, years ago, simply decided to quit — or so I'd always thought. Then there were suggestions he'd been defrocked — probably put about by jealous colleagues. It doesn't matter anyway. What there is no doubt at all about is that his information was always cast-iron reliable.'

Ennis paused to take a drink. Stephen was once again experiencing the feeling that something crucial to the Piers affair could be about to emerge. Ennis started up again as he was putting down his glass.

'I'd kept up some sort of contact with Stefano, purely by way of friendship, but hadn't heard from him for getting on for a year. Then he phoned in October, a few days after the Pope had died. He was in a highly agitated state, calling from a payphone, convinced his home line was being tapped and frightened for his life — as were his Vatican informants. Everything pointed, he said, to the Pope having been poisoned, events immediately following the discovery of his body testifying compellingly to that conclusion. Cover-up and high-level misinformation campaigns were well underway. In typical Italian fashion, witnesses were set to reveal nothing. Stefano was powerless to do anything but wanted to put on record, somewhere secure and out of the way and with someone he could trust, an account of what he knew to have taken place. I was to do nothing with it that could endanger him and his informants. Nor was I to attempt to contact him in any way. He would get back to me when it was safe to do so and we would decide where to go from there.'

A few customers had entered the pub by this time and had settled around the bar, exchanging greetings with the earlier arrivals. Stan swivelled his chair to avoid facing them and risking recognition. Ennis paused in his delivery just long enough to drink deeply from his glass.

'Although Luciani had been completely overlooked before his election by supposedly informed Vatican-watchers,' he continued, 'it soon became apparent that he was well known to the more reform-orientated members of the Conclave, who would have been aware of his contentiously radical views on various sensitive areas of church policy — views he had always taken care to conceal in public pronouncements. I don't really want to go into all this just now — perhaps later in the restaurant. But what is important to appreciate is that Luciani was set on a course for reform that was repugnant to the overwhelming majority of the Curia — that's the papal court, the governing body of the Roman Catholic Church — who, from the moment of his accession, had been forever breathing down his neck. Immediately following his election, he had done the obvious thing of maintaining all the existing functionaries in office, though making it clear that this was a temporary measure while he was deciding on more permanent arrangements. He started working on these almost immediately, consulting widely, conducting interviews, studying documents. So that within a month — up until what turned out to be the last day of his life — he had put together a long list of the changes he was determined to carry out. On that very last day, he discussed these with Cardinal Villot, the Vatican's Secretary of State and "Camerlengo" — effectively the Pope's deputy, the person who, in the event of the Pope's death, comes to assume the temporal powers of the papacy until a successor has been elected. It was at this meeting that Villot was to learn that he was the first one on Luciani's list for the chop. You can imagine how that went down.'

Ennis picked up his briefcase from the floor and started rummaging through it.

'I've a picture of him somewhere,' he said. 'Ah, here it is.'

He took it out, placing it on the table between Stephen and Stan: a seated figure, black cape over black, with jewelled buttons and pendant; cold, piercing eyes through tinted shades, mouth set in an arrogant sneer.

'My God,' said Stan. 'The perfect stage-villain. You couldn't better it.'

They all laughed.

'We shouldn't be judging by appearances,' said Ennis.

'That would be quite unfair. Wait until you've heard the rest of it.'

He put the photo back in his briefcase.

'As you'd expect in a village,' he went on, 'many in the Vatican were aware of Luciani's list and a good bit of what it contained. Stefano had been receiving continual updates from his various well-placed informants. It was a white-hot issue, auguring unprecedented upheaval in the Vatican power structure.'

He stopped to drink, emptying his glass.

'Can I get you a top-up?' said Stephen. His own glass was still more than half full, Stan's much the same.

Ennis declined the offer. He wanted to get on to the Pope's death, he told them, and the immediate reactions to the discovery of his body. Just the bare known facts which Stefano had passed on to him. Then they could go to eat. Afterwards, they could consider the fraught issues surrounding his papacy.

'It was Sister Vincenza, the nun Luciani had brought with him from Venice, who found him. She would enter his study at four-thirty each morning with a pot of coffee, leaving it there and tapping on his bedroom door with a good-morning greeting. He would respond, returning the greeting. On this occasion, there was no response. Worried, not knowing what to do, she went away, returning some minutes later to tap again on his door. Still no response. She tapped again, harder this time and, getting no reply, opened the door. What she saw nearly gave her a heart attack. Luciani was sitting up in bed, wearing his glasses, features frozen in an agonised expression, hands clutching sheets of paper containing the explosive list, which he had discussed with Villot just some ten hours earlier, and notes he had made of that meeting. She pulled herself together, felt his pulse to confirm the obvious and hurried to summon the two priests who acted as Luciani's secretaries; then went to tell the other nuns who served with her in the papal apartments — setting news of the death and the manner of its discovery spreading rapidly through the Vatican village.'

'How many nuns did the Pope have serving him?' Stan interrupted at this point, his mind grasping at previously unimagined scenarios.

'Four or five or so,' said Ennis, 'including Sister Vincenza.'

'Quite a harem,' said Stan. 'You haven't a picture of them by any chance?'

'No, I haven't. Sorry. But I think it would only disappoint you if I had.'

Having dealt with that, Ennis returned to what had to be the crux of his account.

'Fathers Magee and Lorenzi, the Pope's two secretaries, arrived at the bedside within minutes. Magee's first action was to telephone Villot — now effectively head of the Roman Catholic Church. From being informed the previous evening that he was to be put out to grass, Villot had now become, quite literally, lord of all he surveyed. He lost no time in wielding his newly acquired absolute power. On a table beside Luciani's bed was a bottle of the liquid medicine he took each night for a chronic ailment. Villot pocketed this bottle, then removed the papers from Luciani's hands, the glasses from his head, then picked up various other personal objects that lay around. None of these items has ever been seen again. He then decreed that news of the death was to remain secret until he declared otherwise and that its discovery by Sister Vincenza should never be revealed. Instead, he put together a tissue of lies for transmissions to the world at large. This attributed discovery of the body to Father Magee, in concocted circumstances which included, among other fabrications, a sacred book in the dead Pope's hands — in place of the contentious list, which was to vanish without trace. You can well imagine how all this went down with the papal household, many of whom would have been well aware of what had actually taken place and knew that news of it would already have spread widely within the Vatican village and, most likely, beyond.

'Villot then made a number of phone calls, the first being to arrange for the hasty embalming of the Pope's body. He was later to render this gruesome process more difficult for the embalmers by forbidding them to drain blood from the corpse.'

'Why on earth did he do that?' said Stephen.

Ennis hesitated before replying.

'I was going to come on to all that a bit later... but, I suppose this could be as good a place as any. You see, as I told you before, Stefano's informers were convinced the Pope had been poisoned. The medicine he took each night on getting into bed could have provided a convenient means of delivery. Villot's actions certainly add credence to that view. This is not to imply that he was the assassin. It could be that he suspected murder and was set on protecting the church from scandal. In his mindset, if the Pope had been murdered, the best course would be to cover it up, considerations of morality and justice not coming into it. So, to come back to your question, if blood had been drained... well, it would have to be around for a while. They couldn't very well just flush it down the loo. Perhaps that could give someone the idea of getting it tested — clearly something Villot would at all costs want to avoid.

The bigger, more transparent problem he had to face was resisting calls for an autopsy — the inevitable outcome of such a death anywhere else. But not in the Vatican if its absolute ruler decides otherwise. In the event, Villot simply ignored the insistent calls for an autopsy, arranging instead for a hasty lying-in-state and burial.'

'Well,' said Stan, as they were getting ready to leave, 'don't say I didn't warn you. You only have to look at the guy.'

Later, in a Greek restaurant in Charlotte Street, over moussaka and retsina, they talked for a while of other things: of Stan's plans to be written out of his television soap for a few months, so he could participate in a potentially blockbuster Hollywood production.

'Just so long as Broadlands don't decide to kill you off,' said Stephen. 'And have you kiss goodbye to all that easy money.'

Stan assured them of his welcome back with open arms, of the prospect of his fans in impassioned revolt at any other outcome. Then they went on to Ennis's book on the Irish republican movement, which he was coming close to finishing; and finally, to Stephen's decision to say nothing about the Last Theorem problem. Returning then to where they had left off an hour or so earlier.

'The case for Pope John Paul I's murder looks, on the face of it, pretty persuasive,' said Ennis. 'Had what I described earlier occurred anywhere other than in the Vatican, it would undoubtedly have led to a thorough police investigation. The question of motive would have been a key factor: what possible reason could there be for anyone wanting to kill him?'

'That's just what's been bothering me,' said Stephen. 'I

can imagine Luciani perhaps putting noses out of joint. But nothing surely that could amount to that. Didn't Stefano say anything about this? His informants believed he'd been murdered, didn't they? They must have views on what lay behind it.'

'My last conversation with him was focused, of course, on Luciani's death and its discovery by Sister Vincenza and with what happened immediately afterwards. That was what he had phoned in agitation to tell me. The circumstances didn't really leave time for much more. But I'd been aware of the tense atmosphere that had been building up since Luciani's election from other sources: an intensification of the age-old battle between traditionalists — reactionaries, if you like — and modernisers, with the Curia unwaveringly traditionalistic. And now, with a new Pope resolutely on the other side, there was fevered speculation that he was embarking on an unprecedented disruption of the old order, and this was confirmed to Villot on that last evening of his life.'

'Yes,' said Stephen, 'but to have him murdered! It just doesn't seem credible. It's not as though we're talking about some Mafia organisation.'

'I know. But certain insiders feel very differently. And Villot's actions point at the very least to him having suspected foul play. He could have banished all doubts about the cause of death by agreeing to an autopsy. End of problem, if there was nothing to hide. Instead, no autopsy — in the face of clamorous demands for one. No death certificate — just a Vatican health service doctor's stated opinion of probable myocardial infarction, but nothing committed to paper. This is hardly surprising, as myocardial infarction can only be confirmed as a cause of death by an autopsy. But then, the

Vatican's absolute ruler can decide exactly as he pleases. No power on earth can force his hand.'

Stan, who had appeared distracted since speaking about his film plans, brought them back to Luciani's proposed actions that were so upsetting to members of the Curia.

'Can you give us an idea of just what they were?' he asked Ennis.

'Well, there was both a general problem and at least one very specific one. The general one was Luciani's vision of a *poor church*, a church concerned with the secular issues of poverty and disparity of wealth in the world; also, to the further displeasure of the Curia, he was coming out as opposed to the ostentatious displays of riches and ceremony, which they all loved. This much could have been predicted. At one stage in his career, he had made a great point of selling church treasures to finance a centre for the disabled. And, when Patriarch of Venice, he preferred to dress in the simple black clothes of a parish priest, rather than the elaborate robes to which he was entitled. He also took to turning up alone and incognito for such things as visiting the sick in hospital — to the distress of administrators who would have wanted to accompany him and make a great fuss about it.'

'But, you know,' said Stephen, interrupting, 'all this is precisely how Piers anticipated the initial stages of the church's transformation. A shift of emphasis from the pomp and the supernatural to rational concerns for human welfare. Not a revolution. Just a slow, promoted process.'

Ennis was watching Stephen, taking in what he was saying.

'Yes, I can see that,' he said eventually. 'But I can't imagine for a moment that Luciani was abandoning notions of the supernatural.'

'No, of course, he wasn't,' said Stephen. 'But it doesn't matter. Piers believed that that could only come later. And gradually, largely of its own accord once the initial steps had been taken — helped along, perhaps, with a bit of encouragement now and then. The first move had to be simply a renunciation of the superfluous trimmings. At the same time, a strong commitment to conflict with temporal injustices, with the greed of the wealthy, the exploitation of the poor and vulnerable. From what you've said, Luciani's vision of a poor church seems pretty much in line with what Piers saw as the first step in the transformation.'

'Um,' said Ennis, thoughtfully. 'Well anyway, what there can be no doubt at all about is the Curia's deep misgivings at Luciani's liberal leanings and what they thought he had in mind for the church — his list of changes that we talked about earlier, which they'd been aware of from the start. But, to come back to the specific concerns of the Curia, one of the things in particular that had them thoroughly steamed up was what they suspected to be his position on the burning question of artificial birth control.'

'Oh my God!' exclaimed Stan, loudly. 'Not that again!'

Stephen smiled, having a good idea of what lay behind his outburst. Ennis looked puzzled for a moment, deciding then to ignore it.

'It was a battle the traditionalists thought they had finally won ten years ago,' he went on. 'Confirmation of the uncompromising ban on all forms of contraception — a decision that came close to tearing the church apart. It was during my last year in Rome that it all came to a head. I don't know if you can remember the bitterness it caused?'

Ennis was looking at Stephen as he said this. But it was Stan who answered.

'Oh God, yes. That was the last straw. For years, the church's position on bloody birth control had been a constant topic of indignant mealtime bickering at home. I would come back after months away and they would still be at it. You couldn't get away from it.'

'I remember it,' said Stephen, with a laugh. 'Supper in the Firbright household during our St John's days. I was quite shocked by some of the things your family used to come out with. But it was great fun. I'll never forget your mother's "... geriatric Cardinals in silly red hats quoting Genesis and passing round French letters." A foretaste of liberation, I suppose.'

Ennis, though smiling at these asides, wanted to get back to serious matters.

'*Great fun* in no way describes the public reaction to Humanae Vitae, — Of Human Life — Pope Paul VI's encyclical which demolished the hopes of millions expecting a softening of the church's stance on contraception. They were devastated by it.'

He went on to speak on the background to this decision: the setting up of the Pontifical Commission on Birth Control by Pope John XXIII; its expansion to some seventy members by John's successor, Pope Paul VI; its major conclusion, after two years of exhaustive study, agreed overwhelmingly by all but four dissenters, that the prohibition of artificial birth control for married couples should be lifted; the jubilation at this news of Catholics throughout the world.

'But then,' Ennis continued, 'powerful elements within the Curia stepped in, subjecting the Pope to relentless pressure to reject the commission's recommendations. Their most forceful argument was a political one: that, regardless of the strength of the case for making contraception permissible, to do so now would be tantamount to acknowledging that the church had previously got it wrong. Saddled with its absurd doctrine of papal infallibility, this was something it was simply unable to admit; it would undermine, so they insisted, the whole basis of the church's teaching authority. So Paul was torn between these relentlessly opposing views, deciding eventually — reluctantly perhaps, certainly to the widespread dismay of the faithful — to side with the traditionalists. All over and done with, so they must have thought: the comprehensive ban on all forms of artificial birth control firmly re-established, the battle won. But now, ten years later, along comes this new Pope, already suspect in their eyes, set on reopening the whole business, seemingly with a view to reversing the decision. The anxiety... the hostility this engendered among them was at boiling point.'

'Enough to make them want to kill him?' asked Stan.

'Oh, I don't know about that,' said Ennis, looking uncomfortable. 'The bitterness this dispute has provoked... Anything is possible, I suppose. Maybe we will never know.'

TWENTY-SEVEN

Stephen spent the following day at college, conferring with his postgraduate students, checking over some incomplete analysis he was feeling unprepared to take further, generally filling in time. His mind, in the meantime, forever returning to Ennis's account of the mysterious death of Pope John Paul I, to perplexity at the notion of his having been murdered at the behest of members of the Curia, and not getting anywhere with speculation on what bearing this could possibly have on the death of Piers.

He left college early, thinking to call in at The Goose, opting instead to return home on foot — on the unfulfilled expectation that a long walk would help resolve his confusions. It was a hot and humid evening, the sky overcast, a fine drizzle accompanying the final stretch of his journey. He arrived home wet and sweaty, ready for a much-needed shower and change of clothes. As he was stepping out of the cubicle, about to start drying himself, the phone rang, sending him hurrying to it, dripping and cursing, half-wrapped in a towel. He had been expecting Suzie's call somewhat later. She knew he had been out with Stan and his friend the night before and would be wanting to hear what had come of it. But it wasn't Suzie who responded to his greeting.

'Would it by any chance be Wisdom-of-the-West to whom I am speaking?'

Sharif! It must have been three, possibly more, years since they had last been in touch.

'Mystery-of-the-Orient! At last! Where are you, for Christ's sake? I've been wanting to get in touch but with no idea how to find you.'

'Well, you know how it is with my tribe. We move in mysterious ways. Like your God. But right now, I am in London. If you can drag yourself from your exalted labours, we could meet tomorrow evening. Is that at all possible?'

'Yes, of course. That will be good. I've a lecture from three to four but any time after that. How about calling into college? It's changed a bit since you were last there but I'm still in the same place.'

'Better if you come here. It's a humble hotel but it satisfies my basic needs. Say about six o'clock?'

'Yes, that should be fine. It's really good to hear from you, Sharif. And get to meet up with you again at last.'

Sharif gave an address in Park Lane, which didn't sound humble to Stephen.

'Just go to reception and say that Sharif is expecting you. They will look after you.'

This sounded a bit strange, but before he could comment, Sharif had hung up.

Stephen arrived at the Park Lane address a few minutes after the appointed time. It was a large, stately building but with nothing to mark it out as a hotel, making him feel he had somehow misunderstood Sharif's instruction. He nevertheless approached the entrance, where he stood puzzled at there being no bell-push or knocker or any other apparent means of signalling his presence to those inside. But as he made to leave, he heard a loud click, and on turning back, saw that the door was ajar. He pushed it wide and walked into an impressive reception area displaying an abundance of gleaming dark wood, mirrored walls, sumptuous furniture and huge pots filled with exotic plants. The attractive young woman seated behind a counter smiled as he approached hesitantly.

'I have an appointment with Sharif…'

Her smile broadened.

'You must be Stephen,' she said. And, as he nodded, 'I'm so pleased to meet you. I'm Lucy. Sharif phoned to say he'd been held up a little in a business meeting. He said to take you to the bar where he'll join you as soon as he gets back. It shouldn't be many minutes.'

She stepped around from the counter, revealing a tight miniskirt and long, suntanned legs, to lead him through a portrait-bedecked hallway to the bar, situated at the back of the building, overlooking a small walled garden. The only customers were two smartly dressed men seated at a side table, bent over a pile of documents. Lucy introduced Stephen to the barman as a friend of Sharif's and returned to her desk. On being asked what he would like, Stephen requested a beer.

'A Worthington E, sir?' the barman replied with a smile. And on being told that would be fine, 'It's what Sharif always asks for.'

Stephen hadn't long to wait. Halfway through his beer Sharif arrived, arms outstretched for the embrace which followed. He had once told Stephen that "You're looking fat and prosperous" was a polite term of greeting in his region of Pakistan. It was certainly apt for Sharif in his present guise: very elegantly turned out, with dark pinstriped suit perfectly tailored to his much-enlarged body, the overall effect being of conspicuous wealth and self-important power. Then a giggle somewhat diminished the impression, brought back the Sharif of old.

'I must get out of these ridiculous garments,' he said. 'Then we can go out and enjoy ourselves. Come up with me to my apartment while I'm getting changed, then we can decide what to do.'

They first called at the reception desk, where Lucy handed Sharif a stack of mail. Regardless of their being on first name terms, she did this with a great show of reverence, something Stephen remarked on when they were out of earshot.

'They seem to treat you here as though you own the place.'

'A perceptive observation,' Sharif replied with a chuckle.

'What! You mean, you *do* own it?'

It was looking very much as though Sharif's once stated aim of accumulating a large amount of money — his reason for turning his back on a career in academic mathematics — could well have come off, an impression only marginally dented by his reply.

'Not all of it, unfortunately.' Then, with a knowing smile, 'Just a bit.'

Later, in the pub, he was to expand on this statement, explaining that he had teamed up with a small group of well-heeled businessmen to seize an opportunity to buy the plush hotel – in severe financial difficulty – at a very good price. Then they converted a sizable part of it into self-contained apartments, both for their own occasional use and, when otherwise available, for letting on short term contracts at exorbitant rates to wealthy clients — mainly Arabs and Americans.

They had reached the door to Sharif's apartment on the first floor, which he opened with a key and a flourish.

'Have a look round while I get changed,' he said as they walked in. 'I won't be a minute.'

He left Stephen in the spacious, beautifully furnished living room, with two large sash windows facing across the road to Hyde Park. Having taken in the view, his attention turned to a long, glass-fronted bookcase on the rear wall. Among the mixed assortment of books, he saw a substantial space devoted to mathematical texts, spotting among them a newly published volume he had recently ordered for his departmental library. On the shelf below were box files he recognised as Sharif's from his studentship days. As he was reaching for a book that had attracted his attention, Sharif returned. He was wearing jeans and a loose cotton jacket, now looking just a chubbier, if slightly jaded, version of his old self.

'I might have guessed you'd find your way there,' he said with a laugh. 'But don't go jumping to conclusions. I just dabble in that stuff now and then for old times' sake. No way I'm going back to it seriously. For one thing, I'm no longer capable of doing anything original there.'

'I can't believe that,' said Stephen.

'And anyway,' Sharif went on, 'I've other plans, but more of that later. Look, what I really fancy now is a couple of pints in a proper pub and then a curry somewhere. I haven't done that for years. How about that?'

That suited Stephen just fine. As they left the hotel, Sharif hailed a taxi.

'Where to?' he asked Stephen, who, after a few moments' hesitation, directed the driver to the pub near college which he used to frequent with Piers and Natasha. It should fill the bill nicely, he thought. A relaxed setting where they could talk. They had a lot of catching up to do.

A secondary source of satisfaction for Stephen at this renewed encounter was the pleasurable break it provided from his overriding preoccupation with the Piers saga — quite unaware at the time of the extraordinary contribution to it that Sharif would shortly come out with: a bombshell of undoubted significance to speculation on those two mysterious Vatican deaths.

But it hadn't landed yet. And so, it was with a feeling of great contentment that Stephen followed Sharif into the pub, the years since they had last set out like this simply melting away, the closeness returning as though never interrupted. It brought back for Stephen the first time they had met, the sensation, after little more than an hour or two together, of having known each other all their lives.

'Wow, this is really something,' said Sharif, taking in the blazing fire, the beautiful glass-shuttered mahogany bar; stopping to examine an elaborately framed and decorated mirror, one of the several lining the walls. 'How is it we never got round to coming here before?'

'I discovered it by chance, soon after you'd left college.'

Stephen was on the point of saying more — about that first visit... that incredible meeting... the dramatic events it had given rise to — stopping himself in time. Maybe later, he thought, after the more immediate phases of catching-up had been got through.

'Makes a change from The Goose,' he said instead. 'Somewhere quiet where we can sit and talk.'

He bought beer and peanuts and they settled at a secluded

table.

'You must be wondering why I took so long in contacting you, seeing how I'm set up here in London,' said Sharif, as he tipped nuts from a packet to an open palm. 'In fact, I don't suppose I would have spent more than five or six days here last year — and those packed with meetings and general hassle. Like yesterday and today, and what's lined up for me tomorrow. Then off to Tokyo Friday, for more of the same. I can tell you it's killing me.' He stopped to tip the nuts into his mouth.

Immensely curious though Stephen was, he didn't see any point in asking what lay behind all this activity, whatever Sharif was prepared to reveal being sure to come out anyway.

'But at least the end is in sight now,' Sharif went on. 'Another year at the very most, then I should be set up. Able to quit.' Adding with a chuckle, 'Leave all my misdeeds behind.'

He picked up his glass and took a long drink.

'And then what?' asked Stephen, more curious than ever. At which Sharif burst out laughing.

'Just what you predicted, getting on for twenty years ago.'

'What are you talking about.'

'Don't you remember? About me at forty, returning to my village and marrying a young virgin?'

'You can't be serious.'

'I've never been more serious in my life.'

This was true. It wasn't something fantasised, latched on to in a moment of desperation. On the contrary, as Stephen was to learn, a well-planned operation, pursued by Sharif for some years and now in sight of being realised; his 'business dealings' having led to substantial sums being fed into the family coffers in Pakistan, to the purchase of more land around their village, to the expansion and substantial upgrading of their farm and other property.

'We were always regarded as relatively well-to-do,' he said, 'but now we've moved up a notch. Which is what I wanted, of course. But it's all very visible, what we're doing, causing a lot of raised eyebrows. And it was starting to cause problems... but that's been taken care of now.'

He laughed, his look at Stephen soliciting a request to hear more.

'Tell me about the young virgin,' said Stephen, intrigued at this particular development. At which Sharif burst out laughing again.

'I was expecting you to ask about my local problems... about how I dealt with them,' he said. 'Well, you've done so. You've homed right in on it.'

To Stephen's puzzled expression, he explained that Nasreen, the girl he was soon to marry, was from the most affluent family in the neighbourhood — whose elders had been getting seriously concerned at the upturn in Sharif's family fortunes, which were threatening their perceived predominance in the region.

'A trivial local matter, you might think, and rightly so. But these things can run very deep in that society, can lead to no end of bitterness... and worse than that... much worse.'

He went on to describe how his courtship of Nasreen, which though heavily frowned upon at first, had gone on to eliminate the potential for conflict — helped along, so he hinted, by discreet backhanders; the two families to be united in what was set to become a formidable clan.

'I've a picture of Nasreen,' he said, reaching in his jeans

back pocket. 'Perhaps it's not quite what you were expecting.' He handed Stephen a folded leather pouch containing the photo: an outdoor windswept setting for a beautiful young woman in jeans, knitted top and ankle boots, perched on a wooden fence; long black hair blowing out in front of her, over her shoulders, her right hand brushing it from her smiling face.

'No,' said Stephen, with a laugh. 'I had little idea what to expect... a child perhaps... in traditional costume...' He laughed again, Sharif joining in with him. 'But she's beautiful,' he went on. 'And so trendy looking and self-assured. I can begin to understand the attraction of what you're going for. How old is she?' he asked, as he handed back the photo.

'Twenty-two, coming on twenty-three. Getting on a bit for a young virgin,' Sharif replied with a large grin. 'Unusual that, in that part of the world. And a real problem for her parents. She'd been turning down attempts at arranged marriage since her early teens, wouldn't even consider them. They were desperate. Then I came along to make matters worse.' He put the photo back in his pocket. 'But that's all smoothed over now. The wedding is planned for September. We wanted it earlier but this way ties in with the incredibly complex arrangements that have to be made. A huge affair it's going to be. Lasting several days. You have to come, you know, you and Suzie. You'll be put up in style. It's going to be really something.'

'I wouldn't miss it for the world,' said Stephen. 'Nor would Suzie. I can't wait to tell her.'

Hectic times ahead for us this year, he was thinking: Texas, for Karl's session, then Franklin, and now this; and on top of it all their decision to try for a child. Almost too much to take in. But nothing compared to the permanent changes in lifestyle Sharif seemed to be heading for.

'Don't you think village life might be a bit difficult to adjust to?' he asked.

'It's not what you're thinking,' Sharif replied with a grin. 'Sure, we'll spend a lot of time in the village, but I also have a house in Karachi, which Nasreen is busy now having refurbished... spending pots of money, bless her. We'll have to see just how we decide to divide our time.'

From what he went on to say, it was apparent there were other things in the offing: some role in local politics, hinted at offhandedly, but clear to Stephen that groundwork had been carried out and that there was more to it than he was letting on to.

'I'm sorry at not seeing Suzie this time,' said Sharif as they prepared to leave, 'but tell her I asked after her. I often think of those times — and the beautiful Rebecca, of course. Remember my prediction that you and Suzie would eventually come together? At the time when you were convinced it could never happen? So, my prediction for you worked out as well as your one for me.'

They were walking along Tottenham Court Road, heading for a new Indian restaurant in a street somewhere behind Euston Station, when Sharif started to speak about his 'business affairs'. Stephen was later able to add to what he'd learned about them that evening. But impressive and entertaining though the tales were, they revealed only the vaguest outline of how Sharif had gone about securing the lucrative deals that had raised his financial status from penniless to substantially wealthy within a matter of a few years. The Malaysian casino project was where it all started. He had arrived there as the building and related construction work were nearing completion, uncertain of how he would fit in, not at all clear what his duties entailed, and regarded with suspicion by established members of the team he was joining. By no means a happy beginning. A state of affairs that continued for some weeks, causing him to feel the whole adventure to have been a terrible mistake. But then, out of the blue, he experienced an amazing stroke of luck. A serious problem had arisen with a major funding agency, which was threatening, at best, to delay the opening of the casinos for months, giving rise to no end of seemingly insurmountable difficulties. The problem was down to a senior official of the agency who was querying the provenance of certain funds — money laundering being suspected under circumstances that were proving this difficult to refute. Panic reigned. Sharif had been largely excluded from the ensuing wrangle but was by chance to discover the name of the recalcitrant official in question, realising with a jolt that it was someone he knew well — Hakim Bhatia, a close friend from school days he had been out of touch with for some years. He kept his cool, giving no indication of this extraordinarily good hand he had been dealt, working out instead how best to play it. Saying nothing to colleagues, he managed to contact Hakim, who was delighted to hear from him and they arranged to meet. Just what took place at that meeting — the first of several — is anyone's guess, but following it Sharif went on to resolve the intractable problem in a manner which came over to his superiors as pure financial wizardry. After which there was no looking back, his reputation established and set to become amply rewarded.

They had arrived at the restaurant, a pub across the road

from it catching Sharif's eye.

'How about another beer before we eat?' he said. 'It's years since I've enjoyed an evening like this. It brings back the old days, what we used to get up to together. It doesn't happen like that any more.'

They called into the restaurant, booked a table for later and crossed over to the pub.

'So, what happened afterwards?' said Stephen.

They had bought beer and found somewhere to sit. Stephen was intrigued with what he had been hearing, eager for more. Sharif, for his part, in expansive mood: relaxed, business tensions brushed aside, happily expounding the bones of his dealings after receiving reassurance that whatever he would be coming out with would go no further.

'I became really busy. At first with the casino project, which threw up a whole lot of other problems after that initial setback. But then other things started taking over. I had come to be regarded as an expert, to be consulted by all sorts of people on all manner of financial matters... particularly money transfer problems. Things that I knew next to nothing about. My main concern at the start was not to let on to this.' He stopped to drink, starting up again as he was putting down his glass. 'This sort of thing happens all the time in the financial world. Someone is identified as a financial wizard, often on the flimsiest of evidence, and before you know it the punters are queuing up to entrust him with their life savings.' Thoughts of Philips distracting Stephen's attention for a moment. 'That wasn't where I was at, of course. Nobody was losing out from what I was doing. The other parties were happy at getting their huge sums where they wanted them, I was happy with my commissions. Everybody happy.'

'Sounds like money laundering to me,' said Stephen with a grin.

'Not a bit of it. Couldn't be more respectable. There are plenty of perfectly legitimate reasons for people wanting to transfer money and to experience extreme difficulty in doing so. I've always been committed to seeing to it that everything is open and above board — for self-protection if for no other reason.' He smiled on saying this. 'And, in any case,' he went on, 'the main vehicle for most of the transactions has been the Vatican Bank.'

Mention of the word Vatican had the effect of bringing Stephen up with a start.

'What the hell is the Vatican Bank?' he asked.

'It's a bank fully controlled by the Vatican State. Its official title actually translates to something like Institute for Religious Works, but it's known universally as the Vatican Bank. And that's who I deal through most of the time. Now, you couldn't get more respectable than that... What's the matter?'

'It's just that... just that someone I knew well worked in the Vatican. Piers Denney. He died a few weeks ago under mysterious circumstances. He could have been murdered. Just like the previous Pope a couple months before. I know it all sounds crazy, but it's something that's been bothering me ever since it happened. And also bothering Stan... Stan Firbright — remember that rehearsal of his, where you met the beautiful Rebecca? Piers taught at the school we both went to.'

Sharif remained silent following this, giving Stephen a strange look.

'I don't deal *directly* with the Vatican Bank,' he said eventually. 'That's done through an intermediary, an organisation with unfettered access — which they do very nicely out of and good luck to them. But I know a bit about the set-up. And I know that they were all very worried about something a few months back. Very worried indeed. All business halted for a while. I have to say that my relationship with the intermediary is a strictly impersonal one. There's no question of my talking to anyone there about anything other than the specific operation in hand. That wouldn't go down at all. But it nevertheless came over obviously enough that their problem was down to the new Pope, and that it cleared up pretty swiftly after he had conveniently dropped dead.'

They were both silent then, Stephen controlling with difficulty his desire to push Sharif further on the possibility of this convenient outcome having been helped along... But no, don't overreact, he was telling himself. For the first time though, and to his mounting excitement, he felt a plausible scenario for the death, perhaps the two deaths, could be coming into focus.

'Tell me about the Vatican Bank?' he asked, breaking the silence. 'What's so special about it?'

'Quite a lot,' replied Sharif with a laugh. 'But look, it's time we laid claim to that table we booked before they give it to someone else. Let's go and eat. I'll tell you what I know over the curry.'

They crossed the road and entered the restaurant, now crowded and bubbling with activity.

'We really must do this more often,' said Sharif as he picked up the menu. 'Maybe with Suzie next time. I've been so bogged down with my affairs, I'd almost forgotten how good it can feel to switch off like this.'

They gave their order and, while waiting for it to arrive,

Sharif started up on the Vatican Bank. It was an extraordinary tale, to which Stephen listened spellbound.

'As I said before, it is wholly owned by the Vatican State. Which puts it in the unique position of not having other authorities breathing down its neck. Only the Pope has any say in what it gets up to, and he has other things to think about. It has a truly vast portfolio of private and national assets from all over the world, with which it can do what it likes. There are no checks and balances, no niggling controls to contend with. All of which makes it an ideal conduit for transferring whatever quantities of cash to wherever you like — provided that is you can get the necessary access. Once you have that your problems are over... Oh, thank you.' This was to the waiter who had arrived with their starters. 'It only got that way quite recently,' he went on. 'It's an interesting story — especially for you with your Roman Catholic upbringing.'

'Spare me that,' said Stephen with a laugh. 'Just get on with it.'

'Well, it was ten years or so ago when the new Pope, Paul VI — that's the one before the one we were talking about just now who conveniently dropped dead — decided he wanted to sort out the chaotic state of Vatican finances he'd inherited. He found that separate pots of vast sums existed all over the place, each one guarded by someone who didn't know, or wouldn't let on, just how much was in it and where exactly it was all to be found. Pope Paul was completely at a loss. But luckily, or so he thought, he had someone to turn to.'

A waiter arrived with strange-looking bottles of the beer they had ordered. He opened one and poured it into their two glasses.

'Before Paul's elevation to the papacy,' Sharif went on —

after having tasted his beer and grimaced — 'he was Cardinal of the Archdiocese of Milan, where he mixed freely with the great and the good — or, perhaps more accurately, the rich and the powerful. Among these was an immensely wealthy banker, Michele Sindona, who had been making quite a name for himself in financial circles — buying up banks all over the place and expanding his substantial holdings worldwide. It seemed he could do no wrong financially and they got on famously — particularly after Sindona had come up with full funding for a pet project of his he had previously been having difficulty fulfilling. Their friendship continued after he become Pope. So, it was no surprise that he consulted Sindona on the problems he was facing with the Vatican finances. And being a good Catholic boy, Sindona had no hesitation in offering his services. What he was to discover would have had his eyes popping out of his head — only metaphorically though, because Sindona is an exceptionally cool customer who never shows emotion. I met him a couple of times some years back and can confirm that. You never know what he's thinking and it's not a good idea to ask.'

They were interrupted by the arrival of their food, to which they helped themselves from the array of silver dishes set out in front of them.

'Um, this is all right,' said Sharif, tucking in. 'A good find.'

'I'd heard good reports of the place. Been meaning to try it out for some time.'

They ate for a while in contented silence.

'What the Pope didn't know,' Sharif then went on, 'though might have suspected had he cared to think about it, was that Sindona was Mafia up to his eyebrows. How did he think that a Sicilian lad of humble origin could have accumulated the funds to buy that first bank? Well, let's see. He's undoubtedly very bright. He studied law and economics at university and then went on to develop a speciality that was to earn him a very comfortable living: transferring cash around the world in ways that avoided taxation and other unwelcome scrutiny. A very marketable facility.'

'As you discovered for yourself,' interjected Stephen with a grin.

'Well, okay,' replied Sharif, smiling to himself. 'But this is a quite different ball game. What I've been getting up to amounts to dodges that sometimes get close to the limit of legality but never cross it. What we have here though, is massive and indisputably criminal. By the late fifties, Sindona had already become an invaluable accomplice for Mafia criminality, expertly laundering the proceeds of their dealings, including those of the Gambino-Inzerillo family heroin trafficking millions. And then, to top it all, ten years later, we have the Pope effectively offering him the services of his scrutiny-free Vatican Bank.'

A waiter came to ask if they wanted more beer, which they declined.

'So, what happened then?' asked Stephen, his mind still grappling with possible implications of what he was hearing.

'Well, Sindona supervised the setting up of the Vatican Bank as a secure holding zone for Mafia millions, as well as what is probably the world's leading agency for no-questions-asked international money transfer; generating fortunes all round, including of course for the Roman Catholic Church.'

'Hang on a minute,' said Stephen, suddenly breathless, veiled realisation dawning. 'The Vatican Bank... the last

Pope... the one you say was seen to be the problem... He could have put a stop to it all, couldn't he? He had the power to do so... If Sindona and his Mafia paymasters really believed he was going to pull the plug on them... well, what do you think they were going to do about it?'

Sharif was looking a shade uncomfortable, not saying anything. Perhaps, thought Stephen, a result of his having been using the those very facilities himself... blocking out from embarrassment what should have been staring him in the face.

'For Christ's sake, man!' Stephen was fully wound up now, the missing element in Ennis's account sliding into place. 'We know that millions of dollars of Mafia money were at risk. We know that those people wouldn't hesitate for a moment to kill to protect their interests. And there's something else as well. Something you don't know that I only learned myself the other day... about the circumstances surrounding the discovery of the Pope's body... the way they point to the extreme likelihood of his having been murdered.'

TWENTY-EIGHT

Stephen's preoccupation with Piers's death had landed him in altogether deeper water than he could possibly have imagined, his head swimming at the seeming unreality in which he found himself: a scarcely credible twentieth-century papal murder and Vatican participation in the multimillion-dollar laundering of Mafia proceeds from heroin trafficking and prostitution. Time, surely, to wake up from what had to be an over-the-top, anxiety-driven dream. But no, it was all real enough, and showing further signs of coming together: Sharif's disclosures resolving the problem of the absence of a credible assassin in Ennis's account of the discovery of Pope John Paul I's body, and an event reported in the press a few weeks earlier serving to obviate any possible doubt regarding likely Mafia response to a perceived threat to its finances: an Italian magistrate gunned down in broad daylight in Milan soon after embarking on an investigation into some other banker suspected of Mafia affiliation. All this occurring around a bemused Stephen as he pondered ineffectually what possible relation it could have with that other mysterious death, that of Piers Denney.

Thankfully for his peace of mind, other events were to intervene to distract Stephen from what was in danger of becoming a debilitating obsession. In first place, the return of Suzie, determined as ever for a more settled life and, to

Stephen's surprise, in no hurry to start on the fertility tests.

'It's so good to be back,' she had said on arriving home. 'I don't want to think about that or anything else for a while. Just to relax and get used to living normally again.'

This attitude represented the culmination of recent dissatisfaction with her nomadic existence, expressed to Stephen with increasing frequency in her phone calls of the last few weeks and, in no uncertain terms, on his last weekend visit to the dismal room she had rented for the last stop of her latest and, as she would have it, final tour.

'There've been good moments that I wouldn't have missed for the world but it's all gone on for too long.'

This was something with which Stephen couldn't agree more. He remained at home for the next couple of days, enjoying being there with her, cooking and carrying out simple household chores together, and filling her in on the latest developments of the Piers saga: amplifying what had been related over the phone, perhaps even persuading her to keep an open mind on the cause of death; and, in exchange, agreeing to row back on his obsession with it for a while, to concentrate on other things, at least until the arrival of Piers's Vatican colleague with the information they hoped would throw fresh light on the affair. It was during this period at home that Stephen decided to make a regular feature of working there, perhaps a couple of days or so a week, in the small office he had long ago set up in a spare room and hardly ever used. This way, they would be together even more. It almost felt as if they were starting out again. All that was needed, they decided, was a second honeymoon to mark the new beginning.

But, try as he might, concerns with the Piers affair could not for long be brushed aside. It had been three weeks since

Stephen's meeting with Alain and he had heard nothing since. Calling him from college, he was answered by Mrs. Chadderton, who immediately recognised his voice and sounded pleased to hear from him.

'Alain was just talking about you this morning,' she said, 'thinking it was time he got in touch. Can I get him to ring you when he gets back from his rounds? He shouldn't be long.'

Sure enough, Alain returned the call some twenty minutes later, apologising for not contacting him sooner and inviting him and Suzie to dinner the following week.

'Emma has been on at me to do this for some time,' he said. 'She's looking forward to meeting Suzie, and so am I.'

It was the first time Stephen had heard Alain refer to his housekeeper by her first name, which he had never even heard mentioned before. But, although *Emma* sounded far more appropriate for the attractive young woman than *Mrs. Chadderton*, it still seemed strange somehow coming from Alain. And there had been something else slightly odd about his manner — not in any way unpleasant, indeed quite the contrary — that Stephen was aware of but couldn't quite put his finger on. He realised as soon as he had hung up that no mention had been made of the awaited visit by the Vatican colleague, which had been his purpose in calling in the first place. Oh well, he thought, that can wait till our dinner date next week.

Dinner at the St Anthony of Padua presbytery turned out to be a great success, despite Suzie's initial misgivings at being stuck for hours in a priest's house in a dreary South London suburb.

'Strange company you seem to have been keeping while I was away,' she had complained, only half-jokingly. But that all changed within moments of getting there: Alain, in casual mufti, winning her over with his welcome, and Emma surprising them both by her appearance and manner, – no trace of the humble housekeeper role as she emerged from the kitchen to greet them in jeans and T-shirt, looking younger and more attractive than ever – telling Alain to pour drinks for them all, that she would be with them in just a moment after having attended to something on the stove; acting, for all the world, as a young wife, happy to be displaying her culinary skills to welcome guests, setting the scene for the evening to follow. It was a splendid meal, enjoyed by the four of them chatting convivially around the small table, and washed down with the claret Suzie had handed to Emma on arrival, and then with another bottle produced by Alain. They talked of this and that, of Suzie's theatrical career, their forthcoming visit to Texas and California — to which Emma showed particular interest, having lived in Texas for two years with her husband shortly before his untimely death. Feeling the conversation to be preceding a little one-sidedly, Stephen was on the point of asking Alain and Emma about their summer holiday plans, just stopping himself in time. For although in almost every respect they had been comporting themselves as a couple, no explicit expression of what seemed a mind-boggling transformation in their relationship had been forthcoming — despite a gentle, oblique probe by Suzie when a seemingly suitable occasion had arisen. Alain, though friendly enough, was having much less to say for himself, leaving most of their side of the exchanges to Emma, his more subdued manner tying in with the impression Stephen had picked up from their telephone conversation the previous week. Suzie and Emma had clearly hit it off, the seeds of close friendship tentatively sown.

Strangely enough though, what wasn't talked about at all was the Piers affair, except for Alain briefly informing Stephen, without further explanation, that the expected visit from Piers's Vatican colleague was now unlikely to take place before the summer. Clearly, there had been problems there, of which Alain was either unaware or had felt the occasion inappropriate for revealing. Before Stephen and Suzie's departure, in a minicab phoned for by Emma, all expressed the desire to meet again soon. This coming over, however, as having to take place in the presbytery again, a restaurant or Stephen and Suzie's home presenting unspecified, though understandable, difficulties. And so the enigma persisting, occupying the thoughts of Suzie and Stephen on their cab ride home — in silence but for brief exchanges with the driver.

'It looks to be an extremely dangerous journey they're embarking on,' said Suzie as they entered their hallway, alone at last. 'I can't imagine how they can hope to keep it to themselves. Parishioners must be talking about them. You can imagine what that lot are like. No way is it going to go unnoticed... some prig certain to stir things up... complain to the bloody bishop. They must know that, must surely be planning their next move.'

Stephen remained silent, his mind grappling with the enormity of the seemingly inevitable upheaval in Alain's life. Then, wanting to switch off:

'Perhaps we're rather jumping to conclusions.'

'Oh rot!' Suzie was having none of that. 'Can you imagine for one moment that they're not in bed together right now? Come off it!'

'You're right, as usual,' said Stephen, smiling, coming off it. Then taking her into his arms. 'But it's only that I'd rather hear it from them directly, that's all.'

As they made their way to the bedroom, Stephen's mind strayed to competing concerns — for Alain and Emma, to be sure, but something else as well: to a parish scandal leading to the cancellation of that Vatican colleague's visit, putting pay to any hope for further insight into those two deaths.

The long wait for that visit — eventually set to take place in mid-July — was to be broken for Stephen and Suzie in April by their trip to the United States. They were to spend the first week in San Antonio, where Stephen would present his paper on the Last Theorem problem in Karl's conference session. He was planning to attend only one other session, leaving him plenty of free time to enjoy with Suzie — effectively the second honeymoon joked about a month earlier. Then it was on to Franklin, where they were to spend three days on the campus, staying in an apartment for academic visitors fixed up for them by Karl. Both looking forward to it all, Stephen particularly so to his return to Franklin after some sixteen years, to the opportunity to meet up again with Percy Mattingly and colleagues in the Mathematics Department and who knows what other acquaintances of his time there, and to introduce Suzie to them and show her something of his old haunts. Before setting out, Suzie, having by then settled back into what she felt to be a normal routine again, booked a hospital appointment with a fertility consultant for soon after they were due back in London – a further marker for lifestyle changes ahead.

The trip was to proceed pretty well according to plan: San Antonio a delight in many respects, Stephen's presentation going down well, giving rise to enthusiastic discussion with the promise of interesting collaborative exchanges to follow. Touristic excursions with Suzie also living up to expectations: the Tex-Mex restaurants, the beautiful river walk, the San Antonio Museum — where they were able to see, proudly displayed among the preserved artefacts of local historic conflict, the coonskin hat worn by John Wayne playing Davy Crockett in the film The Alamo. A visit to the San Antonio Zoo on their last day rounded off a thoroughly enjoyable week. Stephen had been told of the zoo during his time at Franklin by a large, formidable woman, an active member, as she lost no time informing him, of "Daughters of the British Empire" — an organisation for women with familial links to Great Britain. She had waylaid him at some social gathering on being informed that he was English and, in the course of conversation, had learned that he was thinking of visiting San Antonio.

'In that case, you *must* visit the zoo,' she had said with great emphasis. 'It's such a *happy* place. You really *must* visit it.' Although he never made it to San Antonio at the time, the memory of that insistence stuck.

'Indeed, we must visit it,' said Suzie, on being told of that encounter sixteen years later. It was a fine day as they started out, sunny without being too hot, a few wispy clouds drifting lazily across a blue sky. Though neither of them was particularly fond of zoos, they had to admit that this one came over rather well, with spacious paddocks for the herbivores and imaginatively designed indoor and outdoor facilities for the other animals. And yes, a prevalent air of contentment among the various visitors wandering casually around, clearly enjoying their day out. An amusing incident was to colour their recollection of that visit. It was heralded by an eruption of excited exclamations from a large group of schoolchildren, together with futile exhortations from the nuns accompanying them to come away from what turned out to be the extraordinary spectacle of a pair of copulating penguins — both seemingly oblivious of, or perhaps further stimulated by, their enthusiastic reception. The business was being conducted with much flapping of vestigial wings and in what, surprisingly to Stephen, appeared to be the missionary position — though, due to the near rotational symmetry of penguin anatomy, it was difficult to determine whether the one underneath was in the supine or the prone orientation, or for that matter the sex of either of them.

'Everyone certainly appears to be very happy,' said Suzie, taking in the performance, 'apart from those nuns. Perhaps this is the sort of thing the lady who told you about this place had in mind.'

Despite Stephen's severe misgivings, the Vatican emissary's long-delayed visit to the St Anthony of Padua parish was finally confirmed, Alain phoning Stephen to give notice of the promised meeting for soon after his arrival in mid-July. It was to be a long wait. But following their return from Franklin, Stephen and Suzie's life had taken an unexpected turn, providing something closer to home to distract them from the Piers saga: confirmation that Suzie had become pregnant. It was on the way back to their Franklin campus apartment, after an enjoyable drink-laden dinner with Percy and Patsy Mattingly — at which Suzie had been uncharacteristically abstemious — that she had let on to having missed a period. Though this had happened before, she had a strong feeling that this time it could be different, and it would turn out that she was right. Quite unexpectedly, and without the need for the anticipated medical intervention, their cherished dream was on track to being realised. It was nevertheless with a feeling of burgeoning excitement that Stephen was brought back to the Piers affair by Alain's call; to the opportunity for a meeting with someone in a position to fill in authoritatively on the grim picture painted by Ennis and Sharif, and fully conversant and apparently in tune with Piers's heretical agenda; perhaps even able to provide some inkling of what lay behind his mysterious death.

TWENTY-NINE

On arrival at the St Anthony of Padua presbytery, Stephen was greeted by Alain wearing a dark suit and dog collar and looking a little flustered. A similarly attired, somewhat older, priest rose from an armchair as they entered the living room, introduced himself as Guido, Guido Di Antonio, and declared unsmilingly, and in fluent English, how pleased he was to be meeting Stephen after having heard so much about him from Piers, — not at all something Stephen wanted to hear — then breaking into a warm smile as they shook hands. Stephen was later to learn that Guido had spent most of his childhood in England, attending school there and returning to Italy with his Italian parents in his late teens. At this point, Alain apologised for having to leave them, mumbling something about two very sick parishioners and that he would try not to be too long. He then set off, carrying a small black bag. No sign of Emma though, which Stephen wondered at.

'The corporal works of mercy,' said Guido, smiling to himself as they settled into adjacent armchairs. 'A truly satisfying duty which I much regret hardly ever being called upon to perform these days.'

Withdrawing a packet of cigarettes from his jacket pocket, he offered one to Stephen, who declined.

'You don't mind if I do?'

'Of course not.'

He lit up, inhaled deeply, then sent a perfectly formed smoke ring spinning and hurtling towards the fireplace.

'Brilliant,' said Stephen, genuinely impressed.

'Forgive me,' said Guido, 'but it's my one-and-only party trick. I can't resist showing off with it to new acquaintances.'

After that, they spoke easily together, though by unspoken consent putting off for Alain's return matters concerning Piers and the movement he had given rise to. Eventually, however, Guido touched on to the related long-running controversy in the church between traditionalists and modernisers, fuelled by the ground-breaking papacy of John XXIII and the Second Vatican Council which he had inaugurated.

'Although the arguments were being generally conducted on ideological grounds, there were hard-nosed practical considerations at their core.' He paused to light another cigarette. 'Church attendance dropping off at an alarming rate, wholesale abandonment of the faith throughout the developed world, a trend which has continued, showing no sign of tailing off, calling into question the church's very survival. Well, what's to be done about it? That's what people were asking. How should the church respond?'

He was looking at Stephen as though expecting him to answer.

'But that raises the question of why the tailing off, doesn't it? I know we're putting off talking about Piers for now, but isn't this what he was on about? About the church having to broaden its appeal... ease off on the dogma... all that supernatural stuff that's no longer believable in the modern world.'

'Well yes,' replied Guido with a chuckle. 'What you're saying applies widely for sure. Certainly in Europe. But what about other places? Those vast stretches in Asia and South America, for instance, where the church is thriving, the dogma revered and accepted without question? To go soft on it now risks alienating the very people the church can still count on. That's the practical part of the traditionalist argument. Stick with the contented masses of the undeveloped world, they're saying. The way things are going, before long they'll be all we have left.'

'But you don't agree with them?'

'I wouldn't be here if I did. No, it's the long view that Piers was concerned with. The church's future in the face of growing worldwide acceptance of the baselessness of religious belief. You're looking puzzled.'

'It just seems strange, coming from you... seeing where you're from...' Then, with a smile, 'with how you're dressed.'

Guido smiled in return. 'You would have expected it of Piers though, wouldn't you? What you probably fail to take into account is how many of us in the church have come to feel this way. For most, it's kept well under wraps, a guilty gut reaction we've learnt to suppress. But let us be in no doubt about what lies behind that suppression: the feeling that the basic social structure provided by the church is worth preserving, that it brings comfort and hope in all sorts of ways to countless millions, that humanity would suffer irreparably in both practical and psychological terms from its demise.' He reached in his pocket for his cigarettes, then thought better of it. 'These feelings are widespread now, both within the priesthood and among the faithful in general. Uncomfortable to dwell upon though, and for the most part brushed aside... buried.'

Guido went on to talk about this and other difficulties

priests, in particular, have to contend with in coming to terms with the loss of faith. Then, touching on to Piers's vision, which he admitted having come to share only after having seen how rapidly it was being latched on to by others, the apparent ease with which the proposed opening up process was being accepted. This all went on for some time, until they were interrupted by Alain's return. He was carrying, in addition to his black bag, three takeaway pizza boxes.

'Sorry about this,' he said as he set them down on the table, 'but it seems that everything is happening at once today: two of my parishioners terminally ill, approaching the end, and Emma away with her mother, who's also been taken ill. So it's pizza for lunch, I'm afraid. I know it's a bit early, but perhaps it would be best to eat them now while they're still fairly hot.'

'I'm ready, and quite hungry,' said Guido. 'You're making me feel I haven't left home.'

They made casual exchanges as they ate, starting with Alain inquiring after Suzie, some four months pregnant now, Stephen working at home for the most part, going through the motions of looking after her. Then on to other things, and going on for too long, so it seemed to Stephen. When on earth would they be getting round to Piers? Sensing perhaps his growing impatience, Guido turned to him with a knowing smile and shifted the conversation towards what he had been waiting to hear.

'Did it make the British press, the assassination the other day in Milan of Giorgio Ambrosoli? On July 11th to be precise. The date turns out to be of particular significance.'

Guido was looking at Stephen while saying this, as Alain emerged from the kitchen bearing a tray with cups of coffee.

'I didn't see it if it did. But then I haven't been paying

much attention…'

'He was gunned down in the street,' Guido went on, interrupting him, 'outside his apartment as he was returning home. He was a lawyer, charged by the Italian authorities to investigate the affairs of a banker by the name of Michele Sindona.'

'My God!'

'Oh! That name means something to you?'

'Yes, it does… But this sounds like that other killing… just a few months ago… a magistrate who was investigating some other banker…'

'So, you're aware of that too.' This obviously surprised Guido. 'Yes, the similarities are striking. The magistrate in that case was Emilio Alessandrini. He was shot dead in the street just after he had started an investigation into the dealings of Roberto Calvi and his Banco Ambrosiano.' He stopped to light a cigarette. 'Sindona and Calvi are close associates,' he went on, 'both frequent visitors to the Vatican, embroiled together in all manner of dubious financial activities, at times in league with our very own Bishop Paul Marcinkus, who controls the Vatican Bank.'

Stephen was struck dumb at the relation of this to Sharif's revelations, with clearly more to come. The brief silence that followed was broken by Alain.

'I remember Piers years ago speaking of Marcinkus. Quite respectfully, I seem to remember. I got the impression they were on good terms. But he never mentioned him again after that.'

'They *were* on good terms. Up until the time Piers started getting an inkling of what was going on there… the criminal financial shenanigans under the protective cover of the Vatican

State. Others must have suspected as much and turned a blind eye. But not Piers. You know what he was like. Suspecting that something was seriously wrong there...' Guido broke off in mid-sentence, stubbing out his half-finished cigarette. 'But look,' he went on, 'before coming on to all that, perhaps I should fill you in on the background of the Vatican's key player in all this. Someone Piers was to engage in a quite different ball game from that of his habitual entanglements with the religious establishment.'

And so Guido went on to speak about Paul Marcinkus. An extraordinary tale, spelling out for Stephen what, in the kindest interpretation, was the stupefying naivety of Pope Paul VI in his moves to regulate Vatican finances. Not content with his appointment of Mafioso banker Michele Sindona to oversee the reforms, he had gone on to pave the way for Marcinkus — a man by his own admission with no previous knowledge of banking — to assume control of the Vatican Bank.

Son of an immigrant Lithuanian labourer, Paul Marcinkus was born in 1922 in Cicero, a poor and dangerous industrial suburb of Chicago, set to become the new base for Al Capone's criminal empire. It was against that backdrop that, from an early age and the shelter of strict Roman Catholic schooling, Marcinkus was to embark on the demanding course for ordination to the priesthood, thereafter to prepare the ground for a career of international service to the Roman Catholic Church: attendance at the Pontifical Gregorian University and the Ecclesiastical Academy in Rome, followed by diplomatic stints abroad, and then to a more settled position in the Vatican's Secretariat of State. It was from there, shortly after the accession of Pope Paul VI, that his forceful intervention in a potentially calamitous incident was to bond him firmly in the affection of the new Pope, with far-reaching consequences for his subsequent career.

'I only just missed seeing it for myself,' said Guido with a smile. 'But I have first-hand accounts of reliable witnesses.'

An improvident outdoor encounter with a large gathering of worshippers had got seriously out of hand, brought about, it seems, by an endearing gesture of the new Pope — a feature that was becoming something of a hallmark of his papacy: arms stretched upwards in a great V, then a beckoning action, up and over, repeatedly, with open palms and an engaging smile. A motion flippantly likened to a fledgling testing its wings prior to first flight, but taken by the excited onlookers as an invitation to approach closer. Which they did, hesitantly at first, fast developing into a stampede; the Pope's smile changing precipitously to a look of terror as he turned to find his passage blocked in all directions, his minders nowhere to be seen, pressure from the rear of the mob forcing those in front up against his frail body. But then loud cries of pain and indignation signalled the arrival of the US cavalry: the great bulk of Marcinkus, head and shoulders above the heaving masses, emerging from behind to carve a passage to the terrified pontiff, leaving a trail of injuries in his wake; and then onwards to safety, with more collateral damage, but with the Pope firmly secured under a massive protective wing.

'It was no laughing matter.' This was from Guido to a clearly amused Alain. 'And anyway, you'd have heard it all before.'

'Yes, but not in such picturesque terms.'

'Picturesque maybe, but no exaggeration, I can assure you. Rather the contrary. There was bloodshed... and protests. One fellow threatened legal action but was talked out of it.'

'Probably fobbed off with a plenary indulgence.'

Guido didn't respond to this quip of Stephen's, perhaps feeling that it encroached on his sole right to impious asides. Instead, he turned to something he knew Stephen would be interested to hear.

'By the time of this incident, Piers and Marcinkus had got to know each other quite well — nothing very surprising about that for English speakers in the Vatican village. They would chat together amiably enough on chance meetings and very occasionally dine together in one or other of the smart Roman restaurants frequented by Marcinkus. Both of them were aware, however, of their respective positions across the traditionalist-moderniser divide. This wouldn't have bothered Piers. As you know, he was tolerant to a fault of divergent views, but it may well have irked Marcinkus, who was steadfast in his refusal to even acknowledge the reformist movement Piers was labouring to get off the ground.'

Guido stopped to light a cigarette, then went on to describe the transformation of Marcinkus's status in the Vatican following that fortuitous encounter. Pope Paul had been greatly impressed by his spontaneous initiative. He was also immensely grateful and showed it the following day by assigning him to the role of unofficial papal bodyguard. And from that point on they became ever closer: Marcinkus becoming a key member of the papal entourage, progressively taking over much of the management of the Pope's personal affairs and accompanying him on his frequent overseas missions — acting, as well as unofficial bodyguard, as an interpreter and general factotum for the myriad organisational problems and contingencies that inevitably arise in the planning and implementation of such visits. All in all, a momentous progression for a poor, working-class lad from a criminally rife suburb of Chicago.

'While on the point of that background,' said Guido as he stubbed out his cigarette, 'I think it only fair to point out that suggestions that, as a youth, he was personally involved in the endemic lawlessness of that community are totally without foundation. Yes, he was certainly big and tough and would at times display those attributes. Still does, as on the memorable occasion we've just been talking about — which led, incidentally, to his popular nickname of The Gorilla. But all the indications point to a blameless existence up that time. His corruption occurred a few years later. After which, he was to make up for lost time.'

Guido then turned to Michele Sindona's entry on the scene, an account which confirmed and added detail to what Stephen had learned from Sharif. Pope Paul was desperate to sort out the tangled mess of Vatican finances and had asked Sindona to advise on how to go about this. And so Sindona became a regular visitor to the Vatican, with Marcinkus, in his new administrative role, facilitating his interactions with the custodians of the various Vatican hoards. Of these, the Institute for Religious Works — the Vatican Bank — was soon earmarked by Sindona as prime candidate for his attention. He saw immense possibilities there. Access to its records, however, was proving well-nigh impossible, due to the unhelpful, more often defensively hostile, attitude of its functionaries, in particular its octogenarian head. Sindona was getting nowhere with any of them but was at the same time establishing a good relationship with Marcinkus, whom he knew to be well regarded by Pope Paul for organisational skills exhibited on his behalf. This gave him food for thought. At a subsequent meeting with the Pope to discuss his initial feelings on the Vatican's financial arrangements, he played a subtle hand. Without expressing overt criticism or mentioning names, he floated the idea that perhaps the Vatican Bank could benefit from some fresh administrative input to the organisation of its records and procedures. Pope Paul, with a flash of insight, fed no doubt by Sindona's suggestions for desirable attributes in potential appointees, realised he had on hand the very man for the job. Within a very short space of time, Marcinkus's already elevated status had been formalised by his consecration to Bishop, following which he was assigned the role of Secretary of the Institute for Religious Works. Misgivings with regard to this latter appointment — that he lacked knowledge of banking and financial matters in general — were simply brushed aside: Sindona would be more than happy to instruct him in all he needed to know and be constantly on hand to advise on any problems that might arise. True to his word, Sindona was to become a regular presence in the Vatican village, constantly engaged with Marcinkus in the affairs of the Vatican Bank, the sight of "The Gorilla and The Shark" setting off together for a fashionable restaurant at the end of a working day soon to become a wryly observed feature of the Vatican scene.

In the event, Sindona proved an able teacher and Marcinkus a rapid learner, gradually taking over more and more of the bank's affairs. So much so that Sindona soon felt able to recommend him to Pope Paul as ready to assume full control. And so to the appointment in 1971 of Bishop Paul Marcinkus to President of the Institute for Religious Works. The foundations for Sindona's unfettered access to this secure and uniquely privileged vehicle for money laundering and whatever other nefarious activities he could come up with were well and truly laid.

'It's an extraordinary story,' said Guido as he fumbled in his pocket for his cigarettes, then lit one and inhaled deeply. 'By the time Marcinkus fully realised what he was getting into he would have been too deeply enmeshed to do anything about it — even had he wanted to, which is doubtful. The upside for the church, a big one, was that the bank was making money for it hand over fist. An exemplary justification for his actions, he must have felt. "You can't run the church on Hail Marys," is how he is reputed to have put it. And if others were also raking it in… well… just par for the course. Besides, the really big scams were yet to come. And by the time they had, Marcinkus would have been fully corrupted, and basking in papal approval for the transformation he was bringing about in Vatican finances.'

At this point, Alain, who had been glancing at his watch, announced that he would have to leave them for a while, for a scheduled meeting in the church with a new organist.

'But please carry on,' he said to Guido. 'I know something of the background you're filling us in on — though I have to say I'm enjoying your account of it. In any case, I won't be long.'

'There's just a bit more Stephen needs to be informed about before we get on to Piers,' said Guido, stubbing out his cigarette and reaching in his pocket for another one. 'I'll wait till you get back before getting on to anything you're not already aware of.'

Alain nodded apologetically to them both and left, giving Stephen the opportunity to put to Guido something that was continuing to bother him.

'I'm finding this all quite fascinating, Guido... incredible... a Mafia-Vatican collusion... But what I can't for the life of me make out is why you're taking so much trouble for me. I really appreciate it and feel flattered. But why?'

'I thought Alain had told you why.'

'Well, yes he did... that Piers would have wanted it that way... but it doesn't ring quite true somehow.'

'No, I don't suppose it does.' Guido lit the cigarette he had been holding. 'But then you wouldn't know how bad he had come to feel about the way things had ended with you. He would often talk about it, believe it or not. And also with Natasha, it seems. Shortly before he died, he'd been planning to get in touch with you. Among other things, he wanted to tell you that his vision for the church's future, that he knew you were sceptical about, was getting off the ground. You were the only close friend he had left outside the church... and it meant a lot to him. And he felt it meant a lot to you too.' He was looking intently at Stephen as he said this.

'Yes, it did... does... I really don't know what to say.'

'Well, just leave it then. There's nothing for you to concern yourself about.' He stood up and went over to the window. 'It's a nice day,' he said, looking out, 'and we could both do with a break. How about a breath of fresh air before Alain gets back?'

Leaving the presbytery door on the latch, they turned down the pathway running beside the church to the spacious garden behind it, which sloped down to a large prefabricated building at its lower boundary.

'I wonder what goes on in here,' said Guido as they came up to it.

He tried the door, finding it locked. But then a call from

Alain, who had spotted them as he emerged from the church, announced that he was about to make coffee.

'Should be just time to round off what little you need to know about the Vatican Bank before dinner,' said Guido as they headed back. 'Then afterwards we can get on to the real business.'

'I want to tell you about just one of the financial scams perpetrated by Marcinkus, instigated by Sindona and Roberto Calvi, soon after he had become President of the Vatican Bank.'

Guido had started up no sooner than the three of them had settled around the table. He had placed his cigarettes and lighter in front of him and appeared anxious to get going again.

'Other scams of theirs were a good deal greater in terms of the sums involved. But this was the one which would effectively precipitate the deadly incidents of a few years later that I'll be coming on to this evening.'

Stephen and Alain settled back in silence as Guido went on to describe the lead up to events that were to propel both Piers and the short-lived future Pope into the evolving drama. Piers had, early on, identified Albino Luciani as very much in tune with what he saw as the initial phase of his vision for the church's fundamental transformation — all much in line with what Stephen had learned about him from Ennis. When Luciani became Patriarch of Venice, it appeared likely to Piers that he would soon be made Cardinal, and so an eligible candidate for the papacy on the death of Paul. He began putting out tentative feelers for this eventuality. At the same time, his relationship with Marcinkus had cooled following an invitation to dine with him and Sindona in a restaurant the two of them had taken to frequenting in Rome. As Piers later described to Guido, this had gone reasonably well until he came to question Sindona on something or other, in what was intended as no more than a polite expression of interest in his involvement with the Vatican Bank — only to be answered with a sharp rebuff, effectively telling him to mind his own business, and an abrupt change of subject. The unpleasantness had been smoothed over but left Piers suspicious of what could be going on there. Sometime after this incident, following which he had had virtually no contact with Marcinkus, Piers learned through the Vatican grapevine that Pope Paul had been approached by Luciani about a banking problem that had been causing him some concern. This was of obvious interest to Piers. And it so happened that among Vatican personnel sympathetic to his cause was a priest engaged in work at a relatively minor level at the Vatican Bank. This man, it turned out, had taken to keeping a wary eye on what he saw going on around him there. He was later to play a prominent role in Piers's subsequent investigations. More immediately, he was able to reveal to Piers details of the banking operation which had so upset Luciani.

'Luciani's "banking problem" was to do with the Banca Cattolica del Veneto, a wealthy bank regarded by clergy of the Venice region as effectively their own.' Guido paused for a moment to light a cigarette. 'A number of Venetian dioceses held shares in it, the majority shareholder, however, being the Vatican Bank. The practical outcome of this cosy arrangement was that clergy were able to borrow money for diocesan projects at very low rates of interest. This facility, they were to discover, had been abruptly withdrawn, full interest rates being introduced regardless of the worthiness of purposes for which funding was being sought. They were up in arms, Luciani inundated with complaints of his clergy at this unprecedented additional burden on stretched diocesan finances. Hence his approach to Pope Paul.'

Alain stood up at this point, saying it was getting close to supper time and that he needed to attend to something Emma had left for them in the kitchen.

'But I'll leave the door open,' he said to Guido, 'so I'll be able to hear you perfectly well. I know you've still got quite a bit to get through.'

'Only a couple of things before we eat,' said Guido. 'They shouldn't take long. Just what Piers learned from his informant at the Vatican Bank. I'll call him Oscar, by the way. It's not his name. The less that gets mentioned the better. Well, Oscar was able to throw light on what had happened with Banca Cattolica del Veneto.' He started coughing violently having said this, at the same time stubbing out his cigarette. 'I really need to cut down on these,' he said when he had got his breath back. Stephen thought that was a good idea but didn't say anything.

'What had happened,' Guido continued, when fully recovered, 'was that Marcinkus had sold the Vatican Bank's shares in Banca Cattolica del Veneto to Calvi at what appeared to be a very high price. Pope Paul was delighted, all that lovely money available to the church. Everyone was delighted. Even Calvi, who had seemingly paid through the nose for the deal. "It's been my privilege to have been able to help out in this way," had been his modest response to Pope Paul's fervent expression of gratitude, "...the very least I could do." So you can imagine the Pope being a little put out at Luciani's approach to him some weeks later with the disconcerting news of how Calvi was clawing back on his generous benefaction, and feeling belatedly guilty at the realisation that no one had thought to confer with the Patriarch of Venice about the sale of church assets of such direct concern to his archdiocese.'

Guido went on to describe the Pope's relief on finding that Luciani did not intend to make a fuss, was content to draw a line under the affair. He then suggested that he meet Marcinkus, with a hint that perhaps means could be found to compensate the archdiocese for its loss of privileged treatment. But this was clearly a buck-passing gesture with nothing behind it, and seen as such by Luciani, but followed up nonetheless.

'Luciani's encounter with Marcinkus failed predictably to live up to papal expectations. It was short-lived, acrimonious and abruptly terminated, the more clamorous exchanges being overheard by Oscar in the adjoining office. Still basking in papal approbation for his financial accomplishments, Marcinkus was in no way prepared to submit to moral criticism from a mere archbishop, even one further ennobled with the title of Patriarch. "Just go and concern yourself with your own responsibilities and I'll concern myself with mine," had been his parting shot as Luciani rose to leave.' Guido made to reach for his cigarettes, then changed his mind. 'You can imagine how Luciani felt about Marcinkus following that encounter,' he went on. Then, with a wry smile, 'He was to recall it vividly six years later when, newly installed as Pope John Paul I, he was in a perfect position to settle the score.'

Alain came back from the kitchen with the welcome news that supper was ready and keeping warm in the oven.

'There's just one more thing I'd like to finish up with before we eat,' said Guido, still smiling to himself. 'Something I've been saving till last. Shouldn't take too long.'

It was a remarkable tale he went on to tell, one which was

to provide a rather different perspective from Pope Paul's on Calvi's acquisition of Banca Cattolica del Veneto.

'Banks are particularly useful assets to acquire if you want to get your hands on huge sums of money. This was something Sindona had come to realise early in his career. Starting from scratch, it had taken him quite some time to accumulate the funds to buy his first bank — secured largely by pay-offs from Mafia money laundering and related high-profit illegal activities. But after having done so, there was no stopping him — confirming again for Stephen what he had heard from Sharif.

'With each new acquisition came another vast tranche of investors' money effectively at his disposal,' Guido went on. 'In a relatively short time, he had acquired over a dozen banks, including a couple in Switzerland and one in the United States. Hailed by the President of Italy as "Saviour of the Lira", by America's ambassador to Italy as "Businessman of the Year", there appeared no limit to his prowess and prestige. Calvi likewise was a highly successful operator, his main asset, Banco Ambrosiano, one of the wealthiest banks in Italy. He and Sindona are close partners-in-crime, collaborating in all manner of financial scams to their mutual advantage — both, as it happens, are now in deep trouble with the authorities, but that's another story. Marcinkus, by virtue of the Vatican Bank's provision of confidential means for illicit dealing and, paradoxically, its aura of respectability, was to become a valued additional partner in their schemes. A good illustration of their modus operandi is provided by Oscar's account to Piers of what he was able to uncover concerning Calvi's acquisition of Banca Cattolica del Veneto.'

Guido then gave a brief outline of the operations behind this transaction. They involved two companies owned by

Sindona: Company A, which had obtained an option to buy the Vatican Bank's shares in Banca Cattolica del Veneto from Marcinkus, and Company B, which Calvi had agreed to buy on a specified date. The groundwork thus prepared, Sindona orchestrated — by means of which he and Calvi were past masters — a concerted buying of shares in Company A, setting off a huge surge in demand for its shares, which soared in price, vastly inflating the company's market value. Then, on the agreed sale date, the artificially inflated assets of Company A were transferred to Company B, which Calvi then bought at its massively inflated price. This he was happy to do because it was other people's money he was paying out, and it was going to Sindona, who would surreptitiously pay a substantial amount back to him personally out of the immense profit he was making; and he was also achieving his aim of acquiring Banca Cattolica del Veneto. So, once again, everyone was happy, and Marcinkus, fully corrupted now, was securely locked into the thriving criminal partnership.

'My God!' said Alain, as he got up to fetch the food. 'How on earth could they get away with it? It all seems so blatantly illegal.'

'Don't forget that they were operating from within the Vatican State. Nobody there was the slightest bit interested in questioning what they were up to,' said Guido, as he and Stephen were helping Alain prepare the table. 'And they had the resources of the Vatican Bank to cover up much of what they were doing, and to direct their takings to anonymous bank accounts in the Bahamas.' He held out his glass for Alain to pour into. 'The kickback from Sindona to Calvi amounted to over six million dollars. Calvi then passed half of it to Marcinkus.' He took a sip of wine. 'Three good chums fair-mindedly dividing the spoils. What could be more civilised?'

THIRTY

'That enigmatic remark of yours, after the pizzas this morning...' Stephen was helping the others clear the table while saying this, 'about the date of the murder of that Italian lawyer the other day being of significance...'

Guido appeared briefly irritated at Stephen's unfinished question. The three of them, having eaten, were settling back in their previous positions, and he was clearly anxious to get started on the final phase of his disclosures — and looking somewhat uneasy as though having difficulty in reaching a decision.

'You know,' he said at last, his expression softening, 'perhaps that *is* the right place to begin. July 11th, the feast day of St Benedict of Nursia.' He paused for a moment, taking in Stephen's puzzled expression. 'Founder of the Benedictine monastic order early in the sixth century,' he went on, 'along with some dozen monasteries, including Monte Casino where he's buried. The Benedictines were the first monks to dress in the familiar black robes: a black tunic tied around the waist with a belt of some sort, over it a black scapula. A costume later adopted with small variations by the Dominicans, Augustinians and others. But the Benedictines were the first *black monks* and can rightly or wrongly be proud of that distinction.'

Guido paused again, as though expecting the obvious

question of what on earth this had to do with what they were waiting to hear from him. Alain was saying nothing, his expression suggesting he was less in the dark than Stephen, and content to hear Guido going on as he thought best. Then, just as Stephen was about to take the hint and ask the obvious, Guido started up again.

'An organisation — let us just call it that — with no name but an impressive logo is thought to occupy an abandoned monastic building somewhere in Rome, which it uses for meetings and other administrative functions. The existence of such a facility could be fiction. But letters, purportedly from that organisation, which warn recipients with thinly veiled threats against continuing with activities deemed counterproductive to the organisation's best interests, are well-confirmed facts.' He paused again, collecting his thoughts. 'Giorgio Ambrosoli,' he went on, 'the man gunned down in Milan last Wednesday — July 11th, St Benedict's feast day — had received such a letter a week or so before. It would have looked very much like others issued by that organisation.' He reached in his jacket pocket for an envelope from which he extracted a folded sheet, which he carefully spread out on the table between Alain and Stephen. 'Like this one, for instance.'

Guido's manner in leading up to this disclosure perhaps contributed to Stephen's feeling of extreme unease at the document laid out in front of him: a dozen or so lines of large heavily-seriffed bold black lettering on old-parchment coloured paper, with no indication of source nor intended recipient. But it was the image on the top left of the sheet — crumpled black monastic robes, empty but maintaining a half-seated posture against the suggestion of a chair, or perhaps a wheel — that completed the uncompromisingly sinister impression.

'Not at all a nice thing to receive,' said Alain, breaking the silence, 'even without the veiled threat — which I assume to be there... but, what on earth is that language? I can't make head or tail of it.'

'Chosen by me for that reason,' replied Guido with a grin. 'It's just your immediate impression of the overall image I wanted to get your reactions to. In most cases, the language is rather stilted Italian.'

'Something Nazi about it,' said Stephen after some moments, unsure quite what it was that made him feel this. 'Just the swastika missing. The black robes though... they somehow manage to fill in for that.'

Guido, after nodding approvingly, was looking uneasy again. He removed the document, folded it carefully and put it back in his pocket.

'But that date,' said Stephen, 'July 11th... Who on earth would have made that connection with the black monks? Couldn't it be just coincidence?'

'Not to those to whom the message was addressed. They would be in no doubt whatsoever of its significance.'

This brought back to Stephen something Natasha had said at the time of his summons to her house in Camden, to the upheaval she claimed having been caused by burglars searching for Piers's documents: that *they* — whoever that referred to — weren't interested in covering up what they were doing, quite the contrary.

Guido had lit a cigarette, the first for quite some time, leading Stephen to speculate that his earlier coughing fit might have persuaded him to cut down, at least for a while.

'I had intended to get straight on to what we know of

Piers's last movements.' Guido, having inhaled deeply, was looking more composed. 'But this latest killing provides a fitting introduction in a number of respects. For one... it seems that Piers also received one of those letters.'

'My God!' This was from Alain, who knew something of what Guido was talking about but clearly not this. 'When did you find that out?'

'It was just a few days ago, just as I was leaving to come here, strange as that may sound. I was told it by a colleague who had returned to the Vatican from an assignment abroad. It had been shown to him, along with other of Piers's documents, some apparently of sensitive nature, by the person entrusted with their safe-keeping.'

'Piers's missing 1978 file by the sound of it,' said Alain, looking puzzled. 'I'd been wondering what had become of that.'

'Yes. But look... we can come back to this later. We need to get on now. On to what we know of Piers's last movements. There's quite a lot to get through.' With a look of resigned sadness, he stubbed out his less than half consumed cigarette. 'With the impending death of Pope Paul VI, Piers had been unremittingly engaged in discreet lobbying for the election of his successor. It had been a long-running and largely undercover operation, culminating against all the odds in the elevation of Cardinal Albino Luciani to Pope John Paul I. You can't imagine what this meant to those of us involved in working to bring this about.'

'It was a wonderful feeling,' said Alain, 'even for those like me just looking in from outside. I have to say, though, that I didn't share Piers's enthusiasm for Luciani at the time. His public statements were always so cautious... I couldn't have believed he would turn out the way he did... so bold and decisive. Piers had got it right as usual... had read the man from the start.'

'Yes, indeed,' said Guido. 'Luciani was making his intentions for fundamental changes abundantly clear, to the manifest distress of members of the Curia. They were at a loss at how to react. Also prominent among prospective losers was Marcinkus, of course, and the criminal financial empire that had grown up around him. It was this prospect that was threatening the interests of a vast cohort from among the most wealthy and powerful people in Italy.' He paused, looking concerned again. 'Look, I don't want to spend time going on about the pernicious activities of Propaganda Due — that pseudo-Masonic lodge more often referred to simply as P2. We could be at it all night. But its role in the violent drama that we're seeing being played out here can't be overlooked. Crooked bankers Michele Sindona and Roberto Calvi are both prominent within that organisation, for which the criteria for membership are far-right leanings and possession of power — power either through wealth, however obtained, or position. Its members include senior parliamentarians, government ministers, leading magistrates and journalists, heads of the police and the military and the security services, directors of major banks, billionaire industrialists — such as Silvio Berlusconi. Effectively a state-within-a-state, it wields enormous power, dictating much of government policy and its implementation. Okay, this much is common knowledge, at least to those with an informed interest in such matters. But what came as a complete shock to Luciani, days after his inauguration, was the prevalence of P2 membership in the upper echelons of the Vatican hierarchy — in clear contravention of church directives, which deem freemasonry an evil institution from which Roman Catholics are banned from membership under pain of excommunication. What on earth is going on here? would have been his fully understandable reaction on learning of this — and leaving him in no doubt of what he would have to do about it.'

A thought came to Stephen, who had been listening, fascinated. Guido had paused, giving him the opportunity to interrupt.

'As a matter of interest,' he asked, 'was Cardinal Villot by any chance one of those P2 members?'

Guido looked surprised at the question. He was unaware of Stephen's knowledge of Villot's actions following Luciani's death.

'Yes, he was,' he said, though somewhat dismissively, unwilling to be side-tracked. 'We can talk about him later. But now I really need to get on to Piers's role in all this. I'm sure that's what you've been waiting to hear.'

Guido went on to describe the feeling, emerging within days of Luciani's election, of a major turning point in Vatican affairs — a prospect viewed with satisfaction by Piers and those involved with him in working for Luciani's election, but with severe misgivings by others, in particular those with long-held positions of power and authority which had marked them out as candidates for P2 membership — 'like Villot, for instance,' he said, glancing at Stephen with a faint smile. These individuals were rapidly coming to realise that their days of dominance were coming to an end, giving rise to much anxiety and bitterness. It was in this unsettled, turbulent atmosphere that Piers became alerted by Oscar to disturbing developments in Bishop Marcinkus's response to his impending dismissal.

'Oscar was still engaged on an occasional basis with the Vatican Bank,' said Guido, smiling to himself as he thought about it. 'There's something… *unsubstantial* about his presence there… sitting quietly at his corner desk, poring over his papers. It's almost as though he isn't there.'

It seemed to Guido that it was this persona of Oscar's — 'or should that be lack of persona?' — that gave him access to much sensitive material supposedly kept under wraps, and enabled him to overhear telephone conversations Marcinkus would otherwise have thought necessary to conduct in private. The account of Calvi's purchase of Banca Cattolica del Veneto, given by Guido earlier that evening, represented just one of the Vatican Bank's involvements in fraudulent operations to have come to Oscar's attention in this way. There were many others, to which he had become quite inured by the time of Luciani's accession to the papacy. But then, two weeks or so after that crucial victory, — received ecstatically by proponents of radical Vatican reform, including himself — he was to overhear something that was to cause him deep concern. Marcinkus had, by then, been informed of his impending dismissal and was biding his time in the forlorn hope of some measure of reprieve; in the meantime conferring frequently by phone with Sindona — who was in a furious mood at official probing into his affairs and threatening reprisal, while, at the same time, anxious for reassurance that evidence of his wrongdoings that had not, for whatever reason, been destroyed was being securely concealed. All much in line with what Oscar had heard many times before, the full gist of those previous exchanges easily deducible just from Marcinkus's part in them. But this was not the case for the call which had now perturbed him. He had no idea this time who the caller was, nor what information he was conveying. It was just Marcinkus's reaction to it: the overwhelming impression that something of profound importance was being put to him by an authority to whom he was in awe, his few responses brief and obsequious, in marked contrast with his habitual air of self-confident superiority and disdain in his dealings with others. Who on earth could the caller be? he wondered, and what on earth was he telling him? Following the call, a change in Marcinkus became apparent, a relaxation of his previous tense demeanour, as though the reprieve he had despaired of receiving could be coming through regardless. All very strange and disturbing. In reporting this incident and the feeling it aroused in him to Piers, Oscar was aware of how thin it sounded, how unsupported his ill-defined misgivings. Piers knew him well enough though to trust his instinct and so share his concern.

'All they could do was to keep it in mind, they decided, and await future developments that might shed light on its significance.'

Guido broke off having said this to light a cigarette, giving Alain the opportunity to interject.

'But Marcinkus was right, wasn't he? He's still there.'

'Yes, indeed he is. Very much so, I'm afraid. But you're jumping ahead. I'll be coming on to that later.'

Guido then got on to what Oscar had told Piers about Sindona's concerns with the ongoing investigations into his financial affairs. Although confident that illegalities in his direct stock market dealings had been well enough obscured, he was still worried that something incriminating could come to light. It was then that Piers referred back to the multimillion-dollar kickback paid by Sindona to Calvi and Marcinkus following Calvi's purchase of Banca Cattolica del Veneto. Was there any concrete evidence anywhere, he asked, of this clearly illegal transaction? Oscar thought for a while before saying that perhaps there was, though it might be difficult to get hold of. They left it there; the emerging scope of Pope John Paul's far-reaching reforms was too much on their minds for prolonged consideration of much else. And so the matter rested, until the shattering news of the Pope's sudden death the following week — just over a month after his election — threw everything into grief and disarray. Guido talked briefly of this, confirming in essence what Stephen had learned from Ennis and Sharif. He felt somewhat guilty at not coming out with this prior knowledge, but relieved to find it largely accorded with what Guido had to say. When the initial shock of the Pope's death had passed, Piers was able to take stock with where it left his movement: their hard-earned victory, achieved against the odds, overturned, their opponents barely able to conceal satisfaction at this decisive reversal in the battle for control. And then Oscar's disclosures of the previous week came hurtling back: the image of Marcinkus seemingly receiving reassurance that his position was secure, that papal intention to dismiss him would come to nothing. It could well be, it appeared to Piers, that it was the Pope's death that was being implicitly foretold in that call — which fitted with news emanating from the papal apartment of the suspicious circumstances of that death, of an implausible, hastily assembled cover-up.

Piers arranged a further meeting with Oscar, hopeful that he had arrived at some notion of the identity of Marcinkus's informant. But no, Oscar had nothing to add on that. But what he did have, and passed on to Piers, much to his surprise, was a folder containing what he claimed to be indisputable evidence of the multimillion-dollar kickback paid by Calvi to Sindona and Marcinkus. He had taken Piers's casual enquiry seriously, finding, to his surprised satisfaction, that getting hold of the incriminating material turned out far easier than he had at first imagined. It was all in the folder, he said, including originals of certain key documents — Oscar having replaced these where he found them with "near-perfect copies". Piers was delighted to receive this. He took it away to ponder what best to do with it.

'One can only begin to imagine what was going through Piers's mind,' said Guido as he fumbled in his pocket for his cigarettes. 'He was still in shock at the distressing news of the Pope's death… at the seemingly unthinkable possibility of him having been murdered. But if that was indeed the case, and the more he thought about it, the more likely it was beginning to appear, then Sindona and the Mafia's massive financial interests he represented — which had been terminally threatened by Luciani's avowed intentions — must surely have been behind it. So where did this leave Marcinkus, forever closely engaged with Sindona, and in receipt from him of multimillion-dollar payoffs?'

Piers, so Guido broke off to explain, had a more immediately pressing matter to deal with. He nevertheless initiated enquiries into the ongoing Italian government and Bank of Italy investigations into Sindona's financial affairs, before turning his full attention to preparations for the impending election of Luciani's successor. This was being proceeded with in unseemly haste, in what appeared to Piers a desperate attempt to draw attention away from the murky circumstances of Luciani's death. In the event, Polish Cardinal

Karol Jozef Wojtyla went on to win the election just eighteen days after the death of Luciani, ten days after his funeral. It was a result welcomed with relief by the Curia: the victor a traditionalist through and through, with firm anti-birth control views and, as it turned out, a relaxed position with regard to financial impropriety. Marcinkus and P2 affiliated members of the Vatican hierarchy were able to breathe heartfelt sighs of relief, absolved at a stroke from the punitive intentions of Wojtyla's predecessor. For Piers and the moderniser factions in general, it was a bitter blow. They had thrown their weight behind the candidature of Cardinal Giovanni Benelli, a close associate of Luciani and supporter of his radical agenda. But their efforts were impeded by the confusion following Luciani's sudden death and the short time available for canvassing for Benelli in the face of strong Curial opposition. The result was a setback of the kind Piers had always expected in the long-term pursuit of his aims. Masking his disappointment, he turned his thoughts to what to do with the cast-iron evidence obtained by Oscar of Sindona's criminal dealings.

Enquiries initiated by Piers into the ongoing scrutiny of Sindona's affairs revealed that Giorgio Ambrosoli had uncovered countless examples of patent criminality — though for the most part obscured in tangled webs of complex transactions that could render them difficult to prove categorically in a court of law — especially given the quality of legal representation Sindona could be expected to call upon in his defence. It was probably these enquiries that led to Piers being served the threatening *black monk* communication. More to the point, they clearly revealed Oscar's documented evidence to be of considerable value to Ambrosoli in the pursuit of his investigations. Providing him with it, however, risked exposing Oscar's central role in bringing it to light, with likely disastrous consequences for him. In order to forestall this, Piers had thought up another way, not involving Oscar, in which he could conceivably have come across the incriminating evidence. His strategy for fooling Marcinkus into believing this was going to involve confronting him directly with the evidence, before passing it to Ambrosoli.

'This was typical of Piers,' said Guido, pausing to light a cigarette. 'No thought for his own safety, going to great lengths to protect others. But he couldn't have foreseen just how dangerous what he was proposing would turn out to be.'

Concealing Oscar's role in obtaining the evidence was Piers's prime reason for seeking the confrontation with Marcinkus. But it also satisfied his predisposition to be open in his dealings with people. As he had once enjoyed some sort of sociable relationship with Marcinkus, he felt uncomfortable at the thought of what amounted to reporting on him behind his back. Better to first confront him directly, he decided, get his reaction and then decide what to do next — though he was in little doubt at what this would have to be. He telephoned to arrange the meeting, which was eventually agreed upon for Wednesday evening of the following week — just a day before he had booked the night train for the first leg of his journey to London, and a long-overdue return to Natasha following the Vatican upheavals.

'The only thing we know for certain about that meeting is that it ended in violence.' Guido was looking deadly serious now, Stephen and Alain locked in shocked silence. 'A punch-up is the term I think you would use for it,' he went on, 'an extraordinary thing to have happened... quite unimaginable. It was late in the evening, nobody was around. I had spoken briefly to Piers two days before but never saw or heard from him again. But Oscar saw him the following morning, just before he set off for the arranged meeting with Ambrosoli. He looked in a real mess apparently: cut lip, bruised face... sticking plaster over what appeared to be some damage under one eye. But when Oscar commiserated with him, asked what had happened, he managed a smile of sorts, pointed to his other bandaged hand and said something to the effect of "Wait till you see the other guy." As it happened, Oscar did see Marcinkus later that morning. He too was looking the worse for wear... also with a bruised face... and wearing dark glasses, which he took off at one point to look at something on his desk, revealing a swollen black eye. It must have been one hell of a set-to.'

'What on earth could have started that off?' said Alain. 'There's no way it could have been Piers... must have been Marcinkus... Piers responding in self-defence...'

'Very likely,' said Guido. 'But we'll never know exactly what happened. And we don't even know what Piers was planning to tell Marcinkus about how he got hold of the evidence of his payoff from Calvi. Perhaps it was that though, whatever it was, which provoked Marcinkus into lashing out. But what then seems extraordinary to me is that what followed seems not to have been by any means a one-sided affair. Piers must be a lightweight compared to Marcinkus — the Gorilla! And, what, six, seven years older? That he managed to put up what appears to have been a good fight seems just incredible.'

It was mention of that black eye on Marcinkus that sent Stephen's mind racing back to an incident from St John's days. He smiled to himself at the memory, then broke the brief silence.

'It doesn't surprise me that Piers would stick up for himself in that way if provoked,' he said. 'He was an accomplished boxer in his youth, something of a champion at his school, and always kept himself very fit when I knew him — though without flaunting the fact. So it doesn't surprise me at all.'

It must have been during Stephen's fourth form year or thereabouts that the dubious sport of boxing was to enjoy a brief period of popularity at St John's. So much so that a fully outfitted boxing ring, with ropes and padded corners and the rest of it, came to be installed in a little-used assembly area for the purpose of adding a polished touch to the final tournaments. It was to remain there for some weeks. One morning, during this period, the deputy headmaster, Brother Ignatius, turned up to take his fifth-form class with a black eye — a real shiner, cause of joyous speculation among the boys. Ignatius possessed the harsh features, build and reputation of a bruiser — attributes he revelled in and used with effect in terrorising suspected miscreants. Some hero, it now appeared, had landed him one. Who on earth could this have been? It was left to Philips — inexplicably aware, as usual, of covert goings-on in the school — to point the finger at Brother Carroll. More than that, to divulge the whole story and predict a very probably verifiable further outcome. It went something like this. The brothers were known to make use of the gym and other such amenities during out-of-school hours when they had the place to themselves. The temporary availability of boxing facilities — not an obvious attraction for most — thus presented Brother Ignatius with the opportunity to mark his displeasure at Brother Carroll's open-hearted relationships and evident popularity with the boys, without having to voice such suspect sentiments directly. Ignatius knew of Carroll's school boxing achievements but considered these of little consequence when measured against his own, altogether more impressive, physique and general toughness. His challenge was duly taken up. The contest itself should have convinced him he had got it badly wrong; his complete inability to land a punch, and the indignity of being subjected to many — for the most part little more than pats, which appeared to onlookers as though Carroll was taking care to go easy on him — having the effect of enraging him still further, leading to his demand for a return bout the following evening. This was the "probably verifiable prediction" of Philips' disclosure, which was indeed verified the following day when, to the boys' delight, Ignatius arrived in class with *two* black eyes.

These entertaining recollections were going through Stephen's mind as Guido got on to what he had learned of Sindona's precipitous fall from grace in the United States, where he had been indicted on multiple charges of fraud and related offences for which he was on multimillion-dollar bail; and, at the same time, contesting extradition to Italy to face a jail sentence imposed in his absence, and where his dealings were being subjected to further investigation by government-appointed lawyer Giorgio Ambrosoli, who, four years previously, had acted as liquidator of one of his banks.

'Even in his desperation at the ever more likely prospect of serving a good part of the remainder of his life in jail, Sindona had been railing against Ambrosoli, threatening to have him silenced.' Guido reached for his packet of cigarettes, toyed with it a while, then put it away. 'And now, sure enough, he's been killed… just last Wednesday… St Benedict's feast day! And already Sindona is threatening massive legal reprisal against anyone who so much as suggests he could be behind that killing. But the thing that has really sunk him is that indisputable evidence of Oscar's that Piers delivered to Ambrosoli before he left for London. It's that that has blown a vast hole in the defensive barrier he and Calvi had erected to obscure their criminal dealings. And he knows it. And it's most probably that which drove him to set in train reckless acts of vengeance... that cold-blooded killing for one, which for all his bluster is going to stick with him.'

Guido stopped having said this, looking distressed, his eyes moist. He wiped them with a handkerchief and asked Alain if he could get him a glass of water. After this had arrived and he had drunk from it, he apologised for his show of emotion. He had recently been in contact with Giorgio Ambrosoli, he said; knew him to be a devoted husband and father of three young children, well aware of the danger he was facing, subjected to threats and bribes and persistent pressure from the highest levels of Italian political society, from people who had very probably made use of the facilities Sindona, with the aid of the Vatican Bank, provided for transferring vast sums of money illegally out of Italy; determined nonetheless to persist with his investigations for no other reason than that doing so was what he knew to be right for his country. And there was a further reason for Guido's distress, which, after fumbling for his cigarettes, lighting up and inhaling deeply, he now turned to.

'The evening after Piers had delivered Oscar's file of evidence to Ambrosoli, he set off on his long train journey to London. He was seen off from Roma Termini by a Vatican colleague, arriving in Paris the following evening, then transferring to the Night Ferry from the Gare du Nord to arrive at Victoria Station at about nine the next morning. We've been able to contact someone who travelled in the same carriage for that last leg of the journey. He had exchanged friendly remarks with Piers on disembarking and, as he was making his way to the exit, had seen Piers being approached by two men at the ticket barrier and conferring with them there.' Guido paused to wipe his eyes again and drink from his glass. 'That was the last reported sighting of Piers before his body was discovered two days later in Westminster Cathedral — in a side chapel dedicated to two highly venerated Benedictine monks.'

'Benedictine monks!' Stephen was brought up with a start on hearing this. 'But... but it's dedicated to Pope Gregory I and St Augustine... the first Archbishop of Canterbury...'

Both Guido and Alain were looking at him strangely, Alain with the suggestion of a smile.

'Didn't you know?' he began. Then, his smile broadening, 'No, I don't suppose you would have any reason to...'

'As is well known, and certainly so to the people to whom the message was directed,' said Guido, interrupting somewhat harshly, 'they were both abbots of major Benedictine monasteries before taking on broader responsibilities for the church.'

Stephen was feeling stupid, not knowing what to say next.

'Church history is not a popular topic for outsiders,' said Alain with a chuckle. 'No need to worry about it. The important thing is that you know now.'

True, thought Stephen. The mystery of where Piers's body was found... well, not exactly resolved... but no longer the unfathomable mystery it was before. He was feeling a mixture of strong emotions, which did not include satisfaction at this partial resolution.

'So,' he said eventually, breaking the silence, 'where do you go from here?'

'A good question...' began Alain, Guido cutting in before he could say more.

'The murder, murders, are being investigated by the British and Italian authorities. We are doing everything we can to help, of course. But regardless of that, regardless of how this all ends up, we will carry on as Piers would have wanted us to. Which is to continue promoting his vision, downplaying the dogma, the unreasoned certainty, the superstition; transforming the church and the Christian myth into a generally acceptable force for good in the world, open to all, regardless of belief or lack of belief or anything else; to fight relentlessly against poverty, inequality, injustice, all manner of cruelty and exploitation... What more can I say? Oh, and to plan ahead, to be ready next time, as we were for Albino Luciani. The present incumbent represents a step back, which we will just have to live with for a while. But next time round... to see to it that we are well and truly prepared again.'

It was getting late, Guido was looking tired, as they all were; other matters not dealt with paling into insignificance. Stephen was thinking of Suzie, no longer waiting up for him now — she would give him until eleven, she had said, then go to bed; it was now past midnight. Guido had lit a final cigarette, the ashtray overflowing in front of him. Stephen, on a whim, rousing himself to again break the silence.

'How about blowing us another smoke ring, Guido,' he said, 'to round off the session?'

Guido regarded him blankly for a moment, then broke into a shy smile. Turning in his chair to face the fireplace, he took a long draw. Then out it shot with a whoosh: a real beauty, spinning and speeding over the table, across the room, narrowly missing the head of the Virgin Mary on the mantelpiece, exploding inches from the crucifix on the wall — to applause from Stephen and Alain, and a satisfied smile from Guido which, try as he might, he was unable to restrain.

It was after one o'clock when the minicab deposited Stephen at his home, where he found that Suzie had been waiting up for him. She had fallen asleep on the sofa and was rubbing her eyes as he entered the room.

'Well,' she said, half smilingly, barely awake. 'All resolved then, what happened to Piers?' Her tone implying little expectation of this being so.

He sat down beside her, her head moved instinctively to his shoulder.

'Yes, it is,' he replied, bringing her up with a start. 'A contract murder, one of a spate of them, including, very probably, that of the last Pope.'

She was fully awake now, turning to him in disbelief.

'And Piers's body in the cathedral?'

'No mystery any more... it all fits in... but it's a long story.'

A story Stephen had been anticipating telling the following morning. But, tired though they both were, there was no way now of putting it off any longer.

Suzie listened attentively as he sketched through Guido's account, only interrupting to seek minor clarifications and, at one point, to wonder at the source of those black monk letters.

'They sound like what you might imagine coming from some sort of primitive Masonic guild,' she said, perceptively

— causing Stephen to diverge on to the Vatican's cosy relationship with P2. 'The probable source of those black monk threats and the killings, though that's likely to be well-nigh impossible to prove.'

'Well, it puts pay to the notion of Piers having committed suicide,' said Suzie, when she had heard him through. 'At least that must be some sort of relief.' Then, as they were getting up to go to bed, 'I almost forgot to tell you that there were two calls for you while you were out. One from Stan, anxious for news. He said something about meeting up early next week. I said you'd call him tomorrow.'

Stephen was pleased with her lack of bitterness when referring to Stan. Rebecca's recent attachment to a seriously wealthy businessman — a whirlwind romance it seemed, with talk of near-imminent marriage — was perhaps contributing to this softening.

'And then there was one from Karl,' she went on. 'He says he's got some good news for you but wouldn't let on what it was. Wants us to meet up in the Goose tomorrow evening, then go for a meal somewhere. I said it sounds fine for me but you would phone in the morning to confirm. I've a feeling he's got a new girlfriend in tow and wants to show her off to us.'

They hugged in silence, both having difficulty in keeping their eyes open, then made their way clumsily up the stairs.

EPILOGUE

Suzie gave birth to a healthy boy on New Year's Day 1980, some three months after she and Stephen had attended Sharif and Nasreen's wedding in Pakistan — a lavish affair lasting several days and leading to the start of a long-running friendship between Suzie and Nasreen. Conversations with fellow guests revealed Sharif as having already made something of a name for himself in local politics, with hints of a likely future role on the national stage.

Over a meal in a Greek restaurant in Fitzrovia — an event in itself marking a significant break from previous practice — Alain and Emma revealed to Stephen and Suzie their decision to get married. Alain had already set in train the messy business of renouncing his calling — 'jumping before being pushed,' he had put it, with a smile that didn't quite obscure the discomfort involved — and had applied for and been offered a fellowship at his old Oxford college, 'which should tide us over for a year or so, give us time to work out where to go from there.'

Widely diverse destinies were in store for the separate persons of the Vatican's unholy trinity of crooked bankers. Following the spate of killings, that most probably included that of Pope John Paul I, two of them would go on to suffer violent deaths:

Michele Sindona by poisoning, Roberto Calvi by strangulation. In marked contrast, the third one, Bishop Paul Marcinkus, was to be accorded honour and privilege, being consecrated archbishop just three years following the accession of Karol Jozef Wojtyla to the papacy. Marcinkus was able to repay this favour by providing the new Pope with the wherewithal for illegal transfer of vast sums of dubious origin to the Solidarity movement in Poland.

Sindona had been extradited to Italy from the United States — following conviction there for a raft of criminal financial offences — to stand trial for the contract murder of Giogio Ambrosoli, for which he was found guilty and sentenced by the Italian court to twenty-five years imprisonment. The poison which killed him was in a cup of coffee which he drank in his cell. One hypothesis for the killing has him committing suicide in desperation at the prospect of spending the remainder of his life in gaol; another has him murdered to protect past users of his nefarious services from risk of exposure.

Calvi's death was altogether more dramatic. Following the collapse of Banco Ambrosiano, with debts of over a billion US dollars, and besieged by creditors that included vengeful members of the P2 Masonic lodge and the Mafia, Calvi did a runner. He travelled to London by a circuitous route through several countries, with false identity and passport and without his moustache — and reputedly entertaining a desperate hare-brained scheme for blackmailing former users of his services into bankrolling his losses. All that can be said for certain regarding his plans, whatever they were, is that they failed miserably and he was murdered. His killers, like those of Piers's three years earlier, had taken pains to convey their message to interested parties, this time by hanging his body over the Thames from a rope round his neck under *Blackfriars* bridge.